BABY BOY

Isaac Series – Book 4

Taylor J Gray

Baby Boy

Copyright ©2020 Taylor J Gray

Second Edition Copyright ©2021 Taylor J Gray

ALL RIGHTS RESERVED.

This book contains material protected under International and Federal Copyright Laws and Trusties. Any unauthorized reprint or use of this material is prohibited. No part of this book may be reproduced or transmitted in any form or by any means, electronic or mechanical, including photocopying, recording, or by an information and retrieval system without express written permission from the Author/Publisher.

This is a work of fiction. Names, characters, places, and incidents are the product of the author's imagination or are used fictitiously. Any resemblance to actual persons, living or dead, business establishments, events, or locales is entirely coincidental.

Cover Design: Book Cover by Design

Proofreading: Abrianna Denae

Formatting: Abrianna Denae

BABY BOY

ACKNOWLEDGEMENT

Oh you're still here!...thank you!

DISCLAIMER

Adult only. Explicit and descriptive scenes of BDSM, medical fetish and play and M/m sex.

FOREWORD

Baby Boy is the fourth book in the Isaac Series.

For reader pleasure it is recommended that the Isaac Series is read in order from Book 1 to get the most from the story and understand the characters.

Julian – A stand-alone book but these characters turn up in the Isaac Series

CHAPTER ONE

"What am I going to do with you?..."

I was in the cage trying desperately to lose myself in submission, but I couldn't, it wasn't enough, and I couldn't distance myself from him enough to break this connection with him. I had no answer to his question, but I wasn't sure he was asking me. So here I sat, my hand through the bars of the cage curled in his, waiting, asking him to help me, to not give up on me, and to help me find a way back to him.

"Do you want to come out of the cage, Isaac, and share your time with Julian with me?"

I spoke against his hand. "Yes please, Sir." I could do that, I could share my time with Julian. I wanted comfort from my play and my wounds. Physically they weren't much, a few welts and a sore cock but to me they were huge, my mind was overloaded, I needed to share.

He pulled his hand away and moved to the end of the cage and opened it. I hesitated then crawled quickly out and knelt at his feet, looking down.

"Isaac."

I looked up at him slowly. He didn't ignore me, he just looked at me. I raised my hands that were still connected, slid them under his t-shirt, and touched his skin to quench my need for him.

I whispered my words to him, scared to expect his attention. "I'll behave."

He stroked my face with his fingers, then quickly stood and slipped off his shirt, bending down to me, he picked me up with ease and walked to the mattress. He sat with me between his legs and held me tightly to his body for ages in silence. I soaked up the touch of his body and his smell. When I felt him loosen his hold a little, I looked at him and held out my hands slowly, showing him the welt. He unclasped my restraints, put my hand to his mouth, and kissed it.

"Do you have others?" I nodded and leant forward over my knees.

He ran his hand down my back and touched the three welts that marked the top of my arse. "They are very beautiful, Isaac. Would you like me to bathe them?" I nodded.

They had already been cleaned by Julian, but I wanted him to tend to me, to touch me and care about me. He kissed me before moving me from him. "Wait here."

He left the basement and went to his room as I sat curled over my knees, watching the door for his return. A moment later he returned with a bowl and a first aid box. He sat against the wall, pulled me between his legs so my back was to him, and lifted my hand and took the restraint off my wrist. He gently bathed my hand with a cloth from the bowl even though we both knew that they had already been cleaned. This was trust-building; it was what Keepers did for their slaves, cared for them, bonded with them when they felt low and sore from their visit. They loved you so it didn't hurt so much. He dried my hand, wiping it gently in the towel. I wanted to tell him things…I did. It was just hard…where did you start when so many things were there filling your head?

"I got in the way." He leant his head against mine while he continued to dry my hand. "I didn't misbehave. I was touching Jacob while he was playing and it got caught with the cane."

He kissed the side of my face. "You'll have to be more careful, Isaac. The hand is not a good place to feel the cane." He dried his hands and opened the first aid box and got out the cream that was always used on welts and wounds, he rubbed it gently into the marks.

"I know but he was beautiful, and he felt so good under my hands…and my lips… and because I had that thing on my cock it hurt. I was trying not to let it..." I felt his smile against my skin and I wanted to see it so I turned my head to look at him, but the smile was gone.

"What thing was on your cock?" I looked away.

"Julian put my cock in a cage, to stop me getting hard…to stop me playing." He nodded once in understanding. "He asked me to play, I said I didn't want to play and I didn't… because I didn't trust him…so he didn't trust me..." The words ran out of my mouth like water from a tap as I told him the story.

He sat and listened patiently, never interrupting as I told him how Julian had punished Jacob with the cane and the flogger and the electric in his cock. He just sat rubbing my hand even though the cream had long since gone. "... and I didn't want to play but Jacob looked hot in his binds and my cock kept getting hard... and now it's sore." He slipped his hands between my legs and pushed them open, pulling me back to him so he could look at my cock.

"Okay, well we will see to it in a minute. Lean forward over your knees and let me look at the ones on your back." He pushed me gently forward and I curled myself over my legs, resting my head sideways on my knees.

He bathed them with the cloth, one of them was sore and I drew a breath in between my teeth. He touched his finger to the one that hurt. "This one?" I nodded my head.

It didn't hurt that much but I was hurting, and everything felt harsher and sorer. He rested the warm cloth against it.

"I wanted to stay and touch Jacob... so I took the cane to take the pain away. Is that bad? Am I bad? I wasn't bad." He touched his hand to my head and stroked the hair around my ears.

"No, Baby Boy, you weren't bad, you were very good. Was Julian pleased?" He was drying my back and then put the cream on.

"Maybe, he didn't punish me, and he let me sit with him... but he said not to tell you. Are you angry?" I heard his smile on a breath as he pulled me back to him and wrapped his arms around me and kissed me.

"No. Let me look at your cock." I opened my legs. He reached his hand down to touch it and I pulled my knees together. "It's sore."

He didn't move but held me tighter. "I have you."

I thought about it, then slowly opened my knees to him and he lifted my cock and looked at it. I pushed my face into him, and he held it with his hand while he got the cloth and gently bathed my cock. He dabbed it with the towel to dry it.

"It will feel better tomorrow." I closed my legs and he kissed me, and I felt overwhelmed with his care. I wanted to give him something.

"I wasn't bad… I was just a gay whore and he didn't like it. He caned me every day for it... it made me not like the cane anymore, not that I liked it before, but it was better before. It hurt more every day and now I don't like it... and... and I don't know what to do about it." I looked up at him wanting him to tell me how to fix the things in my head. He looked at me and stroked his hand over my forehead.

"No, Isaac, you were not bad. He was a bad Keeper and he didn't deserve you. You are never bad, and you are not a whore. There are no whores in this world, only in play." I turned, laying my face against him.

"He told Kellen I misbehaved so he could punish me but I didn't. I didn't do anything, I tried really hard not to. I ate my bread every day and drunk my water. When he didn't look after me, I tried to do it myself, I tried to clean my welts under the shower while he was sleeping. The water was so cold because I couldn't let it get warm in case he woke up. I would have been punished for leaving my bed. It was forbidden…I was not allowed to leave my bed, in the daytime, he restrained me to the bed while he wasn't there so I couldn't leave. That was boring and it hurt my arms and shoulders, especially when I fell asleep." Layton made me look at him.

"How were you restrained? How did you lay?" I shook my head at him. He didn't get it.

"I wasn't lying down. I wasn't allowed. I was like this." I put both hands above my head and he frowned at me.

"For a few hours?"

I put my hands down and fiddled with my wrist cuff, I realised that the other one was still missing, and I looked around for it while I spoke. "No, after the morning shower until supper time." He loosened his hold on me, as I moved to look for the cuff. I couldn't see it and I could feel the panic.

"What are looking for?" I held my hands out to him.

"It's missing…I can't find it." I looked at him, worried. He put his hand behind him and pulled out the cuff.

"I have it here, Isaac, you don't need to worry." I held my hand out with relief and watched as he put it on.

"I thought I'd lost it." Once he had buckled it, he clasped my restraints together and I looked at him. "Is it time for me to go back to my cage?" He smiled and shook his head.

"No, come and settle with me." He pulled me back between his legs and wrapped his arms around me. He stroked his fingers over my arm and leant his head against mine. I felt so secure and safe. I felt my whole body relax for the first time in ages. Nothing bad could happen while he held me like this. "Would it matter if you lost your cuff?"

"Yes." They were his and if I wore them then I belonged to him.

"How did you eat your lunch, Isaac, if you were not released all day?"

"No one came. No one brought me lunch, I wanted it, my stomach hurt sometimes but no one ever came... not until supper. That's why it was boring, and I had to sleep." He shook his head against mine and I looked up at him, worried he thought bad things about me. "I was a good slave. He said if we showed Kellen we were getting on, he would be moved and I would get a new Keeper... I wanted a new Keeper... I wanted a Keeper like Leon..." He looked at me and kissed me. I could feel the desolate feeling spreading inside me and I breathed heavily trying to stop the feeling spreading.

"I know you did. Is that why you never said anything to Kellen?" I was still looking at him, remembering.

"I didn't want to be punished." I could feel the tears threatening and looked away. He held me to him and stroked me.

"Oh, Baby Boy, he wouldn't have done that, I told you to trust him if you needed to." I was taking deep breaths to keep the sobs away.

"I tried... I don't want to talk anymore."

He put his lips to my forehead and spoke under his breath. "Because of Beecher..." I nodded.

I was feeling agitated, I didn't want to think about it anymore and I started to pull at my binds and squirm in his hold. He held me tight, still with his mouth against my skin. "A little more, Isaac, then I will make you tea." He rubbed his hands over me firmly but gently, making me feel secure and giving comfort at the same time. "This is just like welts and wounds, it stings and hurts when they are cleaned but I'm right here, Baby Boy. Did you get supper every night?" I nodded feeling the tears threatening.

"Bread and butter... every night, bread and butter, bread and butter, bread and butter and a bottle of water." Layton pulled my face to look at him. His face was tense, not angry, not like a fist, his eyes were dark, almost black, and I pulled back away a little.

"Just bread and butter? You couldn't survive, Isaac, you must have had something else?" He didn't believe me, and I pushed at him for a moment, but he held me tight.

I shook my head and the words spilled from me in panic. "I drank shower water and begged clients for food. They let me earn it, some of them would throw me food while I was restrained and I had to eat it off the floor and they liked it, liked watching me.... and... and…" My thoughts seemed to stop as I thought about him. "… and Marcus fed me... Marcus always looked after me... not as payment, not for anything because he liked to, he wanted to." I felt the tears roll down my face but I didn't move. He was still glaring at me and I felt unsure of him. "Can I go... can I go to my cage please?"

His face softened and he held my face in both his hands and kissed both cheeks of their tears. "I'm sorry... I'm so sorry, I'm not angry, Baby Boy. I didn't mean to frighten you." He pulled away and looked at me, stroking the back of my neck with his fingers.

His face was softer and his eyes had the golden fleck back in them. I lifted my hands and touched his face with my fingertips. I wanted to see if my memory of him was right, he didn't move, just sat and let me touch him. I bit my lip as I ran my fingers over his lips then pulled my hands away, he caught them in his gently, pulled them back to his lips and kissed them.

"Don't go back to the cage, Baby Boy, stay with me. No more talking, not for today... would you like tea?" I breathed deeply and nodded. He pulled me into his arms and kissed me.

"Can I sleep with you in the bed tonight? I told you things you didn't know... you said, you said if I told you things you didn't know then I could earn it, earn a night in your bed." He held me close, wrapping his arms around me again and I felt safe.

"Yes, Isaac. You have been so good today. You can have hot tea and biscuits and sleep with me in the bed. I missed you." He kissed me again. "Would you like to help make it?" I shook my head and he laughed quietly. "That's okay, I'll slave for you just this once."

He carried me through to the bed and covered me with the blanket and made tea. He let me have biscuits and dip them in my tea until they were soggy and broke. Then he let me have his tea to drink. We didn't talk much, he never made me speak anymore, he just sat with me, watching and touching me. He cleared the cups, got undressed and got into bed, pulling me until I was lying virtually on him and wrapped his legs around mine. I held my wrists out for him to disconnect my restraints which he did.

"Tonight Isaac, I have you."

I laid my head on him and pushed my arms under his so I could hold him tightly and I fell asleep.

BABY BOY

CHAPTER TWO

I woke in the middle of the night; it was dark apart from a few lit candles and I was wide awake. I was still laying with Layton, and he was stroking my back with his fingers. I closed my eyes again, wanting the peace I had found in my sleep but it wouldn't come, so I pushed myself up on one arm and looked at him. He had his eyes closed but I knew he wasn't sleeping.

"I'm awake now."

A smile took his lips and he slowly opened his eyes to look at me. "So I can see and hear. Are you not tired anymore?"

I shook my head. "I want to be, I want to go back to sleep here with you."

He touched his fingers to my forehead and tapped them gently. "Are your thoughts bothering you?"

A million yeses to that question but not all of them were to do with my time at Kellen's house. I looked down, ran my fingers over his skin and circled his belly button over and over. I shrugged my shoulders in answer before any words could come out of my mouth.

"You can stay with me here, Isaac, you don't have to sleep. Do you want tea or something to eat?"

I shook my head. My head was full of questions, hoping the answers would help the constant niggles going around and around in there.

"How do you train someone to be a Keeper?"

He sat up a little and held his hand out to me. I took it and he gently pulled me to him. I lay my head down on him.

"It is not something you can train someone to do. They have to be sensitive and open so they can understand their slave. They have to have slaved or served in this world in one capacity or another, so we know they have an understanding of what brings people here. Most of my Keepers here have been in this world for a while, some of them as slaves. They have either run their time as a slave or it's not been the place for them. A lot of Keepers are Switches, meaning their needs and desires are both submissive and dominant at different times. This makes them good Keepers because they understand it from both sides. Some of them play with each other or with me, which I encourage because it reminds them of what their slaves endure on visits. If they taste it now and again, I think it makes them better Keepers for my slaves."

"Does Leon play?"

"Yes, a little. He is not naturally submissive but likes to taste it sometimes, he says it keeps his mind open to the slaves' suffering. He's a challenging playmate and very strong but he can take a lot when he allows himself to get into the right headspace."

"Who looks after him... after playing?"

"I do. I always do, I make sure his mind is back in the right place before he is released and then we will spend the rest of the day together while I care for him and settle him back."

I don't know where it came from, but it was said before I knew it. "I like you."

There was a short silence before he spoke again, and I was thankful he ignored it.

"Usually, he goes back to work the next day." Change the subject.

"Do you think Rourke played?" He hesitated and I looked at him.

"I don't know, Isaac." I lay back down.

"I don't think he did. He liked to see me suffer. I think he liked it more than he admitted to himself, but I don't think he understood it though. Do you think he liked watching me with Beecher?" He stroked my hair in his fingers like he used to.

"Maybe. I thought you had made your peace with him over that?"

"I did... we did, but I'm angry with him now. Him being there made me feel safe... when I wasn't... not safe with my Keeper. I don't think Keepers should play with their slaves, it's confusing. I thought he was trying to help me... but he hurt me, then he left. If he was a good Keeper, he wouldn't have left me... or punished me." I stopped and waited for him to say something, but he didn't, so I continued. "If Leon punished Sim like that, what would you do?" I turned and looked at him.

He looked at me for ages before speaking. "It's not confusing if the Keepers are good with their slaves. If it were one of mine, I would punish him in the same manner so he would always remember the suffering, and then I would send him back to the vanillas. Rourke abused your trust, Isaac... and your need for pain and pleasure, to feed his own need. I think he realised his treatment of you was getting beyond his understanding which is why he left. Julian encouraged him to go away. He could see how unstable he was getting; how much he was pushing you to take. Do you not love him anymore?" I laid my head back on his chest and shook my head.

"I don't think it was love I felt. I think I held on to him in my mind because I was scared, and he was the last normal thing... my normal anyway." He didn't speak and we lay there in silence. I didn't want it to be quiet, it reminded me too much of being on my own, in that room, in that cage. "I'm still awake." He was still stroking his fingers over me.

"I know. I was giving you time to settle your thoughts."

"I already had lots of time to think. I don't like it." I pinched his skin in my fingers and pulled it from him, then let it go and did it again.

"I can tell."

I shook my head. "Am I talking too much now? Would you like me to be quiet?" He moved me to the pillow and lay down in front of me. He looked at me and touched his hand to my face.

"No to both. I like to hear the things in your head, Baby Boy. I can see that there are things that are bothering you and I don't care how jumbled they come out, tell me whatever you like."

"Boots." I looked at him and he half-smiled. He remembered too. "I see them all the time and I miss them. I'm sad that I lost them, even though they hurt me."

"Hurt you? I don't remember them hurting you? Do you mean they rubbed you?" I put my hands together and laid my face on them and looked at him.

"Do you think I'm losing my mind? I thought I was going mad when I used to talk to them."

I could see him struggling to keep up with the things that were coming out of my mouth, but I was just saying the things that were finding their way out of my head. If I thought about them too much and tried to put them in any sort of order, they would hurt me again. I was trying not to let that happen.

"No, I think you are trying to heal, finding your peace bit by bit... I'm trying very hard to stay with you, Baby Boy... but I need you to help me understand. Can you try?" His hand was still touching my face and he stroked his thumb over my cheek. I didn't answer, I didn't know if I could. "I have you." He waited and I nodded, already scared of the feelings and the hurt I knew would come. "Who did you used to talk to?"

I whispered my answer, wary of the memories. "My boots... to share... I never let them see though. If he knew, he would have punished me and taken them away... and I needed them... so I wasn't alone." I was looking at him trying to see if he was understanding. "I used to just tell them silently, in my head but then I think my head got too full... so I started speaking to them, telling them things. Is that going mad? Is that what losing your mind is like? Because you said to share and there was no one there to listen... just them." I watched him. Did he think I was insane?

"I don't think you were losing your mind; I think you were working very hard to save it. It was very clever of you. It was clever of you to know that you needed to do that, so you didn't get lost. You were so brave when I know how scared you must have been, on your own for such a long time." He looked at me for a moment before continuing. "How did the boots hurt you?"

I could feel it starting inside me as I thought about it, the panic I felt as the boot had fallen on the floor, it had sounded so loud in the darkness. My breathing increased with the memory, and I should have kept looking at him, stayed with him, then maybe it wouldn't have spread so quickly but I looked away. I looked up at the headboard where my boots had hung and remembered pulling at them so I could have them when I died.

"They hurt me here." I touched my fingers to the side of my face that had been beaten. I looked back at him and shook my head. "Can you stop it?"

He closed his eyes and I watched as his face crease in pain as he understood. When he opened them again and saw me watching, his face changed, it became softer as he rubbed his fingers over mine, over my face.

"No, Baby Boy... I want to... but I can never change the memory or stop the pain he caused you."

I felt it spreading inside me, the desolation, the fear. I couldn't stop the tap from running now. "You see...I couldn't reach the water. I could feel the new welts eating away at my skin and it was hard, I couldn't breathe, I couldn't move. I knew I was dying, and I was scared... too scared to go on my own. I knew it would be dark...but I wanted it, wanted its peace. I was just scared to go on my own, so I needed something to go with me. I could just about reach my boots without moving and I got them, but I was running out of time... I could feel it pulling me to go, pulling at my body, at my throat but I was so scared. Each breath hurt and got harder and harder to take.

"You said the boots were for me so I wouldn't feel alone in the dark and I didn't want to go on my own. I wanted to take them with me, but the laces were stuck... but then it was alright, I got one on and I pulled at the other... it was so loud...when it dropped to the floor, the noise in the dark was so loud it made my heart stop…and woke him...

"When he picked it up, he said: 'Whores don't wear shoes'... no... no, when he picked it up, he pulled me to him by my other boot and hit me with the one in his hand. He said each word as he smashed the boot into my face…whores…don't…wear… boots! Then I couldn't hear him anymore or feel it, it was dark. I thought it was over, thought that was the end of the pain and I was relieved... but it wasn't. When Kellen woke me, I felt it all over again..." I was breathing quickly, trying to fight it. I put my hands out to Layton wanting him to stop it.

"I can't stop it, Isaac."

I felt the tears and I cried out, pushing him, angry with him for not stopping it. I had managed to go nearly a year, storing it in my head, every day, every hour, every minute of feeling hungry, taking his abuse both mentally and physically. Why had I tried to keep going?

He sat up and grabbed my arms and pulled me to him. I was still crying out as he manhandled me in his arms and wrapped me tightly into his body, wrapping his legs over mine and holding my wrists in his hands.

"I can't stop it, Baby Boy, but I'm here with you, while you hurt, while you suffer. I have you. Cry it out, Baby Boy."

I pulled at my hands, trying to get them free from him. I didn't want to get away, not really, I wouldn't know what to do if he had let me go. I wasn't fighting him; I was fighting the memories. I looked at him and cried out, it was a guttural cry and for a second, I wasn't sure it was me, but it was and came from deep inside and I couldn't stop it.

"I know, I have you. The first memory is always the worst, it will get easier I promise. Every time will get a little easier. I have you, I'm not going to let you go or leave you on your own."

For the last eighteen months, people had said things they didn't mean, made me feel safe when I wasn't... except him. He had never lied, even telling me he couldn't stop the pain and I knew that was true. It didn't matter how much I struggled or how long I needed him to hold me while my mind lost control, he would stay. I didn't have to earn him; I had never had to earn him. That was why I could be myself and that was why out of everyone, I had always trusted him.

I pushed my face into his chest and tried to stamp my feet. He held them tightly in his legs but the effort it took me to try for a few minutes was enough to burn the anger out of me. As my energy drained, my anger lessened, and the pain became an ache in my head; he let go of my wrists and held my hands in one of his. He held my head to him and stroked my face with his thumb. I took a deep staggered breath, trying to settle my breathing as I relaxed into him. He loosened his hold but never let go, as promised. My head felt like I had had some sort of seizure, it was thumping and I groaned.

"Just breathe, Baby Boy."

I shook my head slowly, the pain was horrendous, like nothing I had felt before. "My head."

He pulled my face to look at him. "Headache?" I screwed my face up as it throbbed. "I'm guessing that means yes." I pushed my face back into him and groaned as I felt a little sick.

He held me close and moved, leaning his body sideways. I closed my eyes and wrapped my arm around him to hold myself close to him, clinging to him like a monkey clings to its mother, knowing that was where it was safest. He sat back, opened a bottle, and tipped some tablets into his hand. He leant sideways again then sat back, he held out a bottle of water. I looked at the tablets.

"Will they make me sleep?"

He shook his head. "Strong painkillers left by Kendal, that's all."

I shakily picked up one tablet and put it in my mouth, he offered the water and I took it and swallowed the tablet. He gestured to the other tablet and reluctantly I took it and swallowed it. He drank some water himself then put the lid on the bottle and put it beside him on the bed. He wrapped his arms around me again and kissed the top of my head.

"If I fall asleep then I will know you lied to me."

I could hear his smile as he spoke. "If you fall asleep it will be because you are tired, Baby Boy, that's all. Are you comfortable?" I nodded, then groaned. "It is just the stress that is causing it, try and relax." We sat in silence again and I closed my eyes to ease the pain.

"Do you think he damaged my head?"

"No. Are you worried about the headache?" I could feel him looking at me.

"Yes. I have never had anything like this before…I think something is wrong."

He shifted under me and got out his phone and dialled. I fleetingly looked up at him and he stroked my face and I laid it back on him and closed my eyes.

"Hey, it's Layton. I know I'm sorry... Isaac has a very bad headache and I wondered if you can come over and take a look at him... If you could... thank you." He closed his phone and looked at me. "Kendal is coming, Isaac." I nodded my head a little and then rested it against him.

I never heard her arrive but when I woke, she was sitting on the bed with a cup of tea in her hand. There was a lamp on in the room and I blinked against its glare. I was still with Layton; his arms were still wrapped around me, and she smiled when she saw me open my eyes.

"Hello, poppet. How's the head now?" I moved my head a little.

"Still there." I closed my eyes. It was a little easier, but it was still there, the light wasn't helping.

"Is the light making it worse?" She moved towards me and I nodded. "I need you to look at my light, just for a moment, Isaac." I leant back on Layton, and she shone her torch in my eyes one at a time. "Okay honey, you can rest now." I curled back into him, and he stroked his fingers over my face.

"Well?" Layton was asking.

"I believe it's just a migraine. Probably brought on by stress and nothing to worry about, Isaac. I will give you something to help relax you. Sleep is your best friend at this moment."

I closed my eyes and Layton kissed me.

"See, I knew that's all it was. Try and sleep, Baby Boy, Kendal will give you something. You're like a coiled spring, you're so tense." I didn't want to be put to sleep, it worried me that I wouldn't be able to wake should the nightmares come.

"Don't make me sleep." I opened my eyes and looked at Kendal. "Don't make me please."

She smiled. "No, just a small jab in your arm to ease the pain and relax you. You don't have to sleep, it will just make your body and mind a little heavy, make this world a little easier for you for a while."

I pushed my face into Layton. He increased his hold on me and then I felt the sharp sting in the top of my arm. I moaned into him, not wanting whatever it was I was being given and he kissed me.

"Just let it take you, Isaac. I won't leave you."

I felt it working almost immediately through my body and as hard as I tried to fight it, to push myself into Layton away from the warm feeling that spread through me, I couldn't. My head flopped back to his shoulder and I couldn't lift it back up. I could see him looking at me and feel the ache in my head beating far away. They had paralyzed me, taken all my physical abilities. I didn't like not having control of my body and I tried to lift my hand to him in panic as he looked at me.

"Breathe, Isaac, I have you." He looked at Kendal. "Thank you. He's gone, I can feel his body is relaxed. How long will it last?"

I moved my eyes to watch Kendal. I wanted to know how long I would feel like this too. She walked out of my sight, but I could hear her.

"A few hours. His whole body is so tense, this will ease the strain and that will ease the headache." She came back into sight and touched her hand to my head. All I could do was move my eyes and I looked up at her. "That's it, Isaac. Just lay there and relax, sweetie. Layton will watch over you." She moved away. "I... am off to get some sleep... you will feel better in the morning." I saw Layton nod.

"Thank you for coming out."

"See you later, boys."

I heard the door close and looked back at Layton. He looked down and stroked my face.

"I know it's a little strange, Isaac, it is just letting your body rest. Would you like some water?"

I opened my mouth to speak and slurred the word. "Yesss."

He got the bottle and took the lid and held it to my mouth and tipped it. I could just about swallow the liquid and a little poured out of my mouth. Layton wiped it with his fingers. I tried to fight against the warm feeling inside me and my legs twitched.

"Shh, Baby Boy. Don't fight it, just let your body sink into me. It's like sleeping with no nightmares." I looked at him. "I know you're feeling vulnerable, but this is just like being in restraints, Isaac, just as if I had taken your control away. Just let your mind go with it, like you do when you are bound." If you didn't fight your binds then it was easier.

"Yess...Ssir." He stroked my face.

"That's it, good boy. I'm going to stay with you while you rest."

I let the warm feeling take me, letting it into my head. When you didn't fight it, it kind of felt like you were floating. I watched him the whole time. He touched and soothed me as I gave myself to him and floated in his arms until sleep took me easily.

It was morning. I could see the natural bright light through my eyelids before I opened them.

"Good morning." I opened my eyes slowly and looked at Layton. "How's your head this morning?"

I thought about it and about what he had done, well him and Kendal. I felt violated.

"Gone." I could speak without effort, and I lifted my hand and touched my lip.

"The drug has worn off, Isaac, you are back as you were. Just take it easy."

I pushed myself up to sitting, I was still between his legs, and I pulled my legs into me and sat away from him. I was annoyed about having my body drugged. He touched his fingers to me and ran them down my back.

"I decided to do that, Isaac, I was worried about you. You were caught up in the trauma of what had happened, and it was causing you a lot of stress. I wanted you to relax but still know that you were safe with me. I didn't mean to frighten you." I didn't speak or look at him. He moved from the bed and I turned quickly.

"Don't go... I won't be angry." He smiled at me while he pulled on his trousers. He walked towards me and ruffled my hair.

"You can be angry with me, I'm not leaving. Just giving you a bit of space while I make breakfast... Okay?" I nodded, glad because I was still angry with him.

I sat quietly and watched him as he cooked and made tea. He didn't look at me until it was ready and then he turned, carrying the tray. I looked at him.

"It scared me; can you not do that again?"

He put the tray down on the bed, sat down, and looked at me.

"Would you rather we just put you to sleep?"

I didn't answer him because I couldn't decide. The nightmares were so real.

"I know that the nightmares scare you, I didn't want to force you into that place. You were going to do yourself damage if you didn't calm down. I will not lie to you, Baby Boy, I will do it again if I feel I must for your safety. I know it makes you very vulnerable but know I would never hurt you. I know that trust is something you are struggling with..."

"I trust you." I looked away then back at him. "I don't want to be put to sleep."

He smiled at me, leant forward, and touched my face.

"You want to be friends again and eat breakfast?" He looked at me and smiled. "I have tea." I half smiled at him, he sat back and dragged the tray between us. "Go for it."

I really smiled at him, and he laughed as I took my tea and drank it. He had made eggs and toast. We sat and ate in silence. He made more tea, sat back on the pillows and watched me. "Are you feeling better?"

I looked at him. "Yes." He wanted more, I knew. But I felt mentally exhausted still. I sighed at him. "Can we shower first?"

He climbed forward onto his knees and crawled towards me. He took the cup and put it on the floor and then turned back to me, kneeling in front of me. He touched his fingers to my stomach and trailed them up to my chin, making me look at him. He rubbed his thumb over my lip before leaning in and kissing me.

"Are you in need of some TLC, Baby Boy?"

He rubbed his beaded tongue over my lip, and I opened my mouth to him. He kissed me and teased my tongue with his, wanting to play. I pushed my tongue to him and he pulled away, holding my face in his hands. He licked at my tongue, teasing. "Hmm, Baby Boy? Do you need this?" He pulled away a little and waited.

"Yes." My answer was whispered.

I wanted to feel him touching me, caring for me... desiring me. He took my mouth gently with his and sucked at my tongue, rubbing the bead over its tip. I pulled my mouth from him, wrapped my arms around his neck, and pulled myself to him on my knees. He held me as I kissed his neck, stroking my body with his hands.

I was suddenly frightened by the feelings running through me, old feelings that I hadn't felt in a long time. The need to have it and feel it was strong, it coursed through me, but it was tinged with fear which made me wary. I shook my head and moaned. He took my head in his hands and kissed my face.

"It's okay. I'm going to take care of you." He looked at me. I was a bit bewildered at how quickly the need for him had taken me. "Don't worry, Baby Boy, I have you, okay?" I nodded in his hands then pushed my face to his shoulder and wrapped my arms around him.

"Can you wash me, wash my hair?" He held me to him. "Do I even have hair yet?" His face was next to mine and I felt his smile against my skin.

"You have beautiful hair, Isaac." He ran his hand over my head. "It has grown very quickly, I will show you in a few days, not today. I think your mind is dealing with enough." He held his lips to my head and we stayed like that for a while. "You ready for some special Layton love?" I pulled away from him and frowned, looking at him. He laughed which made me smile. "Okay, that sounds scary." He stopped and looked at me.

I held still, wondering what he was going to say. "Oh, Baby Boy, I forgot what it was like to watch you smile." He kissed me fleetingly. "Come on, time to shower." He took my hand and pulled me from the bed.

When we got to the shower, he let go and I went and sat on the shower floor. Waiting for him to put on the water. When I looked at him, he was undressed and watching me. I loved to look at his body. As a slave, I saw lots of bodies, big, small, muscled, toned, fat, and thin but none of them stayed in my head like his did. It was always his body I saw, complete with tattoos, always with pictures because that was him.

"Why do you cover your skin with tattoos?" He walked towards me and turned on the spray.

I turned my head down and let the water run over me. It was warm and I leant back on my hands, looking up into the spray, enjoying the beating water against my face. He pulled me from behind, sliding me out of the spray and into his body. He tipped some liquid into his hand and ran it over my hair. I thought he was going to ignore the question. He tipped my head back and ran both hands over my scalp, and then rubbed his fingers in my hair. The answer became unimportant as I let him just have me.

"Some things are too precious to forget."

I let his voice soothe me. There was nothing better than this feeling. Being here with him, no pain, no thoughts, not earning anything, just being me. Being loved by him.

He washed me slowly with the sponge, spending time washing fingers and toes, arms and legs. He pulled me forward under the spray with him and used his hands to wash away the lather. I watched him as he watched his hands on my body. His tenderness and care of my body made me cry but I knew he couldn't see my tears in the shower. I was glad because I wanted to keep watching him.

This moment was worth the year I had spent hanging from my bed alone, trying not to think about him because it hurt too much. I reached out my hand to his body and touched my fingertips to him. I had left him before when he had wanted me to stay, not stay with him but stay as a slave in his house. I had left because I didn't want to rely on him, but that's what I had been doing from the moment he had brought me here all those years ago.

Every visit, every client, I had put into practice everything he had taught me because I trusted him. I knew he had taught me those things to keep me safe. He had always been my safety.

He stroked his hand over my head and looked at me. "I know how much they hurt you, Isaac." He wiped his thumbs over my cheeks. "I know."

I reached out my other hand and touched him. I wanted to feel him under my hands, I was drawn to touch him. I knew if he asked, I couldn't give anything to him. I looked at him again, wanting to see what he wanted from me.

He continued to stroke his hands over my head washing away the residue. Nothing, he wasn't asking or expecting or demanding. He looked at me again and I leaned towards him and laid my head on his chest.

"I know it still hurts. It's like a wound, Baby Boy, it needs to be looked after and cleaned many times before it can start getting better. Just a little more and a little more each time. Don't stop trying, Isaac, okay?" I nodded into him, and he stroked my head and my back with his hands.

He turned the water off and held me until I shivered with cold and then covered me with towels and a robe, while he sat behind me and rubbed my hair with a towel until it was dry.

He tipped my head backwards and I looked at him upside down. "There, you are beautiful. Are you warm enough?" I nodded and he kissed my forehead before letting my head go and moving.

I pushed myself back to the wall as he walked over to the shower, put it on, and washed and shaved his body. When he had finished, he wrapped a towel around his lower body, got out an electric shaver from a cupboard and began to shave his face.

"How often do you shave?"

He looked over at me. "It depends. On my body, as often as I need to, my face, every other day if it's a normal day. Unlike you, Isaac, I cannot go for weeks... would you like to try this?" He held out the shaver. I looked away and he came and crouched down in front of me.

He touched my face and I looked at him. "I've never used one of them... I've never really shaved myself, always had it done for me. Do you want me to shave?"

He smiled. "No, not if you're not ready to. It's not like you are turning into some big hairy monster. Kendal shaved you while you were healing... She likes to mother and you were the perfect candidate... still." He smiled again and got up.

He finished shaving and put stuff in his hair although it was already sticking up. He turned and looked at me. "Come on, I'll put the kettle on. Maybe you can tell me about some of your clients." He held out his hand and I took it and he pulled me from the floor.

"Can I have biscuits with my tea if I tell you?" I heard him laugh quietly as he led me into the bedroom.

CHAPTER THREE

I spent the morning telling him about some of the clients I had taken visits with. They were easy memories, being used and punished by clients was normal, my normal and that made it easier to tell him. We had just finished lunch and he cleared the plates and took them to the kitchen. I curled my knees into my body and looked at him. Something was bothering me.

"I don't remember what happened when you picked me up, did you... meet Marcus?" Layton returned carrying a fruit bowl which he put on the bed. He sat down and looked at me.

"I did." He picked up an apple, peeled it, and offered me some.

I shook my head and fell silent, watching as he ate the apple and biting my bottom lip anxiously. He looked at me. "Are you going to tell me about him then?"

I looked down at my toes and touched them with my fingers.

"You didn't like him, I can tell... but I want to tell you about him... be... because he saved me, every time I took a visit with him, he saved my mind."

He leant back on the footboard at the end of the bed, pulled his knees up and leant his arms on them, looking at me between his legs.

"Do you love him?" I looked at him then back at my feet.

I shook my head a little, not understanding what it was I felt for Marcus.

"I don't know what I feel, I'm not even sure I know what love is. I liked him but I don't even know if we were friends." I sat quietly for a while, thinking. "I think in the end we were. He has a foot fetish, and he loved my feet. He loved to hurt them, punish them and then loved making them better but he wasn't like other clients. He wasn't just about inflicting the pain, he liked to talk to me. He used to say that he had never met such a needy slave, but he liked it. He liked that I needed him to look after me, he understood, and for a few hours of punishment, he gave me a day's worth of comfort.

"I never told him my thoughts, never shared any with him... he was a client, and I didn't know if he would tell Kellen." I looked at him. "He is the reason I didn't get lost, that I managed..." My breath caught in my throat as I felt the sadness creeping into my mind. "...That I managed to get back to you... so I could share... with you." I could feel the tears in my eyes, and I looked back at my feet and watched as the teardrops landed on them.

Layton moved towards me and sat with his legs around me, touching his fingers to my hair. I leaned against his chest, and he kissed my head. "I don't want you not to like him." I didn't know why that was important to me, but it was.

He leant his face to mine and whispered. "Then I won't."

I lay against him and settled my mind.

"He always took off my restraints, he said they weren't needed, and he always let me come. One time, he played with my feet for so long that they were so sore... it was the only time he pleasured me with his mouth just so I could come. I didn't mind that he punished me. I gave him what he wanted so I could have what I needed, even though he said I never had to earn the comfort he gave. It felt wrong just to take it from him, to let him soothe my mind of all my other visits. He always fed me, and he had the biggest bath I've ever seen. He liked to kiss my toes in the bath, and he didn't mind that I never had any hair, that it was shaved... he just loved me because he said he liked to."

Layton stroked his fingers through my hair, letting me be but soothing my memories. My legs were still curled into my body, but I was leaning on him.

"How did you end up with Marcus... after your Keeper had hurt you?"

I didn't answer straight away. I ran the memories round in my mind trying to make sense of them and the pain I had felt. I needed to look at him, I needed my anchor to the present so the thoughts wouldn't consume me. I tipped my head back on his shoulder and he touched his lips to my forehead.

"I... I thought I was dead... it was completely dark in my head, not a single thought, just that I was dead. But then he was asking me to open my eyes, wake up look at him. It was the most pain I had ever felt... I kept breathing, hoping it would go away, like that moment when the whip touches and you can't catch your breath, but you keep consciously breathing and it fades away... but it didn't, it wouldn't stop. I was scared at first when I saw him, but he soothed me, gave me something for the pain and it eased it a little. He talked to me; told me I should have told him while he cleaned my wounds." Layton stroked my face.

"Who, Baby Boy? Who found you? Marcus?"

I shook my head. "Kellen... Kellen found me. He said Marcus had come back for me, but Devon had sent me to another client. He kept ringing Kellen to find out why I hadn't arrived... that's why he came, that's why he found me, but he wasn't angry... he was nice..." I took deep breaths and looked away from Layton down across the bed. "I asked to go back but he said I needed to wait... he said I could go to Julian's to heal..." I was pulling at my wrist cuffs and pushing at Layton's leg with my feet, agitated by the painful memories. I had wanted to go to Layton, I had desperately wanted him, needed him to soothe the pain.

"Isaac?... Isaac, come settle with me." He took my wrist, and I pulled my hand from him, pushing at his chest, pushing myself away from him.

I didn't want to hurt him, but I needed to vent my anger. It was too big, it needed room, the pain I had felt was too much. I grabbed the covers in my fists and pulled at them, yelling loudly into the room. He moved away from me, and I looked at the bed, lost in the memories.

"They all hurt me. I gave my body and my mind to them, and they hurt me, hurt them... I didn't want to go to any of them... I wanted you to come for me... the pain was so bad..." I creased my face up and pushed my fists into the bed, the pain was torrential, and it wouldn't stop. I growled out my words, then cried out into the room again. "I wanted to be dead... so it didn't hurt... so no one could hurt me again. Don't send me back..."

"Isaac!" I looked at him. "I'm going to help you."

I stared at him, caught in the memory that wouldn't stop hurting me. I wanted him to stop it, then and now. I couldn't help myself, any more than I had been able to then. I needed him to stop it. I watched as he jabbed the needle in my arm and I looked at him scared, knowing what was coming.

I pulled at the covers angry again, with him, with the needle, and took deep breaths as I felt the warm feeling spreading through me. I felt myself sinking into the bed and I tried to fight against it. He touched his fingers to my hair and stroked it.

"I'm... scared." I looked at him as I tried to stay upright.

"I have you, Baby Boy, just like before, don't fight it. Just breathe. Nothing bad is going to happen, your body is just going to rest."

I felt my strength drain from me and he held my head while the rest of my body fought for control until the drug finally did its job and I sunk over my knees to the bed. I moaned out distressed at the paralysis.

He came into view and stroked my face. "I'm here, I have you." He pulled my legs out from under me and took the bedclothes from my fists, stroking my hands. I tried to hold onto him, but my fingers just twitched.

"Shh, I'm not going anywhere. Would you like me to hold you, Isaac, until it wears off?" I couldn't even answer.

He pulled me onto him, my body across his legs, my head in his arms and he wrapped his arms around me. "Comfortable?" He kissed the side of my face and stroked my hair. "Good boy... just relax, I have you. You're not alone, Isaac. No darkness, no nightmares, just resting here with me." I gave in to it and let it take my mind. "That's it, just let it take you, Baby Boy."

I didn't answer, my only thoughts were what I could see and that was him. I was safe.

I slept a little again. The sleep was peaceful apart from the small niggle that lingered in my mind. It was like I knew there were things I should be thinking about, but the drug was stopping me from getting to them, it was frustrating, and I found it easier not to try. I opened my eyes when I could hear him calling my name. I was laying on the pillow and he was leaning over me, stroking my face.

"Hey there. Are you ready to come back?"

I moved my arm, it felt heavy, but I brought it to my face and touched my lips with my fingers. I was glad that I had control again over my body.

"I've made tea."

I felt a little disorientated, thoughts rushing back into my head and remembering how they had consumed me, and I had lost myself in them. I closed my eyes and shook my head. I was still distressed at him having taken my body again.

"Come on, Isaac. Warm tea will make it feel better."

I opened my eyes and looked at him. "Can you promise not to do it again... please, I don't like it, I don't like not being able to move... it scares me." He kissed my face and looked at me again.

He sighed. "I will not promise but I will give you some more time to try and sort it in your head. If I feel you are causing yourself too much stress and trauma though, I will intervene... agreed?" I sulked for a moment and then nodded. He ruffled my hair and sat up. "Come on, sit up and drink this tea before it's cold. I want to talk to you some more about Marcus."

I sighed and pushed myself slowly to sitting feeling groggy. I didn't want to talk anymore, I just wanted to forget it for a while.

"Can we not? I'm still feeling the effects of the last one... and I don't want you to make me a vegetable again."

He laughed quietly and shook his head. "Safe subjects only, I promise. It wasn't talking about Marcus that made you catatonic." He passed my tea and sat cross-legged in front of me.

He took my foot and looked at it and rubbed his fingers over the fading scars. "You liked Marcus, didn't you?" I nodded while drinking my tea. "And he likes you too. He said he had never met anyone like you." He looked up at me and then back at my foot. "No one, he said, allowed him to play like you did and still looked at him without fear in your eyes. He said he could see you were desperate for comfort and touch and the more he gave, the more you offered yourself to him." He fell silent for a moment before continuing. "Did the punishment he gave on your feet not scare you?" He looked at me again.

I shrugged my shoulders. "A little... at first. I have never had just my feet punished before, I didn't know what it would be like to feel it, but he watched me the whole time, I felt safe. He never made me hold myself, he always bound me, so I had to submit to it."

I always found it harder on the mind if you were made to hold yourself for punishment rather than just having to take it.

"The single tail hurt the most, that's what caused the scars, but he never left me without looking after the wounds. In the hours I spent with him, most of them were like being with my Keeper while he looked after me." Layton nodded in understanding. "I don't know a lot about him, but I know I always felt safe with him."

He looked at me. "Is that why you asked to go to him?"

I didn't remember much of that time, but I could only think it was. I nodded and he looked away. There was silence for a while and I hoped that that was it for today, that we could just do this, be together and not think or talk.

He sat rubbing my foot and his words came out of nowhere. "He calls for you." He put my foot down and lifted the other foot and I stared at him confused by his words.

My heart rate increased, and I waited for him to look at me or say something else, but he didn't, he just sat rubbing my foot. I couldn't remember the time I had spent with him in the end, I didn't know what I had said or what he thought, it was all a blur. A million questions piled into my head, I closed my eyes and groaned quietly.

Why couldn't my head be empty for once? It seemed as soon as I emptied it of one thing, it was filled with a million other things that wanted attention and I didn't want any of them. I just wanted to stay here with Layton, wanted to empty my head of everything, not add more. Being a slave was an easy, simple life but he was making me free and that's why everything hurt so much. I didn't want it.

"Can you jab me with that thing again please?"

He looked up. "No..."

I held my hands out to him, putting my wrists together, and dropped my head. It was an easy place to go.

"Can I go back in the cage then please?"

He took my hands and I thought he was going to clasp my restraints together, but he undid the buckle and took them off. I looked up at him.

"No." I dropped my hands to the bed agitated.

I felt like a fish, flapping around in a puddle trying to find a way to get under the water. I was breathing heavily staring at the bed.

"Isaac, look at me." I slowly raised my eyes to him. "There is no reason for you to hide. I'm sitting right here; all you have to do is talk to me. Tell me what's making you so agitated and look so sad?" I sat for a minute and just looked at him. "Tell me one thing, Baby Boy, and we will deal with it."

"My head is filling with things and I don't want to think about them."

"Things to do with Marcus?" I nodded. He dropped my foot and moved closer in front of me. "Then don't think about them, just say them so they are not in your head."

Well, that kind of made sense. It was what I used to do, with him. I used to just say what came into my head and it never bothered him. I sighed.

"I don't remember what happened when Kellen took me to Marcus. I don't know what he thought. I don't understand why he calls, what does he want? Does he know what happened?" Layton was just about to speak when something else occurred to me. "Does he want me... to visit him? I... I can't... do it, he needs to know... then he won't call, he'll stop calling." Layton took my hand and held it in his.

"Okay, now breathe." He looked at me. "These are not terrible things, Isaac. Let me tell you what I know and then, if anything else bothers you, we can talk about it as we go along, okay?" I nodded, relying on him now to sort these thoughts. "Marcus was extremely worried for you when you got dropped off, all he knew was that you had asked for him. He didn't know what had happened and when Kellen called to say they were going to pick you up to take you back the next day, he worried for your safety with them.

"You were unconscious for most of the time you were with him, but you kept saying things like you didn't want to go back and calling out random things, one of those things was my name. He decided that he wasn't convinced about you going back with Kellen. so he did some searching and somehow, he managed to find me. He has some good connections, Baby Boy.

"When I got there, he was so worried about you but there wasn't time to explain things to him, you were in desperate need of medical attention, and I didn't understand why you were there. I could see he cared for you, and he asked if he could call to find out how you were. I agreed, believing that he wouldn't want anything to do with you. He left the country on business that same day and honestly, I didn't think he would call but he did.

"He called a few days later and has called for you every few days since. I have explained what happened and he was angry, angry with himself for not realising. He thinks you were very brave, Isaac, and thinks you are very special and wants to see you, not as a visit, not to punish you, but as a friend to see that you are alright. I have already informed him that you are no longer a slave, Baby Boy, that you are not to be punished. He still calls every week to check on you. His persistence makes me believe he cares about you a great deal." He looked at me.

"Can I see him?"

He forced a smile. "He wants to see you... he has asked if you would like to spend a few days with him. Would you like to go?" I shook my head which made him smile. "Would you like to see him at least?"

"I'm not sure... why does he want to take me away? Do you want me to go with him? Do you want me to go away?"

Was this the start of him moving me on? I was gripped by panic and pulled my knees into my body, wrapping my arms around them. He took my hand again and kissed it before pulling me to him. I lay with my head on his lap and he stroked my hair around my ears.

"I want you to be settled and safe, Isaac. He says he wants to spend some time with you, look after you. No one is going to make you go. I think seeing him would be good for you and him. You shared something special, something that needs to find an understanding if it's to end or maybe… it's not finished between you."

I frowned trying to work things out in my head. I didn't understand what we had shared but I owed him something.

"I think I need to say thank you to him. Here though, can he come here? Not away from here." Layton looked down at me and I moved to look up at him to see if he thought it was okay. Was it the right decision?

"Of course. He will be glad to see you, I think he has started to think that I kidnapped you and kept you hostage. It would put his mind at rest to see you fit and well."

I laid my head back on him and moved my arm around him to hold him. I felt a little unsure now. I liked Marcus but I wasn't a slave anymore and I wasn't sure where that left our relationship.

"I will call him later, make arrangements."

I didn't say anything, I still got the feeling that Layton didn't like him and that worried me.

"Why don't you like him?" I could feel him looking at me but I didn't turn.

"Is that why you're unsure, Isaac?" I didn't answer and he continued. "I don't dislike him really... I believe he's a good person because of what he did for you. I do not doubt that without him, you would have been lost many months ago. I have never come across a client so understanding of their slave, or someone who... sees you the way I see you... and it makes me... feel things about him that I shouldn't, and that he probably doesn't deserve."

I moved a little so I could see him. "I don't understand? So, you do like him?"

He smiled down at me. "I think you shouldn't worry so much. Marcus can come here and see you and I can still watch over you in case you find it... difficult. Okay?" I turned my face back to his lap and nodded.

I found some peace in the fact that he would be here ready to turn me into a vegetable should I need him. It made me smile and he must have noticed because he touched his finger to my lip, but he didn't speak. I reached out my hand and picked up my wrist cuffs.

"Can I have them back?"

He took them from me and started to put them on. "For now, Baby Boy."

I felt safe again.

The next two days were a lot calmer. We spoke a little about my time at Kellen's but nothing that made me want to hide. Every night I asked for my restraints to be connected but he always said I didn't need them because I was with him.

It was morning and I was awake before him for the first time. I spent ages just watching him. I rarely saw him sleep, he was always awake, even if I woke in the night, he was there to soothe me, and I began to wonder if he ever slept at all.

I needed the bathroom and after a long mental conversation with myself about whether to wake him to ask him if I could go, I reluctantly left the bed and him. Marcus was coming today, and I wasn't sure how I felt about it. I used the toilet, brushed my teeth, and with my thoughts taken with Marcus's arrival, I found myself standing under the shower touching my body.

I could feel it was different from what I had seen in the mirror that first time Layton had taken me from the hospital room. I wanted to see but he had had all the mirrors covered. I looked over at the basin and saw the razors he had been using. I wanted to shave, he had made it look easy when I had watched him, and I had never shaved myself. I left the shower and got the razor and came back under the spray and soaped my body.

I sat on the floor next to the running water and shaved my legs and under my arms, then I opened my legs and looked at my cock. I rubbed my fingers over it and around my balls and could feel the small stubble that had started to grow, I wanted it gone. I wanted to feel smooth like his skin was. I lifted my balls and hesitated, he had done his quickly and I couldn't even put the razor to my skin.

The last time Devon had shaved me it had been rough, and my skin had been sore, it had taken all my will not to close my legs to him or I knew I would have earned some punishment. I gave up, annoyed with myself for the thoughts, I dropped the razor on the floor between my legs and looked at my cock. It had been off-limits to me for many years and now it was off-limits for different reasons, for myself and others since I had recovered.

The only time I had wanted to feed it, I had been forbidden by Julian. Having it touched and pleasured and punished had been part of my daily life and now I had ignored it for weeks, fearing the loss of control that would come from touching it. Now I couldn't even shave it. I rubbed my hand over it absently, and without conscious thought or will it became hard and pulsing within moments. It was screaming for attention, I released it and leaned back on my hands, pulling my knees up and spreading them wide.

I moaned as I looked at it, protruding from my body. I wasn't body shy, only sometimes against more well-built slaves but once I started playing, it got forgotten. I always loved my cock though, I always considered it to be my best offering and was always proud of it when I was asked to present it to any Dom. These last few weeks since I had woken up, I had done everything to ignore it and forget it. Any slight bit of need or excitement I had felt had caused me to recoil from it, but it wouldn't be ignored now, and I thrust my hips into it.

The rush of feeling it gave me spooked me, and I pushed myself forward onto my hands and knees, tipped my head back and blew my breaths out quickly. I was torn between wanting it and fearing the memories and thoughts that would come with touching it.

Pleasure and pain, they were the same, well, that's how it usually worked for me. They ran through my body and mind with equal need and if I took one, then I knew I would want the other. That's where things became confusing. Where would that leave me? Back to being a slave to them? I didn't want to give them my body and mind to play with anymore, I couldn't trust them to keep me safe while I played and sated my need.

I felt my cock pulsing, asking to be touched and I spread my knees, sinking further towards the floor and thrust my hips into the feeling. My body was working against my mind, and I let out a sob as I was consumed with the feeling. My sane thoughts, the ones that had kept my need from me these last few weeks, that kept me protected, were being smothered. I could feel the urgency in my body, in my blood, as it raced through me, chasing the orgasm and the release it sought.

I wanted so much to give into it and touch my cock and I breathed hard, trying to give myself time to decide as the battle continued in my mind. I turned my head panting, trying not to engage the feeling and looked at the shower as my body thrust again towards the floor, begging.

My last sane thought was a cold shower as I sobbed again and pushed myself back to sit on my feet and took my cock in my hand. I cried as I stroked it in my hand and felt the orgasm ask, my hips thrust forward, and I fell back onto my other hand as my body took what it wanted. The orgasm raced through my mind and body, burning me, making my body jolt violently at the intensity of it as it coiled ready to explode.

I threw my head back, my mind lost in it as it took control of me, as my mind, body and soul gave themselves to it. I could hear my cries as my life shot from me, but they were far away. For that single moment, my mind and body were one and they took me to a place so sweet and pleasurable that it was painful to feel it again.

As I drifted back to reality, I moaned and looked at my cock as the last of my life left me, my body still jolting as it tried to hold onto the sweet feeling. Finally, it gave up and I dropped my hand from my cock, leaned back on them, and gasped noisily. My breaths turned into sobs as my mind came back. I closed my eyes against the harshness of it, knowing I would always be a slave to it.

I felt fingers touch my face. I opened my eyes and looked at him. He was kneeling naked beside me, and I let my body fall into him and cried quietly on him, while my body still twitched and jerked from its exertion. He never spoke, he soothed my body with his touch, stroking my hair and back with his fingers, letting my body and mind slowly return from its high.

I felt him move and I wrapped my arms around him not ready to be away from him.

"Shh, Baby Boy, I have you." He stretched his legs out in front of him and around me.

I pulled my legs further into my body. I wasn't ready to talk or look at him yet. We stayed there for a while in silence, the only sound was the cascading water from the shower. He stroked his hand over my forehead back over my hair and I knew he was looking at me.

"Isaac?" I didn't open my eyes. "Look at me, Baby Boy." I slowly opened my eyes and looked at him, then looked away.

I wondered how much he had witnessed. I knew he would understand what had happened, he would know that I hadn't been able to fight against my own need for it. I felt like my last defence against this world and what it wanted from me had been broken and now I felt vulnerable again.

He stroked my hair in his fingers. "It's okay, Baby Boy."

I shook my head against him. "I don't want to be their slave anymore... they hurt me. Not just marks on my skin, not just that... inside me, it hurt inside." I closed my eyes trying to shut out the thoughts.

"Shh, slow down, Isaac. No one is sending you back, you're here with me and I have you. You have just taken your first taste in a long time, and I know it's a little overwhelming to have those feelings rushing back to you when you fought so hard to deny them. Just breathe, you're safe here. We will work through it together bit by bit until it doesn't scare you. Now that you have let it in, it will feel a little unsettling for a while but try and trust what you feel."

"I felt that... it was painful." He smiled and rubbed his hand over my arm pulling me tighter to him.

"I saw, Baby Boy, I saw the sweetness it held. I wish shaving brought me that sweetness."

So, he had been there a while then, watching me. I pushed myself up to sitting but still leant against him, I still needed the contact. He kissed my forehead.

"I tried to shave..." I opened my legs and then closed them again. "I got scared. How long were you watching me, I didn't see you."

He smiled, his lips were still at my forehead and I could feel them as his spoke.

"I woke and heard the shower, so I came to join you. As I walked in you were just getting the razor and so I decided to let you be. Your mind was busy, and I didn't want to disturb you, so I sat by the door and watched you. I wanted to be here in case you needed me. I thought for a moment that you weren't going to take it... I loved watching you, you were very beautiful."

He kissed me again and I snuggled into him feeling vulnerable at having been watched. He laughed under his breath "Would you like me to finish shaving you?"

I sighed and nodded. "Can you make it so it's not sore, last time he did it, I was sore for a week." I shivered a little, the air making the dampness of my body cold.

"No, it won't be sore, come on under the warm water before you catch a cold." He moved me from him and I floundered a little at having my comfort taken.

He stood and pulled me up and made me look at him. He looked at me for ages and it made me uncomfortable, then he swept his hand over my face, leant in and kissed my lips.

"Just a little more time, Baby Boy, and things won't seem so difficult, I promise. There's no rush." He took my hand and kissed my fingers, then led me under the shower and washed me, soothing me like he always did before he sat me on the floor and got another razor and bowl.

When he knelt in front of me, I looked away and opened my legs to him. He touched my face and I turned to look at him. "Let's start with your face?" I nodded and he kissed me. "I understand giving your body to someone demands great trust on your part, even though I know you trust me, I know it's still difficult."

He was soaping my face with lather, sitting with his legs over mine then stopped and looked at me. "If I shave your face without leaving one mark, it will make it easier for you to accept it when I shave the rest of you, okay?" I nodded. He picked up the razor and rinsed it in the bowl. He looked at me as he raised it to my face. "It's a new razor, sharp as a knife so it won't make you sore, I promise."

I closed my eyes and let him have me. He shaved my face and then he shaved the rest of my body. He was so gentle and careful. He did it slowly, not like he had done his own when I had watched.

He took me under the shower again and kissed me on the mouth. "Beautiful, Isaac, touching and watching you has made me hard. I want it, I want you to watch." He rubbed his cock in his hand and slid the other over my body pulling me towards him as he kissed my mouth and I put my hands behind me to the wall to steady myself.

I was still reeling from my own venture, but I felt the desire to touch him as I watched him. I kissed him back, tentatively at first, unsure of my own feelings but he opened his mouth to me, and a moan of pleasure left him. I moved my mouth to his neck, and I could feel his body tensing under me, chasing his pleasure. I pulled my hands from behind me and touched him gently with my fingertips, running them down his body and then I watched them run across his skin as his body twitched and jerked from my touch. His cock was hard in his fist as he rubbed it. I watched as he thrust into it over and over.

I looked at him and he looked back at me, but I could see he was being taken by his pleasure and I wanted to be part of it. I dipped my head and took his ringed nipple into my mouth and sucked at it. He swore under his breath and put his hand to the back of my head, holding me there gently.

I could hear his orgasm was close and I sucked and bit at his nipple harder, trying to tip him over the edge. He gripped my hair in his hand tightly and I did it again fleetingly, before looking up at him to watch as his body shook with his pleasure. His lips were parted as he gasped. and I pushed myself up on my toes so I could cover his mouth with my own. I felt his orgasm pulse through him as I pushed my tongue into his mouth and I knew when his mind had come back because he took my mouth roughly, pushing me against the wall and holding my head in his hand as he ploughed my mouth with his tongue.

I dropped my hands from him as my body submitted to the onslaught and I let him have me. He pulled away and trailed kisses down my neck before nipping my skin gently in his teeth, which made me flinch.

When he looked at me, I was breathing quickly as was he and he smiled at me. "The nip was for touching when I said you could only watch." I dropped my eyes from him and he pulled my chin up to make me look at him. "You made me come, Isaac." He leant forward and kissed my lips while watching me. "Are you sorry?"

I looked at him, I didn't know what he wanted me to say so I nodded my head and then shook it. He laughed and kissed me again. "I have missed you so much." He was playing his fingers in my hair, watching me. "It's okay, Baby Boy."

I was overwhelmed and confused by him, and I tipped my head towards him to show him. The use of my pet name told me that my part in his orgasm was over and I was free to ask for comfort. He held my head against him and kissed the top of my head. He pulled me back under the shower to keep warm while he washed quickly.

After, he sat with me and dried my hair like before and kissed the top of my head when it was done. He pulled me round to look at him. "Are you settled, Baby Boy?"

I nodded. I felt better, grounded, my thoughts were quiet again apart from one thing.

"I'm hungry."

He smiled and kissed me again. "Me too. Have you remembered that Marcus is coming today?" My quiet thoughts suddenly burst and filled my head. I looked away from him. "Don't hide, tell me what's in your head?"

I turned my head towards him talking to him over my shoulder. "I'm not sure, I want to see him. I'm worried. I don't want him to take me away." Layton sighed and turned me to face him.

"You're a little unsettled by this morning, that's all. No one is taking you away, Isaac. I know you're still struggling with the thoughts in your head." He reached out and stroked the side of my face with his hand. "Has Marcus ever given you a reason not to trust him?" I shook my head. "Then there is nothing to worry you. He is coming as a friend, to see you, not to punish you." I nodded. "Come on, let us get breakfast." He took my hand and led me to the bedroom.

CHAPTER FOUR

By the time we had eaten, it was nearly time for Marcus to arrive. Layton found me some new white linen trousers to wear for when Marcus arrived, although he had seen me naked before, Layton insisted I wear them.

We both sat on the sofa waiting. I sat cross-legged looking at the cage and he sat next to me holding my hand to stop me fidgeting, he said. As the waiting time went on, I pulled my legs into my body and leant my chin on them, staring out into the room. Layton was reading something to do with work and he was absently stroking his fingers through my hair. I closed my eyes trying to lose myself in his touch, but I was still bothered by the morning and Marcus's impending visit.

The orgasm had been so intense, my mind was still buzzing from it and my body seemed to be constantly reminding me of it. The feeling was almost like it wanted more or wanted it again, but I didn't want to feed it again especially as I didn't know what was expected of me now, what my place was with any of them. I didn't even know what I wanted.

Should I just let Layton punish me? Should I go away with Marcus and maybe let him play? The idea scared me. I didn't feel ready but then I didn't even know what being ready felt like. I had always been able to turn my suffering into pleasure for them because they liked to watch and then turn the pain into my pleasure but the last pain I remember hadn't been for any of those reasons. It had been given out of hatred for me, for what I was.

If I felt any pain, would I think of him? I wasn't sure if I even wanted to come again, to lose the little control I seemed to have and was only just getting back. I wondered what Marcus would want from me now? Could a slave and client be just friends? I felt like I was waiting to go on a visit, gripped by the nervous energy that came from the waiting and I turned to look at Layton who was watching me, still rubbing his fingers through my hair. I stuck out my bottom lip showing him my anxiety and he smiled.

"Come here, Baby Boy." He tugged my hair gently and I turned and huddled into his body. "I have you." He stroked his fingers over my face and hair. "It's been a long day already, hasn't it? I can see your mind is very busy. Are you tired?" I nodded.

He wrapped his arms around me and held me, kissing the top of my head. His phone rang making me jump and he held me tightly while he fished it from his pocket and answered it. "Okay... no, send him straight down Leon, thank you." He closed the phone and looked at me. "He's here, Isaac." I didn't move. "Come on, let's go and meet him and he can see how beautiful you look."

He moved from me and stood up and held out his hand. I couldn't decide if I wanted to stay on the safety of the sofa alone or go with him. I decided that with him was better and I nervously took his hand. He pulled me from the sofa, and we walked across the basement to the far door. It was the door that led to upstairs and his other slaves, his other life, one that I was not part of anymore.

I padded behind him looking down at the floor trying to stop my heart pounding. When I heard the door open, I stopped in panic and he stopped in front of me. I didn't look up as he spoke. My heart was beating so fast I thought I might faint.

"Hello, Marcus. It's good to see you again." Layton stepped forward a little and from under my lashes, I saw him shake his hand. Then I saw Marcus and my breath caught.

He tipped his head, peering to look around Layton to see me and he was exactly as I remembered him with his tanned skin and soft black hair. He was immaculately dressed in a suit and long heavy overcoat. I gripped Layton's hand tighter.

"As you will understand, Isaac is a little nervous."

I saw Marcus nod his head in understanding but still trying to see me properly around Layton, who hadn't moved. Still holding Layton's hand, I tipped my head slowly to see him.

"Oh, my god, Isaac, look at you!"

I dropped back, startled by his outburst and tried to step back but Layton held my hand firmly, forbidding the action as Marcus sidestepped around him and stood looking at me.

I realised then that he had never seen me properly, I had a little hair now and Marcus had only ever seen me when my head had been shaved. I looked up at him slowly, wanting to see what he thought. He gave one of those smiles that took my air for a second.

"Look how beautiful you are." He stepped closer and reached out his hand and put his palm to my face.

I was nervous about the touch at first and then I recalled all the times he had comforted me in that way when I had been in pain. I closed my eyes and leaned my head into his touch. He stepped to me further until he was close, right in front of me.

I slowly looked at him and his name whispered from me questioningly. "Marcus?"

He nodded slowly and I tipped my head towards him, he wrapped his arm around me. I remembered everything about him then, the feel of his body, his smell, the relief every time he had come for me. I wasn't sure when I had let go of Layton's hand or he mine, but Marcus scooped his arm under my legs and carried me to the sofa. I sat across him with my legs and feet over his legs and looked up at him, my senses flooded with the sight and feel of him again. I touched my hand to his face and leaned into him and kissed his cheek whispering his name again. He looked at me smiling.

"Hello, Isaac." He pulled me to his body and I remembered the safety that I had found there before in my suffering.

I lay against him and watched as Layton stood looking at us. He wasn't a Keeper; he had never felt like that but there was a small part of me that would always be his and as I embraced having him back Layton turned away speaking.

"I will make tea." He left the basement, turning to look again just before he disappeared through the door.

I couldn't see his face properly; I couldn't see what he was thinking but he seemed to leave quickly. I wondered if he was glad to be free of me for a while. Two of them together was confusing anyway so I was glad of the freedom, and I snuggled deeper into Marcus. He kissed my face and stroked my arm with his hand.

"I can't believe how well you look, Isaac. I worried about you for so long." He pulled away a little and looked at me, looked at my hair, running his hand over it. "I can't believe how different you look." I looked at him remembering everything I had taken from him.

"I'm sorry... I'm sorry that I asked Kellen to bring me to you that day, that I caused you so much trouble. You always made me safe, and I didn't know... I didn't have anyone... anywhere else…" I floundered a little, not knowing the right words to express what I wanted to say. "I'm sorry that you worried."

He smiled again and pulled me to him. I went willingly into the comfort of him and his touches. I closed my eyes and remembered how much he had saved my mind when I had been with him. "Thank you... for looking after my mind when I was with you... for saving me."

The words seemed so small for what he had done for me, and I doubted that he understood the whole of it. Layton understood, he knew that Marcus had saved me, he knew that without Marcus's love and tenderness, I would not have been able to endure the months of cruelty and abuse that Devon had given. Marcus held me tighter.

"Layton has informed me of the weeks of neglect that you suffered, Isaac. Why didn't you say something to me? I could have helped you; I would have helped you. Don't you know that?"

I hadn't known that, not then. As a slave you were so sheltered, even your thoughts were guided by their will.

"You were a client and I was a... slave. I didn't have anywhere to go... and you did help me."

I felt him shake his head. "I wouldn't have punished you, Isaac, if I had known the pain you were already suffering."

I looked at him. "I liked it, I needed it. It was the only payment I could give for what you gave me... that's how it works." I waited and when he never said anything I continued. "I can't... I'm not sure I can pay you anymore... not now, not yet... maybe one day...maybe not ever. It scares me."

He looked pained and shook his head. "Fuck, Isaac. You never had to pay me. I would have cared for you. You are a little addictive." He smiled. "So vulnerable and needy. Every day I have people rushing around after me, making sure my every need is catered for but you, you are so different to anyone else in my life. I liked spending time with you, being with you, watching over you, taking care of you. I liked our talks and bathing with you and yes, I love your feet..." He ran his hand down my leg and rubbed my toes. He pulled one foot up and leaned to kiss my toes before letting it fall back to the sofa. "...but I would never let my need of it hurt you, Isaac. I would never wish you to look at me with fear in your eyes." He was certainly different from most clients. I gave him a soft smile and leaned in and kissed his lips gently.

"I'm not scared of you... I was worried about seeing you because...I didn't know why you wanted to see me? I'm not sure clients and slaves can be friends, can they?"

He smiled and squeezed my foot which he still held in his hand. "We were friends, Isaac, we are friends. Nothing would stop me from being your friend. I like you... I have a need of you too, to be with you... even if you don't have feet." He made me smile and he kissed my lips.

"Layton is helping me heal. I know I still want it, I just can't... have it, not yet, not without fear. Maybe soon... maybe never, I don't know." I shrugged my shoulders.

"But you are safe with him, you feel safe to be here?"

I nodded. "Always, he has always kept me safe. I can't go from here yet... I know you want me to go with you, but I can't be away from him, not yet. Do you understand?"

He smiled. "I do and that's okay. Maybe soon... If he lets me take you that is. I get the impression he is not fond of me. I have been asking for weeks to come and see you and he has been putting me off." He looked at me and ran his hands over my head. "I know why. Do you love him? You told me that you loved him when I wasn't sure if I had done the right thing by finding him. You said it was okay because you loved him."

I looked away. I didn't know I had said that I didn't remember.

"If you are bound and at someone's mercy and can still look at them and think they are beautiful, still feel safe with a person, even though your mind is so lost and confused. Is that love? When I'm not with him, something is missing inside me. I don't understand it, but it hurts."

Marcus lifted my face to him and smiled. "Do you not think I'm beautiful?"

I leant and kissed him. "Yes, I do but when you're not here, it doesn't hurt. I think about you, I thought about you a lot... can friends love each other and just be friends?"

He laughed at me. "Yes, they can. I love you and I miss you, I missed seeing you. When I was away, I thought about you constantly. Layton updated me every time I called, and I hoped I would see you again. Now I can relax and know that you are happy where you are."

I wasn't sure if happy was the right word, but I didn't say. Everything I had said was true, but I didn't know if I was allowed to stay here, Layton had a job, a life away from me and this basement. I knew it was only a matter of time before things changed. He was giving me time to heal but he couldn't stay with me forever down here. I pushed it from my mind and looked at Marcus. I was very sure now what I felt for him and could tell him and know he understood.

"I didn't know who you were to me, but I love you. In a different way I think but it feels like love. I think you are going to be my best foot friend." I smiled at him.

He laughed and kissed me.

"You are funny. I love you too and always, always friends and especially foot friends."

We chatted for ages. It was just like before, he told me of the trips he had been on. Half the time I didn't understand the things he spoke of, but I loved listening to him and the way he tried to explain when he could see I didn't understand. He said that he would tell me more about his life and his world every time we saw each other so I could know him a little better.

I wanted to tell him more about being here, about Leon and Sim and Jacob but I was so tired, the thoughts and words were jumbled in my head, so I lay quietly on him and closed my eyes. He was rubbing my feet gently with his hand.

"I think it is time for me to leave, Isaac." I opened my eyes and looked at him, sad.

I didn't want him to leave, I loved the way he made me feel when I was with him. Now I knew he understood where I was, where our relationship was, I was relaxed with him again.

He smiled at me and touched me soothingly across my neck. "You are very tired, I can see. My visit made you anxious and I promised Layton I would keep it short."

Layton. He had gone to make tea and never returned. I sat up quickly looking for him.

"I don't know where he is?"

Marcus pulled me back. "He was very graciously giving us time alone I think, so we could get to know each other again. I am quite sure he has not gone far." I relaxed again in his arms. "I have to go away again soon... I can see you are not ready to come and spend time with me before I go, but I would like to come and see you again. Would that be okay?"

I curled into him. "How long will you be gone?" I wrapped my arm around his neck as he rubbed his hand over my back.

"A month... maybe a little less. I will let you know as soon as I return, Isaac. Maybe you will feel ready to come away with me for a few days?" I shrugged my shoulders not really knowing anything.

"Maybe..." Maybe by then, I wouldn't have a choice, ready or not. "I... feel sad that you're leaving." He kissed me and I sat back and lay against him.

"I feel sad too, but I will think about you while I am away and now, I have a reason to look forward to coming home."

"If I'm allowed to come away with you... will we play? Can friends play? Do they have to play?"

He laughed. "We will only play, Isaac, if you want to and yes, in this world, friends can do whatever makes them happy. I'm happy just to be with you and look after you, I do not expect your obedience and you are free to do as you please with me."

Yes, I was and always had been, the subservience was always mine. He had only ever bound me when he knew the pain would not let me stay for him. That was why we were only friends. Layton did expect my obedience, he liked to control me, and I liked it. I wanted to be dominated... by him. It was where I felt safe and comfortable and loved.

I looked at Marcus and touched his face with my fingers. He turned and looked at me and I held his face while I kissed him. He took my hand in his and then pulled it away, looking at the restraint then looked at me, questioning why I still wore them.

"I just want them... for a little while longer."

I knew I couldn't go back to being a slave. Too much trust had been broken and I knew I would never completely be able to give myself over to clients. It was the only life I knew though and wearing the restraints made me feel like I still belonged here in this world, even if I couldn't take part in it.

He kissed me on the back of my hand. "Time for me to go, Isaac." I nodded.

My memories of such a painful time would always be a little better and easier because of him. I hoped that one day I would be able to give myself to him again and even out our friendship. I moved from his lap, slipped to the floor, and looked up at him as he stroked his hand over my head.

"Do you want to wait here for Layton?"

I nodded and he moved from the sofa and stood. I caught his hand and he turned again and looked at me.

"I'm sorry I couldn't come away with you today. You will come back, won't you?" He crouched down and touched my face. I held his hand and kissed it.

"Of course, Isaac, are you worried?" I looked at him and touched his face.

"I'm trying not to be."

Layton's voice when he spoke, startled me but not Marcus, which made me wonder if he already knew he was there and whether his presence had made Marcus uncomfortable and that's why he was leaving.

"Isaac has some trust issues." Marcus turned to look at him and I dropped my hands and lowered my head. "People who Isaac trusted to care for him, and who he thought were his friends have either left him or caused him a great deal of harm physically and mentally. He is very fond of you but has lost trust in his own judgement." Marcus turned and kissed the top of my head before standing and turning towards Layton.

"I understand. I kind of get the feeling that you are not fond of me, and I think I understand the reasons. I mean Isaac no harm or you. My friendship with him doesn't come with conditions and I hope I can earn the trust of you both over time. Isaac's relationship with you is very clear and it is not my wish to come between you." Marcus stepped back and touched his hand to my hair. "Not that I could, of course. Isaac has been very clear and honest with me about where his loyalties lie. His trust in you has not wavered."

I felt so confused with them both here.

"I have never given him a reason not to trust me." I looked at Layton under my eyelashes and saw him briefly look at me then back at Marcus.

This was so confusing. It felt like they were fighting but I didn't understand why. I wanted Marcus to be my friend but if Layton didn't like him, then I knew I would have to give him up. I waited and listened almost holding my breath.

"He still struggles sometimes. I know you have never given him a reason either. When he speaks of you, I can see how much you mean to him." Layton smiled at Marcus then. "I believe it is only you and I that see and understand him... I would not deny that makes me a little uncomfortable, but it also makes me easy with the knowledge that I know you would never harm him." Marcus stepped towards Layton and held out his hand.

"I would like us to become friends."

I tipped my head slightly to see Layton around Marcus and Layton was looking at me and smiling. He stepped forward and took Marcus's hand and shook it. "I have to go away again on business, but I would like to call now and again and if it's alright with you, maybe speak to Isaac?"

"Of course, but please understand that it may not always be possible for Isaac to come to the phone." He looked at me as he said that, and I dropped my eyes from him.

"I understand. I will arrange with you when I can next visit and maybe if it is okay with you and he is happy to, maybe spend a few days with me?"

I didn't hear Layton answer, but I wasn't so worried now. They had seemed to come to an understanding in their friendship and that made me feel better about being with Marcus.

"I have made some supper. You are welcome to join Isaac and I?"

I looked up at Marcus hopeful that he would stay a little longer, but he shook his head.

"I think it has been a long day for him and I can see he is very tired. I will leave you alone so he may settle for the night, but I would very much like to join you next time."

Layton smiled. "I think Isaac is disappointed, but you are right and I appreciate your understanding. Thank you, Marcus... thank you for looking after him and finding me when you did. You without a doubt have played a huge part in saving his life."

Marcus turned as he spoke. "No thanks needed." He crouched down to me again and held my face to him. "Just seeing you look so beautiful is all I need. Goodbye, Isaac. I love you very much and I promise I will come and see you again." He kissed my face and I leant into him. "Be good." He looked at me before standing and turning. "Goodbye, Layton, I will call soon."

Layton nodded at him. "Goodbye, Marcus."

I watched as Marcus went out of my sight and then listened as I heard the door at the far end of the basement close. I looked back at Layton who was watching me. I sighed heavily and Layton came and sat on the sofa and put his fingers in my hair. I leant my head against his leg.

"Are you feeling sad, Baby Boy?" I nodded.

The use of my name told me I was free to speak. "He found me and now he has gone again."

Layton stroked my hair through his fingers. "He will come back. I can promise you." I closed my eyes. "Do not sleep yet. I want you to eat supper first."

I didn't open my eyes. "Can I just stay here for a while?"

I heard his smile. "Just for a minute, Baby Boy, just for a minute."

I let the sad feeling settle inside me, knowing I was not alone but safe with him at his feet. He was in control of me, and I was comforted by that. He didn't let me stay there long. He took me to the bed where we sat and ate supper before using the bathroom and getting undressed for bed.

I fell asleep almost immediately but was woken in the night by a bad dream. I dreamt that I had gone with Marcus to his house, and he was punishing me, punishing my feet. The pain of it hurt and then it wasn't Marcus anymore, it was Devon and the pain wouldn't stop, he was asking me to come like a good whore. I woke scared and sat up, and then because it was dark it made me panic even more that I couldn't see who was in the room.

I moved across the bed, holding my hand out into the darkness, trying to shield my face from any more punishment. The lamp was switched on and a hand took mine. I slowly turned to see him. It took my mind a minute or two to come back and realise it had been a dream and not real. I let the air out of my lungs that I had unconsciously held in my panic and panted to catch my breath while looking at him. He hadn't spoken, just gently held my hand and watched me as I dealt with it. He touched my face.

"Are you with me, Isaac? I have you, nothing can hurt you."

I nodded at him, trying to calm myself.

"Bad things happen though, when you're not here, when you don't have my mind. I don't like it when he is in my dreams. I don't like the dark, can you leave the lamp on?"

He smiled at me. "Of course. I cannot have your mind when you sleep, Isaac, but I will always be here when they wake you. Has Marcus's visit upset you?" I looked away and shook my head. I didn't want him to stop Marcus from coming back. He turned my face to him. "Isaac?"

"Don't take him away. He's my friend... please."

He sat up and crossed his legs in front of me. "I will always do what I think is best for you, you know that don't you?"

I looked at him and nodded. "He was in my dream, but he didn't hurt me... Devon did..." I felt the tear run down my face and I wiped it with my fingers. "Does that mean he can't come anymore?" He reached out and wiped my damp cheek.

"Come here and settle with me." I lay down and put my head in his lap and took a staggered breath. He stroked his fingers through my hair. "Don't ever feel you need to hide things from me."

"Sorry." He lifted my fingers to his mouth and kissed them.

"I have never given you a reason not to trust me and I would never. You have found someone important to you, I would never hurt you by taking that away from you."

"Yes, Sir... thank you." I pushed my face into his leg and kissed him. "I'm sorry. Are you angry? I can go in the cage if you are trying not to be angry with me." He stroked his hand down my back.

"I have never been angry with you, Isaac. After everything that has happened to you, I think you are very brave and strong to trust anyone and yet you let me have you easily. I will not ever be angry with you if your trust wavers. It just means I have to try harder. Would you like to tell me what is worrying you so much, that it bothers you in your sleep?"

I sighed and turned on his lap, so I was looking up at him. I had to trust him. "I don't know where I'm going. I know I can't stay here forever. You said I can't go back to the vanillas... are you going to make me a slave again? To slave here for you?"

He looked down on me and half-smiled. "No, Baby Boy, you will never slave for them again. You are to stay here with me, so I can keep you out of trouble."

My heart raced with excitement, but my head was more cautious. He was going to let me stay here with him, but I was unsure what that meant.

"Do you want me to play?"

"Yes... I know it scares you. When I watched you this morning, I could see you are very strong, but this need you have inside you is stronger. I know you're still fighting it, but you cannot deny it forever, you know it still burns inside you. It is only a matter of time before you have to sate it and I will be here to keep you safe while you do."

I turned into him and curled myself into a ball and he held me to him. "I understand that when that time comes, Isaac, it's going to be scary. You will give your mind and body to me, and I want you to know that I will not betray that trust. I will work very hard to make you feel safe and loved, while you salve your need." Just talking about it made me scared as I nodded into his body. He had been honest with me. "Tell me what's in your head?"

"I'm scared. I want to stay here with you but what if I can't please you, will you send me away?"

He pulled my face to his. "I love you, Isaac. There are no conditions for my love. I will never send you away so you have nothing to fear. I do not doubt that when you are ready, you will be able to give yourself over to your need and desires freely. You could never disappoint me, Baby Boy, you never have."

I was still stuck on the part where he loved me. I had told Marcus I loved him and now I was confused. Were Layton and I friends? Other questions came into my head.

"What about your work?" He let my face go and I let it fall against him needing the contact.

"I do have to return to work shortly, not yet. You have my undivided attention for a few more days. We will discuss it further when the time comes. You are very important to me, Isaac, I will make sure that your needs are catered for at all times, even when I am not with you."

I wrapped my arms around his body not wanting to be apart from him. He laughed a little and held me tightly while he moved us to lie on the bed. We lay looking at each other. He looked beautiful; I could see the flecks in his eyes from the lamp. I reached out and touched my fingers to his face. I couldn't tell him I loved him. I wanted to but if you loved someone then you had to share everything with them and I wasn't sure if I could yet, despite what he said about playing, I still wasn't sure. I ran my fingers over his lip ring and licked my lips.

He noted the action and smiled. "You can have whatever you want tonight, Baby Boy. It will not always be free." I looked at him and he smiled. "I still love you. Are you worried?"

I swept my hand around his face. He was my life. I had, for a moment today, doubted him. Looking at him now, I didn't know why.

"Do you have me?"

He touched my face. "Always."

I moved towards him, kissed his bottom lip, and then looked at him, unsure. He ran his hand over my hair, and I closed my eyes. My heart was beating fast in my chest, and I was sure he knew. I opened my eyes and looked at him again. If I lost myself in it, he had me, he would keep me safe.

I kissed him again and touched my tongue to his lips. He parted his lips and touched his tongue to mine. He held my hair in one hand and my face in the other while he teased my mouth and lips with his tongue before letting me go so I could take his mouth with mine.

I moved over him pushing him to the bed, my hands sliding over his body quickly. I moved my mouth down to his neck, licking and tasting him gently before moving down across his chest and licking his nipple. I took the ring in my teeth and pulled it from his body, stretching his small bud and areola. Then I took it into my mouth and sucked at it, feeling his body tense under me.

I pushed my hand into his chest, pushing myself up and looked at him. I was kneeling on one leg beside him, my other was across his body, my cock was already hard, reaching out touching him. He looked at me and swept his hands up my body, brushing my nipples under his palms.

I couldn't decide what path to follow. The desire and need screaming inside me like yesterday or the one that was telling me to ignore it, fearing it. He brushed his hands down my body and over my thighs, then back again, framing my cock in his fingers but not touching it. He swept his hands down to my knees before repeating the action, watching his hands as they sat framing my cock.

I covered his hands with mine and looked at him, shaking my head uncertain, breathing heavily. He closed his hands around mine and looked at me.

"You can lose yourself, Baby Boy, you're with me... it's just you and me."

I looked at his hands underneath mine and my cock as it pulsed gently with my breathing. I was struggling and I looked back at him wanting him to take control, I needed him to lead me so I wouldn't think so much until I didn't have to think.

He pulled me forward putting my hands either side of him and then pushed my head to his stomach. "Love me, Isaac."

I kissed him gently, trailing tiny soft kisses across his body, never letting my lips leave him. I let my tongue taste him now and again as I deepened the kisses against him, dragging his skin between my lips. I moved down his body, sweeping my leg over his hard cock and touching my lips to his hips. I could see his cock dancing above his body asking to be touched, his hard shaft pulsing, supporting the mushroom head that bloomed above it. It glistened with precome, tiny droplets of his life sat in the crease and without thinking, I licked it while looking at him.

He was watching me, his lips parted with his breathing, and I touched my lips to it again, still with my eyes on him, watching him drag in a breath at my touch. I wanted to suck him, I liked sucking cocks, I had always been good with my mouth, and I wanted—needed—to have it.

Gay whores sucked cocks.

I had had that drilled into me day after day by Devon and I could hear his voice as I looked at Layton's wet mushroom head asking. I ran my tongue around it, and I heard him moan but I didn't look at him. My mind was busy. I wanted it, I wanted to feel it pulsing over my tongue, feel it choking me, take his life from him but I wasn't ready for the memories that were bombarding me making me feel like a whore. I didn't want the pain and punishment that came with that feeling.

I was sitting astride his legs, my cock hard between my legs, fighting the voice in my head. I dug my fingers into his skin as I held his hips in my hands. Layton wouldn't hurt me, I knew this, yet I was stuck in that time, in that moment and place in my head and I couldn't move beyond it... not without help, not without him. I needed him to control this moment, take my mind, I wasn't ready to lose myself in it alone, without him. I pushed my hands on him, lifted my body and looked at him.

"He's in my head, his voice... I can't... help me... I need you to take me there."

In one quick movement, he sat up, making me sit back on his legs. He put his hands against my body and dragged them up to my shoulders and down my arms until he reached my wrists, then he pushed them behind my back and connected them. As soon as he did it, I pulled at them, fear running through me. He swept his hands up to my head and pushed it down, so I was leant over him, his cock under my face. He held me there with one hand and stroked the other down my back as my mind battled against him in panic.

"Breathe, Isaac, just stay there and breathe."

I closed my eyes and breathed deeply, slowly letting him have me, have my mind. I could feel his hand running over and over on my back, his other pushing gently on my head. I let my head drop slowly under his hand, no longer pushing against him. He grabbed my hair and forced my head back to look at him.

I opened my eyes, completely relaxed in my binds and in his hands, my mind free from any thoughts, just him.

He looked at me and stroked his other hand over my face. "That's it, Baby Boy, now you're with me, now you can have what you want." He leant back on one hand and pushed my head back down with the other. He opened his legs wider, making mine stretch around him, and he thrust his cock towards me. "Take it, take what you want."

My mouth was already open for him and as he released his hold on my hair, my need for him carried me forward until I closed my lips around his cock and sucked him. I moaned in my throat at the feel of him inside me and I wanted more. Pushing myself further on him, sucking him as I swept my tongue up and down his shaft. I wanted my hands now, I wanted to hold him and pleasure him, I pulled at them and the excitement at not being able to have them washed through me. I pushed his cock into my throat making myself gag and heave around him and then I felt his hand forcing me, holding me there as he moaned.

He released me and let me draw my air. I put my mouth to his shaft and stroked it up and down until I was ready to have him again. I sucked him rhythmically over and over, taking as much as I could of him into my mouth before drawing my mouth up around him. His juices leaked from him as his orgasm grew closer. I sucked at his cock head, driven by the taste of him. I could feel his body straining under me and he held my head as he thrust his hips.

"Fuck, Isaac, I'm going to come..."

I sucked him until he forced his cock into my throat as his orgasm shook his body and I closed my lips tightly around him to feel his life pulsing up his shaft and into me. He cried out his pleasure as his body shook and as soon as I was able, I sucked him again, taking every last drop from him. I still wanted him, I moved my mouth from his cock and trailed it down his veined member licking his balls before sucking at them.

I had forgotten what it was like to enjoy someone else's pleasure, to be their desire, to have their orgasm burn a need inside me. I moaned as his body twitched under me, I didn't want his pleasure to be over with, I still wanted it.

He pushed me to sit back on my arse again and took my mouth with his, he sucked and licked the drool and cum from my lips. I felt his hand rub around the base of my cock. I tensed under him, but he grabbed my hair in his hand and held me to his mouth. I immediately relaxed again for him letting him have me so I could serve him.

He pushed his hand under my open legs and rubbed my balls in his palm and I moaned into his mouth with pleasure. I was pushed forcefully to the side and laid on the bed with him between my legs. His hand was around my throat, pushing my head against the bed, and his body lay across my right leg, holding it to the bed. He rubbed his fingers over my cock head and held it in his hand.

"Precome, Isaac. That is why your need is not sated."

I was breathing heavily from panic and when I felt his tongue touch my wet, sensitive head, I jerked and tried to pull away from him. He held me still and the only limb I had movement in was my left leg. I pulled it into my body, but he pushed it back, his hand opening my legs to him. He kissed around the base of my cock with gentle tender kisses as I squirmed under him and panted my breaths, trying to get my air.

He pushed harder at my throat, not quite choking me but pushing my face further into the bed, stretching my body out taut.

"I'm going to take you there, Isaac. You are so fucking beautiful." More gentle kisses moving up onto my hard cock. "...Don't fight me, just let me have you."

I pulled at my wrists, which were still connected under me, as he took my cock in his mouth and gently sucked the precome from its head. My body jolted at the pure ecstasy of it, and I felt him push his hand harder into my leg, holding me open to his mouth. I let my body sink into the bed, giving myself over to him, to take me where he pleased.

I was panting hard, letting the pleasure wash through me as his mouth rubbed over my cock, teasing the orgasm that waited. Usually, I would feed it, breathe into it and spur it to take me but I just lay and let him take me there slowly. I could feel my mind slowly being drawn from this world and knew that when I came, I would be taken from it, lost to it, like this morning.

As it asked inside me, I called out to him uncertainly. "Lay...ton?"

He went from holding my throat to cupping my face, stoking his fingers over my cheek, soothing my journey into ecstasy, letting me know he was with me every step. The continued pleasure of his mouth tipped my orgasm over the edge and my mind and body were thrown into spasm.

My thoughts were taken. I cried out as I lost control. Like electric sparks, it fired through my body over and over until it burnt out and ebbed away leaving my body and mind spent. I closed my eyes to stop the tears, not from pain but the sweetness of it. I could feel his fingers stroking my face and I needed him. I felt so raw, so open, it had been months since anyone had touched me and made me feel like that. I pushed my foot into the bed trying to turn and see him and then I felt him pull me to him.

"I have you, Isaac." He pulled me onto my side, I looked at him as he stroked my face and kissed me gently at the corner of my mouth. "Good boy, settle now, I have you."

I let my head fall forward towards him and he kissed it and rubbed his hands over my shoulder and arm.

"Just breathe, I will release you in a while." He pushed his arm under my head and played his fingers through my hair. "So beautiful, Baby Boy." I opened my eyes and looked sideways up at him. He was looking down on me. "Your eyes are electric blue, dancing, like before."

"Was I...? Was it beautiful?"

He smiled at me and bent and kissed me. "No one makes me feel it the way you do, Baby Boy. The way you look and touch, it burns me inside. I love to watch you suck me... I love to watch you."

He leant over and undid my restraints, but I didn't move. I knew when I did my arms and shoulders would protest painfully and I wasn't ready.

He smiled. "Not ready to move yet?" I shook my head. He started to rub my shoulders. "Who was in your head? Devon?" I closed my eyes and nodded, remembering what I had said. "Tell me."

I sighed not wishing to share. He stroked his hand across my forehead and I pushed my face into him. I went to move my arm, I wanted to hold him, but my muscles wouldn't work, and I creased my face at the ache.

He went back to rubbing my shoulder. "Tell me, or I will just be mean and pull your arm forward." I turned my head and looked at him and he was smiling. "Don't try and test me, Baby Boy. You know I never lie to you."

I didn't say anything, he reached behind me and took my arm.

"Okay!...okay…" He rubbed his fingers over my skin, waiting. "He used to tell me that I was a whore... every day, he caned me and told me that gay whores sucked cocks and got fucked by cocks and I should be a good whore boy when I went on my visits. He made me feel dirty, he used to call viewing day my whore day... Julian called me a whore too... and Rourke, when I stayed with them. I think that's what I am.... when I want it so bad... I think I'm a whore and I don't want to be."

He was looking at me, I could feel him staring and I looked at him quickly before pushing my face back into his shoulder. He didn't speak and I waited for ages till I needed to see his face to see what he was thinking. I turned and looked at him again. He sighed.

"Do you think Julian treats Jacob like a whore, Baby Boy?" I shook my head. There was no doubt in my mind that he ever thought that of Jacob. "Do you think Kellen thought of you as a whore?" I thought about it. No. He had treated me like a prized possession, a slave, yes but a prized one. I shook my head. "And Marcus?" I shook my head straight away. He had become angry when I had said that word. "Me?" I felt a smile pass my lips fleetingly. No, never, ever. I shook my head.

"There are whores, in the vanilla world. They are not bad people; they are people who are lost. They are fulfilling their need either for sex or money or both. Whores do not give their minds and bodies to others. What they do is more like a business transaction, and it requires great thought on their part. When you play in this world, clients or Masters and Mistresses use the word to make your mind submissive to them. When Devon called you that every day, I think it is because he was threatened by you.

"He was trying to keep you submissive to him, his place in this world is not... was not as assured as yours, Isaac. If he did not cane you and keep you there, you would not have suffered like he wanted you to suffer." He stopped talking for a moment and touched his fingers to my face gently. "He is sick, Baby Boy, his mind is sick, and it has made him a bad person. When people are sick like that, they cannot be believed... As for Rourke, he was playing with you. He was playing at being your Master when he really should have been your Keeper, your friend.

"Many clients have probably called you a whore over the years, but I suspect your mind was so taken with the play that you did not give it a thought. The only reason it still sits in your mind now is that no one was looking after you, no one had you, and he made you associate that word with pain. Now you associate pain with Devon, understandably after what he did. We just need to make new associations in your head, Baby Boy, heal the damage he did to your mind." He kissed me and I looked at him.

"Can you do that?" He smiled.

"We can, together. It may take a while. You spent a day with Beecher, and it took your mind weeks to heal. You have spent almost a year with Devon. You cannot expect your mind and body to forget the things it has been made to learn. You have done so well, come so far. You have such a beautiful nature and a strong mind, it already knows what it wants. You have to be patient; your mind will remember the pleasure it found in playing and being punished I promise.

"Trust your own instincts, Baby Boy, like today. I will help you whenever you get stuck, okay?" I nodded and he kissed me quickly. "Right come on, let's get you straightened out before you seize up in this position forever." I creased my face and then stuck out my bottom lip and he laughed. "Sulking is not going to help but I love your beautiful mouth."

He ran his thumb over my protruding bottom lip then moved from me, taking his arm from under my head. I tipped forward on the bed and moaned as my blood vessels were finally allowed to feed my arms again. He sat behind me and rubbed his fingers into my shoulders, digging them deep into the muscles, bringing them back to life. Slowly he moved my arms back to my sides and rubbed them until I could move them again.

"What's the time?" He lay beside me on the bed stroking his fingers over my face.

"I have no idea... Are you hungry?" I nodded and he smiled. "I'm too tired to cook, Baby Boy. What about a bowl of cereal?" I nodded. He went to leave and I put my hand out to stop him. He looked back at me. "I have to go and get it, Isaac, or I will have to call Beatrice down to bring food." I shook my head at him. I had no idea who Beatrice was, but I didn't want anyone to intrude on our time here.

"I changed my mind; I just want to lay here with you." I touched his face with my fingertips, he kissed them and moved closer. "Do you have bad things in your head?" I shook my head.

"No, just you." He smiled

"Good, that's how it should be. Try and sleep now."

He pulled me towards him and wrapped his arm around me. It had been a long time since my mind had been this peaceful and quiet.

"Can you leave the lamp on?"

He kissed me. "Yes, Baby Boy."

I laid my head against him and listened to his heart beating gently. I didn't feel tired, but I did fall asleep.

BABY BOY

CHAPTER FIVE

The following days were quiet and peaceful, spent with just Layton and me. He fussed over me endlessly and I loved it, my mind loved it. There was no room to think about anything except him.

He answered my never-ending questions about Julian, Jacob, and Kendal and how they had become friends with each other and about the slave world.

I may have lived in it for years but there were things that I didn't know. When I was just lying or sitting quietly, I would see him watching me and it would make me smile. I had never felt so safe, knowing I wasn't going to be sent away made me feel so secure with him, although I hadn't thought about that in detail yet and wasn't completely sure what my place would be.

Every morning in the shower he became hard, I would kneel and pleasure him with my mouth, not because he made me but because I wanted to pleasure and please him. He let me take what I wanted and never pushed me to take more, even though my cock would be hard between my legs just from watching him and feeling him take his pleasure.

He would always ask if I needed to come but I was content, for the moment, just to be with him. This was new to me, being settled somewhere, knowing every day I would be safe, knowing that I wasn't going to be taken somewhere and used by strangers. It was what I had wished for, in those long, lonely days where I had sat on my bed talking to my boots.

I could feel my need building in me and knew it was just a matter of time until I would want it sated, until it got the better of me and what little control I had. Thinking about it scared me. I had never had to think about it before, never worried that it would be too much or never stop. I had always just trusted my body and mind to use what I was given to satisfy my need for it.

Trust. It was something else that I had never had to think about. From the minute Layton brought me here and offered me slavery as a way of life, I had just trusted. Now I couldn't imagine trusting anyone... except him.

He was clearing away the stuff in the kitchen, his back was to me as I sat on the bed and watched him. I had no doubt that he knew I was watching him, he always seemed to know. We had just eaten breakfast, even though I knew it was late in the day, time was nothing here. The only time that it mattered was when you had a client to visit and since I wasn't a slave anymore and had no schedules to keep to, it didn't matter.

I still had an issue with the dark nights, they made me restless, so he would sit and talk with me well into the night until sleep took me. I still wore my leather restraints, I found comfort in them even though he said I could take them off. When I had told him I wasn't ready to not wear them, he had accepted it. I used to believe they kept me here and I wasn't sure if that was the reason I still felt the need to wear them. Did I still doubt him? I didn't feel like I did but I hadn't let him play with me yet, hadn't ventured beyond touching and cock sucking, and I had only let him do that to me that one time. He had said it was going to take a long time to heal but now I worried that I wasn't healing at all.

Layton had done nothing to me that I should doubt him, yet the fact that I still wore my restraints and didn't join him in the shower when he took his pleasure, made me wonder if I was making any progress. I sighed and pulled my legs into me, wrapping my arms around them, not feeling so secure now. I was still watching him, and he turned and dried his hands, looking at me. He was wearing black jeans but was shirtless and when he leant back on the counter, his skin stretched across his body showing how toned he was.

"Something has taken your mind, Isaac. Tell me."

How could I tell him that I wasn't sure if I trusted him? That maybe I still doubted him?

"Am I healing?"

He pushed himself from the counter and came and stood next to the bed. He touched his hand over my head. "Yes, Baby Boy. Tell me what's bothering you?"

I looked at him. "What if I can't anymore? I feel like I'm stuck..."

He sat down on the edge of the bed and kissed me. "Stuck with me?" I looked at him and he smiled. "Your thoughts are not making any sense, Baby Boy. Help me understand."

Would he understand? Would he be angry? No, he said he wouldn't get angry.

"I trust you... I know I do... so why can't I... why can't I give up my restraints? Why can't I take my pleasure with you in the shower? Maybe this is a far as I can go, maybe I can't be the same as before?"

He moved and sat behind me and wrapped his arms around me. "Let's talk about it. Tell me why you want to keep the restraints?" He lifted my hand and touched the leather around my wrist. I sighed as I watched him. He ran his thumb over my pulse point and kissed the side of my face. "You can be honest with me."

"You gave them to me when I was struggling and I thought that if I kept them, then I could stay here with you, be part of your life. I don't want to be a slave anymore, but I don't want to leave this world... or you. Now you said I can stay... with you so why can't I just take them off? Why does it fill me with panic not to have them? So now I think maybe I don't trust you... and that scares me because... because if I don't trust you then I'm alone and I don't want to be. I need you."

He put his face next to mine and spoke quietly near my ear. "Shh, I have you, Baby Boy. I said healing would take a long time and you would have to be patient, do you remember?" I nodded feeling agitated by my thoughts. "You have worn these restraints for many years, Isaac. You have learnt to find comfort in them when you were agitated, like now." He picked up the other hand and connected them and I felt my arms relax in his hands. "Your mind has been trained to give itself up to the binds whenever your movement is restricted, making you more submissive and pliable to your user or Keeper. A slave that fights their binds, causes themselves damage and is no good to clients." He took my hands in his and rubbed them gently. "It's your first lesson, do you remember? Remember the time when they felt uncomfortable and having your movement taken scared you?"

I nodded. Yes, I remembered struggling against them the first time my Keeper had put them on and connected them. It was my first time forcefully having my will taken from me and being at someone else's mercy. On the streets you kind of got to decide, even if the choices weren't the best. I had been scared.

"New slaves are kept like that for a long time while their mind adjusts and settles. It becomes normal to sleep and find peace in them." I turned my face towards him, but he was so close, I couldn't actually see him.

"That was the first time you brought me down here."

He nodded slowly. "That's right. Your Keeper, James, was worried because you wouldn't settle, so I brought you down here, bound your wrists and ankles behind you, and sat with you. Do you remember it?"

I nodded. I had been distressed and cried and he had sat and soothed me until I was quiet.

"You were very brave, Isaac. You gave your mind to me very quickly once you understood the place I wanted you to be in." He was still holding my hands, his chin leaning on my shoulder. I loved his face next to mine and I leant against him.

"You made me feel safe. Every time you brought me down here, you made me feel safe. You were scary too... but always safe." He touched his lips to my face and kissed me tenderly.

"As hard as it was to accept them and give your mind to me, it is no different going back, Baby Boy."

I turned towards him. "I don't understand. Don't you want my mind?... I need you to have me... No... I don't understand." I went to move, panicked, and he wrapped his arms around me to keep me with him.

"Hush now... I always have you, always." I relaxed into him again, breathing quickly. "Just because you do not wear the restraints, doesn't mean I don't have you, Baby Boy. You are still the same person. You are naturally submissive, Isaac, what you feel is who you are, the binds don't make you feel that way, they just made it easier for you to go there. You are not a slave anymore, I do not need you to be constantly restrained to know your place... when I want you, I have ropes that do a perfectly good job at keeping you where I want you." He kissed me. "Are you ready to let me take them?" I shook my head. I needed to think about it more and I wished I had never said anything. "Okay, there is no rush. When you are ready to give them up, I have something for you, a gift for you."

I looked at him. No one had ever given me a gift before.

"What is it?"

He smiled and shook his head. "No, Isaac. You cannot have it while you are a slave." I turned my face away from him. "And sulking will not get it either."

Now I didn't know what to do. I wanted my gift.

"But I really want it."

He reached down and disconnected my restraints. I lay relaxed on him and thought about it.

"The gift is not going away. It will be waiting for you when you feel ready."

I sat quietly while he stroked my body and ran his fingers through my hair. His face was still next to mine and now and again he kissed me. I was excited about my gift and wondered what it could be.

"Will I like it?" He laughed and I turned my face to see him. "Are you being mean to me?"

He smiled again. "Yes... to both questions. Yes, you will love it and yes, I am being mean but only because I love you and I want you to keep moving forward in your mind. I don't want you to get stuck. I know it's hard to give up your restraints, but you did it before when you were here, remember?" I hadn't had a choice then.

"I didn't give them up, you took them from me. I always knew I would have them back." I thought about that then spoke again. "If I give them to you for a little while, can I have my gift?" I really wanted it. He didn't answer and I turned my body sideways so I could look at him properly.

He sighed and stroked my face. "No, Baby Boy. You need to find your comfort in other things. I am not going to take them from you by force, this has to be your choice and it will be less traumatic if you do it when you're ready. I promise the gift will be waiting for you."

I screwed my face up and jerked my body and then stuck out my bottom lip. I leant my head on him.

"But I want it... I don't like you today." He laughed quietly and stroked my hair and kissed my head.

"I can tell."

I worried then that he wouldn't love me if I didn't like him.

"If I don't like you, will you still love me?"

He wrapped his arms around me and held me tightly.

"You have my love always, Isaac, it never has to be earned. This is a difficult time for you. Your mind will take you through lots of different emotions and feelings as it fights to keep you submissive, and I push you to be free of them. I mean you no harm. I am here for you when you need me, when it seems confusing. Even if you don't like me." He kissed my head.

"I don't understand what you want, I'm already confused." I felt him smile "I don't want to be free of you. Who will look after me and comfort me? How will I play, if you don't have my mind?"

"I know it seems confusing and I'm sorry that it hurts you. I want you to stay with me, but you need to be able to be apart from me. You need to be free to do simple things like making tea for yourself and using the toilet instead of waiting to be told. I will always comfort you when you need it and I will take your will and look after your submissive side when I need to, so you can play without worry."

It didn't seem possible. How could you be free of rules and punishment and then play? It felt like he was pushing me away, yet he was holding me and soothing me. "Tell me what thoughts are in your head?"

I shrugged my shoulders. "I feel sad like you don't want me anymore and it makes me scared. Bad things happen when you're not with me. I want to be good for you and now I don't know how to because you already love me and said I could stay but you want to be apart from me. I don't understand, I don't want it, it doesn't feel safe." I buried my face deeper into him trying to shut out all of it. He stroked my hair over and over.

"I know it's hard and it feels strange and wrong to you. It is not my wish to be apart from you, but there will be times when I cannot be with you and you will have to try and learn to trust that I will always come back for you, always. I will not leave you on your own until you feel secure. I have to go back to work very soon, Isaac, but I will have someone come stay with you for now when I cannot be with you. Your mind is telling you it is wrong and not safe because you were trained to feel that. It will make you feel like that for a while, but you know, don't you, that I would never do anything to harm you?"

I did know, as much as I didn't like it and it all felt wrong, I knew I could trust him. I nodded to him.

"Good boy, Isaac. It is not my wish that you become my equal, I know you would never manage that, but it is my wish that you find some independence, try and find a balance in what you feel." He kissed my head. "I know you don't feel very secure right now. We can stay here a while until you feel better about the things in your head." He wrapped his arms around me and pulled me closer to him. I curled my body into him, needing his comfort and the safeness of him more than ever.

"Can I still have my gift if I give you my restraints?"

"Of course."

I sighed. "Maybe later... or tomorrow. I just want to stay here for a little while longer." He kissed me and stroked my hair.

"Yes, Baby Boy. This is not the last time you will be in this place. I will bring you here when you need it and when we play, when you're ready to play. Starting tomorrow, Isaac, I'm going to push you a little more, so you don't feel so stuck. From tomorrow, you will no longer wait for me to tell you what to do, if you want tea then you can make it, if you need the toilet then you can go without request or asking. Do you understand?"

My stomach somersaulted but I nodded. Not today though, today I wanted to stay right here with him. To let him have me and take care of me and know I was safe.

We didn't do anything more that day. He didn't talk anymore about me being free or independent, for which I was glad. It filled me with fear and talking about it made me think about it. I let him smother me with love and comfort and laid with him most of the day, losing myself in his touch.

Now it was morning again and I wasn't sure how to even start this new independence. I had never been very good at looking after myself, it was one of the reasons I had taken the slavery offer.

I sat on the bed trying to decide whether I needed to pee. If I took myself there it would be a start and I would please him... maybe. I had never had to think about it for the past five or six years, I had used the toilet when I was taken there or told. I put my head in my hands. It was the simplest of things and yet I couldn't decide if I needed it or not. How was I ever going to be apart from him if I couldn't use the bloody toilet!

He walked towards me with breakfast, and I got off the bed, then stopped and turned back again. Maybe I should eat breakfast first, then make tea... or go to the toilet. I was standing naked next to the bed, struggling with what to do. He sat down and looked at me.

"Breathe, Baby Boy."

I let out the breath that I seemed to be holding. Now it seemed I couldn't breathe properly without him. This was not going well. I wanted to hold out my wrists to him and sink to my knees and just let him take it all away.

"Where were you going?"

I felt my shoulders sink, this was going to seem so stupid to him. I looked away from him.

"To the toilet... I think. I mean I don't know if I need to go but I always get taken there in the mornings... so I think I should go... or should I make tea first? Because I want tea and you said I had to make it but now you have breakfast so I decided to eat that first. Well, I haven't decided yet, that's what I'm doing..." I looked at him. I felt stupid and I could feel the tears prickling at my lashes. "...I think... I'm not good at this... I'm trying to be good... I'm trying."

He held out his hand. "Come here, Baby Boy." I dropped my head stepped back to the bed and sat down with him. He took my hand and kissed it. "I know this is difficult for you but don't stop trying okay?" I nodded and he touched his fingers to my face and pulled it to look at him. "I love you, Isaac. Would you like a little help?"

I nodded. "Yes... please because I feel stupid."

He smiled at me and wiped the tears he could see with his thumb. He leant over and kissed me. "You are not stupid. You haven't had to make these decisions for a very long time and as simple as they seem to me, I know they seem hard to you. I have made the tea and breakfast; they will wait if you need to use the toilet?" I didn't answer because I wasn't really sure. "This will get easier, I promise." He was looking at me, waiting.

"Err... I'm going to go to the toilet... do you think that's best? Can I ask you that?"

He smiled at me. "You can ask me anything you need to, and yes I think that is a good choice."

I smiled at him feeling a little elated at my good decision. I leant forward and kissed him, then got up to go and turned back.

"Thank you...for helping and making tea." I stood and he tapped my arse with his hand.

"Go and hurry up before it gets cold."

I used the toilet and washed my hands. I wished the mirrors were back so I could see what I looked like. I looked down at my body and it seemed like it was before. My restraints on my wrists and ankles stood out against my pale skin and I wondered if I would be able to give them up today, I wasn't so sure. I really wanted my gift but there were too many changes, too many things to think about. I had only been awake for half an hour and I was already struggling. Giving up the restraints would mean the end of my slavery days with clients, the end of time with Keepers to comfort me and the end of just thoughts of pain and pleasure.

I sat down on the tiled floor and rubbed my feet and ankles around the restraint. Marcus had always taken my restraints when I had visited him and I had thought nothing of it. It had been a client's request and you always did what the clients wanted or got a bad report and then your Keeper would administer punishment on request of the house owner.

This wasn't a passing request from a client though, this wasn't temporary. When I took them off this time, it was the end of slave Isaac. I held my ankle restraint in my hand and gently pulled at it. I wanted to stay with Layton and be who he wanted me to be, I did, but I already missed the serenity that came from being a slave.

I pushed my feet to each other and clasped my ankle restraints together. I pulled my feet apart to feel their restraint and was so drawn to the feeling, I clasped my wrist to my ankle and then with difficulty, I managed to attach the other one.

My knees were spread out to the sides and my arms lay between them and now that I had attached the clasps, I couldn't free myself. I found a strange peace and safety in that; I closed my eyes and felt my whole body relax. It was so easy to shut everything out, to drift off in my head and not have a care.

I didn't know where I went but it was very similar to flying, that place he had taken me to once except I wasn't flying, I knew I was on the bathroom floor. It just seemed very far away, like I was so tiny in the room, and nothing hurt or bothered me, just the pull of the restraints keeping me here, keeping me safe.

"Isaac?"

I let my head tip back to the far-away voice, I was so relaxed, it kind of flopped and I stared vacantly up at him. I felt him stroke his fingers over my hair and gradually I let him into my safe cocooned headspace.

"I'm sorry... I... I just wanted it."

He sat on the floor with me, put his legs around me, and stroked my body and head with his fingers. He kissed me now and again and I closed my eyes and found my peace again.

"That's okay, Baby Boy, I have you. I'll watch over you until you're ready to come back."

I stayed there for ages, even though somewhere in my head I knew I shouldn't, I knew he didn't want me to. It felt so nice, it felt like freedom to my mind, but I felt alone and I didn't want to be. I wanted to see him. I turned and looked at him. He was sitting close, but he wasn't touching me. I felt very vulnerable and I tipped my head and body against him, seeking the comfort and security of him.

I pulled at my binds wanting the freedom to hold him.

"Shh, wait just a minute."

I felt his hands touch mine and he released my wrists. I wrapped my arms around him and held him tightly.

"I'm sorry... I'm sorry... I was trying... it got too much..." I buried my face into him so scared he was going to just give up. "Please let me stay here." I felt him release my ankles and he wrapped his leg over both of mine and held me.

"Oh, Isaac. I know you're trying. I know this feels hard. It hurts just as much as it did when you were learning to be a slave. You tried so hard, too hard, that you made yourself panic, that's all. Next time you need to tell me, it's not a good place to go on your own, Baby Boy." I nodded to him. "Settle now, just breathe and rest with me. I will make more tea in a while." I took a deep breath.

"I didn't even make it past breakfast, I'm sorry." He laughed. "I thought you would be mad."

"Not at all. I am amazed that you were able to get yourself in such a submissive place, it's very clever of you. You must not ever do it again when you are alone though, only with me or someone... someone like Marcus. When you let your mind go like that, it's makes you vulnerable, Baby Boy. You're tripping off of the sub feelings. Promise me, the next time you want to go there you will tell me."

I nodded. "I didn't mean to go, not really and it's not like when you took me, that was sweet, like doughnuts with sugar. This was missing the sugar." He laughed again and I looked at him and sort of smiled. "I'm sorry." He kissed me and rubbed his thumb over my cheek.

"Sugar or no sugar, you were tripping and alone." He smiled at me. "Are you ready to have tea now?"

I nodded. "Do I have to make it?"

He smiled. "I will make this one, you can help make the next one. Breakfast will have to be toast or cereal now."

He sighed heavily and I looked at him. He was tired I could see by his face. Did he worry about things? He never seemed to. I sat up and looked at him properly. I looked at him questioningly. "Tell me?"

"Do you worry?" I touched my fingers to his forehead. "Do your thoughts hurt you?"

He smiled gently. "Yes sometimes."

"Do I hurt you?"

Did I make his thoughts hurt him? I didn't want to. He took my hand and kissed my fingers.

"No, not in the way you're thinking. You make the worry worth it, make it better. Like now, Baby Boy. The way you look at me, I see you, I can see the person you are. You show me your mind even after everything that you have seen and done and endured and it's beautiful, you are very beautiful."

I took his face in my hands and kissed his forehead as he did to me so often. I didn't know how to ease his thoughts but when he kissed me it always made me feel better.

"I'm going to try hard today. I promise I won't fly or trip or whatever it is you call it. I will just stay here with you. Is that good? Is that okay?" He smiled a smile that made me feel so loved. Well, that's what it felt like.

"That, Baby Boy, would be very good."

He nuzzled my neck with his face and it made me smile because I had made him happy and it tickled a little. "Ready?" I nodded and he stood and pulled me with him to the bedroom.

I did try really hard. I made tea and helped make dinner for us both, I took myself to the toilet without being asked. I had worried that I couldn't be with him and talk to him if he didn't have my mind and I had free will, but he was no different. He touched me and held me and soothed me just like before. I tested this by pulling away from him and going to the kitchen to get a glass of water before returning to him. He took me back in his arms and said nothing, just loved me again.

I settled a lot and I slept the night peacefully naked in his arms. The next morning when I woke, he was already gone from the bed. I listened for him before I opened my eyes to see him in the kitchen. I got up and used the bathroom and came straight back to him and stood at the side in the kitchen. He turned and looked at me smiling and then walked over and kissed me.

"Good morning, Baby Boy. I love seeing you in the mornings with your sleepy eyes and fuzzy bed hair."

I looked at him hungrily. He never had fuzzy hair or sleepy eyes. I reached out and touched his naked body and then leant in and kissed his smooth skin and he moaned his pleasure of my touch. He liked to come in the mornings, usually in the shower but I wanted him now. I dropped to my knees, spread them around him, took his cock in my mouth and sucked him. He didn't stop me, I thought he would but he didn't, he just let me take him while he stood clutching the kitchen counter in one hand and took hold of my head in the other.

He looked down and watched as I sucked him and rubbed my hand over his balls, squeezing them in my fingers. I looked up at him with his cock in my mouth, wanting to watch his pleasure as I rubbed my mouth over his hardening shaft.

"Fuck, Isaac, you're going to make me come right here. Is that what you want?"

I nodded my head to him, my mouth still full of his cock and I slid my hands up his body, taking his nipples in my fingers and playing with them, squeezing and pulling at them. I wanted him to come but I wanted him to want it, to lose control in it so when I heard him hold his breath to feed his orgasm, I took my mouth from him and looked up to him, licking my lips.

I watched as his pleasure abated and he looked down, stroking his hand over my head shakily. He was breathing hard trying to contain his need, but I didn't want him to. I wanted him to want it, I wanted him to want it so bad that he took it without thought. I wanted him to force his cock in my throat and make me take it.

I took him back into my mouth and sucked him again. He started to thrust gently, moaning his pleasure and I took my mouth from him again.

"Fuck, Isaac, stop playing, take me there, take me all the way." He pushed my face back onto his cock and I sucked at him again with his hand pushing the back of my head.

It excited me and I felt my cock get hard, but I wanted more. He was still letting me control this, holding back to protect me. I sucked him quickly rubbing my tongue against his cock head as I slid my mouth up and down him.

"Oh Isaac, that's it, boy, just like that...I'm coming..."

I slipped my head out from under his hand and my mouth from his cock. I heard him growl his need. I looked at him again, breathing hard. I touched my hand to my cock and rubbed it, just watching his need play across his face turned me on. I moved backwards and leant back against the cupboard, spreading my legs, playing with my cock. I looked up at him as he watched me. He stepped towards me, offering me his cock to suck. I leant forward and took it in my mouth again while stroking my own and his orgasm asked immediately.

I took my mouth from him again and he stepped further forward, reached for my head, and pushed it back onto his cock. I sucked him again and then pulled my mouth from him.

He stepped right into me. "Isaac!"

He pushed his cock into my mouth and thrust. I tried to pull away, but he grabbed my hair, pushed my head back to the cupboard, and thrust deep into my mouth. My orgasm ignited inside me as I struggled to pull my mouth from him, but he pushed harder and deeper inside me, making me gag on him.

"Now take it!" He held my head to him with both his hands and thrust over and over in my throat. The more I struggled, the more he held me there and the more I wanted to come.

"That's it, open your throat to me, you fucking little cock tease. Now you're going to take it." His orgasm was now controlling him as he held my face and thrust himself voraciously in me.

I struggled a little more to make him hold me harder and tighter, I wanted him to force me, to deny me my air and as he pushed his cock in my throat choking me, my orgasm tipped over the edge. My body jolted and my cry of pleasure was growled and spluttered around his cock.

He stepped forward and pushed further. "Oh fuck... fuck... suck me while you come, boy, suck it." I sucked him as my orgasm screamed around my body. He shoved me forcefully against the cupboard and pushed himself as deep as he could as his life shot into me. "That's it, take it... take it... like a fucking good boy..." I struggled for air, he held me tighter. "No...no, this is what you wanted." He held my head while he thrust again. "Choke on it, then swallow it, then suck it clean."

I heaved around his mushroom head while pushing at his legs as spit, cum, and bile from my stomach were forced from my mouth around him. As he allowed me to take my air, I swallowed what was left and sucked him clean. He looked down and held his cock in my mouth, letting me take a few breaths before pushing his cock in again and watched as I retched a few times before taking it out. I tipped forward, leaning on my knees and gasped as it drooled down my chin onto the floor to join the splatters of my cum that lay between my legs.

He pulled my head up and looked at me, grabbing a towel from the side, he roughly wiped my mouth before dropping it in between my legs. He dropped to the floor beside me and sat with his back to the counter next to me, breathing heavily.

He put his hand around my neck and pulled me to him roughly and kissing my head. "Did I hurt you?" I shook my head. "You are a sneaky little fuck, Baby Boy, when you want something bad enough." He was panting and settled his breathing while he stroked my hair in his fingers. "I can see I will have to keep more on top of things. I didn't want to take you like that."

"I wanted it like that, it makes me hot when you make me." He laughed a little.

"So I saw." He pulled my face to look at him. "You're not hurt?" I shook my head and he rubbed his thumb over my lips. "Such a beautiful mouth."

He bent and kissed it, licking the residual cum from my lips before taking my mouth again. I was covered in my spit and cum and when he released my mouth I looked down at it.

"I came without permission." I looked back at him, wondering if he would punish me.

"Yes." He looked at me for a moment before continuing. "Things are different now; I will always tell you when I wish you to ask for it. You are not a slave now, Isaac, you will not always have to ask, sometimes…most times but not always. You are healing faster than you think, Baby Boy. It won't be long... until you want it all again." He kissed me. "Shower time, you want me to wash you?" I smiled at him and nodded. "Come on. Then you can make me tea."

CHAPTER SIX

Despite telling me I could make him tea; he made me breakfast and tea, and then cleared the kitchen of our play while I slept. Now I was sitting between his legs while he played with my hands after we had just eaten lunch. There was nothing like this time with him. When we were both happy to sit quietly and just touch each other, it seemed even more peaceful now, after this morning.

He spread my hand out and put his up against it and then linked his fingers through mine and took it to his mouth and kissed them. His legs were on either side of me and I put my other hand to his leg to stroked it. I tipped my head up to him, he looked at me asking, and kissed me. I lay my head on his body and watched as he continued to touch and play with my hand.

If this is what being free of slavery felt like then I wanted it, I wanted more of it. His arms were leaning on his knees, and I touched my hand to his wrist and stroked it.

"Have you ever been a slave?" I felt him shake his head.

"No, Baby Boy. Not like you. I did submit to someone for a while."

I turned and looked at him. "Did you get punished?"

He smiled, not looking at me and absently carried on rubbing my hand. "Yes... a lot. I was not a very good bottom. I wanted to top but I wasn't permitted to at the time."

"Is that why you understand so much about slaves and their minds?"

He nodded. "Maybe. It taught me a lot. Pain teaches you a lot about yourself, especially when you have to endure it for a long time. It taught me a lot about being a Dom too." He still hadn't looked at me.

"Who punished you? Kellen?"

He smiled and shook his head. "God forbid, no." He looked at me. "Julian."

I thought about it for a minute. "Do you love him?"

Was that who he loved? When we had spoken before, and I had asked him if he had loved anyone, he said he did. He never had told me who and I wondered if it was because Julian didn't know. He sighed and turned me so my back was to him again and wrapped his arms around me.

"He's a friend. He needed to vent a little when things in his head got confusing. I offered myself, saw it as an opportunity to play with one of the most demanding clients. I wanted to learn a few things about myself and about being a bottom, a slave. I love him for the things he taught me and the trust we still share."

It didn't really answer my question.

"Do you love him as you love me?" he laughed and kissed my face.

"No. You are far more important. I love you more."

"Is that because I am the bottom?"

He laughed for a long time that it made me smile.

"Yes, one of the reasons. I prefer to dominate not submit. Sometimes, Baby Boy, I don't know where your mind will take me next. You are always surprising me... and that's another reason why I love you."

Feeling quite brave with my place and a little cocky I smiled and patted his leg. "It's a good job I found you then."

I picked his hand up and kissed it. He held my face and turned it, putting his lips to my neck. He bit me gently and then blew a raspberry against my skin while I struggled and giggled. He didn't let me go for ages and I was panting for air by the time he released me. He held me tightly and gave me tiny tender kisses across the side of my face and spoke quietly in my ear.

"I love you, Baby Boy."

I knew then that I didn't need my restraints or my slave status to be with him. I was his. I would submit to him when he asked, suffer anything he wanted me to, so I could have him dominate me, the way he liked to, the way I wanted to be dominated. I felt like I had found my place with him, safe, sane, and definitely where I wanted to be.

"Can you take them off now? I don't think I need them anymore." I held my wrist up to him.

He held my wrists in his hands and looked at me. "You can't go back this time, Isaac. If I take them, I will never let you go back to being a slave." He made me look at him.

I nodded at him. "I won't need to will I? You will give me what I need, what I want? You'll take me there and bring me back so I can be free with you... like this, like now?" He kissed the restraint still holding them in his hands.

"Yes, Isaac. I will look after you. I will look after your needs, all of them. You must never doubt me, even when you suffer... I will always keep you safe." I knew that. I nodded.

He undid one of the restraints, kissed the pulse at my wrist, and then did the other one. He sat and rubbed them free of their six-year prison. I was fine with it until he dropped my hands. I lifted them and touched my pulse on each one and then I touched them together. I would never be restrained while I rested or find my peace in them again. I would only be restrained when I played.

I looked at him and he touched my face, stroking his thumb across my cheek. He was looking at me, watching me and I tried hard not to show him how it bothered me. I thought I had been ready, now they were gone I doubted if I had made a good decision.

He pulled my leg up to my body so he could reach my ankle and took the leather restraint, dropping it on the bed with the others. I was breathing hard as he lifted the other leg and did the same. I tipped my head against his arm.

"Good boy, you're just feeling a little overwhelmed. Six years is a long time to be a slave. I have you." He stroked his hand over my hair and kissed me.

The more I thought about it, the more I felt the need to get away and keep myself safe, the panic took the sane thoughts and I tried to move away from him. He wrapped his arms around me and held my wrists, hooking his legs around mine, making me immobile.

"Find your safety here with me, Baby Boy." I tipped my head back and looked at him, I wanted to go, I wanted to go in my mind. "Can you try and stay, Isaac?"

I creased my face as the thoughts in my head made it difficult to deal with and to stay. I pulled against his hold, finding comfort in it and hoped he wouldn't let me go. I looked at him again, asking him if I could go and find my safety from my thoughts, taking it, even though I knew he wanted me to stay.

When he spoke, I had already gone, taken myself away from reality and the harsh thoughts in my head. I was completely relaxed on him; I could see him and feel him but from really far away and I was separated from the world he wanted me to stay in.

"I have you, stay there as long as you need." And that was all I needed to take me deeper into my submissive state of mind and my safety from my thoughts.

I don't know how long I went for. I never really knew. It always felt like a long time, but I knew sometimes it was only minutes. I felt my body jerk and knew it was a sign that I was on my way back. I groaned and felt him stroke my face.

"Welcome back, Baby Boy." I looked at him, my mind still far away as he looked back at me. "Just breathe slowly, I have you." I lifted my hand and touched my fingers to my wrist. "You don't need them, Isaac. No one is going to make you stay anywhere you don't want to be, not anymore."

I nodded turning slowly into him and whispered my question. "Was I gone long?"

He smiled and nodded. "Yes, a couple of hours. I am guessing that's how long it took you to feel safe with me and without them."

I was laying sideways on him and I wrapped my arm around him and kissed his body awakening from my escapism.

"Thank you. For letting me go... I know you didn't want me to. Sometimes I can't stop the things in my head." He played his fingers in my hair and stroked my arm.

"When did you used to take yourself away like this? During visits?" I shook my head.

"No. That would have been scary and clients wouldn't like it. Usually, when I'm healing, it stops the pain from hurting my mind, stops my thoughts. I think it kept me sane. I never went there when I was with Devon. It wasn't safe."

"Not safe?"

I shook my head. "No. Like being with a client. You have to stay, I have to stay in the room, stay with them, otherwise, they could damage me. You taught me that. I'm not aware of what is going on when I go, I can feel things, I could feel you but it's like I can't feel the world. I wouldn't be able to follow instructions... and that would mean getting punished. I always tried to be good with Devon, do whatever he said so he wouldn't get angry." I smiled a little. "Never really worked, he always found something to punish me for. I think maybe... when he was hitting me with my boots... I think I went then because I didn't try and stop him. I could see him but it didn't hurt after a while." I moved further up his body and snuggled into him. "Do you know where it is I go?" I wondered if he understood from when he was punished by Julian.

"Maybe, a little. It's a very submissive state of mind. I'm not sure it's healthy, Baby Boy, and you must promise to not go there when I am not around. I may speak to Kendal about it, would you mind?"

I looked at him. "Do I have a choice?" He smiled down at me.

"Yes...but if you say no then I will ask her secretly."

I tipped my head back into him. "She will think I'm mad."

"No, she won't. She'll probably blame me." I smiled and he laughed and for that, I got a kiss and a hug. "Would you like your gift now?"

I looked at him. I wanted it but I wanted to enjoy it and I was still reeling from my mind warp.

"Can I have it later? I still feel a bit loopy. No one has ever brought me a gift before. I think the waiting is exciting, it makes me feel warm inside, it makes me smile." He shook his head and smiled.

"Yes, I know those feelings. It can wait until you're ready. Do you want to sleep a while, then we can have tea when you wake?" I nodded and closed my eyes as he played with my hair. Sleeping with him was always safe.

As I stirred, I could feel something touching my face and I turned away from it, but it followed me. I realised then that he was kissing me and when he touched his tongue to my lips, I touched mine to his and smiled, still with my eyes closed. I opened my eyes slowly to see him leaning over me. He was so close, leaning on his elbows, arms on either side of my face, his hands in my hair, his knees on either side of me and his cock hanging, barely touching my stomach.

"Did I frighten you?" I shook my head.

"No. Was I asleep long?" I stretched under him and stroked my hands over his legs and up his body.

"Long enough. You looked too beautiful, I had to touch you." I smiled at him.

"Good... I like it. I like waking up and you being here. Did you sleep with me?" He shook his head as he spoke.

"Nope, I was busy." He sat up and climbed off me and held out his hand. "Come on, I'll show you." I smiled at him and took his hand and he pulled me from the bed.

He took me into the bathroom and gestured to the walls. I followed his hand with my eyes and then saw what he was pointing to. All the mirrors were back as they had been, no covers hiding them away. I walked slowly over to the basin and looked at my reflection.

I stood there for a while before he walked up behind me and wrapped his arms around me, putting his head on my shoulder and spoke to my reflection. "Beautiful, Baby Boy." He kissed the side of my face and then looked back at me.

The last time I had seen my reflection, I had been covered in bruises, skinny, and bald. Now I was the same as before, my white hair sticking out all over the place, my skin pale, and I couldn't see my bones. Well, not like before, not quite like before, I had some shape to my arms and my body, nothing big, no big muscles but more toned. I had never seen myself as beautiful and still now, with him standing behind me, I still couldn't see it, but I could see me and I loved it. I put my hands up and touched his hands, linking my fingers through his, leaning my head against him. I looked at his reflection.

"Thank you... For bringing me back. For bringing me back here and being with me. I think... I think I would have died if Kellen had sent me back to the vanillas." He turned me around and kissed me.

"I would never have let that happen. I would have come and found you. I was already searching for you when Marcus found me." I thought about that.

"I don't understand. You knew I was at Kellen's, didn't you?" He nodded.

"Yes, but I never heard what happened until Kellen was telling the councillors as he asked for your freedom, he had already moved you by then. I never imagined he would have moved you to a client's house and as clients are kept confidential, I probably would have never found you... can I ask you something?" I nodded still looking at his reflection. "When Kellen gave you the choice of where you wanted to go, to wait for him... why didn't you ask to come here?"

I looked away from him. He hadn't told me everything. He had loved someone else, maybe still loved someone. He said it wasn't important back then, but I wanted to know, did he love me the way I loved Marcus? How did you know the answer to those questions? I was where I wanted to be but was he?

I felt uncomfortable and I dropped my hands from him as he tipped my head up to meet his eyes in our reflections. He was so beautiful, his eyes, his voice, his body, his mind. He kissed my face while looking at me. "I can see the answer to that is eluding you." I didn't want him to think I hadn't wanted to come here.

"There were reasons... If I don't tell you, will you be angry?" He closed his eyes for a moment before holding me tighter and looking back at my reflection.

"I'm trying to understand." So was I. "You say you're not ready to go with Marcus but there is where you requested to go. He was safe then but not now?" I nodded slowly.

I was never meant to come here.

"It's safer here... but I will do what you want me to do, I'll go with him... can I come back? I don't think he wants me forever."

He shook his head and a million thoughts flew through my mind at once. I couldn't come back? He didn't want me forever? He said he would have me always. Did always not mean forever? I clasped my hands together.

He looked pained. "Isaac, your mind is so complex, your thoughts are so deep and change so fast. I think I understand you and then the things you tell me don't make any sense." He sort of smiled at me and kissed me again.

The action went against the way the conversation was making me feel. Feeling insecure I turned in his arms and wrapped mine around him. I kissed his neck, trying to make things better.

"I don't understand either. I will do what you want, whatever you want, can I stay? Are you angry?" I didn't want to look at him.

"I think, Isaac, that you need to tell me why you didn't ask to come here but for whatever reason, I can see that you don't want to. I can't decide whether to push you for an answer or let it be." He sighed and rubbed his hand over my head as he pushed me away. He took my hand and walked back to the bedroom. "I have tried to make you feel secure and safe. I love you and still, you doubt me." He sat me on the bed.

I looked up at him and shook my head worriedly. "I don't doubt you." He walked away and I stood and took a step towards him then stopped.

He had his back to me, and I didn't know whether to follow him or not. I wanted to but he seemed like he wanted to be away from me. I felt lost and I could feel the tears threatening. I went to call after him but when I looked up for him, he was walking out into the basement and spoke.

"Stay on the bed, Isaac." The bedroom door shut behind him and I let my tears fall.

I turned slowly, crawled onto the bed, and sat watching the door, crying while I waited for him to come back. After a while, I stopped crying and sat and just watched the door. I had made him angry, and he was trying not to be angry with me, like before. I should have just told him.

It wasn't him I doubted, it was me, my feelings, my thoughts. I didn't doubt that he loved me, I felt loved, I felt things I had never felt before with anyone. What I felt for Layton was different to what I felt for Marcus. Marcus and I had the same feelings for each other, we were friends, maybe friends that played… I wasn't sure about that yet, for lots of reasons. Layton was one of them. The things that happened in this world, slavery, the punishments and pain... and the pleasure, it distorted things.

A year of pain had distorted my view of things, my thoughts. I did not doubt that I wanted to be with Layton or what I felt for him was greater than anything I had felt for any other person. I doubted that it was right though. A slave couldn't love a Dominant, not here in this world, it was against all the rules to even have private slaves. Maybe it was time to just tell him everything and stop trying to protect myself.

He had been honest and open with me, apart from not telling me who he loved, which wasn't a surprise really, I was just a slave. Patient too, he definitely had been patient. I had to make it up to him and say sorry. I brushed my face with my fingers and headed to the kitchen, made tea, and waited for him to come back. For a while, I started to worry that he had left me alone, left the basement completely but I knew, I knew he wouldn't do that. Settled with the knowledge that he hadn't left me, was just outside the door I re-boiled the kettle.

I would make him a fresh tea and this time take it to him. He had said to stay on the bed but if I took it to him as a peace offering, surely he wouldn't be angry? I opened the cupboard to get a fresh cup out and as I reached up for it, my hand caught a glass and knocked it from the shelf. It was one of those things that seemed to happen in slow motion.

The glass fell, I tried to grab it with my other hand, and I did, I caught it in its downward motion. Just as I wrapped my hand round it, it smashed against the counter edge. It didn't hurt, I didn't really feel it, I just saw the blood, lots of blood. It had me frozen to the spot as I watched it dripping out of my clenched hand and then I realised I was still holding the shattered glass, so I opened my hand and let it drop to the counter.

I turned my hand over and saw the embedded glass in my palm just under my thumb and quickly pulled it out and let it drop. Panic had me frozen as a million thoughts filled my head, the first being was that I was certainly going to be punished for this. I stood for ages not knowing what to do, there was so much blood and I turned towards the door to shout for him, then I froze, mouth open... I didn't call his name.

The last time I had seen this much blood was when I had watched my balls sliced open and I had called for Rourke. I was frozen in the moment as I remembered thinking that I should never have called him. Wasn't it that, that had started this whole rollercoaster? That precise moment when instead of just letting them have me, let them do what they wanted, I had tried to stop it to protect myself.

I looked back at my hand. I was still holding it over the counter and the blood was now pooling around the broken glass and dripping off the end of the counter to the floor. I couldn't think properly, couldn't think what to do. I looked at the bedroom door and hoped he would come for me.

My hand throbbed and it brought my thoughts back from just waiting. I had to figure it out, all of it. Rourke had not been a good Keeper. He had given me a collar, humiliated and degraded me into submission until my mind had been completely his to do his will. Here, Layton had taken my restraints and said he wanted me to be independent of him... and yet, I felt safer with him than I had Rourke.

Layton always had me, the whole time, even when I wasn't playing, even when he wasn't with me and when he wanted nothing from me, he still loved me. What that meant I didn't know but I had to try and sort this out myself to show him I could do it; I could be independent.

I looked around, saw the tea towel, grabbed it off the side, and wrapped my hand in it. Now that I had done that, I couldn't decide what to do. Should I clean up first? Yes, that would be better, that would be the adult thing. I picked up a bit of the broken glass off the side and the blood made it slide through my fingers. I dropped it as my finger started to bleed.

I put it into my mouth and sucked it before taking it out and looking at it. It was just a small nick but now I was in a mess. I would have to go and get him and tell him what I had done. I didn't know how to fix it and he was already angry with me anyway. I wondered if he would punish me? No... what I had with him was different, I needed to trust my own thinking, know that I was right to trust him.

I turned and walked towards the door, holding my tea towel wrapped hand against my chest, and opened the door really slowly and peered out. I couldn't see him on the sofa. I wondered whether I should say sorry for earlier before I told him about the glass? When I did see him, all my thoughts were taken.

He had rope wrapped around both his hands from the ceiling and he was doing pull-ups. He had his back to me and his beautiful naked body was beaded in sweat, his ankles were crossed behind him as he pulled himself up. I knelt on the floor quietly, not wishing to disturb him. His whole body flexed, as over and over he pulled himself up and slowly let himself down.

It was like watching someone being punished as he pushed himself to complete each one, his arms and body shook as each one pained him to complete, and he moaned with exertion. Had I made him so mad that he needed to punish himself? I didn't want to say anything now, I wanted to let him be and just wait for him to come back.

I made to move, and he stopped, letting himself hang from the rope as he spoke, panting. "I told you... to stay on the bed."

I knelt back on the floor. I had no idea how he knew I was there. My heart was beating fast. "I... I wanted to say sorry."

He never spoke, just hung, swinging gently. I waited and watched as he dropped his head forward. "It's okay, Isaac. Go back to the bedroom... I will be there in a while."

I didn't know what to do now. I could hear his breathing heavy and fast from his exercise. He wanted to be left alone but I had to tell him about the mess in the kitchen.

"I'm sorry... I made you tea and..."

He interrupted. "You want me to tell you what to do and when I do, you don't do it!" He jumped from the rope he was holding and stood with his back to me, his body moving with his exertion. His words and his actions made me jump.

"I... I made a mess and... I've hurt myself." He swung around then, so fast that it made me look away. He stormed over to me and I panicked. "I'm sorry... I'm sorry."

"Jesus, fuck, Isaac... shit what have you done?"

I cowered down as he knelt beside me and put his hands over my body. I watched to see what he was doing. The tea towel was soaked in blood now and it had covered my body where I had been holding it.

He scooped me up in his arms. "Shit, Isaac, I'm so sorry."

He walked me quickly through the bedroom and into the shower and turned on the water before sitting on the floor with me. The water washed over us both gently and he looked at me and pulled my face to him. "God, I'm so sorry, Baby Boy."

I felt the tears again. I was the one that was sorry. He unwrapped my hand and held it under the water and I watched the red water running away. I grimaced as the water made it sting but I didn't pull it away. He held it as he tipped his head against mine.

"Okay, I just need to clean it, Baby Boy. Is it anywhere else?" He rubbed his hand over my body, washing the blood away, checking.

I shook my head and looked at him. He looked worried as he stroked his hand over me, checking all of me. He even found the small cut on my other finger, looked at me, and kissed me.

"I wanted to make you tea to say sorry..." He pulled my head into him.

"It doesn't matter, none of it matters. Can you stand up?" I nodded and he helped me to my feet.

He turned the shower off and wrapped my hand in a small towel then wrapped me in a towel and walked me to the bed. I sat where he had put me earlier as he quickly went and got the first aid box. I didn't move this time. He was still naked and wet as he unwrapped a piece of gauze and opened the towel and placed it on the cut. He held it tightly while he bandaged my hand.

"It's going to need stitches, I think. I will have to call Kendal." He reached into the bedroom draw and got his phone and quickly called her.

"Hey, I need you. Isaac has had an accident...cut his hand, I think it needs stitches...thank you." He put the phone down and looked at me.

I felt so bad for the trouble I was causing. "I'm really sorry." I moved towards him. "I made tea, but you didn't come back... so I was going to make you another one and come and say sorry, but the glass fell out of the cupboard. I caught it but not before it hit the counter... I tried to clear it up, but it cut my finger." I held up my finger on my right hand. He took it in his fingers and looked at it.

He got a plaster from the box, put it on, and kissed it. I looked at him, I wanted to sit with him so I knew we were still alright. "I know you're still angry, but can I sit with you? I'm a bit worried." He reached out and touched my face.

"I am the one that's sorry, Isaac. I shouldn't have walked out like that and just left you. Did I scare you? Did you think I had gone?" I shook my head.

"No, I knew you would be close by. I thought you went on the sofa so you wouldn't get angry. I got upset and I waited for you to come back and when you didn't, I thought I would make it better with tea."

He pulled me across his lap. I wrapped my arms around him and he kissed me. We sat in silence for a while before I spoke. "I'm sorry for not telling you things. Did I make you punish yourself?"

He half laughed. "You are very astute, Baby Boy... something like that, yes. It doesn't matter. When I saw you covered in blood..." He shook his head.

I didn't know what that meant but I didn't ask.

"I was worried when I saw all the blood." I lifted my head and looked over to the kitchen.

"It's everywhere." He stroked my hair.

"I will see to it when Kendal gets here. As long as you're okay." He looked at me. "We had an argument... kind of. We are still friends and I still love you, you understand that, don't you?" I shrugged my shoulders then nodded slowly.

I had never had an argument with anyone. I touched my plastered finger to his face.

"I don't want to argue." He smiled

"Well you see, Baby Boy. When two people live together and they are thinking their own thoughts... when one person is not following the other's will... it happens, sometimes. I got angry because you decided not to share something with me, and I should not have done. I want you to make your own choices and I should have accepted your answer." He kissed me. "This is new to me; I have some things to learn too. So, we may have arguments, but it doesn't mean I don't love you okay?" I nodded.

"Next time I will sit on the bed and wait for you, I promise." He smiled at me.

"Oh, Baby Boy. Next time I won't walk away. When you cut yourself, you should have called for me, I would have come."

I didn't know what to tell him. Not being honest with him had led us to argue and I didn't want that again.

"Can I tell you something?" He nodded looking at me. "I tried, I went to call out your name and... with the blood everywhere... I... it... it was like that time I called Rourke's name to help me... and that changed everything. I didn't want things to change again. I thought you would be mad, I thought you would see I couldn't be independent and maybe you would make me be a slave again. I don't want to go back to them, I don't want them to have me, I just want you to have me."

He pulled my face to his lips and kissed me and spoke. "I do have you, Isaac. No one else I promise. I'm sorry I wasn't here but you made a good decision about coming to find me when you knew you couldn't get through it on your own. That was being independent, although it doesn't seem like it, I know." He shivered a little.

"You're still wet." He pulled the towel around my shoulders more.

"Yes, I need to get us a robe before we both catch a cold." He looked at me and I nodded and got up from his lap, sitting on the bed cross-legged. He left the bedroom, heading towards the bathroom.

While Layton was getting his robe, the basement door opened, and Jacob and Kendal walked in. I was so pleased to see Jacob. He was wearing jeans and a t-shirt with a jacket, but I remembered how his body had looked hanging for Julian. He came straight to the bed and sat, touching my face before kissing me and I smiled at him.

"I made a mess." Kendal sat then and took my hand. "I'm sorry, Kendal." She looked at me for a moment before a smile took her face and she shook her head.

"He is meant to be keeping you out of trouble." She started to unwrap the bandage and I looked back at Jacob.

The last time we had met, he had been submitting to Julian and I had been trying to lose myself in staying a slave. He stroked my face. "Did it hurt?"

I shook my head. "Not the cut, I argued with Layton... that hurt..." I dragged my breath in through my teeth as Kendal pulled at the wound and I tried hard not to pull my hand away.

Layton came into the room. "Ahh, great you're here. Hello, Jacob." He leant down and kissed Jacob's head. He had a robe on now and carried another in his hands. He helped me into the robe as he spoke to Kendal. "Thank you for coming. Is Julian with you?"

Kendal shook her head. "No. He's away and I'm staying with Jacob for a few days. Where's my kiss hello? It does nothing for me when you both are more pleased to see Jacob than me."

Layton hooked the robe around my shoulder and leant down and kissed her, smiling. "Hello, Kendal. It is always a pleasure to see you. You know that."

She grabbed her bag and dragged it across the bed. "Only because I clear up after you." She looked fleetingly at Layton before looking in her bag. She was holding my wrist in one hand and rummaging in her bag with the other. "Now honey, this is going to smart a little." She looked at me. "I need to clean it and check for glass before I can stitch it so I'm just going to make it numb with a little injection."

I looked worryingly up at Layton and pulled my hand from Kendal. I didn't like the injections they gave me; I usually couldn't move.

He smiled at me. "Just your hand, Baby Boy..." He stroked my face. I shook my head at him, he knelt next to me and pulled me to him. "I know you're worried. It's Kendal and you know she won't hurt you."

I pushed my face into him, I could already feel it, the need to go away, my mind wanting to take me. The place where I went when things overwhelmed and bothered me, like people and pain. I didn't want any needles stuck in me again. I moved my hands, agitated, and felt someone hold my good hand and take my hold of my other wrist.

I felt restrained and I pulled at them and felt my panic which then caused me to drift further into my safety. "Are you tripping, Isaac? Do you want to go?" I nodded and he stroked my face. "Okay, Baby Boy, I have you."

It was my signal that I was safe to go. I let my mind drift, while I listened to him speaking. "Just give him a minute. He has this very neat little party trick that I wanted to speak...." His words drifted off far away, muffled in my head. I knew he was talking but they no longer made sense.

It was kind of like putting my head in a pillow or that bit when you wake up and open your eyes and see everything, but your mind is not awake to process what is going on. I didn't want to know what they were doing; this was better. He was here and he had me and I knew I was safe with him, that's all I needed. At one point, I could feel a warm sensation running through me and I just hid from it further. Years of dealing with pain on my own had made it easy to do. When you felt it, you just took yourself a little further from it.

GRAY

CHAPTER SEVEN

I drifted back to voices and looking around for him I turned my head to the hand that stroked my face and followed it until I found him. I was laying on the bed with him sitting next to me and it eased my foggy mind to know he was here. He was looking at me and he smiled.

"Hey, Baby Boy... breathe, I have you."

Someone spoke behind me, and I moved in closer to him. I remembered then that we had been in company and although it hadn't bothered me at the time, it bothered me now. I had never drifted off when in the presence of people, only him. He continued to stroke my face easing my mind back to reality.

"You're safe." I looked at him. "With friends remember? Jacob and Kendal."

I nodded letting him know I was back but wasn't quite ready to speak yet. I sat up so I was leaning on him, and could see Jacob and Kendal sitting, and drinking tea at the end of the bed. I was wrapped in the robe and my hand was fully bandaged. I sat and watched them for a while before I felt part of the room again.

"Is my hand fixed? Did you have tea?" I wanted tea, I wanted to have tea with them like Jacob was doing. Layton tipped my face to him.

"Yes, it's stitched up and we are, would you like one?" I nodded and Kendal spoke.

"I'll make you a fresh one, honey, yours has gone cold." She left the bed and headed to the kitchen. I could hear her humming.

I looked at Jacob and smiled weakly. Did he think I was strange now?

Layton spoke. "I think Jacob was a little worried."

He sat cross-legged at my curled feet and legs. I wondered if he had ever felt the need to submit to the world around him.

"Are you ready to sit with Jacob while I speak to Kendal?" I nodded and pushed myself up from him. Jacob moved beside me as Layton stood. "I will still be able to see you." I nodded to him, and he turned and joined Kendal in the kitchen as I looked up at Jacob.

"Hey, I'm sorry, I didn't mean to worry you." I smiled at him.

"Where do you go?"

I shook my head. "I'm not sure. It's like flying... without the sugar."

I wondered if he knew about flying, whether his mind had ever been taken with pleasure and pain like mine had that once with Layton. "Do you know flying? Has Julian ever taken you there?"

He nodded and smiled. "Yes, a few times. I'm not really sure about the sugar bit though." He looked at me and laughed.

I shrugged my shoulders. "Well, Layton made me fly once and it was sweet. There was pain and pleasure and it was a buzz…sweet. My mind left the room, which it never does when I play but I couldn't control it, I just went, and it was sweet. When I drift off like that, it's very similar I think, it's not as sweet, not so addictive... so, no sugar." I looked at him to see if he was following me.

"Why do you go then?"

I sighed. "I don't know it's like I panic…and then I think I do it to protect myself. I have been a slave for a long time and taken lots of visits and punishments. Healing was always the worst times, lonely. After my Keeper had tended to my wounds and given me a little comfort, I was usually left alone so, I think I learnt to take myself away from it. Don't you need to do it when your healing?"

He shook his head. "No, Julian looks after me. Before he allowed me to stay with him, I used to go for a walk in the woods…and think about things."

I thought about it. Walking in the woods sounded awful, especially alone. Now I guessed, unlike Keepers, Julian would not leave him to suffer alone. Layton had never left me to suffer alone after playing and thinking about it now, I had never felt the need to go after playing and healing with him.

"I remember though, when I had spent time as a slave, the long hours healing, left alone. My Keeper was Pierre and he was nice, he stayed with me a lot, looked after me. He was friends with Julian, so I think he was a bit nicer to me. I don't know how you were a slave for so long, I didn't like the clients or viewing day. I don't like people looking at me."

Kendal laughed from the kitchen and I looked over to see Layton smiling, looking at me. I stayed looking at him while I spoke to Jacob.

"I was trained well. You were lucky to have Pierre, he's looked after me a few times, just temporary. I know he looks after Joel now. They have a thing for each other, they have been together a long time. Not all Keepers are nice though."

Jacob sat up and I looked at him. "I know Joel... Julian brings him to play sometimes, he's funny. He always talks when Julian wishes him to be silent and he makes Julian mad, but I think, really, Julian likes him. He lets me play with him sometimes, even fuck him. I always get punished for it, but I like it. I'm not allowed to fuck anyone."

No subs were not allowed to take their Dominants. Layton had allowed me to have him once, when I was struggling after Beecher. I doubted I would ever be allowed that pleasure again. I looked at Jacob and smiled, I liked hearing about his time in slavery and his play times.

"Do you play with any other slaves?" He shook his head.

"No. Joel is the only one and you the other day. I didn't know we were coming here; it was hot. I so wanted you to suck me when we were playing... Julian says you have a beautiful mouth." I smiled a little embarrassed and he half laughed. "Sorry, I don't usually have anyone to speak to about things. I get shy around people, they make me uncomfortable, except you, I always just want to touch you."

I lifted my face to him, and he bent and kissed me. He touched his tongue to my mouth while he held my face and I willingly opened it and let him taste me. I pulled away and feeling eyes upon me, I looked across at Layton who was watching us. He shook his head, and I dropped my face from him and Jacob. I could quite easily lay with Jacob and lose myself in him, he loved to touch and I loved to be touched, caressed, and soothed. I rested my head against him and stroked my hand over him, trying to feel him.

"I'm not really shy, only when I don't know where I fit in with people. Like you and Sim, I know that we are the same and I feel free to touch. I submit to Layton..." Well, I hoped to soon. "...So, I know my place with him. I'm not sure about Julian or Kendal, I don't know how to be with them. Do you understand?"

He nodded. "Yes, it can feel complicated sometimes. I try and do what I want until someone... usually Julian, tells me I can't. You should do what you want, they'll soon tell you if they forbid it or not. Like just now when Layton didn't want us kissing." I looked up at him. He had seen that?

"You saw him? I don't know why we can't touch?" He shrugged his shoulders.

"Who knows. When they want it, we're allowed, when they don't, we're not." It was kind of like still being a slave. This whole being free and independent thing was confusing. "Don't let it worry you. It used to confuse me too."

So how did you behave if you didn't know what the rules were? I looked over at Layton and he was hugging Kendal, he kissed her on her head and then looked over at me. They had been talking but I hadn't been listening. Kendal turned and walked towards me, tea in hand. I sat up and crossed my legs. She passed me the mug and looked at Jacob.

"Layton would like to speak to you Jacob." I put my hand out to Jacob.

"Is he going to punish him?" Was he in trouble for kissing me? Kendal smiled and shook her head.

"No, of course not." Jacob leaned in and kissed the side of my face.

"Kendal wouldn't allow it here... and anyway, it was worth it." He smiled at me before springing off the bed. I watched him go and then looked back at Kendal.

"I don't understand this world. I did, when I was a slave but now it doesn't make sense." She sort of laughed and held out her hand and took my bandaged hand in hers.

"That's exactly how I feel about it sometimes, Isaac."

I drank my tea and watched over Kendal's shoulder as Layton touched Jacob's face with his fingers. He was talking to him, but I couldn't hear what was being said. Jacob's body was slouched and his head was lowered, so I knew he was being chastised in some way. Kendal looked over her shoulder and then back to me.

"We haven't really talked since you came back." I pulled my eyes from them and looked at her.

I knew what this was, he had spoken to her about my mind wondering thing. I didn't know why people were so worried, I had been doing it a long time.

"You have made such a brilliant recovery. I was amazed to see you looking so healthy when I last came here." When she had jabbed me with the needle and made me a vegetable, yeah I remembered it too.

"Can you not leave any of those needles here that make me a vegetable? I don't like them."

She smiled. "No, they are not nice are they, honey, but it was just to help you get through difficult time." She paused and I didn't say anything so she continued. "Layton tells me you have your own way of dealing with things. Drifting off like you did today?" I shrugged my shoulders. Did she think I was mad? "He's worried that it hurts you."

"It doesn't feel like it hurts, it feels safe. I've been doing it a long time. Am I forbidden now?" Kendal shook her head.

"No, not at all. Can you stop yourself from going, if you wanted to?" I chewed the inside of my mouth while I thought about it. I had never needed or wanted to stop it before.

"Maybe. I used to go there while I was healing in my room, when I was alone. I don't know how it started; I don't purposely go... just when I'm on my own but Layton said it's not safe to go when I'm on my own. Do you think it's bad?"

She smiled. "No, not really. I think it's a very submissive place and that's why it feels safe." I nodded. "I think that you've perfected it down to a fine art, like meditation only it's a very submissive space. You can feel things and follow instruction so I think it would be wise not to go there with strangers or when you're alone as it makes you very vulnerable to them.

"You used to take yourself there when you were healing from physical pain because it made it easier to deal with. You are still healing, Isaac, your mind is healing and dealing with a lot of things that maybe scare you or don't make sense. I think as the days go by you won't need to go there so much but I don't see any harm in it."

"I went there twice today." She smiled and touched her palm to my face.

"Then it must have been a very difficult day, poppet. Is there anything you want to talk about?" I really liked Kendal.

I felt normal around her and she always treated me like I was...normal.

"Do you argue with Julian or Jacob?" She sat back and pulled one leg under her.

"Yes. I argue with Julian all the time. Not really Jacob though."

"Do Julian and Jacob argue?"

"No. Their relationship is different. Even I have trouble understanding it sometimes. Jacob finds things difficult sometimes when Julian is not around, especially if he goes away for days. He relies on Julian a lot more than even he realises, and he loves him very much. He does what Julian tells him to do without question, he would never question or argue with him. Layton told me you had a bit of an argument... is it bothering you?" I nodded and put down my cup and looked at my lap.

"I didn't like it and he wasn't here to help me. I want to do what he says but sometimes I can't."

"Oh honey, there is nothing wrong in arguing but there is a difference between can't and won't. I'm not sure what sort of relationship you have with Layton and maybe you don't either yet, it's still early days for you, you're still dealing with not being a slave anymore and I know how hard that is. If you can't do what he says, then there has to be a reason why you can't do it." She sighed "Do you want to do whatever it is he was asking for?" I nodded. "Okay, then if you're finding it difficult maybe you should tell him why. I think Layton wants you to be his, Isaac, but you have to decide if that's what you want too."

I looked at her. "I do, I am his. I want to stay here with him, but he says I have to be independent and I can't seem to do them both." She nodded in understanding.

"Yes, it is difficult, I can see why you struggle. I think if you want to be his then you need to be honest with him and tell him everything, even when you think you can't, when it seems difficult. I'm not sure what sort of independence he wants but you should try and do your best. I'm sure he will let you know if you are forbidden to do something and then you will have an understanding of what is expected of you.

"You and Jacob are very different. He has not seen the things you've seen and not done the things you've been asked to do. Apart from a short and very uncomfortable time in slavery, he has only ever known Julian and has been independent. Your mind is different, Isaac, your relationship with others and Layton is different. You should not think that you have to be like Jacob, you need to be yourself." She smiled. "I shall enjoy watching Layton try and keep you in your place. I think he has his work cut out for him."

"I do try and stay out of trouble." She laughed.

"I know you do, Isaac, your mind is always busy. He will find it very hard to deny you what you want... I'm sure you will both be very happy." I put out my hand and touched hers and she held on to it. "We are friends, Isaac. You can chat to me whenever you like, even if it's about sex or private play or your slave days."

"I thought you didn't like those things?" She smiled

"I tell them that, so I don't have to listen to them talk about it twenty-four hours a day. I don't like the thought of you or Jacob being punished or the slaves, but I understand their need of it, I understand it serves a need. I know the slaves are kept submissive so it doesn't damage their minds. Jacob doesn't like to share with me but if you ever need me to treat your wounds or help you deal with things then I will always be here to help you. I like chatting with you because you actually talk back to me." She laughed and kissed my hand. "You have had a long journey, but I think now you are where you're supposed to be. I think you're home, Isaac. It feels right that you are here, and I know things feel strange and new and different, but just give it a little time... you'll find your place. I will come and patch you up when you get into trouble." She smiled and I smiled back at her. "You good now?"

I nodded "Can you do something for me?" She looked at me. "Layton always listens to you…"

"I'm not sure about that."

"Well when you asked him to give me milk instead of tea, he followed that like his life depended on it... can you tell him I need chocolate cake or something nice." She laughed out really loud and hard.

"You boys... you have me wrapped around your little fingers... I will see what I can do."

I smiled at her and leaned over and wrapped my arms around her. I felt more comfortable with her every time we met and had no doubt that we were going to be friends, if we weren't already.

"Thank you." I hugged her tighter, thanking her for everything she had done for me and she hugged me back.

"You are always welcome, honey." I sat back down. "Look after this hand now, okay. I just gave it two stitches. Layton can take them out in a week or I can come back and check it."

"Can you come back and take them out, I promise I won't go off." She smiled.

"Okay... save me some cake?" I smiled and nodded.

She stood up and Jacob came over and hugged her from behind. Everybody loved Kendal, she was safe for people like Jacob and I and posed no threat to people like Layton and Julian.

Layton came and sat next to me and I snuggled next to him. "Thanks for coming Kendal."

She smiled and held Jacob's arm as he held her. "Oh, you're welcome. He still a bit underweight and needs building up a bit though. You need to feed him up, especially while he's healing and now with the hand, it saps the energy. Maybe a little chocolate cake or something."

"Really, underweight? Chocolate cake?" He kissed my head "…. Okay… will doughnuts with sugar do?" Oh shit, I had been busted! I tried hard not to smile. Kendal was completely oblivious to the secret meaning.

"Yes, that sounds fine." She grinned at us. "Come on, Jacob, time to go, Julian should be home soon. I will come back and take the stitches out and check on him." She winked at me.

"Bye." Kendal got up and leant over and kissed me and then Layton. Jacob looked down at me.

"Bye, Isaac. I hope your hand feels better." He bent and kissed Layton.

"Goodbye, Jacob. Thank you for your help." They both left leaving the room silent.

Layton lifted my hand and studied the bandage.

"So, Baby Boy, chocolate cake eh?" I stayed silent and looked at him under my lashes. "Do you think you deserve chocolate cake?"

I stuck out my bottom lip. "No." I actually didn't. I had caused a lot of trouble today and had made him angry.

He rubbed his thumb over my bottom lip. "It has been a really long day. How about we save the chocolate cake for another day?"

I nodded. "I really want cake though, I can't remember the last time I tasted it."

He laughed. "I know, there's a lot of things. You go to some extraordinary lengths, Isaac, to get things you want. Now you have involved Kendal in your scheming." He shook his head. "I shall have to speak to her." I sat up and turned and looked at him.

"Don't be angry with her. We are going to be friends and chat; I didn't mean to get her in trouble. What if she doesn't like me anymore?" He tipped his head sideways and looked at me.

"I'm not angry, Baby Boy. I think it's funny." He smiled at me, then reached out and fiddled with my hair. "You know, I would never take away any friends you have, Isaac, don't you?" I nodded. "Anyway, do you think Kendal would take any notice of anything I said to her?" I smiled at him.

"Can we have cake when she comes around? I said I would save her some." He shook his head and smiled and pulled me back to him.

"I will think about it. Did Kendal talk to you about your little mind trips that you do?" I nodded without looking at him.

I was sitting with my back to him and his arm was draped round my shoulders. My bandaged hand sat in his lap and he held it in his gently.

"She said I submit, only I do it better than anyone else... you shouldn't worry though, she thinks I won't do it so much anymore and I will try not to... I don't mean to cause trouble for you, or argue with you. Kendal says that Julian and Jacob never argue but she said that I wasn't the same as Jacob."

"No, you are really not." He tipped my face round to his. "Are you still bothered about the argument?" I nodded and fiddled with my bandage.

He put his hand over mine, pushed them to my lap and held them gently.

"I've never had an argument with anyone and I didn't know what to do. You always help me, but you wanted to be away from me... I don't want to make you feel like that." He kissed me on the lips gently.

"It was wrong of me, Isaac. I should not have walked away from you when things are still so new and difficult. You did not make me feel like I wanted to be away from you, I never want that. I was pushing too hard and going too fast." He waited a minute before continuing. "I don't want you to stop being you. I know you feel like you shouldn't do things to make me angry or go against my wishes, but I also understand that sometimes, Baby Boy, your need and want of things gets the better of you. It makes you misbehave..." He laughed and I looked at him to let him know I was sorry. He kissed me. "It's one of the reasons I love you and as much as I will endeavour to keep you in your place, I don't want to stop your mind from working. Because I have you, Isaac, whatever you do. And you know there will always be consequences when you misbehave." I looked at him a little worried and he smiled. "But you already know that and it hasn't stopped you so far." He pulled me to him and kissed my head.

"You have spent so many years doing the will of others and you like it; you like to give your mind and body over to someone else but every now and again something in you rebels a little. I don't think you understand it either, after so many years of being a very good slave. I like the fact that you have these rebellious moments that you can't seem to control, it keeps me busy and amused trying to keep up with your mind. I promise the next time we have an argument I will stay with you and not leave you to deal with it alone, okay?"

I nodded. I didn't want to argue though, I would rather he punished me. I hadn't felt that in a while, the want to be punished. The thought of it made my stomach somersault and I looked up at him, wanting him to take my mouth with his. He touched my lips with his fingers but didn't give me what I asked for, even though I think he knew I wanted it.

"Always pushing, Baby Boy." I pulled my face away from him, sulking and he laughed. "How about you have something you have already earned?" I looked back at him, not understanding. "Your gift?"

My gift! I had forgotten about it. I smiled and nodded at him, excited.

"Now? Can I have it now?" He smiled.

"Yes. You need to get up though." I jumped from the bed and looked at him.

"Where is it?" He moved slowly from the bed, and I had to hold back the urge to pull at him. He stood behind me, took my robe from me, and threw it on the bed. He put his hands over my eyes.

"Hold your hands behind your back." I did as he asked and held my bandaged hand in my good hand. "Good boy. I like that you did that without question. Now just let me take you."

He pushed me forward and the urge to hold out my hands to feel my way was strong, but I wanted my gift more, so I held them tightly behind me. We walked slowly forward and I let him guide me.

"Is this gift going to hurt?"

I heard his smile. "No, Baby Boy."

He turned me around and we walked forward again and then he turned me again, then we stopped and did it a few more times but I knew we were in his room with his clothes and the toys.

"Are you sure it's not going to hurt?" He kissed the back of my neck and it made me shiver.

"I'm sure. Do you know where you are?" I smiled under his hands.

"Yes. I know, you tried to trick me but we're in your room with your clothes and... things." I heard him smile again. "I'm right, aren't I? I've worn blindfolds a lot."

"Yes, Baby Boy. What do you think it is?" I shrugged my shoulders.

"Are you going to try and get me to have doughnuts with sugar by tempting me with a new toy?" He laughed.

"Nope. Do want to guess again?" I shook my head.

"Can I just have it please?" He laughed.

"I love it when you beg." I turned my face a little to him

"Please can I have it, please... please!" He dropped his hands from my face and stepped back to the side of me.

I looked at the wall in front of me, expecting to see toys and whips, maybe a wrapped gift. Instead, there were two rows of clothes. On top, were about twenty white t-shirts all hanging neatly and below was about ten pairs of jeans. I pushed my hand between the shirts to look at the wall behind wondering where all the toys had gone then turned and looked at him.

"You got new clothes? Where are the whips and toys?" He smiled, enjoying something but I didn't know what.

"I have moved them into my... weird, funny little room to make room... for your clothes."

I looked at him confused and then his words sunk in. I looked back at the clothes and touched one of the shirts with my fingers. Mine. My clothes. My stomach flipped over. I had never had clothes, well I did once, a long time ago but not since I was an adult. Not to mention the twenty or so items that hung from the hangers. I stroked my hands across them one by one. They were mine. My own clothes.

I looked at him. "These are mine?"

He smiled. "Yes, Baby Boy. Do you like them?"

I looked back at the row of white t-shirts and touched one again. It was mine. I looked back at him again.

"Mine to wear?"

He was smiling still and he broke into a small laugh. "Yes, yours to wear. As much as I like it, you cannot stay naked forever. Here." He stepped towards me and opened a draw which was full of socks and boxer shorts and a few jockstraps, among other things. "All yours, Baby Boy."

I ran my hand over them and then looked back to the shirts. "They are all the same? Same colour?"

He stepped towards me and wrapped his arms round me, leaning his chin on my shoulder. "Yes, on purpose. I know how difficult you find making decisions... this way you don't have to worry."

I let a smile take my lips.

"Thank you." I kissed his arm that held me and leant my head against him. "I think you saved me; I think you save me from my own self... always. If you had never found me in the back alleys, never taught me to be a slave, never asked for me back after Beecher and never looked after me now, I think my need and my mind would have hurt me." I kissed him again still looking at my clothes. "Why do you keep saving me when I can't give you what you need?"

"Because I love you and you give me so much just by being with you. I have what I want and what I need can wait, for as long as you need to, until you want it, until you're ready. It runs through your blood and through your body and your mind. Devon caused you a great deal of pain but every day, Baby Boy, every day I know you feel it asking a little more. One day, you will feel ready to taste it again and you will remember the pleasure it brings. It will not be part of our relationship until you want it to be." He pulled my face round to his and kissed my mouth gently. "Do you want to try on your clothes?" I smiled at him and nodded. He smiled back. "Go on then, I want to see you."

He let me go and sat on the floor cross-legged and watched as I pulled a shirt from its hanger and put it on. It was tighter than his clothes had been on me and I ran my hands down my body feeling it against my skin.

"When did you get these? You have been with me the whole time?" He looked at me and smiled.

"When you stayed with Julian. I took the opportunity to shop for you and you were asleep when I returned, so you never knew. The rails were built while you were recovering, you just never noticed. I'm glad they fit. When you are more comfortable with your place, Isaac, we will go shopping again and you can choose some different colours and maybe different clothes."

I pulled the jeans over my body and looked at him. "I like these, I don't want different ones. I want these ones that you chose." I fumbled with the buttons with my bandaged hand, he got to his knees and pulled me towards him. He lifted the t-shirt and kissed the skin just above my cock before doing up the buttons on the jeans then sat back down.

"Fucking gorgeous, Baby Boy."

I looked at him, feeling unsure in my new clothes. Now I that was in them, I wanted to take them off. I pulled at the material around my cock.

"Are they too tight?"

I looked at him and screwed my face up. "Yes...no... I don't know. What do you think?"

He laughed out and held out his hand which I took. "I think you look fucking beautiful and I think it is going to take you a bit of time to get used to being... confined." He pulled me down to the floor and I dropped to my knees. "Sit. I have something else for you."

Two gifts? Was this one going to hurt? No, not till I was ready. I sat down and struggled a little to cross my legs, which made him smile.

"Can I take them off?"

He shook his head. "No, not yet. Do you like your clothes?"

I smiled. "I love them! I just need to get used to wearing them... we won't have to wear them all the time, will we?" He laughed and shook his head.

"No, only when we need to, when we leave this room." I sat up straighter.

"Where are we going? I don't think I want to go." He reached out and touched my face and stroked his thumb over my cheek.

"Nowhere for now, Baby Boy, but there are things I want to share with you and those things are not down here. I will stay with you the whole time..." He smiled at me. "...so you don't get in trouble." I didn't like the idea of leaving this room or the basement. He frowned. "I thought maybe you could come upstairs with me soon and say hello to Sim?" I liked that idea, seeing Sim.

"Will I be allowed to speak to him?" He smiled still holding my hands.

"We will see. He may be healing when we go but I'm sure he would like to see you."

"I'd like that. Is that my other gift?" He shook his head.

"No." He reached over to his side of the room and brought out a box covered in paper and ribbons.

It was a proper gift, wrapped with tape, the kind I had imagined as a child but never got. He placed it on the floor between us and I stared at it. I had never had a present that looked so lovely, I couldn't believe that it was mine. I looked at him.

"You can open it."

I touched it gently with my fingers of my good hand, running them across the patterned paper and feeling the ribbon that hung from it.

"It's a real gift." I looked at him and he sat watching me. I sat touching it with my hands and staring at it for ages.

"Are you going to open it?"

I looked back at him. I wanted to know what was inside, but I didn't want to ruin the beautiful box. I looked back at it then back at Layton.

"I don't want to spoil it. Can you do it?" He smiled at me.

"There will be other gifts, Isaac. This is not the last one you will ever see. I will do the tape and you can do the ribbon." He held out a piece of the ribbon for me. "Here, pull this."

I took it in my fingers and pulled at it gently and watched the bow disappear from the top. I dropped the ribbon and he laughed. He opened the taped that held the paper and then sat back and looked at me.

"Let me watch you while you do the rest."

I looked down at it. It didn't look beautiful anymore and I pushed the paper open. There was a brown box with a lid and I ran my hand over it till I came to the edge, and then wrapped my fingers round it. I pulled it back slowly and then saw what was inside. Boots! I looked at Layton quickly and then looked back at them.

"My boots." The words were whispered.

"Yes, Baby Boy. These are your very own boots."

I lifted one out of the box and touched it with my fingers. These were not the ones I had shared my thoughts with, they were lost.

"I know the other boots were very important to you and they helped you through a difficult time. These are new boots... for new memories."

Yes, new boots for new memories. I looked at him with tears in my eyes.

"Thank you." The words didn't seem enough for the feelings they gave me. He smiled at me.

"Do you want to put them on?"

I nodded and tried to hold the boot while I did the laces, he took it from me and sorted it out. He passed it to me while he did the other one and then passed that to me. I looked at them in my arms. I bent and kissed them and told them the first thought in my head. I loved him. I looked back at Layton, he was watching me.

"I just wanted to tell them something... something new."

144

He smiled at me and held out his hand for the boots, I gave them to him and then leant back on my good hand, while he put them on my feet.

"You can just try them, Isaac, but you need to wear socks with them otherwise they will give you blisters, okay?" I nodded to him and watched as he put them on my feet and did up the laces.

"I used to talk to my boots because it was like talking to you. I told them things I wanted to tell you." He looked at me and I paused for a moment then decided it was right that I should tell him.

"The reason…the reason I never asked to come here…" His hands stilled and he just sat looking at me. "…was because I wanted to so badly." We sat staring at each other for a moment. He never spoke, just frowned a little so I continued. "I knew it was wrong for a slave to feel the things I did. To see your face in my mind every day and wish that you would come for me. I didn't want to get you in trouble. I didn't want to come here and heal and leave again. I thought if I went back to the vanillas, I would be able to forget about you so when he asked where I wanted to wait, the only person I could think of in that moment was Marcus.

"I was very broken and couldn't think properly but when I woke up, I was here, the place I was trying to avoid. I tried hard not to think the things I was thinking about you, not to feel them. I tried to keep my distance from you, so when I left it wouldn't hurt so much like before, but you said I couldn't leave. You wouldn't let me keep my distance from you. I tried so hard to sort it out, but it got confusing so I went where it was safe, where I didn't have to think but you wouldn't let me stay there either, not comfortably.

"You took everything I needed away, your touch, your comfort and I couldn't stay there anymore because I wanted and needed those things, I wanted them from you. I don't know if it's right to tell you now, but I know that you are my whole world and when I'm not with you, I feel like I can't breathe and it hurts." I was still looking at him and he at me. "I always feel that way, even when we play, even when I'm bound at your feet. I always feel safe and I know you will always look after me. Sometimes when I look at you, I can't breathe. I think that's love, isn't it? When it hurts like that?"

I thought it was. Never having been in love I didn't know, and no one seemed to be able to give me an answer when I had asked them. He was just sitting watching me now. Maybe I was wrong, maybe those things weren't love. I just knew that the things I felt for him I had never felt for another person.

I looked away from him and looked at my boots on my feet. "Can you say something? Even if I have made you angry and you want to be away from me. Can you say something before you go?" I was unsure now; I shouldn't have said anything.

I should have just told my boots and left it there with them but that hadn't made any sense anymore. I told them things I wanted him to know, and he was here sitting in front of me so surely, it was right to just tell him.

We sat in silence. I was breathing heavily and could feel my tears prickling at my eyes. I didn't want to feel stupid, so I got up and walked over to the long mirror and looked at myself. The jeans and the shirt were quite tight and made my body look even smaller, but I loved the boots, I loved the way they made me feel when I looked at myself wearing them.

I looked back at him still sitting on the floor looking at me. He still hadn't said a word and I needed him to. I turned and dropped to my knees, crawling over to him. I looked at him a little breathless before kissing his feet, then I laid down and put my head in his lap. I wanted to show him my place, show him I knew my place and it was exactly where I wanted to be.

He stroked my hair with his fingers and held me with his other hand. "I have you, Baby Boy."

I pushed myself further into him and curled my body into myself and wrapped my arms around him. It didn't matter, when I was here with him safe, nothing mattered. He didn't need to say anything, I didn't need him to say anything, I knew I loved him, I didn't need him to tell me that's what I felt when I was with him like this.

We stayed there for ages while he touched and stroked me, letting me feel the things I had forbidden myself for so long in the safety of his arms.

I closed my eyes and he spoke. "Hey, no sleeping, not here."

I turned my face a little towards him and slowly opened my eyes and he smiled at me. He was still stroking his finger through my hair. "I want to sleep naked with you in the bed." I wanted to stay exactly where I was. "You want to help make supper?" I shook my head and he laughed.

"I prefer the sleeping naked with you." I looked away from him. "Okay, I'll help." He bent and kissed me and scooped me in his arms and stood up.

He looked at me. "You know you're mine now, don't you, Baby Boy?" I smiled at him and nodded. Exactly where I wanted to be. I just had to start earning my place…

GRAY

CHAPTER EIGHT

We cooked and ate supper, then he undressed me and we slept naked together. We didn't talk much, and nothing was said about my earlier declaration, but I felt better for having shared it with him. We just enjoyed each other's company, touching and kissing and being close. I felt freer with him than I had ever felt before, even in the darkness of the night, when it came, didn't bother me as much as it had.

When morning came and he was still sleeping, I took myself to the bathroom. I picked up my boots and took them with me, although I didn't wear them, I wanted to do something that would require me to recall painful memories and I hoped I would find comfort in them. I used the toilet and brushed my teeth and wrapped my hand in the same stuff Layton had wrapped my cast in when I had showered, so it wouldn't get wet. I kissed my boots and put them on the shower floor where they wouldn't get wet but were where I could see them.

I wanted to cleanse myself so I could give him my body, but I knew it was going to be tough. My need for him to have me had been growing for a few days and now I wanted to feel him inside me, the need for him had outgrown my fear of what I needed to do.

I turned on the shower, picked up the cleansing nozzle from the side, and sat on the shower room floor holding it for a while. It had been ages since I had had my hole filled with anything and being cleansed held bad memories. I took a deep breath and looked at my boots, trying to visualize what I wanted. There was no one here but me and them and no one was going to punish me if I couldn't do it.

I whispered out to them. "I have to make new memories."

I stood up and turned the nozzle on until the water ran warm from the plug then stood facing the wall and let the water run between my arse. I rubbed my fingers over my hole, spreading my legs wider and then pulled at my hole, trying to let some of the water warm and lubricate my ring. I stayed like that for a while enjoying the sensation of the water, then I pushed my finger in a little and closed my eyes as my body remembered what it was like to open when asked.

I blew my breaths out slowly and looked across at my boots for mental support. I spread my arse open and with one hand, rolled the shower nozzle between my arse cheeks over my hole, trying to tempt it, remind it what was coming. I ran it over my hole and looked at the wall as I felt the tip of the plug find the hole it sought. I pushed my arse out further to it and pushed the plug inside.

I lay my head on my arm and looked at my boots as I pushed the plug further until my hole gripped its stem. I let it go and pushed my hand against the shower wall as I felt the water slowly fill me. I moved my feet, agitated at the feel of it, and then made an effort to spread them again as my mind started to remember the times I had endured the cane with this same feeling. Without realizing, I had started to cower and get caught up in my upset, pushing my arse into the feel of it remembering and waiting for the pain…then he stepped between me and the wall and pulled my face up to his.

"I'm here, stand up and breathe into the feeling." I looked at him, breathing quickly and he stroked his fingers over my face. "I have you." I nodded trying to hold back my upset now he was me. "Breathe slowly."

I tipped my head forward to him and he rubbed his hand down my back and over my arse, holding his hands there until I lifted my head.

"I need to empty." He swept his hand round and took the plug and pulled at it.

"Relax, Baby Boy." He pulled it from me and I immediately clenched my arse to hold the water in.

I looked at him and went to move to the toilet, but he held me there looking at me, then lifted his hand and held my face, stroking his thumb over my bottom lip before leaning down and kissing me gently. When he let me go, I moved to the toilet and emptied. When I returned he was leaning against the wall with the plug in his hand. I walked slowly towards him, face turned down, looking over at my boots quickly then back to the floor. As I reached him, he lifted my face to him.

I used to enjoy being cleansed, it used to make me hard with the feel of it, now it was something I had to do, to get something I wanted. I looked at him and put my hands on his chest, I spread my feet and tipped my head on him. I felt his hands stroke my arse over and over, pulling it open. He rubbed the plug across my hole, I pushed my arse out to him and he pushed the plug inside me.

He lifted my face. "This is making new memories, Baby Boy." He took my mouth with his as the water filled me, flicking his tongue in and out of my mouth, tasting me, taking my mind.

I wrapped my fingers behind his head and held him there before I dragged my lips from him and whispered to him. "I need to empty."

Not the most romantic words I had ever hoped to say to him, but need wasn't always what you wanted. I tipped my head against him and let him take the plug from me before I walked off to the toilet. By the time it came to be filled again, I already knew the memories I wanted.

I took his mouth with mine and this time it was my tongue that did the tasting. He decided to take it a step further and he rubbed my cock with his hand. When I tried to pull away, he held me to him.

"Look at your boots, Baby Boy, do you remember that day in front of the mirror, how you felt wearing my boots that very first time?" I turned my face and looked at them as he spoke. "Remember how it felt, you looked so hot with your cock hanging under the t-shirt and those big boots…as you thrust yourself at the mirror. Remember my mouth on you? Remember that feeling and how much you wanted it?"

I fought against the feelings for a second then as he kept filling my head with the memories of that day, I slowly let them take me. I grew hard under his hand and I lay against him as the remembered feelings washed through me.

"You looked so hot, just like now when your body remembers what it likes, Baby Boy."

He took his hand from me and kissed me again. I moaned under his mouth as my body ran with so many different feelings, I couldn't decide if I wanted to kiss him, suck him, or just get him to fuck me right here. Completely forgetting the water that filled me it wasn't till I felt myself nearly expel with fullness, that I recalled the feeling and I pushed away from him.

"Fuck... take it out." He smiled and pulled the plug slowly from me and I leaned into him and moaned with the feeling. I stayed there breathing in the feeling of it and he tipped my face and looked at me.

"Go." He gestured to the toilet and I shook my head at him.

"Not yet." I was breathing heavily, holding the water inside me, enjoying the full feeling and I looked up at him and smiled.

I wanted him to just take me now, I felt so turned on. This was the memory I wanted to have every time I was cleansed, my mind awash with need, the blood pumping through my body making me feel hot, burning with desire for the man that stood in front of me. "I'm making a new memory." I slid my hand to his face and took his mouth with mine and he took mine with his.

He slid his hands over my back and down to my arse and back again until they stilled on my back holding me. I moaned as the water asked for its release. I needed to go but I wanted to stay.

He pushed me away. "No more... Go."

I walked quickly to the toilet and emptied. When I returned, he was already under the shower and he held out his hand for me to join him. When I reached him and put my hand in his, he pulled me under the shower and kissed me again, grinding himself against me roughly before turning me around and I thought he was just going to take me... I wanted him to take me.

Instead, he hugged me and kissed me and started to wash me. I looked up at him confused by the feelings running in me.

"One new memory at a time, Baby Boy."

I sighed deeply a little disappointed and leant my head back against him, letting him have my mind to look after for a while.

"Why didn't you ask me to help you?" We were sitting on the bed and he was drying my hair in his usual way, rubbing the towel roughly over my head.

I turned my head and looked at him and then looked back at my boots which sat between my legs on the bed. I touched them with my fingers. He reached for my hand and pulled it to his lips and kissed it.

"Are you telling them things you don't want to tell me?"

I turned and looked at him quickly and shook my head. "No. Sometimes I find it difficult to answer your questions." He pulled me back to his body and kissed my face.

"That, Baby Boy, is because you think about what you're going to say rather than just saying it. Nothing you ever say will change the way I feel about you."

I sighed. "Yes, I know but I don't want you to think I'm stupid. I don't want you to love a stupid person." He laughed and laid back on the bed.

I was sitting between his legs. I moved my boots aside and turned on the bed to look at him before allowing a small smile to take my lips. He was funny when he laughed. I poked a finger in his stomach. "Don't laugh at me."

He looked at me and continued to smile. When he looked at me like he was, that's when I found it hard to breathe. I pulled the towel from his hands and threw it over his face and then crawled up the bed as he pulled it from himself. I looked down at him and then kissed him.

He stroked his hand over my body.

"I wanted... I wanted you to fuck me... again... like you did that night before I left to go back to Kellen's. Devon didn't make it very pleasant to be cleansed while I was with him, and I wanted to try and get rid of the fear I had of the memory of it. I used to enjoy it... once. I thought if I did it on my own, I would remember what it was like to enjoy it again. I want to learn to do it myself... can I?"

He pushed himself from the bed and kissed me.

"Of course, I will teach you." He held my face in his hand and looked at me. "What we did that night wasn't fucking, Baby Boy. It was much sweeter than that. We loved each other."

I looked at him confused. "But... we didn't then... did we? You didn't love me then?" I thought I had loved him then but didn't know at the time that it was love. Was it the same for him?

He smiled at me. "Yes, Baby Boy, I loved you then."

Well, that didn't make sense. He sent me away... well he let me go, let me go back... to slave for them.

"But you took me to Kellen's. You let me go?"

He nodded. "Because you asked to, because you said you needed to. You hadn't found what you were looking for here so I let you go so you could find it. I wanted you to stay here but you weren't ready, and I wasn't going to force you to be with me. I am sorry that I let you go now. I thought you would be safe with your new Keeper while you sated your need and decided where you were supposed to be. I never thought for one minute that you were being abused and neglected by your Keeper, otherwise I would have come for you sooner. I gave you a year, do you remember?" I shook my head. "In the car on the way to Kellen, I asked you how long you needed... I told you I loved you then too."

I tried to think. All I remembered of that journey was feeling scared that my security and time with him was coming to an end. I had convinced myself that I needed a new Keeper, that it was that that was causing the ache inside me. I had thought that he had healed me, and the missing piece of my life was a Keeper to love and comfort me when I needed him.

I knew now that he had loved me but because such an idea was so beyond my imagination I hadn't realised then, I had thought he was just doing his job.

He spoke and stroked my face. "It's not surprising you didn't hear what I said. You were already in slave mode, protecting your mind until you found someone to look after it, to have you."

I felt sad. What I had wanted to have was what I had witnessed Sim and Leon sharing, the adoration and love they clearly felt for each other. I hadn't realised I already had that... with him.

I looked at him. "I was searching for something I was never going to find though... because I already had it, didn't I? You have always had me." He smiled softly. "I'm sorry I left you, I thought I had to."

He pulled me down to him and kissed me. "Don't look so sad, Baby Boy, I have you and this time I'm not letting you go... you get into too much trouble without me." He smiled again as I sat looking at him, thinking about the wasted year.

A year where I had nearly lost my life when I could have been here loving him and having him love me. I didn't want to think about it anymore, I wanted him to have me. I wanted to find my place again with him. Kneeling beside him I held out my hands to him. He looked at me for a moment before turning and collecting rope from the draw beside him. My heart fluttered when I saw it, the smallest doubt flickered across my mind, but I kept my hands out to him.

If you wanted someone to control you, you couldn't half-heartedly give that control. To allow someone to have you in the manner I wanted, you had to trust them implicitly...and I did.

He took my wrists and looked at me. "Trust me."

Although it was more of a statement than a question, I sensed his hesitation, giving me the chance to back down. I gave him a small smile and nodded filled with excitement and a little fear.

He pushed his legs out either side of me. "Then use that beautiful mouth of yours to make me hard."

Without thought, I slipped down the bed between his legs, still with him holding my wrists. I waited for him to let go and I looked at him and he shook his head. "No hands, just your mouth."

I leant forward over my knees, bent my head between my arms and took him in my mouth. It wasn't very comfortable with both my arms stretched out to him but that was what giving yourself to someone was about. Sometimes you had to endure difficult poses or situations to please your Master and if you pleased them, then they might give you a little pleasure in return.

The aim was always to please them without thought and if you were lucky, they in turn, may allow you to come for them. If they didn't, you accepted it and tried harder, worked harder, and took more for them next time. Accepting that though was hard when you were so turned on.

I started to enjoy the dull ache that was beginning in my shoulders, it made me suck him harder in the hope he wouldn't keep me there long. I took my mouth from him to catch my breath and looked at his beautiful, hard cock stretching from his body towards my mouth, asking for more.

I felt a hand on the back of my head. "I did not ask you to stop, Isaac. If you need to breathe you will do it with my cock in your mouth." He gently pushed my head back down until my mouth was wrapped around him again and I worked his cock through the simmering pain that was now working its way down my back.

I didn't dare take my mouth from him again. I wanted him inside me and I liked that he was making me earn it... I liked earning it. It always tasted better when you earned it.

I could feel him pulling at my wrists, but I didn't look up until he asked me to. "Enough... kneel up in the centre of the bed." I moved from him and looked at my wrists bound in rope.

They were separate from each other and the rope hung down from each wrist to the bed as I held my hands out. He sat up, turned and knelt next to me, his hard cock rubbing across my thigh as he rubbed his hands over my back and up to my head. He tipped my face towards him and looked in my eyes before taking my mouth with his. I kissed him back until he took his mouth from me.

He rubbed his hand down my back and across my arse, gently teasing his fingers over my arse crack. He tipped my upper body forward slightly with one hand while he stroked my hole and my arse with the other while he gently rubbed his cock against me. "Are you nervous?"

I turned my face in his direction but didn't look at him as I answered breathlessly. "A little...Sir." It had been a long time since I had been intimate with anyone and had had my arse filled. Add that to being dominated, it was all a little scary, especially having seen and felt the abuse of those situations but I trusted him.

He kissed me and continued to rub his hand over my body, soothing me, but also exciting me.

"Your mouth made me hard..." He kissed my neck under my ear. "Your hole makes me hard." I took a deep breath, breathing in the excitement and fear his words made me feel. "Put your hands behind your head."

I did as he asked and linked my fingers behind my head, letting my good hand take the pressure and letting the hanging rope dangle down my back. I looked straight ahead at the ornate wooden headboard that rose halfway up the wall to the ceiling while his hands ran over my body. He pulled me back to sit on my feet and knelt around me. I could feel his cock stroking across my arse as he pulled himself closer and kissed my back. Stroking his hands to the front of my body, he rubbed my nipples under his palms and I lifted my head in response, panting gently as he touched his lips to my back and ran his tongue over my skin.

He took my nipples in his fingers and pinched them gently. "So beautiful, Isaac, I have missed you." He ran his tongue over my skin and under my arm and turned my upper body around to him a little so he could take my nipple in his mouth.

He sucked at it gently at first and then bit it in his teeth. I drew my breath in quickly as I felt my cock react to the sweet pain and I heard him smile as he took his mouth from me and stroked his hand from my chest down to my cock.

"Mm, you remember don't you." It wasn't a question and I didn't answer as he ground his cock against my arse. "It's been a long time, your body is hypersensitive, waiting, wanting, it will remember just like your cock does... look at it."

I looked down as he stroked his hand over my cock and it began to grow harder in his hand. My breathing was short and quick as the pleasurable feelings ran through my body. He ran his finger over the crease on my cock head making my cock swell even more as I opened my mouth and sucked my air in quickly.

"Nice and slow, Baby Boy, I haven't loved you yet." It felt like he was, the expectation of his touches, of what was to come had me reacting to his every touch.

Over the last few months, I had thought I was broken, void of feeling and desire and need but now, under his hands, under his control, I felt very much alive.

He had one hand stroking my cock and the other slipped under my arse and his fingers rubbed gently over my hole, his lips licked and kissed the sensitive skin under my arm and down my side. Three extremely sensitive areas all being pleasured at the same time, my body was definitely alive, it was on fire with pleasure and my mind was working with it to the point it was almost overwhelming. His hands moved and stroked their way up my body, one at the front of me and one behind.

"Kneel up." I lifted myself onto my knees and he took the rope and pulled my hands above my head. "Move forward towards the headboard." I looked ahead of me and shuffled forward on my knees as he pulled my hands up and looped the rope through a ring on the top of the headboard and tied it ornately round itself.

My arms were bent a little at the elbow, so I wasn't totally strung out and I held the rope in each hand as he checked the fall of the rope across my bad hand. I was apprehensive now; my body was still awash with pleasure, but I wondered if I was going to have to endure some form of punishment to get what I wanted. My stomach lurched and my breathing became quick and loud as my anxiety grew.

"Shh, Isaac, I'm just going to love you... my way." He ran his hands down my arms and my back and over my arse and I tipped my head back, unsure now.

He wrapped his hands around my hips and pulled me back across the bed towards him and I moaned, whispering his name as he kissed the small of my back and pulled my arse open. He ran his tongue down to my hole and I closed my eyes, pushing my arse out to him further to have the exquisite feeling as he pleasured my sensitive hole with his tongue and his lips.

He sucked and licked and ran his metal bead over it until a moan left me with the painful need that was building inside me. He pushed the tip of his tongue into the tight crease over and over making me want more of him inside me. When he took his mouth from me, I moaned gently at losing his touch, then I felt him stroking my cock. I dropped my head forward between my arms and let the pleasure of it wash through me and take my mind so that when he lubricated my hole and pushed his finger inside me, I felt no hesitation at letting him in, I wanted it.

He finger fucked me slowly while he rubbed my cock and I found myself rocking gently onto his finger until he pulled it slowly from me. I moaned at the pleasure as my ring closed around him. He asked for entry again with two fingers and at first, I could feel the resistance, but he pushed them slowly in and held them there while he stroked my cock. I felt my orgasm ask and I rocked my body again onto his fingers lost in it.

"May I come...?" My words moaned from me, and he took his hand from my cock and stroked my body with it.

The orgasm simmered inside me as his fingers gently fucked my hole, it still asked but it was like it couldn't find its way and so raced around my body burning me with its need. He took his fingers from me and I pushed my hands flat against the headboard at their loss. He knelt either side of my legs and pushed my knees closer together and then I felt him asking to be let in.

I felt a slight burning sensation as my hole stretched around him and I moved my knees forward away from it, moaning but he wrapped his hand under my body and pulled me to him while he guided his cock forward.

"Relax... it will just be a few seconds, I promise."

I cried out as he pushed a little harder and then my hole opened to him, making me jolt from the burning spasm as it stretched around his mushroom head. I cried and pulled at the ropes as he gently pushed his cock inside me, stealing my pleasure as he held my arse to him.

"A little more, Isaac, your body will remember."

I moaned quickly with each breath as I felt him start to thrust inside me and he stroked my arched back with his other hand soothing the sensation. When I felt his body up against mine, I knew he was all the way in. He held me there for a while and stroked my cock, waiting for the angry burn of my ring stretching around him to subside.

As I started to feel the pleasure again, I tipped my head forward as my body relaxed, he released his hold on my cock and held my body either side as he started to gently thrust. At first, each movement was a little uncomfortable, but very quickly, each thrust turned into sparks of pleasure as he slowly pulled out and then gently thrust inside me again. My moans of pain turned to moans of pleasure as with each thrust, I felt the orgasm inside me looking for its escape. I felt like I was going to come and when the feeling increased, I tipped my head back and moaned to him.

"I want to come... I want to come... please."

He stroked his hands up my back running his fingers gently over my skin. "Not yet, Baby Boy, it's just making you feel like that, just enjoy the ride. I know it feels intense."

He leant forward and kissed my back and wrapped his hands under my arms and held my shoulders while he gently thrust in and out of my hole and I quivered and moaned each time I felt the orgasm looking for its release. He kept me in the state of heightened pleasure for ages while he stroked and touched my body and I completely lost myself in it.

He moved us both forward while still inside me and pushed his knees between mine, spreading my knees around his legs. When he released the ropes from the ring he pulled me back against his body, wrapping his arms around me tightly. I let my head fall back on his shoulder and looked up at him vacantly. My whole body and mind were consumed with him and the need to come. He smiled at me and kissed me on my parted lips but I couldn't kiss him back.

"I have you, Baby Boy." I raised my hand to his face, completely drugged by the sensation and desire running around my body and whispered to him, begging him to free me.

"Please may I come...?" He wrapped his arms around my body and held me firmly to him as he gently thrust beneath me, kissing my neck and face when I quivered under his confinement.

"I'm going to take you there, Baby Boy." I could feel his body flexing beneath mine, but I couldn't move, it took all my energy just to deal with the orgasm that was now shooting around my body looking for its release.

I moaned out to him, the feeling was so sweet it made my emotions lose control and I cried quietly with every thrust of him inside me. He caressed his hand down my body and took my cock in his hand, stroking it over and over while still gently thrusting inside of me.

"You are beautiful, Isaac. I love being wrapped around you feeling your body quiver under my touch." He kissed me again, small gentle kisses that seemed to draw me deeper and deeper into him. He was breathing heavily, watching me as my hands gripped his thighs on either side of me as I felt the orgasm ask. "Keep your eyes open to me, Isaac."

Still laying with my head back on his shoulder I turned a little to him and dazedly looked at him, whimpering as I felt it rushing at me before I spoke the words.

"May I... I'm coming... I'm coming." Without any effort, without me even chasing it a little, my orgasm exploded through me, making me cry out as my body tremored on him, making me push my hole onto him.

He held me tightly watching me. "God, Isaac, that's beautiful, I can feel your pleasure..."

I cried and strained my body, pushing my hole over him as if the orgasm itself was coming from him into me. My cum burst intermittently from my cock over and over as the orgasm pulsed through me and I gripped him tightly.

He kissed my open mouth, still watching me and then held me to him as he moaned at the feel of my hole gripping him rhythmically. "Fuck, Isaac...you're making me come..."

He held me tightly and ground his cock into me, crying out as his orgasm shook his body. He looked at me as I had done to him as his pleasure ripped through his body and mind and he gave me his life. I let go of his leg and lifted my hand to his face before I let it drop to the bed exhausted.

He pulled me to him tighter, kissed the corner of my mouth, and I looked at him completely sated. I couldn't remember having an orgasm so sweet, that had simmered inside me for so long before erupting.

"I love you."

He smiled and put his mouth to my ear and whispered. "That doesn't count when your body is trembling in pleasure, but I know you do." He licked my ear and nibbled it before kissing it.

I realised then that that was the first time I had said it to him properly. My legs quivered at being stretched across his, but I didn't want to leave him.

"Can I stay here a while?" He smiled and stroked my hair with his fingers.

"Just for a moment more, otherwise your legs will cramp." I wrapped my arms around his, the rope still hanging from my wrists. I could still feel him inside me, I closed my eyes and tipped my head against the side of his face.

"I like making love, it's like one long orgasm." He laughed and I felt his cock move inside me.

"I could see. You look very beautiful when you come, I love to watch you. Were you worried when I bound your hands?"

I shook my head then shrugged. "No, not then...when you hung me on the wall I was worried. I thought you were going to make me earn it by taking some punishment... I don't think I'm ready for that yet; although I wouldn't have said anything to you, I was kind of like just…trusting you to know what to do." He kissed me again. I didn't want him to think I wasn't trying hard to get there so I continued. "Not yet, I'm not ready yet... I am trying really hard though. I liked you making me suck you and the rope." I smiled at him and he laughed.

"That doesn't count either because you always like to use your mouth, Isaac." He looked at me seriously, stroking the side of my face. "I know you are trying but it cannot be rushed or forced, when you're ready you will know. If you taste it too soon we could end up two steps back. There is no rush."

My legs shook again and he pushed me from him to the bed. I stuck my bottom lip out at him at the loss of his cock and his touch. He half smiled and I lay on the bed looking at him. He crawled up the bed beside me, took my hand and started to undo the rope binds. I watched him as he checked my bandaged hand. It had felt good to be bound again and I wished I could keep them on for a while.

I saw him glance at me and then back at the rope. "No is the answer to your next question." I poked my tongue out at him. "I saw that!"

"Why did you forbid me to kiss Jacob? And did he get in trouble?" He sighed as he took the rope and I gave him my other hand.

"Baby Boy, your bed manners are appalling. Must you speak of other men when we have just made love?" He took my other hand and looked at me and I gave him my sorry face. He leant over and kissed me, smiled and then started to undo the rope. "Because I didn't want you kissing him. Your mouth is mine for the time being. Okay?" I nodded. "He didn't get in trouble, I just reminded him of his place with Julian. Julian is possessive and I cannot allow him to overstep the very clear boundaries that Julian gives him."

It was like Jacob had said, when they wanted it, you could have it and when they didn't you were forbidden. I held back the urge to ask why again.

He looked at me as he took the rope off and put it on the floor. "Would you like tea?" I shook my head. "Are you sulking?" I turned on my side away from him.

"A little."

"Why?"

I didn't really know the answer to that. I shrugged my shoulders.

"I feel lost."

He laid down beside me and wrapped his arm around me.

"You're feeling vulnerable, Isaac. I'm sorry I forgot your neediness. I didn't want you to get rope burn." He kissed the back of my neck and I shivered. "Come, turn around and lay with me." I did it immediately, he pulled me into his body and kissed my head and stroked his fingers through my hair. "Better?"

I nodded. Yes, it was better. I felt so safe when he wrapped me in his body. I stroked my fingers across his chest.

"Was it beautiful? I mean... I know it was to me, it was amazing, but you like to fuck and I know it's different without…toys and play…?"

He looked at me. "Are you feeling insecure?" I shrugged my shoulders. "It was extremely beautiful, making love is always beautiful. Fucking is different, it is for sating a need and not thinking so much about each other. This was your first time in a while and for the time being, we will only make love not fuck or play."

I sighed. "It doesn't sate your need though, does it?" And that bothered me.

He smiled and kissed me. "Not always and soon it will not be enough for you either."

I pushed myself up on my arm and looked at him.

"Is it burning inside you? Does it hurt?" He smiled and pulled me back down to his body.

"You make me burn, you make me hard and you make me come. That is all that matters." I half laughed. "What?"

"It sounds very… vanilla." He laughed and kissed me and I smiled.

"It is but there is nothing wrong with vanilla now and again, the main thing is that you still remember there is more to be had."

"Oh, I remember..." I remembered taking it and suffering and... that was it.

I couldn't seem to move on from that. There was more to it, I just couldn't get there in my head. "I just don't seem to be able to move past the 'it's going to hurt' bit."

"You did for a moment when Julian and Jacob played here. You took the cane and it didn't damage your mind or make you ask for mercy, you still wanted to play... with Jacob."

Was he jealous? I was just about to ask when his phone rang. It made me jump as it hadn't made a sound in days. He moved me from him and left the bed and I lay watching him as he stood naked talking on the phone.

"Leon... I can't." He looked at me. "Fuck sake, Leon, he wasn't meant to be here yet, I was going to bring him in myself... shit, is Sim here?" He turned away and put his fingers to his forehead while he listened to Leon. Something had happened and he wasn't happy about it. I sat up on the bed and crossed my legs. "No, no, I will have to come up. Leave him in there for now, hopefully being left alone will calm him down. I just need to shower."

He closed his phone and looked at me. I wasn't sure what to do or say when he was focused on other things and wasn't happy so I just sat.

He walked towards me, smiled and held out his hand. "Come on we need to shower." I took his hand and he led me from the room.

He washed me quickly and then he washed and as he dried me, I watched him. He was distant and hadn't spoken much since the call and it was making me worried.

"Is something wrong upstairs?"

He nodded as he started to dry himself. "Not wrong but yes something has come up and I need to go up and deal with it." He stopped drying and touched my face gently. "I need you to get dressed. You will have to come with me." I shook my head. I didn't want to leave here.

He pulled me to him and wrapped his arm around me. "I know it scares you, leaving the safety of here but a new slave has come in and he is very scared. He doesn't know anyone upstairs. He only knows me, and I need to go to him, to help him. There is no time to get someone to stay with you, so you are going to have to come with me... or stay here on your own?"

I shook my head to that idea and pulled away to look at him. He smiled at me and kissed me. "I'll look after you. Go, get dressed quickly."

I moved away from him towards the dressing room with my new clothes in and he called after me. "Remember to put socks on before putting your boots on."

Slightly panicked and excited, I left him drying himself.

CHAPTER NINE

I was in the clothes room, dressed, looking in the mirror and feeling worried about leaving the basement. Nothing good came from being away from here, but if a slave needed him, I had to let him go and if he was going, then I wanted to stay with him.

The last time I had been left here alone Kellen had come for me and although Kellen didn't scare me now, being away from Layton worried me. This was his job and I was going to have to get used to him being called away at short notice or for urgent matters. When I had been a new slave, he had been the only one that had been able to soothe me, and I didn't want other slaves to suffer because of me. I looked at my boots in the reflection.

I had put socks on but then I had taken them off again. I liked the feel of the leather boots against my skin, and they felt more comfortable without the socks. I would tell him later when he wasn't worried so much. I looked up and saw him standing in the doorway in the reflection of the mirror.

"You look fucking gorgeous. I wish I could take you again, right here." My heart skipped a beat at his words and I smiled at him. "Baby Boy, there are rules for being upstairs."

My heart skipped another beat for a completely different reason. His tone of voice had changed which made me feel I needed to be clear in my understanding too.

"Yes, Sir."

He walked towards me, already dressed in jeans and a black t-shirt and stood behind me while he spoke. "It can be a dangerous place for a submissive, there are lots of people around, clients and slaves. You must stay with me or Leon at all times unless I request otherwise, do you understand?"

Feeling anxious with his tone, I turned to him and nodded. "Yes, Sir... but you're scaring me. I don't want to be away from you." He held out his hand and I took it.

"Good, then you will behave?" I nodded at him and he smiled. "It's not the way I wanted to introduce you to everyone or meet the family but sometimes these very special people who I bring into this world need me."

"I'll do whatever you say... I'm a little excited too." I smiled at him.

He pulled me to him and kissed me. He turned and we walked through the bedroom into the basement as we approached the door to upstairs I slowed and he turned and looked at me.

"My excitement just left me." He half laughed.

"Leon is waiting for us."

I looked at him hopefully. "And Sim?"

He shook his head. "Unfortunately, Sim is on a visit." He stopped pulling me and turned to face me. "Breathe, Baby Boy. I understand this is difficult. There are slaves upstairs and I know that is difficult for you, but they are all very secure in their space with good Keepers. My house is a little different from the ones you've frequented, I'm sure. Nevertheless some things are still the same. There may be slaves on a viewing day and you may see clients but you must not speak to them. Just stay with me. Everyone knows who I am and you will be quite safe."

I just stood looking at him trying to think of all the reasons I should leave the safety of the basement and put myself back in a place, I didn't particularly want to go.

"What's his name?"

He answered immediately. "Orion."

"Who is he?"

"He's a very new boy. I met him on the streets about six months ago. He was selling himself for money, trying to survive on the streets by letting people... hurt him. I will tell you all about him, I promise, but we need to go now. He is scared and I need to help him before he hurts himself."

I nodded to him and gripped his hand tightly. "Will they mind that I'm holding your hand? Because I don't want to let go." He stepped towards me, kissed me and looked at me.

"No, no one will care, I promise. No one will ever hurt you here for loving and touching another man..." He smiled at me. "Especially, when that man is me. The people in my house know you're here, they know who you are. No one will hurt you here."

I smiled weakly back at him and he turned and opened the door. Straight in front of us was a short hallway and a flight of stairs. My heart was beating quicker the further we walked. There were bad people and I hoped we didn't meet any of them.

He stopped at a door and glanced back at me. "Breathe, Baby Boy." I nodded and my stomach somersaulted as he opened the door.

The house was sort of how I remembered it. Long corridors, with large oak doors running along both sides. Some of the doors were closed and some were open. It was quiet, apart from the odd chattering of voices I could hear now and again but it was calm. It made me take a deep breath to settle in its calmness. Layton shut the door behind us and then when we didn't move I looked at him. He was watching me.

"Do you remember?" I nodded to him and he smiled. "Come on, I need to find Leon."

We walked away down to the end of the corridor and I looked back at the doors. Slaves lived here. This was their home, where they suffered and healed and got comforted by their Keepers. As I turned to look the way we were walking, two men turned the corner and walked towards us. One in a Keeper's outfit the other, I guessed, must have been a client as he was dressed in a casual suit. He smiled at Layton as they approached and held out his hand.

"Layton! Where have you been hiding, I haven't seen you in months?"

Layton took his hand and shook it before leaning in and half hugged him. He smiled at the man as they parted.

"Jeremy. Good to see you. Are you viewing?" Layton never answered his question. I looked at Jeremy and he glanced at me, and I just froze to the spot.

He smiled again at Layton. "Yes, one of your newer ones, I think. Finn?"

Layton nodded. "Yes, he's still learning so be patient with him." He looked at the Keeper that stood waiting patiently for the exchange to finish. "Rae." He nodded at him in greeting. "I will come and see you and Finn later. Is everything in order for his viewing?"

Rae nodded. "Yes, Sir. He's all settled, doing really well."

Layton looked back at Jeremy. "When do you plan on taking him?"

Jeremy laughed. "I haven't seen him yet, I may not want him."

Layton smiled back "Oh, you'll want him, he has exceptional physic. When I first saw him, I thought of you."

Jeremy glanced another look at me and this time I dropped my eyes to the floor. It was a natural reaction, one that I had been taught for many years. You never looked a client in the eyes unless they requested it.

"And this one?" He reached out his hand to touch my face, I didn't move but my heart hammered in my chest so hard I thought he could probably see it.

Layton moved slightly in front of me as he turned and introduced us, stopping the intended touch. I don't think I had ever been introduced to anyone in my life, usually, I was left on the floor.

"This is Isaac, Isaac this is Jeremy." I half looked at him as he withdrew his outstretched hand.

"Hello...Sir." Did I call him Sir? I didn't know. Then I remembered he said I shouldn't speak to them. I squeezed Layton's hand in panic.

"Isaac is owned...by me."

Jeremy held his hand up in surrender to Layton. "Of course, my apologies, no offence meant."

Layton smiled at him. "None taken."

I saw Rae's mouth twitch as he tried to hold back a smile and he winked at me. It seemed, as Layton's property, I was off-limits to his touch, which I was grateful for. I liked being Layton's a whole lot.

"Right then, Rae, let's go see this boy that I'm assured I will like." He smiled at Layton and then at me. "Good day to you, Layton, Isaac." He nodded his head and looked at Rae.

"Yes, Sir, if you would like to follow me." Rae led him off down the corridor and I let my breath go that I had been holding.

I saw Layton's smile as he looked down at me. "I wasn't sure how much longer you could hold your breath." I smiled and he pulled me forward, making me step in towards him. He kissed my lips gently. "You did brilliantly, Isaac. Just try and breathe next time and you don't call him Sir, you use his name."

"Why?" Sir felt more comfortable, I didn't know these people enough to use their name.

"Because you are mine, not a slave. Soon word will spread of your arrival here and people and clients will not feel they have the right to just touch you... not without my permission anyway." I nodded but I wasn't sure. He smiled again. "It will take time to find your place, Isaac." He looked at me. "Are you breathing?" It made me smile and he returned it. "Come on." He led the way into another corridor and then another off that.

"Are all these doors slaves' rooms?" He glanced back at me.

"Not in this corridor. This one is staff quarters if they need them." We passed another corridor. "Down there is kitchen, laundry, and maintenance rooms. There's also a large dining room and lounge off of the kitchen for Keepers to relax and for us to eat together when we can." I sniffed the air and he smiled. "Hungry?" I nodded. "I will get Leon to feed you. Beatrice runs the kitchen. Do you remember her?" I shook my head. "You'll love her."

As he spoke a young girl came out of one of the doors at the end. She was wearing a bright orange sundress, even though it wasn't that warm and carrying freshly laundered sheets. Layton smiled at her. "And this is Hazel. She helps Bea run this place."

She was smiling as she approached. "You'll be in trouble if she hears you call her that." She walked straight up to Layton and hugged him, kissing him on the cheek as she pulled away.

Layton smiled at her. "Hello Hazel, this is Isaac."

She looked at me and smiled. "So, you're the person who's been holding him captive then?" She looked at Layton. "Cat got the cream?" She smiled at him and looked back at me. "It is very nice to meet you, Isaac. Bea and I love visitors, so you feel free to come and see us anytime... when you get fed up with him." She nodded at Layton.

I smiled at her. She was very pretty with very long reddish-brown hair pulled back into a ponytail on the back of her head and large brown eyes. She was the same height as me.

"Aren't you cold?" Layton laughed and I looked at him then back at Hazel. "Sorry, I didn't mean to be rude."

She smiled at me. "That's not rude, you can say whatever you like. I like to brighten this place up with a bit of colour and to be honest, it gets warm in the kitchen."

I felt bad so said the next thought that came into my head. "You do look pretty."

Her mouth fell open and the next thing I knew she had her arm wrapped around me. I looked at Layton who was smiling at me.

"Hazel, be gentle with him. Isaac is part of this house now so you will get used to him speaking his mind and not making a lot of sense. On this occasion though, he seems to have it spot on."

She let me go and kissed my cheek. "Aww, you guys! I like you, Isaac."

I smiled at her.

"Where is Leon?"

She looked at Layton. "In your office. Have you come up about the new boy, Orion?" Layton nodded. "Bea has made him lunch, but he wasn't very happy, so Leon told us to keep it for him. I can bring it up when he's ready. I can't wait to tell Bea I met you, Isaac." She touched my arm and smiled.

Layton looked at her nodding. "Maybe in a while, I need to settle him first. Can you make Isaac some lunch please? And ask Bea to replace the bed sheets downstairs please."

She nodded. "Sure I can. I just need to sort out Sim's room first while he's away. Any ideas when the others are going to return home?"

Layton shook his head. "No, maybe a week. Tell Bea I will come and see her later."

He pulled me with him as I turned and smiled at Hazel. I liked her. She was a bit overwhelming but nice, friendly, and pretty. I turned to face Layton and followed after him.

We walked to the end of the corridor through some double doors into a large room where Leon was sitting at a desk. He was exactly as I remembered him and as Layton shut the doors behind us, Leon got up.

"I'm sorry, Layton."

Layton dropped my hand and I stopped where he left me. Leon came up and wrapped his arms around me and hugged me. "Hello, Isaac, it's good to see you looking so well."

A little overwhelmed with it all, I whispered my reply. "Hello."

He left me and walked over to Layton but he didn't hug him, instead, Layton turned and kissed him on the cheek.

"Tell me how he ended up here now? We weren't ready for him. What room have you put him in?"

Leon moved to the desk and handed Layton a file. Layton turned to me and held out his other hand and I walked towards him and took it in mine, grateful to have the contact again. He took me over to the sofa that sat opposite the desk and sat down, pulling me to sit next to him, letting go of my hand he pulled me towards his body and wrapped his arm around me.

I moved so my back was to him slightly so I could see what was in his hand. He kissed the top of my head, opened the file, and started reading. I stared at the boy whose picture sat inside the cover. He looked young, really young. He had short dark curled hair and dark skin.

The picture was taken of him on the streets, as he was bending down to a car. He was probably setting up a fix for himself, offering his services, offering his body for money. I remembered how it worked on the streets.

"He's currently still in the quiet room." Layton flicked a look at Leon and then back to the paper in his hand. "It seems he ended up with a client on Mistress Scarlett's books and got taken to an open party at hers. You know, the bring your own type of thing?" Layton nodded. "She said that when all the guests had left, he was still there, hanging naked and exhausted with a hundred pounds stuck in the crack of his arse." Layton creased his face at Leon's words. I pushed my head against Layton for comfort.

He rubbed my arm. "It's okay, I'm going to sort him out." He kissed me again. "Wounds?"

Leon nodded. "Yes, but I'm not sure how bad, he wouldn't let me see to them. She got him down and dressed him and was looking for some ID so she could have him dropped home but all she found was your card in his pocket. So, she had one of her Keepers drop him here.

"I was going to clean him up and feed him and send him back, but he's in a bad mind space. I know you said he's not ready but any longer out there on the street with the vanillas and he's going to end up doing himself real damage." Layton sighed. "I'm sorry, Layton, I know you have a lot going on at the moment."

Layton shook his head. "No, Leon, you did the right thing. I was hoping to wait a while, ease him into the idea but if he can't behave…" I touched his picture with my fingers that poked out of my bandaged hand. Layton pulled my face up to look at him. "He's safe now."

"How old is he? He looks so young."

Layton nodded. "That picture was taken a while ago, but he is, he's only seventeen. He's too young to slave."

I looked at the photo then back at him. "So was I but you saved me." I had been seventeen when he had brought me here and with that memory, a worrying thought occurred to me. "Can you help him... but don't keep him…or love him as you love me?" He smiled at me and kissed my forehead.

"I could never do that, there's no one like you." He looked at Leon, who was smiling. "Can you make me a shortlist of available Keepers? I need you to source ones with a real sadistic side so probably no one here will be suitable. I know this is not the norm for our house, but he is going to need a Keeper that understands all his needs. His Keeper will be his life for a good while until he's able to go to clients." Leon nodded.

I didn't understand. Sadists like to punish as Devon had. I looked at Layton worried. "Can't you have him? Keepers shouldn't punish, it hurts…and it's confusing."

He closed the file on his lap. "I will have him, Baby Boy, until we can find him a suitable Keeper. But as he is not old enough to be a slave, he will need to be given his fix. If I don't feed it, he will find some way to feed it himself and look where that's got him." He looked at Leon. "I know a few, not sure that they are free though." He looked back at me as I was still worried and looking at him. "I promise I will find him the right Keeper, Isaac. Someone who'll love him." Feeling out of my comfort zone I nodded. "Right let's go and meet our new lodger then." He moved me from him and stood up, handing back the file to Leon. "Has he spoken to anyone?"

Leon shook his head. "He was exhausted when he got here and a bit out of it. When I tried to look at his wounds, he got anxious and flipped out. He got difficult so I thought it better to put him in the quiet room."

Layton smiled and looked at Leon. "Remember what I said, Leon. They are difficult for a reason. He doesn't know how to deal with the things in his head or the pain he is in. Do we have cigarettes anywhere?"

My mind was jumping around with all the information. Orion was suffering. I knew that suffering when the things in your head didn't make sense, it was not a good place to be. Now Layton wanted a cigarette? I had never seen him smoke, ever. I sat up and crossed my legs and looked at him. Leon handed him a packet of cigarettes and a lighter.

"They were in his pocket." He looked in the packet and emptied some into a small bin beside the desk. He looked at me and smiled.

"Not for me, Baby Boy. Orion is a street boy, and he has street habits. At the moment, the cigarette will be the thing he wants most. He has been on the streets far longer than you were, it is going to take a while to break those habits. The cigarette will ensure he behaves, to begin with. It will give him something to work for."

Now I understood. He would make Orion earn it.

"The quiet room will do for now but it's not suitable for a permanent stay. We will see how it goes. If he lets me in, I would like him moved to the first corridor today. The sooner he gets there the sooner he can settle."

Leon nodded. "I'll get Bea and Hazel to set the room up ready in case. Do you want the double room? With the playroom?"

"Yes, he'll need it."

"Why is it called a quiet room?" I had never heard of such a room when I had lived here.

"It's just an empty room with nothing in it, just a mattress. It is like putting the mind in time out when things get too much."

I didn't like it and I was sure that Orion wouldn't.

"It doesn't sound very nice, he will be scared, being alone."

Layton walked towards me stuffing the cigarette box in his jeans. He leaned down and touched my face with his fingers.

"Actually, I think he will find comfort in it. He has been alone for a long time. It is what he's used to." He lifted my face to him. "Your mind is different, Isaac. I would never leave you alone." I gave him a weak smile and he crouched down and looked at me. "I'm sorry that you have been pushed into leaving the basement. I know you weren't ready. If you're worried about seeing Orion, you can stay with Leon?"

I shook my head. Things were moving fast and I was struggling to get my head around everything that was going on, but it was still safer to stay with him.

"I want to stay with you. I won't frighten him."

He smiled at me. "That's not what I'm worried about…Come on then, let's go and see him." He smiled at me and pulled me from the couch. Not for the first time today my insides somersaulted. I held Layton's hand tighter as we left the room.

CHAPTER TEN

We left the office and walked back along the corridor. We passed the kitchen passageway but instead of turning back the way we came, we carried on walking. Layton stopped and I looked at him. He pointed to some double doors which were big and decorative and had a glass at their top edges.

"See those doors, Isaac?" I looked over to them and then back at him. "You must never go beyond them, it's not safe. Do you understand?"

I nodded. The likelihood of me ever finding them on my own was slim. Opening and going through them was even slimmer. The possibility that I would be here without him scared the hell out of me.

My face must have shown exactly what I was thinking because he smiled and kissed me. "Just checking."

He moved on and I followed, still holding his hand and Leon walked behind us. We stopped at a door, it was different from the others, the corridor we were in was shorter and painted differently from the others too. Leon stepped forward and unlocked the door, then stepped back.

Layton looked at him. "You best not come in, Leon. He saw you when he was confused and worried and I want to allow him to start again. Can you help with his room, get his box set up then maybe in a while, come with some lunch for Isaac and Orion."

Leon nodded. "Certainly. Tea?"

Layton smiled. "Yes. Tea for Isaac and myself with biscuits but can you bring a can of coke for Orion. I know he prefers it. Also, he will need a fresh robe and make sure that Hazel puts out linens for him in his room...and bring a first aid box back with you. Actually, can you call Kendal? As he's fresh off the street so we better let her check him over. Put the first aid box in his room and I'll try and attend to anything serious."

Leon nodded. He seemed to take all of that in his stride, I had already forgotten most of the instructions.

Leon left and Layton looked at me. "I'm not sure where his mind is at, Isaac. I need you to sit quietly while I look after him for a while."

"So you can have him?"

He smiled. "Yes, so I can have him for a while. Just till he settles okay?"

I nodded. No one understood the importance of Layton taking your mind more than me. He was my safety and security and I knew, if Orion let him, he would find that same comfort from him. He opened the door and walked in taking me with him. Once inside he kissed me and let go of my hand.

I looked around the room and it was as he had said, empty of everything. Plain white walls and a wooden floor with a mattress in the corner. Orion sat on the mattress, his knees pulled into his body, his forehead on his knees which meant I couldn't see his face, but his hair was longer than in the photo I had seen.

He had no shoes on and his feet were dirty as were his clothes. Jeans and a denim jacket with what looked like a blue t-shirt underneath. Layton never spoke as he walked closer to him, but he didn't go onto the mattress, he sat cross-legged on the floor at the edge of it.

I already felt like I was intruding, I turned and sat against the wall by the door and watched Orion. He was the first submissive I had seen in ages, and I was so curious about him. He hadn't moved or looked up and the only reason I knew he was aware of our arrival was that he curled his toes into the mattress.

We all sat in silence, and I found it hard to stay where I was. It was these quiet times that I would usually find myself crawling to Layton to find comfort but this time, it wasn't for me, it was for Orion. I waited and watched, wondering how this worked. Layton looked at me and must have understood my need. He held his hand up to still me in my place. Forbidden to move, I looked at Orion.

"Orion is not ready to share." Orion lifted his head and looked at me, then turned and looked at Layton who looked back at him. "You're safe, Orion, you're in a mess but you're safe here. This is where I live, the place I told you about. Where people can play safely."

Orion looked at me and I dropped my head but still watched him under my lashes. He looked angry and that scared me a little.

"This is Isaac, he means you no harm, he lives here."

"I want my money and my ciggies." He sounded angry too, I wanted to go to Layton, but Layton had said he needed to be with Orion for a while, so I stayed where I was.

Layton sighed. "That's not how we ask for things here. I can see you're in pain, will you let me tend to your wounds?" Orion shook his head. "Were you taken against your will?"

"No, I wanted it…I needed it."

Layton nodded his head. "I told you if you wanted it badly to call me."

Orion tipped his head forward again into his knees. "I lost your card."

Layton smiled. "Well, I know that's not true because it was in your jacket, that's how you're here and not in a police cell or rotting on the street somewhere."

Orion lifted his head defiantly. He looked older than seventeen, but the street did that to you. You grew up way before your time. His hair, which was much longer than I previously thought, hung in clumped curled ringlets down across his face. His hair was dirty and his face was dirty, streaked with lines which I then realised were old, dried tears. He wasn't crying now but he must have been when he had been alone.

I felt sad for him now and not scared.

Layton spoke again. "Why didn't you call me?"

"He offered more money." Layton sighed heavily and closed his eyes briefly. "I told you I needed money!"

"And I said, Orion, that I would help you when you needed it. You could have played safely with me and I would have helped you. Now you are hurt and moneyless. Were you used?"

"What?" He didn't understand.

"Fucked? Were you fucked?" Orion shrugged his shoulders. He didn't want to share. I got it too. On the street you didn't share things, that's why it got overwhelming.

"At the party they took you to, were you used by others?" Orion just stared at him. "Did they offer you more money for it?" I saw the tear before he wiped his palm across his face. Layton spoke quickly to him. "You know such things don't bother me, what bothers me is the hurt they have caused you. You let me tend to your wounds before, Orion, on the street. Will you please let me look at them?" Orion sat quietly.

Layton took the cigarettes from his pocket and put them on the mattress. Orion went to take them, and Layton put his hand on them. "You want one, you have to let me see to your wounds... all of them."

Orion sat back on the mattress. "You're just like the rest of them, I give you what you want and then you won't pay up. Put me back on the street, I'll earn my own fucking cigarettes. Bet you stole my money too."

Layton didn't seem deterred. "Your money that they bribed you with, no doubt to take more for them, is safe and yours when you are ready. I know you are confused about being here, but you know me, you know I always tell you the truth and I always do what I say I will do." He waited for a minute before continuing. "When did you last eat?"

Orion shrugged his shoulders. "I can look after myself."

"Yes, I know but wouldn't it be nice just for a little while, to let someone else look after you?"

Orion turned his face to me and stared at me. "Are you a whore then?"

I shook my head and looked at Layton.

"There are no whores here, Orion. If you ever speak to Isaac like that again you will not see me again." Orion looked quickly at Layton as he moved and got up. He walked over to me and crouched down and touched his fingers to my face. "Are you worried?" I shook my head and he kissed me. He got up and looked at Orion. "Understand?"

Orion nodded. He had panicked when Layton had moved. He knew he was safe with him.

Layton walked back to the mattress and sat back on the floor, crossing his legs. He looked at Orion. "I know you don't want to go back to the vanillas... the streets, as much as you protest about being here, there is no other place you will be able to sate your need and be safe. This world is different from the one that has hurt you, hurt your mind. You will find it difficult at first, but I will help you as will others that live here. Your first year will be spent with just a friend, someone who understands you and what you want. He will be your Keeper; he will care for your every need as you learn the rules of my house. No one here will abuse you or abuse your trust.

"You will find it hard to be submissive at first but that's because the street has not allowed you to be. You have spent many years trying to sate your need to submit to people but knowing you could not give yourself completely because you had to take care of yourself. Once you learn to trust your Keeper, you will find it easier and more comfortable and natural."

Orion's tears which he had been holding back now rolled down his face silently. He was looking at Layton, his arms wrapped around his legs and his chin leaning on his knees. He looked tired and his street bravado was waning with every word that Layton spoke. It was hard to accept it and let it have you when you had fought for so long to deny it. I remembered.

I curled my legs into me mimicking his pose as I watched the street boy start his journey into slavery. I knew Layton was saving him from himself, knew there was no place for people like him or me in the vanilla world, but it still made me sad.

Layton glanced over at me and then back to Orion.

"What's a Keeper?" He wiped half his face against his knee.

"A friend. He will be your friend and family while you find your way. You have a lot to learn, Orion, but first, we must get you fed and cleaned up." He held his hand out to Orion, it was his first offer of comfort and I watched Orion to see what he would do.

He moved his hand to the mattress and his fingers clawed at it, agitated. I found myself wanting to take Layton's hand and wrap myself in his comfort, but I already trusted him. Orion had never trusted or given himself to anyone and I felt his turmoil. I wanted to say something, but I knew this had to be his choice. Layton dropped his hand to the mattress, and I looked at him hoping he wasn't giving up on him, he needed more time.

Layton moved to sit beside him, still on the floor but closing the gap between them. He slipped his hand across the mattress towards Orion's but did not attempt to touch him just making it a little easier for him. Moments later, Orion stretched out his fingers and touched Layton's.

"I'm scared."

Layton brushed his fingertips with his thumb. "I know you are. No one will hurt you here, I promise." He sat for a moment, just brushing his thumb over his fingers and then Orion curled his fingers around Layton's. It was Orion's way of asking for more and Layton held his hand and pulled gently at it. "Come, Orion, I have you." Orion shuffled forward towards him, then creased his face in pain and he stopped and looked at him.

"It hurts to move."

Layton softly smiled at him and moved towards him on the mattress. He sat facing him with one leg around him and brushed the hair across the top of his head away from his face and looked at him.

"Okay, we're going to sort that out. Is it very sore?" Orion nodded and leant his head to Layton. His pain making him scrunch his toes and catch his breath. Layton stroked his hand over his hair. "Try and breathe through it. I know that seems hard, but you will soon learn to deal with it, we will teach you very quickly how to process your pain so it doesn't hurt your mind." Orion nodded.

I found myself breathing his pain, trying in some way to lessen it for him. Layton just held him gently and stroked his hand over his hair. "That's it, Orion, just breathe it away, I have you." He kissed his forehead and looked at me and I smiled at him.

There was something beautiful about watching Layton work his will on another mind. It was the same when I watched him play, the way he punished yet loved at the same time, always making the sub feel safe and yet subservient to him. Even at this early stage, Layton was already taking his mind and whether Orion knew it not, he was already submitting to Layton's will.

There was a gentle knock at the door before it slowly opened and Leon poked his head in, looking at Layton.

Layton nodded to him, answering his silent question and then things got busy. "Is the room ready?"

I could see Hazel through the crack of the door standing outside with a tray of food. We had been busy this morning and hadn't eaten and now I was starving. I smiled, remembering the morning with Layton and then saw Hazel watching me and she smiled so I smiled back.

Leon spoke and I got brought back into the room. "Yes. You want to move now?" Layton looked at Orion who was struggling with the intrusion into the room. "Yes, let's just go before he fights or flees, he's hurting. Is Kendal coming?"

"Yes, on her way." Layton nodded and Orion went to move away but Layton scooped his hand under his legs and pulled him to his body. Orion cried out in pain and he ignored him as he stood with him.

"Take, Isaac." Layton headed out of the room as Leon came over and held out his hand.

"Come, Isaac."

We followed Layton and Orion through the corridors and back to where Layton and I had come from the basement. It seemed Orion's room was to be the room next to the basement door. As we headed in, I realised this room was different from any room I had stayed in. It had two rooms but that was all I could see as Layton took Orion straight through to the bathroom and I followed, having been left at the door by Leon.

I watched as he took his dirty clothes from him and only then I understood why he was in such pain. He was completely marked from head to toe, deep welts across his legs, arms, and across his back. His skin was rosy red. A couple of his welts had bled as there was dried blood crusted around them. Across his back was a multitude of criss-cross lines that were probably from a whip.

Orion was distressed and very submissive to Layton as Layton tried to clean all of his wounds with fresh, warm water. In the end, Layton ran a bath and put him in it. Orion moaned and squirmed from the sting of the water against his newly marked skin.

"Breath, Orion, this will be the worst I promise."

I sat on the floor and watched as Layton patiently washed his curly hair and sponged his body clean, stopping when Orion cowered away from him and waiting for him to calm down before continuing. When he was done, he helped him out of the bath and gently wrapped him in a towel.

"Were you fucked, Orion?" Orion ignored the question. He was so distraught, shaking and shivering on the bathroom floor. "Orion, I need to check your hole. I know you don't like all this but the sooner we get your body sorted, the sooner we can look after you."

He pulled Orion over his knees and touched his arse, gently pulling apart his arse cheeks but Orion's submission had been lost. He cried out and moved from him, sitting beside me, shaking his head at Layton.

"Please don't... please... wait." He looked at me. "Please."

Drawn to his sadness, I touched my fingers to his frightened face. I remembered being scared when I first came here and having my body poked and examined on arrival.

I looked at Layton. "He needs to wait a minute, can it wait?"

Layton shook his head. "No, it can't wait, not if there's damage."

I turned back to look at him and his frightened tears that were running down his cheeks. I had been used at slave parties before, they were long hours of constant use and some people were rough, forgetting lube and manhandling you.

"Were they rough?" He nodded and another tear ran down his cheek. "I've been to those parties before; they are hard work and hurt a lot. My hole got torn and they fixed it." I looked at Layton and then back to him. "He just wants to look, so he can help you." I looked at Layton. "Can he lay on his side? Lay on your side and hold your knees, it won't seem so bad." I looked from Orion to Layton who was still sitting on the bathroom floor in front of us, watching. "It's better curled up on your side."

Layton smiled at me and then looked at Orion. "Orion? Do you want to try Isaac's way?"

Orion shook his head. He was so frightened, so I turned towards him a little.

"Was it your first time?" He shook his head and moved agitatedly.

I moved my hand to his and held it. The person that sat with me was miles from the street boy that had been so aggressive in the quiet room. "Did lots of people fuck you?" He turned his head slightly towards me and looked at me. I could see the answer in his eyes. "Having your hole checked won't hurt like that..." I looked at Layton quickly and then back to Orion. "Now that he knows why you're scared, he can help you. If they hurt you, he can make it better." I watched him, he was still scared. "Can you just try?" I looked at Layton. "If it hurts him, can you not do it?"

He looked at Orion. "I promise, Orion, if it's too painful I will stop."

I stroked my bandaged hand down his face. Slowly he pushed himself to the floor, curled on his side, and pulled his knees into his body. He tipped his head forward against my leg and I stroked his damp hair.

Layton moved across the floor and opened his arse so he could see his hole. He reached for some lubricant and I looked at Layton. "I just need to check inside." I touched Orion's face.

"Hold your legs tight Orion. It's just a finger."

I watched as he separated his arse and felt Orion jolt as his finger touched his hole. Orion moaned into my leg and I held him as Layton slipped his finger inside him.

Orion cried out. "Please!"

"Breathe, Orion, just for a minute."

I watched as Orion blew his breaths out and then moaned as Layton withdrew his finger. As soon as he was free, he moved to sit next to me again and Layton got up and washed his hands.

He looked at Layton. "Am I damaged?"

Layton dried his hands as he spoke. "How many times were you fucked?"

Orion shrugged his shoulders.

"More than five?"

Orion nodded. "They put money in my mouth to keep me quiet... because I was crying, it was hurting a lot. I asked to be released but they wouldn't let me down. Can I have a cigarette now?" He was agitated, pulling at his fingers.

Layton fished the cigarettes out of his pocket and handed it to him. Orion opened the packet and looked at Layton. "There is only one in there."

Layton walked over and crouched down and gave him a lighter and stroked his face.

"That's it. You have had a rough time so you can have one as promised. I do not allow smoking in my house, Orion, so it will be your last one."

He took the cigarette out of the box and threw the box at Layton. "Fuck you."

Layton quickly took the cigarette from his fingers and held it up for him to see. "We also don't allow disrespect."

Orion dropped his head as did I and Layton reached out and ruffled my hair. "Your anger is rude and disrespectful and will get you nowhere, but you will soon learn that. Your days will soon be full and you won't need to smoke, until then I will get Hazel to get you a nicotine patch to ease the addiction."

"You got a patch for my other addiction?" Orion was still looking down and Layton laughed, leaned over to him and kissing his head.

"You smell so much better. Here." He held the cigarette out for him. Orion slowly lifted his head and took it. "We need to get your hair cut too... all of it." I smiled a little. Slaves were always shaved. "I need to get a doctor to look at your hole and check you over, you're very thin."

"Have they damaged me?"

Layton shook his head. "No, I think it's just a graze, but I want it checked. How did you end up at such a party? They are very dangerous."

Orion lit his cigarette. "A rich man pulled up and asked me to a party." He shrugged. "When we got there, he said I would be whipped and flogged, I asked for more money, he agreed... there was some cock sucking in there as well."

I smiled and Layton spoke. "Do not encourage him, Isaac."

195

I wiped the smile from my face. He was funny though.

"I got offered more money to fuck, I agreed... then it got out of hand."

"As parties have a habit of doing. Who was the client?"

Orion sucked on his cigarette. "How the fucking hell should I know? It's not like we swapped friendship bracelets."

I held back a smile. He seemed to be the smart street kid again, Layton sighed.

"I suggest you watch your language when you speak to me. Had you seen him before?" Orion shook his head and then winced and sat forward from the wall, sucking on his cigarette. Layton stepped forward and pushed him forward further to look at his back. "I need to see to your welts."

Orion looked at him. "They knew him though, at the party." He sucked on the last of his cigarette and threw it into a pool of water on the shower floor.

I had never witnessed such disrespect since I had been on the streets. I looked at Layton nervous and unsure of how he would react.

"Orion, you are not on the streets now. You make a mess here you clear it up... go get tissue from the toilet, pick up the cigarette, and flush it."

Orion looked at him. "He can do it." He nodded, gesturing to me. "I'm wounded remember... You'll do it, won't you? He must keep you around for a reason." He looked at me and I looked down to my lap not sure what to do or think.

I liked him but I didn't like this side to him when he was horrible.

Layton picked up his clothes and threw them at him.

"Get dressed!"

Orion looked at him shocked. "Why, where we going?"

"Just get dressed." Orion didn't move.

Layton grabbed him by the arm and pulled him up. "Fine, go back to the street naked... let's see how many times you get fucked this time." Layton dragged him out of the bathroom and towards the door.

I got to my feet and followed them into the room and then stood and watched as Layton opened the door. "Stay here, Isaac!"

Orion was shouting, apologising and begging while Layton dragged him out the door. I put my hands to my ears, overwhelmed at the noise and the words. I was starting to feel upset. I had never seen a slave that was healing being treated in such a manner. His welts on his back rippled and stretched as he squirmed and struggled in Layton's hand.

"I'm sorry, I was just kidding...No....no, please...." Layton dragged him down the hallway naked as he dropped to his knees, trying to stop his forced journey back to the streets.

I walked and stood in the doorway of his room, not knowing what to do. His cries echoed in the hallway, and I looked around to see if anyone was going to come out and stop it. No one came so I walked a little way after them, stopping again and watched. They turned the corner out of sight, and I became distraught, and feeling lost, I sat on the floor. I pulled my knees into my body and wrapped my arms around them.

I felt the tears come as I listened to Orion's pitiful cries, and I covered my ears. Surely Layton wouldn't put him back on the streets? Orion was a good person, I was sure. I had never seen Layton treat someone so badly and I was so confused. I could hear Layton's voice through my hands.

"I said if you disrespected Isaac, you would not see me again. You know, I always keep my word, Orion!" I could hear Orion's begging cries, they were hurt cries, cries of pain but not physical pain. The sort of pain you lived with on the street.

"Isaac?" I immediately looked up at the voice. Julian.

He looked up the corridor towards the shouting and then back at me. He touched my face with his hand. "New slave?" I nodded and then shook my head.

I wasn't sure what was going on anymore.

Julian smiled. "I came to see Layton. I was surprised when you weren't both in the basement..."

Orion cried out and I winced, ducking my face and covering my ears.

Julian took his phone from his pocket; he spoke a moment later. "Hey Leon, it's Julian...yes I know, I'm here. Can you get word to Layton that I have Isaac? I'm taking him downstairs... Thank you." He closed his phone and crouched down and looked at me.

He touched his fingers to my cheek and wiped the wetness from my face. "You look very beautiful in your clothes." I could hear Orion begging and looked down the corridor towards the sound and bit my lip. "It's okay...come on." He held his hand out.

I wanted Layton but he was busy, and I wasn't sure what to do. Would I be in trouble for going with Julian? Would I be in trouble with Julian?

"He told me to stay in the room. Am I in trouble?" I covered my ears again as I heard Layton's stern voice.

Julian took my hand and smiled. "And yet, I find you alone in the corridor? Come on, you can tell me all about it. Leon will let him know where you are."

He pulled me up and took me through the door down to the basement and I relaxed immediately. This was home.

He let go of my hand, taking off his coat and shirt and chucking them over the sofa. He was wearing black jeans and a black t-shirt. I wondered what I would look like in black. He took my hand and sat on the sofa and pulled me to sit beside him, wrapping his arm around me and stroking my arm with his fingers. "Tell me the story, Isaac."

I sighed, relaxing against him, feeling safe and comforted once more. I told him about Orion and how he came here and how Layton had to have him to keep him safe.

"Now I think he's put him back on the street naked... and he didn't want to go, not really. Orion's not a bad person. He could be good; he could be a good slave. Do you think Layton has put him back?" I looked at Julian for answers. "He was healing too."

Julian smiled. "He misbehaved, Isaac. He was rude to you and disrespectful."

"I know but he didn't mean it, not really. His mind was hurting him." I laid my head on him.

"Do you think Layton knows his mind is hurting him?" I nodded. Layton knew everything. "I think Layton was teaching him his first lesson and while we sit here talking, I do not doubt that Layton is now carrying him back to his room so he can start healing."

I hoped so.

"Sometimes, he's mean though." Julian laughed a little.

"Really?" I nodded at him. "I have never known him to be mean. I am sure he is never mean to you."

"He looked mean when he was dragging Orion down the hallway, it scared me."

He sat up and pulled me closer to him, kissing my cheek.

"Well, you don't need to worry anymore because you are here with me and I will stay with you until he can come back." My stomach growled loudly. "Are you hungry, Isaac?" I nodded.

"Hazel made me lunch but just when we were going to eat, it got taken away. I do like it upstairs, I met lots of nice people and Hazel was pretty. I felt sad for the slaves though."

"Why were you sad for them? You were one of them. Were you sad when you were a slave?"

I thought about that. No, I hadn't been, not till my time with Devon. I shook my head.

"No but I don't know why I wasn't then."

He tipped my face to his. "The slaves are secure and comfortable in their world, Isaac. As you were when you were a slave. They have no reason to be sad and you shouldn't be sad for them. Do you want to help me make pancakes?"

I smiled at him. "I'm not very good in the kitchen." I held up my bandaged hand that was looking a little worse for wear. "I smashed a glass. Layton and I argued, and I was trying to make him tea to say sorry because he wanted to be away from me…"

He cut me off. "Yes, Jacob told me all about it. Are you worried about being here with me?"

I looked away from him.

"No... I don't think so. I get into trouble a lot... I don't want to get into trouble with you." I looked at him. "I'm going to be good."

He smiled at me. "That's good then but you talk a lot."

"Sorry. Layton says it's because my mind is always busy." He laughed a little.

"I think Layton is right. Come on, let's get you some food and then I will change your bandage. You can tell me all about the people you met today."

Surprisingly, I felt very comfortable with Julian after a while. He let me make a pancake for Layton which he put in a container for him and then he made ours because it took a long time for me to make one, he said. We ate our food on the floor in the bedroom and he made me two teas, one for drinking and one for biscuits.

When he had washed up, he got the first aid kit and sat cross-legged with me on the floor. He unwrapped my bandage on my hand and started to put a fresh one on.

"Thank you for bringing me down here. I didn't like listening to Orion." He smiled at me.

"You're welcome and he'll be fine, he'll soon find his place. Layton will find him a Keeper to take care of him."

I looked at him. "Do you think Orion and I could be friends? He was upset when Layton was cleaning and checking him and then he got angry again. He made me smile and I got into trouble for finding him funny, but he was."

Julian touched my face and stroked it. "No, you and Orion cannot be friends. He is very confused and needs to find his way here with Layton and then eventually his Keeper. His mind will soon let go of the other world and all the harm it did to him. He is still trying to keep himself safe that's why he goes from being sad and then angry. You know you're safe here, don't you? You know that Layton will always watch over you?" I nodded.

"Will you keep me safe when he's not here? I don't have a Keeper anymore, but I feel safe with you and I'm not very good at being independent, I don't like it, it hurts my mind." He half laughed and ruffled his hand over my hair. "Please though, can you not make me walk in the nettles again, I didn't like that."

He leant forward and kissed my mouth. I needed to share something else with him, but I knew I would get in trouble for it and to make me feel better about it, I needed him to comfort me. "Can I sit with you?" He smiled and pulled my hand. I turned and sat in between his crossed legs while he finished off the bandage.

I leant my head against him and closed my eyes. He wrapped his arms around me.

"Are you worried about something, Isaac?" I nodded. "Tell me."

I turned slightly in his arms. "I did a bad thing. I didn't mean to, but Layton is going to be angry. If I tell you, can you not tell him?" Julian rested his chin on my shoulder.

"I can't promise that, Isaac, but if something is worrying you, you should tell me until Layton gets here. What is it?" I didn't want to share now but I was in pain, and I didn't know what to do. "Isaac?"

"I have new boots... and I know he said wear socks, but they didn't feel right, they squashed my toes, so I took them off again."

I heard him smile. "So now you have blisters?" I stuck out my bottom lip but didn't answer. "Come on, jump off, let me see." I moved off and sat against the bed while he undid the laces on both boots.

He pulled one slowly off and I winced as the leather dragged across my raw skin. I looked at the sore red patches on my heels and toes. "Isaac, have they been hurting you all day?" I nodded sheepishly.

"It's okay though, I didn't really feel it... only now because I'm tired and I don't want to wear my clothes anymore. Can I take them off please?"

He pulled the other boot and I drew my breath in between my teeth. The other foot was a little worse. I looked at Julian worried. "He's going to be very angry, isn't he?"

Julian smiled. "I'm sure he will be feeling far too guilty about leaving you, to be very angry. I think the pain of having them washed will be punishment enough." I grimaced at him, and he nodded "Yes, it's going to sting like a bastard, you know that don't you?" I nodded and stuck out my bottom lip.

"Can't we just leave them?" Julian sat back and looked at me.

"What do you think?" I looked down at them. Years of taking punishment meant I knew the answer to that.

"No, because they will get infected." He nodded.

"Very clever, Isaac. Take your clothes off, then we'll clean them in the shower."

I took my t-shirt off and undid my trousers which he helped me out of, so they didn't touch my feet. He stood up and held out his hand. "Come on... trouble."

I took his hand and hobbled to the bathroom and sat on the shower floor while he got the shower on. I leaned back on my hands and moaned a little. "Breathe, Isaac, the sting will only last a minute. Next time maybe you will do as you're told."

I scrunched my face as he put the shower over my feet. The pain was searing like knives. I pulled my feet away and then put them back under the water. I closed my eyes, breathing hard out until it didn't hurt so much. Julian sponged them clean which hurt a lot, then turned off the shower and bent to kiss my head. "Good boy."

He wrapped me in a towel, lifted me in his arms, and carried me to the bed, drying my feet gently and then the rest of me.

"Can you tell him that I already got punished for not listening then?" Julian smiled.

"I think he will know that. It is very late and you have had a long day. I think you should sleep now. Get in the covers." He pulled the blanket back and covered me. He brushed his hand over my face and kissed me. "I will be outside on the sofa if you need me." He picked up a blanket and turned.

"When will he come back?"

"Very soon, I'm sure. As soon as Orion is settled." He walked across the room and left, shutting the door.

The room wasn't dark as the lamp was on, but I knew I couldn't stay here on my own. I carefully lifted the covers from my feet and walked to the door and opened it. Julian looked at me. I dropped my eyes from his stare.

"I can't sleep on my own, I don't like it."

"It's not even been a minute, Isaac."

I walked towards him, feeling more comfortable and confident with him now, after spending the evening with him. As I got to the sofa, he pulled back his blanket and I climbed in between his legs and laid on him.

He covered me and wrapped his arms around me. "Do you do anything you're told?"

I closed my eyes. "I'm sorry." He kissed me and stroked his hand over my head.

"Comfortable?" I nodded slowly.

I felt completely safe and could feel sleep taking me. I wrapped my hands around the arm that held me. "Goodnight, Isaac."

CHAPTER ELEVEN

When I woke, I was still laying with Julian. I shivered and he pulled the blanket over me.

"Is he back?" Julian stroked my face with his fingers.

"Yes." I went to move and he held me to him. "But… he's sleeping. He needs to rest for a little while." I relaxed back on him, feeling a little upset that I had slept through his return.

"Didn't he want to say hello to me?"

Julian smiled. "He did. He kissed you and stroked your hair and… looked at your feet."

I closed my eyes. I had forgotten about that.

"Was he angry?"

Julian pushed himself up to sitting, still holding me to him. "A little. Would you like tea?"

I nodded and he pushed me from him and stood up. I wrapped myself in the blanket and watched to see whether he would go into the bedroom to make it, but he walked over to the side and got a kettle from the cupboard. I got up and walked towards the bedroom. I just needed to see him, just to look and make sure he was here. I reached and touched the handle.

Julian called out. "Isaac! Go back to the sofa." I froze and looked at the door. I really wanted to see him. I waited and when he didn't come over, I turned the handle. "Isaac!" Julian turned towards me and stood watching. After a moment I dropped my hand from the door and looked down.

"Do you want to spend the time waiting for him in the cage?" I shook my head. I turned slowly and walked towards Julian and walked right up to him.

"But I want to see him." Julian wrapped his arm around me and kissed the top of my head.

"I know but he is very tired and if he doesn't get a little sleep, he will get sick. Then you would have to come to stay with me."

I certainly didn't want to go home with him. I wasn't sure I liked this being free and independent stuff. Maybe I would wait in the cage.

"Now come on, we will have tea then we will go and see Bea for breakfast." I looked at him.

"Upstairs?" He nodded. I wasn't sure that was the best idea either. "I'm not supposed to go without him." Julian smiled.

"Well, we're not waking him so I guess we will have to go hungry." I thought about that.

"I think he wouldn't mind if I went with you." Julian laughed and I smiled at him.

"I am so glad that Jacob is not like you, Isaac. You bring chaos to my life." My smile disappeared.

"Do I hurt your mind?" Julian smiled.

"No. You make me work very hard to keep up with yours. It's good for me and makes me appreciate my world of calm. Now go sit on the sofa and I will bring the tea."

I walked off towards the sofa and looked at the bedroom as I went. Knowing he was on the other side sleeping and I couldn't touch him was hard. I looked at Julian and he was watching me. I didn't want to get into trouble so I would have to behave. I sat on the sofa as Julian made the tea and brought it over.

"Can I have biscuits?" Julian shook his head.

"No, because we are having breakfast."

I sat drinking my tea trying to not talk.

"I'm not sure how you were a slave for so long, Isaac." I looked at him.

"Why? Because I like biscuits?" Julian laughed and shook his head.

"Because you want everything. I know you were a good slave; I just don't know how. Did you want these things when you were a slave?" I shook my head.

"No, I don't think so. I wanted different things then." He looked at me questioningly. "I wanted to be fucked, punished... and I always wanted to come." I finished my tea. "I didn't always get them. Now I want... I just want to be here with Layton and I have that."

"So now you want other things? What about fucking and punishment and coming?" I smiled at him and gave him my cup.

"I don't know why I want the other things, like chocolate cake. I don't remember what it tastes like, but I want it. The things I wanted before...as a slave, they are still there, I can feel them, but they scare me. I think chocolate cake will taste like that feeling... you know, that feeling you get before you come." Julian laughed and shook his head.

"Isaac, your mind baffles me and... only some chocolate cakes taste like that."

"Are you trying to get Julian to get you cake now?" I turned, excited by his voice.

He was leaning against the doorway in just his jeans with his arms crossed and I felt such relief at seeing him. I went to move, to go to him, but remembering my place, I looked at Julian.

"May I go now?" He smiled and nodded.

I moved from the sofa as quickly as my sore feet would take me and threw myself at Layton.

He wrapped his arms around me and kissed me. "I'm sorry for not staying in the room and… for not wearing socks." I kissed his neck in my show of my apology.

He pulled my face away and looked at me. "Were you worried?" I nodded. He kissed me on the lips and then rubbed them gently across mine then spoke in a whisper. "I'm sorry, Baby Boy."

He scooped me up and walked towards the sofa and sat with me with my legs over his lap. I curled into him, it felt so good to be back with him. He kissed my head and played his fingers through my hair. "You want to stay there a while?" I nodded so content again now I was with him I let my mind drift off.

This was when I didn't want anything else when nothing else mattered when he had me, had my mind. I lay quietly and let my mind drift while they talked.

"Thank you for letting me sleep. I hope he hasn't been too demanding?" Julian smiled.

"Extremely but he is very entertaining to listen to and watch. The food connection is very interesting, something you taught him?" Layton shook his head.

"No, all of his own making. His mind is very busy like he's worried his freedom won't last so he has to get everything out. He likes his food and I think the pleasure it gives him reminds him of other pleasures he is denying himself at the moment. He is getting very close to understanding that there is no substitute for this need and desire he has. The misbehaving and not following instructions are part of him searching, he remembers the punishment he used to get. I think even the blistered feet are appeasing his need a little."

"Then punish him, sate his need." Layton shook his head.

"I want him to want it, not just need it. This will be his first taste since Devon inflicted his misery on Isaac's mind and damaged him. This has to be sweet for him, it has to be doughnuts with sugar, or it will damage him beyond even my help." Julian shook his head, smiling.

"Now you are talking about food?" Layton smiled at him.

"I just understand him. If I punish him now, it will just be pain on top of pain he still remembers, given in hatred and not of love or the need of it. The damage Devon caused was extreme, you saw it, this healing cannot be rushed or forced."

"Then he will become the obedient houseboy?" Layton laughed.

"No. He has always been needy. I'm afraid Isaac is Isaac, and you will never have peace when he is around. What did he talk about yesterday when you found him?"

"The boy Orion mostly, you, and how being upstairs made him sad for the slaves. I think he wants to be their friend... you know you must forbid that to him, no good can come of that."

"Maybe, he has made friends with one of the slaves, it doesn't seem to have caused any damage to either of them. When I watch Isaac with another slave, I learn things. New slaves follow his lead and trust him quickly. Sim and Isaac play well together, they trust each other."

"Well, you were always better at understanding the slaves than anyone else I know. I take it the street boy is safe in his room and not naked on the streets?" Layton kissed my head.

"Of course. I would never give up so easily. He is asleep and Rae is going to watch over him until Finn returns from his visit. I will need to spend some time with him though, until I find a Keeper for him. You don't know of any Keepers with a little sadistic side, do you? I usually do not allow the Keepers here to play with their slaves in such a manner, but Orion is different. He understands his need very well and knows how to play people to get it." Julian shook his head.

"If you want a Keeper with a sadistic side, you need to ask Kellen. I know you and he have your differences, but he is the best person to ask." Layton held me tighter. "Would you like me to watch over Isaac while you spend time with the street boy?" Layton smiled.

"You're kidding, right? On both counts?"

"Not at all. On both counts. You know I'm right about Kellen and while Isaac messes with my life's equilibrium, I find his demanding nature strangely intriguing. He is safe with me and despite his reservations, he has shown he trusts me. He seeks attention and Jacob loves to give it, so the two will amuse each other."

"Yes, about those two. There is a desire between them, they'll end up fucking if they are given the opportunity. I have forbidden Isaac to kiss Jacob, but Isaac is easily distracted by his need and want of such things at the moment. You will have to watch him very closely; he can be very sneaky when he wants something bad enough." Julian laughed.

"Jacob will not play if I forbid it, he would not like the consequences."

"Isaac is one of the first subs Jacob has met and he's very smitten. You've opened up his world bringing him here and despite his good behaviour before, I think you'll find he won't mind taking a few consequences for a taste of Isaac. He was the one who instigated the kissing and Isaac can't say no."

"I shall make a note and watch them. Isaac looks pretty submissive now though?"

"Yes. This is one of those moments when Isaac doesn't want the things in his head. Yesterday he took a huge step forward, cleansed and loved for the first time since Devon and then the visit upstairs. This is him trying not to think about it all and letting me know he trusts me to have him. Can you pass the blanket, he is already on his way back, I can feel him shivering."

I felt the blanket cover me and I looked at Julian. I hated coming back from such a safe and peaceful place and seeing people. I shook my head a little as all my thoughts all shot back into my mind. I pushed my head into Layton and moaned. He stroked his hand over my head, knowing exactly where it hurt most.

"We were going to go and have breakfast with Bea but now you're up, I can make something for you both?" Food. I moved my head to look at Julian and he smiled at me. "Hungry Isaac?" I nodded.

Layton kissed me and pulled my face up to his so he could look at me. "Hey, Baby Boy. Were you good for Julian?" I nodded and he looked at Julian and smiled. "I can get Bea to send breakfast down, you have done more than enough, thank you, Julian. Please stay and eat with us though."

Julian moved from the sofa and stood and stretched his half-naked body.

"Can I have pancakes?" I looked at Layton and he shook his head.

"Pancakes? No not today." Julian laughed and both Layton and I looked at him.

"Can I have pancakes please?" He had made them yesterday for me.

Julian shook his head. "You cannot play me against Layton. That will never work." I stuck my bottom lip out. Julian looked at Layton. "We made them yesterday. I will go upstairs and collect breakfast; I would like to see Bea it has been ages. You can chat to Isaac about yesterday."

Knowing now I wasn't going to get my way; I lay back on Layton. Julian pulled his t-shirt on and walked off, stopping to kiss the top of my head on the way. When he was gone, Layton pulled my face up to look at him.

"Why did you ask Julian for pancakes when I had said no?" I shrugged my shoulders.

If you played with two clients and you didn't get what you wanted from one you asked the other. It worked sometimes.

"Does it confuse you when Julian and I are both here?" I shook my head.

"No. You both watch me, you're both Dominant. I just wanted them. I will do what you both want, I just wanted them that's all." Layton looked at me and smiled.

"So you made pancakes then?" I nodded and smiled.

"I made you one but then Julian wouldn't let me make any more because it took too long. He wanted me to sleep but I got up because I didn't want to sleep on my own. He wasn't angry. Did you send Orion back to the streets because he was misbehaving?"

Layton stroked my face with his fingers. "I was going to, but he has learnt his lesson and is learning his place. He is safe in his room, sleeping. Were you worried about him?" I nodded.

"He was hurting. Julian said Orion and I can't be friends. Is that because he is a slave?" Layton nodded.

"Yes. I think Orion needs to learn lots of new things just like you are doing. I think it would be confusing for you both to see each other. Your paths are different and neither of you are secure with your places yet. Do you understand, Isaac?" I felt sad and nodded. He kissed me. "You know I will look after both of you, don't you?" I nodded again. "Julian said the slaves made you feel sad?"

I thought about it before answering him.

"What if they are sad? Who will comfort them? I was sad in the end... not before but at the end." Layton sighed.

"My slaves have good Keepers, Baby Boy. All my Keepers love their slaves very much and rarely use punishment to make them behave. If a slave requires a firmer hand, then it usually means it is time for them to move onto a different house, it usually means their needs are not being met here."

"Is that why you moved me?" He nodded.

"Yes, your need outgrew my house. The more you wanted it and understood it, the more you misbehaved so you could have what you wanted. I do not move slaves because I don't like them, I move them so they can continue to fulfil their need and find what it is they are looking for. My house is a tasting house. New slaves come here to taste it a little, learn the rules of our world, and become accustomed to what is expected of them. For some, it is enough and they stay here, some have particular needs that means they are better to stay here. For others they want more punishment, harsher clients, and stronger Keepers to keep them completely submissive."

"Orion will not stay here, will he?" Layton shook his head.

"He will stay for a year or two maybe, while he learns the rules and finds the peace and security in his place, but Orion already understands his need for punishment. What he doesn't understand is submitting to it and those that play with him. He's also not had a lot of love or comfort in his life. He still thinks he must fight to get what he wants; he doesn't understand the balance that is needed to keep his mind safe. Funny, as you are both in the same mind space but reverse. He is searching for comfort to balance his mind and you are searching for punishment to balance yours."

I knew what he was saying was true but talking about me and being punished made me agitated. I wriggled in his arms and pulled at the bandage on my hand.

He stroked my hair with his fingers. "You are mine, Isaac, nothing will change that now. You will not be sent away and I will take care of all your needs, it doesn't matter how much you misbehave. When you are ready, we can explore different paths to sate your needs but you will always come back here to me."

Come back? Where would I go?

"I don't want to go... anywhere." He smiled and kissed me.

"And you are not going anywhere. I know eventually, your needs will outgrow what I can give you, Baby Boy, even if you don't know it yet. You will never go anywhere you are not happy to go, okay?" I nodded.

I just wanted to be here with him.

"Will Sim stay here?" He smiled.

"For now. Sim is settled here and some of the clients push his limits. If he gets to the point where his limits are not being tested, he may have to move but not at the moment. My Keepers would never let their slaves be sad, Baby Boy, and if that happens, they tell me immediately so I can find out what the problem is. You must never feel sad for them. Even Orion, who is struggling now, will find his peace soon and be secure in his mind and this life. Okay?"

I nodded again and wrapped my arms around him to find my comfort. "Now, we have to talk about me going back to work. You know Orion doesn't have a Keeper yet and I have to look after him, with the other Keepers, until I find one. It means I will have to spend hours away from you so I can do my job properly and help him."

I sat up and looked at him, worried.

"I don't want you to be away for hours." Layton nodded.

"Okay but then that means I cannot help Orion."

No. That wasn't what I wanted, I wanted him to be with both of us.

"I will come with you... I'll behave this time and do what you say. I can be good."

He smiled at me and cupped my face in his hand. "I know you can, but I think yesterday was too soon for you to go upstairs and be so involved, maybe in a few weeks, when you have found your way a little. It might happen again, Isaac, something might happen that means I have to leave you alone again and I don't think you're ready for that yet."

No, I wasn't. It was strange to me, his side of this world, and I wasn't ready to be alone in it. The house upstairs had seemed strange to me, even though I had lived there for many years, lived in this world all my adult life. It was different being on the other side of the doors. The corridors, although empty, had seemed busy to me like I could hear everyone's thoughts.

"I wish I had a Keeper." I sighed heavily. "I don't think I can stay with anyone else because I hurt their mind. Julian said I cause him chaos."

Layton laughed at me and I bit my bottom lip. He touched his finger to it and pulled it gently from my teeth.

"It is true, you are very busy, Isaac, but that is because your mind is not quite content. Julian lives a quiet life with no slaves and a very obedient companion. I think he likes the chaos you bring. He likes you very much and I would be happy for you to stay with him. Do you trust him?" I nodded slowly, looking at him.

"He was nice to me and he let me sleep with him. Do you think Jacob is good because Julian punishes him? I don't want him to punish me. If I misbehave can you punish me?"

He played with my hair in his fingers, looking at me.

"I think Jacob is very settled in his mind and with his place at Julian's side. His life has been very different from yours. When you are with Julian you should try hard to do what he tells you and behave."

I could feel the tears in my eyes and I nodded at Layton. I was worried. "Are you going now?"

Layton smiled at me and shook his head. "Nope, we are going to have breakfast and then you and I will spend some time together today. Julian will collect you later and I will see you tomorrow." So it had already been decided. "That way, most of the time you are away from me, you will be asleep and it will go quickly. You will get to see Jacob as well."

"Is Jacob coming here?" Layton smiled.

"Maybe. I think you may go to Jacob's house or Julian's. We shall ask him when he comes back."

I nodded again. I didn't want to go but I knew I didn't have a choice, so I stayed silent and just lay on Layton, letting him soothe me, just like my Keeper used to do before a visit.

When Julian returned, I didn't look at him, keeping my eyes down.

Layton moved me from him and helped unpack the breakfast then left to get trays from the kitchen. Julian sat cross-legged on the floor.

"Isaac?" I looked at him.

He held out his hand. I didn't want to go, I didn't want him to have me, I wanted to stay here with Layton. I looked back and fiddled with my bandage. He got to his knees and knelt in front of me.

"Hey, I thought you were hungry?" I didn't answer. "Look at me, Isaac." I lifted my face to him. "Has Layton said something that has bothered you?"

My eyes searched for Layton, but he hadn't returned from the bedroom, so I looked back at Julian.

"You can tell me. If something is bothering you, even if it is about me, which I think this is, you can still tell me."

I chewed the inside of my lip. He reached his hand to my face, and I flinched. He dropped his hand to the sofa and looked at me.

"You don't want me to touch you?" I shook my head. "Do you think I will hurt you?"

I looked at my lap. "If I'm not good like Jacob, will you punish me? If I cause chaos, will I be punished? Can you bring me back here to sleep?" Julian nodded.

"I see. Layton has told you that I will be taking you while he is busy, and you think I'm taking you away to punish you?" I nodded. "Punish you like I punish Jacob?" I shrugged my shoulders.

I didn't know what he did to Jacob to make him behave but I had tasted his punishments and it scared me. It seemed the only way I could behave was when I was a slave and my mind was empty of all my own thoughts, but Layton didn't want me to stay there.

"Jacob doesn't cause you chaos, does he?" Julian laughed and shook his head.

"No, he doesn't but that is not because we play or because I punish him. He has never known the slave world like you do, Isaac, his world is just me and he likes it like that. When I ask him to do something, he doesn't feel he needs to question it because he knows I have reasons for it, and he trusts me.

"That is just Jacob, the only thing he is sure about is me. He likes you though I hear. He is always talking about you, always asking about you and your life. He has never met a submissive like you, whose mind is always busy. I would like to watch you while Layton cannot be with you. I know your mind works differently to Jacob's, but I am sure we can get along like we did yesterday." I looked at him.

"I liked being with you. I did feel safe but when Layton is not with me, bad things happen and being away from here worries me."

Julian touched my hand, brought it to his lips, and kissed it. "I promise I will not let anything bad happen. I would like to take you to Jacob's place tonight. He has something for you."

"A gift?" Julian smiled and nodded unsurely.

"Yes, I think it is a gift from him. We will spend the night there and come back tomorrow evening. If you feel worried while we are there you need to tell me so I can look after you, okay?" I nodded "Just until I get to know you better, Isaac, until I understand you better." He reached his hand up to my face and stroked my cheek with his thumb. "Come here to me."

He took my hand and pulled me from the sofa and sat with me between his legs. He laid his face against mine, wrapped his arms around me, and I leant my head into him. This wasn't like when Layton had me, it was different, but it was very close. I felt myself relax in his arms.

"Is Jacob with Kendal?" I felt him shake his head.

"No, he is spending some time with Eden at his place. I think he has her working on your... gift."

I couldn't remember who Eden was and I was going to ask, but then thought I would stay quiet as Jacob would. Julian looked at me and smiled. "You can ask, Isaac, I can almost feel your mind working." I smiled sheepishly.

"I don't know who Eden is?" Julian nodded his understanding.

"She is a very good friend of Jacob's. I am sure you will meet her soon."

Layton walked back into the basement and I felt the need to go to him but stayed with Julian to show my trust. We all sat on the floor to eat the cooked breakfast that Bea had made. I stayed with Julian, well, Layton never asked for me back. It felt good and while eating I forgot about it and after a while, it felt natural to be with him even though Layton was in the room. He also shared his toast with me which made Layton scowl a little and made me smile.

Julian left after breakfast and Layton took me to the shower. We had already washed and were just sitting under the spray, enjoying each other. He was sitting behind me but kept pulling my face back to kiss me, so I turned between his legs putting my legs over his so I could see him. I stroked my hand down the side of his face and kissed the corner of his mouth, then ran my finger over his lip.

"There is no one like you, you're beautiful."

I loved the freedom of being able to tell him and in response, he leant down and took my mouth with his, holding the back of my head with his hand. When he released me, I was breathless and I could feel my cock stirring, feel the pleasure starting to burn inside me.

I wanted to feel more, I looked at him. "I need it, I can feel it asking."

He stroked his hand down my face. "Are you scared by your need, Baby Boy?" I nodded. "Then maybe it's not quite the right time." He leant and kissed my mouth.

"But I can feel it burning inside me... I need you to fix it... make it go away." I looked at him beggingly.

He smiled at me and shook his head. "I will love you, Baby Boy. I think you are worried about going away with Julian and not being here with me, it has sent your mind into a panic. We're not going to play today, because although you may need it, if it still scares you so much then I know you don't want it. You will have to be patient a little longer. Let me love you, it will sate a little of this need you have." He pushed me back from him and I leant back on my hands.

He followed me, laying on me and kissing my mouth, grinding his cock with mine. The water spray ran down his back and he leant forward to turn off the shower before coming back and kissing me again.

His face was so close to mine as he looked at me. "Do you want my cock, Baby Boy?" I shook my head and looked at him. "No? Are you sulking like a brat?"

I looked at him but didn't answer. He ground his cock into mine again and smiled. He kissed my face, dragged his tongue across my cheek, and then touched it to my mouth. "You want this on your cock?"

He kissed me and then took my lip in his teeth, biting down, and it made me draw my breath in. He dragged his teeth across it before letting it go. I could feel my cock growing harder the whole time and I knew he could feel it under his. He smiled at me, kissed my neck and then my shoulder and chest, moving his mouth over my nipple and sucking at it hard, playing the nipple with his teeth.

I moaned out a breath and my legs opened to him as he moved his knees between mine, spreading mine further apart. He moved his mouth to the other nipple and played his tongue over it. My head dropped back as he took it in his mouth and sucked it. He took his mouth from me and kissed my body. I lifted my head and watched him as he worked his way down my stomach with his mouth.

My cock was asking him to touch, reaching out to him, to his mouth. He looked at me and smiled, sticking his tongue out, he stroked it up the shaft of my cock from my balls to the crease of my cock head. My breaths panted from me as I watched him tease it until it leaked its juices for him to suck. I lifted my legs to my body, offering him my hole.

"Fuck me."

He took his mouth from my cock and looked at me, shaking his head and stroking my stomach with his hand. He kissed my hard, wet cock. He turned quickly, grabbed a bottle of gel from the rail and squeezed some in his hand. He looked at me as he rubbed his fingers across my hole, and I lifted my legs further, dropping back onto my elbows to allow him access.

I looked at him, trying to get him to bite. "Fuck me…please."

He shook his head again and smiled as he pushed his finger inside me. My breath caught as I watched him slowly thrust his finger in and out of my hole. A moan left me, making him smile. I dropped one of my feet to the floor and pushed myself across the floor trying to get away from him, but he followed still with his finger inside me.

"I know you want me to love you, Baby Boy."

I pushed away from him again and the back of my head and shoulders touched the shower wall. He pulled his finger from me and knelt between my legs. I dropped my other leg to the floor, he scooped his hands under my thighs and pulled me up towards him, sliding me down the shower wall and onto the floor.

I lifted my head and looked at him as he pushed his cock into my hole. I moaned as I felt the slight burning sensation as he pushed himself in. When he was all the way in, he just knelt there and watched me as he stroked my cock. My legs spread of their own accord, and I reached my hands above my head and pushed against the shower wall, trying to fuck myself on him.

He just waited and watched my efforts as he stroked my cock in his hand. "What do you want, Baby Boy?"

I could feel my pleasure building but it wasn't enough. I moaned at him, wanting him to thrust inside me, my arms laying on the floor now above my head, completely weak with the pleasure coursing through me.

"Tell me to do it and I will, just tell me to love you." He stroked one hand up my body and squeezed the nipple in his fingers while still stroking my cock with the other hand.

I let my head drop to the floor and looked up at the ceiling as my body was consumed with pleasure. I reached for the wall again with my hands, but he had pulled me forward and I could only just touch it with my fingers, so I let my hands lay again beside my head as he pleasured my cock with his hand.

I could come like this, just lying here, his cock inside me, his hand pleasuring me, but it would be empty and mean nothing. I opened my mouth and breathed slowly, letting it simmer inside me. If I chased it now I would come and I didn't want to come, not when I felt so distant from him. I wanted him to force me, to sate the need that burned in me, but he wouldn't and as much as I had tried, I couldn't break his control.

He withdrew a little and then gently thrust inside me and my orgasm asked. I opened my mouth and moaned into the air.

"Mm, your body is already beginning to pulse around me, Baby Boy. I could come now just looking at you, looking so fucking hot and sexy spread under me. I know you want me to love you and I will... you just have to ask."

I blew my breaths out and felt a tear run down the side of my face.

"Love me please." I was looking up to the ceiling.

He took his hand from my cock. "Look at me, Isaac."

I lifted my head and looked at him, I was already breathless with the need of my orgasm.
"Love me... I want you to love me."

He stroked both hands up my body and thrust gently inside me, while we looked at each other. I pushed myself up onto my elbows and looked at him while he loved me. I moaned quietly with each slow thrust as each one tried to make me take my orgasm. He reached out one of his hands and touched my face, stroking his thumb over my cheek. I looked back and showed him what I felt, I showed him where his love had taken my mind.

"That's it, Isaac, look at me while your mind and body are consumed with pleasure so you will always know where my love can take you. There is nothing like this feeling."

I spoke in a whisper so as not to breathe into the orgasm that fluttered teasingly below the surface of my body and mind. "Chocolate... cake."

I smiled weakly at him and opened my mouth as I breathed in the feeling, letting it scorch my mind. He smiled at me as he watched my body move gently with his thrusts. He stroked my body with his hands, and I held his gaze for as long as I could, riding the waves of pleasure he gave until I could not stand the sweetness of it any longer. I shook my head at him and moaned loudly as reality began to fade.

"Show me, Baby Boy, look at me." I kept my eyes open to him as he took my cock in his hand and stroked it slowly. I pushed my hands into the floor as I felt it begin.

"Who's taking you, Baby Boy? Say my name." I could hear his words breathless with need.

"Layton... Layton..." I whispered his name as I looked at him and then I left the world and cried out as my air was taken and the orgasm ripped through my body.

"Yes... fuck... yes, Isaac..." As I came back from mine, I watched him take his.

With his hands wrapped around my hips, pulling me onto him, looking at me as his air was stolen and his eyes glazed over, yet they burnt me with their stare. It was like seeing his soul flicker across his eyes just for a moment.

I collapsed back on the floor and gasped as he pulled his cock from me and joined me, lying next to me. I let my feet fall to the floor. As always, he regained his reality before me and stroked his hand over my hair, I tipped my head to the side and looked at him. No one loved me as he did, no one made me feel it the way he did.

"I like that look, Baby Boy." He smiled at me. "You look loved and sated." He played his fingers through my hair. "You don't know how beautiful you are, Isaac, especially when you are consumed with pleasure."

My mind had returned to reality and I turned my body into him, putting my head on his shoulder. He wrapped his arm around me and kissed my head. "I have you."

He let me settle there for a while until I shivered with cold, even though I tried not to because I knew it would make him move and I didn't want to move. He washed us under the warm shower before wrapping me in a robe and taking me to the bedroom. He changed my bandage, made tea, and joined me on the bed.

"You are very quiet, Baby Boy. Is your need for punishment still burning you?"

I shrugged my shoulders and nodded a little. It felt like something was missing from the pleasure I had taken, even as intense as it was. He stroked his hand over the side of my face and kissed me.

"Why wouldn't you let me have it? I can still feel it like something is missing." He smiled at me.

"Because just feeling it is making you edgy, uncomfortable, and worried. I do not want to fuel those feelings. I asked if you were scared and you gave me your answer without thought. I know these feelings are burning you, calling to you. You are scared because you know what you need to endure to sate them and as much as you need it, you don't want it, do you?"

No, I didn't want to feel the pain, it scared me. The pain I remembered was not pleasurable and didn't make me want it. So, I didn't know why my mind and body were asking to feel it, why the need for it was burning inside of me. I shook my head, looking down into my tea.

"It's because of what he did isn't it?" Layton nodded. "It's what I remember. When he first caned me in the shower for getting hard, I used to find the pleasure in it. The more he caned and punished me, the harder I got. Then after days, I couldn't find the pleasure in it anymore and I don't know why... after that it just all hurt... my visits became difficult. Not with Marcus though, I still liked them." I looked at my sore blistered feet. "I wonder what he would think if he saw my feet looking like this, he would probably like it, like to look after them."

I drank my tea and looked at Layton. "I can't move past the pain he caused... I don't know how to move it from my head. I don't want it to burn in me like this. I don't want to need it when I'm too scared to even taste it."

He took his robe off and sat with his legs around me. He took my tea, put it down, and then took my robe from me. He gave my tea back and stroked my hair with one hand, wrapping the other around my body.

"How do you make a new memory of pain?"

He kissed my shoulder and pulled me to him, laying his face next to mine. "He wanted to hurt you, Baby Boy. He didn't punish you because you were bad or misbehaved, or that you even needed it, he just wanted to hurt you. You took pleasure from it in the beginning because of your mind and body's natural drive for it. As the punishment increased and continued and your limits were ignored, each strike of the cane became just that, a strike of the cane. If I rubbed your cock continuously what would happen?" I turned slightly and smiled.

"I would come." He smiled and kissed my cheek.

"And then if I continued to stroke it?"

"It would be sore." He nodded.

"And if I continued to stroke it?" I creased my face.

"It would be painful."

"Exactly. What once gave you pleasure is now lost to your mind because of the continued abuse of the action. It is exactly what he did to you, Baby Boy. He did the same thing every day until your mind no longer remembered the pleasure it found in it. To make it good again, we must be patient. We have to let your mind heal until the memories are so faint that when you taste it again, it doesn't fuel old memories but smothers it with a new one. Part of that healing is letting your need burn inside you because the more it asks and the more it is denied the more you will want it.

"I will make you look at me every time we make love, so while your orgasm pulses through your body, your mind will see only me and learn that it is me that gives you such intense beautiful feelings, given because I love you. When we play and you look at me, your mind will remember the pleasure I bring and it will want to appease me to have that pleasure. It will associate me only with the love of you, regardless of the punishment I give. Do you understand?"

I nodded and smiled a little. "Yes... you're brainwashing me with your cock."

He laughed out and hugged me. "Something like that." He kissed me. "I know what it's like to need something and not have it sated. The need of it simmers inside and consumes your thoughts. You will have to learn to control it and not let it control you. I will inform Julian when he comes for you, let him know that your mind is looking to appease the need you feel."

We sat on the bed for ages and he soothed my body with his touches, kissing me and telling me he loved me.

I was laying back on him almost sleeping when he spoke again. "Chocolate cake."

A smile took my lips but I didn't look at him. I turned a little and snuggled into him.

"That's where you take me in my mind when you love me."

He held my face to him and kissed the top of my head. I could hear the smile in his voice. "I love your mind, Isaac. Are you hungry?"

I smiled at him. "Only if you are going to give me chocolate cake?"

He pulled me from him and held my face while he looked at me. He stroked the side of my face and kissed me gently on the lips. "Do you want seconds, Baby Boy?"

Always. I would always want him to love me. I stroked my hand up to his body and kissed his chest and then his lips. I looked at him as I moved to sit astride his legs and pushed my cock into his.

"Please, Sir, may I have some more."

He smiled at me as he thrust his hips under me. I shuffled back and took his cock in my hand. Stroking it until it was hard and pulsing in my fist. I looked at him as I watched his pleasure build. "Say my name." He smiled at me.

"Isaac." I shook my head.

"Say my name, my name that only you call me." I stroked my thumb over the crease of his cock and looked down on it, letting my spit drool from my lips over his cock head.

I looked back at him. "Say it. I want to hear it."

He spoke breathlessly. "Baby Boy... love me." He reached over and picked up the gel, squeezing it over his cock as I continued to rub my hand over him. "Love me, Baby Boy."

I rubbed my oiled fingers over my hole and then shuffled forward. I had never loved anyone with my body, I had only ever fucked. I wasn't sure what I was doing but I wanted to feel him inside me. I held his cock and rubbed it over my hole.

"Oh, fuck Baby Boy... yes." I pushed my hole around his cock and slowly sat down on him, moaning at the feel of him deep inside me.

I put my hands to his chest and looked at him, breathing heavily. I touched my hand to his face as I rocked gently forward and back, over and over until I could feel my orgasm asking.

I moaned and dropped my hand back to his body as I continued to move on him slowly while looking at him. I could see he was in the same place as me, his orgasm asking, and I watched as he kept it away.

He lifted his hands to my body and stroked my face and neck. "Baby Boy." He whispered my name and his voice made me moan with need.

He pulled me forward to his body and held me tightly to him while he thrust inside me. I moaned and tried to move so I could take my cock, but he held me there and loved me slowly, teasing my orgasm.

"Is this chocolate cake, Baby Boy? What you're feeling now?"

I nodded against him, moaning and digging my fingers into his body.

"Yes... yes..." I tried to move again but he held me to him, curled under his arms and into his body, my arse stuck out for him to love with his cock.

"Just let me brainwash you a little longer, Baby Boy."

I relaxed against him and let him have me while I moaned with the pleasure of him filling me slowly over and over. He let me go and I pushed my hands into his chest, lifting my torso from his and sitting, pushing my hole deep over his cock. He took my cock in his hand and stroked it as I rocked on him.

"Make me come, Baby Boy, love me and make me come."

I increased my rhythm as my orgasm drew closer and closer and he thrust beneath me, matching my movements. He pushed me back to sit on him as he cried out, looking at me as his orgasm took him. I felt his body pulsing beneath mine and I leant forward, gripping his body as my orgasm exploded through me.

I looked at him and whispered his name fleetingly before my mind left the world and my body pulsed around him, making my whole body spasm over and over until the orgasm ebbed away. I collapsed on him, gasping and we both lay there with him still inside me. I lifted my head to look at him. I couldn't move, my legs had seized up from the exertion. He smiled at me and put his hands to my arse, pulling me forward and withdrawing his cock from me.

"I can't move." He laughed quietly and kissed my head, wrapping his arms around me.

"Good, I don't want you to."

I laid my head back on his body and stayed there until my legs burned and then I still didn't move.

"I don't want to go with Julian." He stroked his fingers through my hair.

"I know. Lots of different emotions and insecurities are running through your head. Those are never going to get better or go away unless you go there and learn that nothing bad will happen while you are away from me. You will not be alone, Baby Boy, Julian will have you and you are definitely coming back... so I can have chocolate cake with you." He kissed my head again. "Just one night, Baby Boy, and then you will be back, I promise. Can you try for me?" I nodded to him.

"What if I have a nightmare? What if he makes me sleep in the dark? What if I make him angry and he doesn't have me?"

"Oh, Baby Boy, your thoughts are causing chaos in your head. I have never seen Julian angry, ever. Not even with Kellen when he took Jacob from him. I trust Julian to take you and keep you safe. I trust him to look after your mind. I trust him more than I trust Marcus."

"You don't know him; Marcus would never hurt me."

"I know and I know that you will want to go with him soon. I want the first time you are away from me to be with someone who I trust, so if you panic or struggle with your thoughts, I know that you are still safe. You need to trust me on this occasion and trust Julian to watch over you until you feel secure away from me. Okay?"

I nodded but it wasn't okay. When I was with Julian here, I was still secure in my mind because I was home, surrounded by things that were familiar and safe. Just thinking of being away from everything I knew made me want to take my mind away from it all and go and find my safety. I relaxed on him and let my mind drift, the ache in my legs made it easy to go.

"No, Isaac." He moved me, rolling me over onto the bed and I moaned at the pain, as gravity pulled my legs from their seized position.

He looked down at me and shook his head. "I don't want you to go off and get all submissive, I want your mind to stay with me. Can you stop it?"

I was breathing deeply, looking at him. I could stay with him, that was safe. I nodded and took a deep breath to clear my unsure thoughts.

He smiled at me. "Good boy. Now come on, let's sort the ache in your legs and then clean you up... again. As much as I like you filled with my life and have you covered in yours, it will make you uncomfortable." He knelt back on his knees and started to rub my legs.

I creased my face as he released the seized muscles with his fingers.

He smiled. "Breathe into it, Isaac, it will appease a little of your need."

I relaxed my legs and let him rub his fingers into the sore muscles while I watched him.

CHAPTER TWELVE

We showered again and he cleansed my hole with the shower spray rather than using the butt plug. I hadn't wanted to be cleansed properly; I wanted his life inside me when he wasn't with me. We made lunch and then we dressed. He made sure there were socks on my feet before putting my boots on.

I sat on the bed waiting as he got ready in his dressing room, feeling uncomfortable. I didn't want my clothes on and I undid the buttons on my jeans. I could feel my sore feet squashed in my boots, so I undid the laces. When he came back into the bedroom he stood and stared at me. I looked down at my boots and fiddled with my laces, just his look told me how unhappy he was.

"Would you rather wear your linens?"

I shook my head even though I wanted to. They would be more comfortable, but I didn't want to feel like a slave going on a visit, even though that's how I felt inside.

"It doesn't matter how many times you undress, Isaac. It is not going to stop Julian coming for you."

I felt a wave of dread churn my stomach which then made me angry, and I swept the t-shirt over my head and threw it on the bed.

"I know you don't want to go but this behaviour is not going to make it go away…or make me punish you how you want." His phone rang and he fished it from his pocket and answered it. "Hello Leon... thank you... I will be there as soon as I can... No just let him be, he can clean it up when I get there. Just make sure Rae stays with him... I won't be too long... okay." He closed his phone and stood for a minute before turning towards me. "At least your unhappiness at the situation is not so volatile."

"Who's unhappy?" Both Layton and I looked towards the bedroom door. Julian stood there, leaning on the door frame. He had a long brown coat on over a suit and looked very smart.

"Orion and Isaac. Hello, Julian." Layton walked towards him and kissed him as Julian stepped into the room. "Orion is throwing things upstairs and Isaac is being… difficult."

Julian laughed and looked at me. I looked away and down at my boots. I felt stupid now and half heartedly tried to undo the knot I had made in the lace of my boot, while watching them under my lashes.

"Isaac being difficult... surely not?"

Layton smiled at him and turned away and looked at me as he walked back into the clothes room.

"Yes, even though I gave him chocolate cake. Can you get dressed, Isaac, I have to go."

I looked at Julian and he raised his eyebrows at me. Layton was not aware that I had told Julian about chocolate cake.

"Chocolate cake?"

I bit my lip and Layton came back carrying a jacket.

"Yes." Layton looked at me and smiled. "Two whole delicious helpings and he's still not happy."

I looked back at Julian, wondering if he would say something but he just smiled at me. His attention to me made me drawn towards him. I moved off the bed and went to him, wanting some comfort from the chaos in my head.

I didn't want to go with him but right at this moment he felt the most Dominant and in control and I needed that. Unsure about my decision, I stopped when I got to him, and he looked at me as I stood asking.

"Isaac, can you please get dressed!" I flinched at Layton's impatience.

Julian watched me for a moment then touched my face. "Hello, Isaac. Do you want to say goodbye to Layton and then we can sort you out?" I shook my head.

I didn't know what I wanted. Layton was leaving me and being impatient, but I didn't want to say goodbye.

"He has got himself into a panic about leaving here and me. His need to be punished and feel something more is burning him, so he is unsettled which is making him difficult." I was now difficult! "Isaac, come here and sit with me on the bed for a moment."

I didn't want to, I wanted Julian to comfort me, I looked at him, begging him with my eyes to have me. Julian just stood looking at me. Not getting my way, I sighed heavily, I turned and walked slowly to Layton who was sitting on the edge of the bed and dropped to the floor at his feet.

I looked up at him but my submission to him was ignored as he reached for the t-shirt and pulled it over my head and then left me to do the rest.

He touched my face to make me look at him. "I'm sorry, Baby Boy, I didn't mean to be impatient." He pulled me up to sit beside him then pulled my booted foot up to the bed and undid the knotted lace before retying it. "Are you angry with me?" I nodded. "Because I'm being mean or because you are going to Julian's?" He tied my other lace.

"I don't want to go; I don't want to be away from here. I will behave if you let me stay with you." He shook his head and held my face.

"We have been through this, Isaac. If something bad happens Julian will bring you straight back here but nothing bad is going to happen, I promise. You need to go and learn that. Julian will have you the whole time. If you come with me, I cannot have you the whole time, you know that. I have to help Orion and that distracts me from you, and you may get into trouble, and I may not be there for you. Do you understand?" I nodded.

He pulled me to him and kissed me. "Good boy, be good for Julian, okay?" I nodded again. "Here I brought you a jacket."

I looked at the leather coat as he put it on me. I didn't want gifts in his place.

He pulled me to him and kissed me again. "I will see you tomorrow." I got up and he turned me to him and buttoned my jeans. "Are your shoes hurting?"

I shook my head not looking at him. They were, I could feel the blisters sticking to the socks and rubbing against the inside of the boots.

"Okay, Baby Boy." He kissed my fingers of my bandaged hand. "I love you."

I stared at him then turned and walked towards Julian who held out his hand, at least someone wanted me. Maybe he would give me something more… punish me… When I looked at him, I changed my mind and tried to think about being good.

"Come, Isaac, let him go and do his thing."

I nodded agreeing with my new Dominant and walked out the bedroom door with him, looking back towards Layton my heart jumped, missing a few beats.

Julian stopped walking and looked at me pulling my face to meet his gaze. "Do you want to say goodbye properly?"

I nodded already feeling bereft and breathless. He nodded and let go of my hand.

I almost ran back into the bedroom as Layton stood from the bed. He held his hand out and I walked into him and wrapped my arms around him.

"I'm sorry, I'll behave... I love you. Please don't forget me, please don't forget to come for me." He kissed me and held me.

"Of course I won't forget you and I promise I'll come for you. You're just staying with friends, Baby Boy, that's all."

I pulled away and looked at him and he smiled and stroked his fingers down my face before kissing my mouth.

He looked at Julian who was waiting by the door again. "Watch him please, he doesn't like the dark, it gives him nightmares and he can make his mind leave the room if he's overwhelmed. Call me if…"

Julian held his hand up. "Isaac and I will be fine, please stop worrying."

He pulled my face to look at him again and kissed me gently on the lips. "Off you go, Baby Boy, he'll watch over you, just until tomorrow."

I nodded and looked at Julian. He smiled at me and held out his hand. I looked back at Layton one last time and then moved to Julian. I didn't take his hand but walked into his body. He wrapped his arm around me and kissed the top of my head. He walked with me still hiding in his body.

"Isaac?" I looked up at him and he looked at me a moment before speaking. "It's going to be okay." I nodded. "Come on, Peter is waiting at the car and Jacob is very excited about seeing you." He smiled at me and held my hand while we climbed the stairs that took us outside.

I didn't like being outside much. Years of being kept in a room pretty much twenty-four hours a day made the outside feel unsafe. Usually, I would keep my head down and follow whoever was leading me, but Julian said Peter was waiting outside and I wanted to see him again. I remembered him from when I had been in the weird hospital room. I had this memory of him bathed in light, standing in the doorway looking rather beautiful and sexy and although the memory had got a bit fanciful in my head, it wasn't far off the real thing.

I stared at him as Julian pulled me to the car and he smiled, making me look away for a moment. He was wearing a dark blue short-sleeved linen shirt with jeans and his arms were so big, they seemed to be stretching the material to its limit. His skin was the colour of chocolate and his eyes even darker, his black hair trimmed short to his head. He had thick pink lips surrounded by short black facial hair, tidy and neat. I wondered what they would feel like on my skin…and what his large hands would feel like holding me down while he…

"Well look at you in clothes and with hair, looking so well. When Jacob said you had made a full recovery, I couldn't believe it."

I squeezed Julian's hand tighter, not ready to talk to the stranger. I knew Peter was good though as Jacob had said he stayed with him sometimes and that they were friends, which made me feel more curious about him, but not quite ready to talk with him.

Julian opened the car door wider. "Isaac isn't very happy about leaving here or Layton. He has a very limited view of our world so things are a bit overwhelming at the moment."

Peter smiled at me softly. "Of course, I'm sorry, Isaac. I forgot how different things must be for you. Jacob speaks of you all the time; I feel like I've known you for ages." He smiled at me. "You can ask me anything and if you need anything, food, drink, just ask and I will sort it for you." I found myself staring at him and nodded in answer to whatever he had just said.

He gestured to the car and Julian got in and I followed. Peter shut the door after us and got in the driver's seat. In the car, I sat with my legs crossed on the seat and watched Peter in the mirror until he made eye contact with me and smiled. I decided it best not to look at him anymore in case I ended up in trouble with him or Julian.

The journey was long and I was glad for the darkened windows in the car but I felt uncomfortable and fidgeted constantly until finally Julian turned and looked at me.

"Why can't you sit still? Did you fidget like this as a slave?" I tried to look sorry and looked down. "Is it your clothes?" I nodded.

He took the jacket from me and then took both my boots off. "When we get to Jacob's you can take your socks off and your clothes if you wish. Okay?"

I nodded and he watched me for a while. "Are you worried?"

I nodded and leant my head into him. I felt lost, I didn't know what my thoughts were. I couldn't seem to think about one thing, there were so many things in my head. I didn't know these people or where I was going or what they were going to do with me. He wrapped his arm around me and pulled me into his body.

"Is Jacob's house far?" He stroked my face.

Maybe when I was inside again I wouldn't feel so lost and unsafe. Travelling to visits was always worrying but then I knew where I was going and knew what was expected of me. Apart from yesterday, the only time I had spent with Julian was when I had been a slave and he had been testing me for slavery after Beecher.

"No, not too far. Do you remember much of the place where you and I stayed when you were a slave?"

I shook my head. The room and the shower were all I could recall and even then, I couldn't remember what was in those rooms.

"I didn't think you would. That is a good thing."

"I remember the nettles. Is that where we are going?"

"If I said yes would it worry you?"

I closed my eyes. The one thing about Julian was he was honest and wasn't concerned with talking about my slavery days.

"Layton said I was to behave so I will do whatever you say. I don't want to think anymore."

I knew my journey was out of my hands. My head was full of questions, but I wasn't sure I wanted the answers to them, and I didn't feel free to ask them. I wanted to go to my safe place but wasn't sure it was safe when I was with Julian. I curled my body into myself and him.

"Peter, can you find somewhere to stop for a while? Somewhere we can get a warm drink."

"Of course."

Julian stroked my face. "This whole journey is not going well for you, is it? Maybe you should go back to staring at Peter?" I didn't answer, I didn't know whether to or not or what to say. "We are going to stop and try and get your mind back and settled. I seem to have lost you, Isaac, between the basement and the car. Your mind moves quickly and I shall have to learn to keep up. I have made you feel unsafe and that was not my intention. Are you still with me?"

I nodded. Only just, hanging by a thread, I was battling hard in my mind to stay. I felt the car swing over and stop and Peter turned in his seat and looked back but I kept my eyes from him.

"A tea I think Peter."

"They do really good hot chocolate here, with cream and marshmallows…remember?"

Julian looked down on me and smiled. "I think just the tea on this occasion. I want to ease him back into our world, not fill his thoughts with erotic thoughts."

I wanted hot chocolate! I wanted the erotic thoughts…! I think.

"Okay."

Peter left the car and Julian looked at me.

"Okay... let's go back."

I sat up and looked at him hopefully. "Back to the basement? To Layton?"

Julian smiled. "Not exactly what I meant but now I have you again, let's talk about it." I leant my head against the back of the seat. "I thought we were friends, Isaac, or working towards it at least?"

"I want to be." He pulled my face around to look at him.

"But?"

I shrugged my shoulders and shook my head. I didn't know what else he wanted me to say.

"If we went back to the basement now do you think we could be friends?" I thought about it.

We had been okay when we were there. I had felt safe there with him and he had comforted me and let me be me and not punished me when I hadn't been able to do what he had asked me to.

"Yes, I think so... can we go?" Julian smiled at me.

"Maybe, let's talk a little more and then you can decide. If you feel the need to go back, we will go back" I wanted to go back. "When we were in the basement today, did you feel safe with me?" I nodded and smiled a little as a thought came to me.

"You didn't tell about chocolate cake." He laughed.

"No, I didn't, you will have to tell Layton tomorrow that you told me about that. As entertaining as it is for me to be on your sneaky side, it is not right that he doesn't know." I smiled a little.

"He probably knows, he knows everything." Julian looked at me amused.

"Really?" I nodded "Mm... in which case he was playing with me." I bit my lip.

"Are you angry with him?" Julian smiled and touched my face fleetingly.

"No, not at all. Layton and I are friends." He sighed and took my hand in his. "Layton understands you, Isaac, he has known you a long time. You and I know each other but in a different way, as Master and slave, yes?" I nodded and looked down at the seat as the car door opened and Peter got back in the car. "When we left the basement and I spoke of the place we stayed, did it make you feel like you needed to be that person again?" I shrugged my shoulders. He lifted my face again to his. "Do you think it is safer to be a slave when you are with me?"

"I think it's a good thing that you are honest to me. If you want me to do those things again, I'm not ready. Layton said to try and do what you say but I don't want them, they scare me. If you want me to do those things... I need... I can't be your friend; I have to be your slave."

Julian nodded. "Because you understand your place when you're a slave. You were very good at it, a perfect slave." I looked at him sideways a little, enjoying his praise of me. "Your place with me then was very clear and now everything has changed and you're not sure where you fit."

"I know you're Dominant, I always know that." I didn't want him to think I had forgotten.

I heard him smile on a breath rather than saw him. "Yes, and you are a submissive. So, we are both clear that that hasn't changed. The place of a slave is very different, Isaac, and I am very strict with them to keep their mind subservient to me and their place. If they leave that place, they will feel exactly like you do now, confused."

I turned my face to him. "I can imagine that you feel very vulnerable out of the security of your slave place and people must be overwhelming. So let's make things clear between us. I am the dominant and you are the submissive and we are friends. It means I will watch over you and protect you, it means when you get stuck or find things overwhelming, you can ask me for help, or Peter here." I had to work at not looking at him.

"The house we are going to is the same one you stayed at when you were a slave. There's nothing I can do to change that, although Jacob is working hard to make it feel different, I was asking if you remembered so I could help you if it became overwhelming. Our places are the same, but our relationship has changed so I will not be punishing you or playing with you. Your mind is now free from the containment of your slavery. I know it's going to make the world overwhelming but because our places haven't changed, you are protected from anything bad happening, even if you find yourself dropping out of it for a while."

"Leaving the room?" he smiled and nodded.

"Yes, leaving the room. The Dominant that played with you is now the Dominant that protects you. The same Dominant that looked after you yesterday in the basement. Just because we are not there doesn't mean it's changed."

Well, that made sense. He had been a mean and strong Dominant when I had been his slave, now that I knew I was under his protection, I felt safe. Who wouldn't want him protecting them?

I fiddled with my bandage on my hand until Peter spoke and broke the silence. "Seeing as we're having an intermission in proceedings, here you go, Isaac."

Julian smiled and I looked at him fleetingly then looked back to my hand.

"And I saw this and thought you might like it." He held out a bag in his other hand and I looked at Julian, unsure.

He nodded. "It's okay, Peter is my very good friend. Everything he does is nice."

Peter looked at Julian and smiled. I slowly lifted my hand and took the bag. Julian took the tea and put it in a round holder on the back of Peter's chair.

Peter looked at me. "Go on, Isaac, you'll like it."

I looked from him to the bag and opened it, pulling out the biggest biscuit I had ever seen. It was the same size as my hand, and I stared at it for ages before looking at Julian.

"Look." He smiled at me.

"I told you he was nice." I heard Peter laugh.

"Not as nice as I could have been. That's a giant oatmeal cookie, they had chocolate chip ones, but they had sold out, next time, Isaac, I'll get you one of those."

I decided I liked Peter a lot and watched as he drank his tea then burnt his mouth, making him huff and puff before taking another sip. It made me smile.

"I think Isaac has had enough chocolate for one day." I looked at Julian and he winked at me.

"Can I eat it?"

"Of course." I looked at it for a while and then put it back in the bag as Peter spoke.

"Aww, don't you like it?" I nodded and smiled at him.

"I do, thank you. I want to show Layton though."

Peter smiled and I found myself smiling back before he turned in his seat and started the engine. I looked at him in the mirror and he winked at me which made me look away.

"Right, what are we doing then?" Peter's question made me look at Julian to see if he had decided if I could go home or not.

He reached out and stroked my arm. "If you need to go back, Isaac, Peter can take us back and we can try again another day." I wanted to go back. I looked at my biscuit in the bag, I couldn't wait to show Layton. He wouldn't be happy though if I went back now and had not even tried to stay with Julian.

I held my biscuit out to Julian. "Can you look after it, so it doesn't break?" He took the bag and looked at me, asking. "I want to go back... but I don't need to. I just need you to have me because being away from there is really... different and I'm worried."

He smiled at me and pulled me to him, kissing my head. "I know, Isaac. I am going to try hard to keep up with your mind but if I miss something just touch my hand and then I will know things are not right, okay? We will sort it out." I nodded. "Peter, to Jacob's please."

Peter smiled at me in the mirror and spoke, making me feel really good. "Well done, Isaac, good decision."

My stomach somersaulted as the car moved off. Julian stretched his legs out and handed me the plastic cup with my tea. I took it and sat back in the seat, sipped it, and then looked at it.

"Can I have hot chocolate next time too? So I can have erotic thoughts, instead of my thoughts."

Julian and Peter both laughed and I shrank back into the seat. He leaned over and kissed the top of my head.

"That's funny, Isaac."

I looked at him feeling stupid. "I meant it though."

He stroked my face.

"I know which makes it a very beautiful thought too, like your mind."

I liked that and smiled at him. The rest of the journey was easier.

When the car pulled to a standstill, I was nearly asleep, curled into Julian's body. I opened my eyes and looked up at him.

"We are here, Isaac. You are dealing with a lot and it is making you tired, but this is the last part of your journey today."

I pushed myself up and wiped my good hand across my eyes. "Can I sleep here with you?" I was comfortable and felt safe, it didn't matter that we were in the car.

He touched my face and smiled. "No, we can't spend the night here. Kendal and Jacob are inside waiting."

I looked out the window and could just make out the outline of the house. I didn't remember it at all which I wasn't sure was a good thing or bad. I looked back at Julian, feeling nervous about leaving the car.

"I know it's scary but inside is safe. You'll feel better with walls around you again. It's just Kendal and Jacob and you know both of them." After a moment's pause, I nodded.

He reached down and got my boots, giving them to me. I bent down and put them on, tucking the laces into the sides and then looked at Julian for his approval.

He smiled at me. "That will do, you can take them off when you get inside." He held out his hand and I gave him mine. "Ready?" I shook my head and he smiled. "Just breathe, that's all I want you to do is just breathe. You don't have to talk to anyone or let go of me, but I want you to stay with me. Do you understand?" I nodded.

He didn't want my mind wandering off. Usually, when I was with a client that was easy to do, it was safer to stay in the room with them. If your mind wandered off then they could take you beyond your limits without you even knowing, until the pain of it hurt your mind.

Peter opened the car door and Julian looked at me again and spoke. "Breathe." I took a deep breath and followed as he got out of the car and headed for the door. I stopped and looked back at Peter.

"Bye, Peter, thank you for my biscuit."

He smiled at me. "You're welcome, Isaac, but I will see you in a moment. I promised Jacob I would come and have tea before I left."

I felt stupid again. Of course, they were friends and friends liked to be with each other. I wondered if I would ever understand all the different relationships people had with each other. I bit my lip and nodded.

"Isaac?" I looked at Julian. "Don't worry... come on." He gave a little tug on my hand and I turned and walked with him towards the door.

He stopped just before he opened it and pulled my face up to meet his eyes. "They are friends, Isaac, just breathe." He turned, opened the door and stepped inside. I walked behind him.

It was quiet inside and I gripped Julian's hand tightly as we moved forward down the hallway. As we reached a corner, I could hear Kendal's voice.

"You will have to ask J, it's not up to me." We turned the corner, and I could see Jacob and Kendal standing by the sink in the kitchen.

Julian stopped in the doorway and I stepped a little behind him with my heart beating so fast. "Ask me what?"

I saw Jacob move immediately towards us. Julian raised his hand and stroked it across Jacob's face before kissing him. "I was a little longer than planned, Jacob, I'm sorry." Jacob leant his head into him and Julian kissed the side of his face. "Everything good, Kendal?"

Kendal dried her hands and looked fleetingly at me and I stepped back behind Julian. She walked towards Julian and kissed him on the cheek.

"Everything is fine, is Peter coming in?" Julian nodded.

"Yes, he's on his way. He will drop you back home later." Kendal peered around Julian.

"Hello, honey. Are you feeling a little overwhelmed?"

Breathe. I wanted to sink to the floor and be ignored.

"Isaac is way out of his comfort zone. Tea, I think will help."

Kendal smiled at me and moved away to the other side of the kitchen. Jacob stepped from Julian and looked at me.

"Hey, Isaac." I tipped my head to see him.

We were the same Jacob and I. We had taken different paths, but we had ended up in the same place. He seemed so confident with his place even when he was away from Julian, and I envied him that. He filled me with confidence just seeing how at ease he was with these people and in this place, even so, my reply was whispered.

"Hello." I squeezed Julian's hand.

"Let's move to the sitting room." Jacob looked at Julian.

"Can I show Isaac around first?"

Julian smiled at him and then looked at me. "Would you like to go with Jacob?"

I shook my head and stepped towards Julian. He looked back at Jacob. "I think Isaac needs some time, Jacob. Maybe later or tomorrow."

It was bad enough not being with Layton, I didn't want to be away from Julian as well. Jacob gave me comfort, but he was like me, and I didn't feel secure with him. He looked disappointed but nodded, accepting his answer without question.

The sound of the front door closing down the hallway made me jump and Jacob look at Julian.

"Peter?" Julian nodded and Jacob walked past us.

I stayed with Julian but watched him go and then heard him greet Peter in the hallway.

Peter laughed. "I know. Give him some time, show me."

Julian stepped into the kitchen and I went with him. He pulled me beside him and looked at me.

"Jacob is very fond of Peter and they haven't seen each other for a few days. He's gone to hog his attention for a bit." He looked at Kendal. "Was he anxious that I was late?"

Kendal smiled at him while she loaded the tray. "Not like usual. He thought Isaac wouldn't come. I think now that he is here, he thinks everything is fine." Kendal looked at me. "He doesn't understand how hard this is for you, Isaac. Can I look at your hand?"

I shook my head. I just wanted to stand here and be with Julian. His hand in mine was all that was keeping me here, it all felt wrong.

I looked at Julian. "I want to go back."

He pulled me to him and wrapped his arms around me. "Breathe Isaac. Is it the people?"

I looked at Kendal who was now busy with the tea again. "No... I don't know. Can we go back to the car?"

I heard Julian smile. He stroked his hand over my head. "Well, you're talking to me, so I didn't lose you between the car and here. Talk to me some more, tell me something."

I pushed myself into him.

"I'll take the tea in." Kendal moved passed us and left.

Julian took me further into the kitchen and sat me in a chair and then pulled another chair so that he sat opposite with his legs around mine. He looked at me.

"This is Jacob's kitchen... well actually it is probably more Kendal's. She cooks here more than he does. Jacob can't cook." He smiled at me. "Kendal has tried very hard to teach him, but I think he prefers Kendal to look after him rather than fend for himself, so he makes it difficult for Kendal. She knows though, she never says anything, but she knows he doesn't try very hard."

I looked around the kitchen for the first time since we entered. It was large and bright, the biggest kitchen I had ever seen.

I looked back at Julian and he smiled. "I can feel your mind working, Isaac. You have a natural curiosity which you're struggling to keep under control. You are free to do as you wish here and when you feel more secure, I am sure you will find your way around. It's a strange place for you and I understand that you do not feel safe here, but you are. For now, you can stay with me until your mind settles."

I sighed feeling a little better now we were alone. "It all feels wrong."

He shook his head. "It's not wrong, it's different and that's making it feel wrong to you. This is just like the car. That felt wrong too but after a while, you felt safe there. This house has many rooms and they will all feel different because it is not your room or the basement. The longer you stay here, the more settled you will become and learn to feel safe. If you really need to, we can go back to the basement, but you will come here again and feel the same. I know this seems hard, Isaac, and it makes you want to hide but I promise if you stay, it will get easier and you will feel more comfortable. It would please both Layton and I if you stay."

I nodded. My desire to please was so strong, years of earning praise and comfort were not just down to training, it was who I was.

"Before Kendal leaves, I would like her to look at your hand too." I nodded again. "Now let's go and join them in the sitting room and have tea." He held out his hand and I put mine in his reluctantly. He kissed it and then touched a hand to my face. "Good boy. Come on." He stood and I followed.

We walked out into the hallway and turned left, entering the first door. It was the sitting room, and Kendal, Peter, and Jacob were all sitting drinking tea. Jacob was sitting with Peter on the couch and Kendal was sitting on the floor by Jacob. He was playing his fingers in her hair while she drank her tea.

Julian walked over to a bean bag and took his coat off before he sat down and pulled me to sit between his legs on the floor. I sat, crossed my legs and looked at Kendal. She smiled at me and passed my tea.

"There you go, honey, just as you like it."

I took the tea and sipped it as Julian wrapped his hands around my shoulders and kissed the top of my head. I slowly lifted my head and looked at them all. Peter was rubbing Jacob's shoulders and Jacob was looking at me.

"Are you going to stay?" I pushed myself into Julian and nodded to Jacob.

He smiled at me. "Good. I want to show you something."

Julian stroked his hand over my chest and spoke at Jacob.

"Tomorrow, Jacob." Jacob nodded, still smiling.

"Can Isaac sleep with me tonight?" He looked at me. "You can sleep with me if you want, if Julian says." He looked back at Julian.

Peter pulled his head back to look at him. "We just spoke about this. Let Isaac breathe a little." Peter let go of his head and Jacob looked at me.

"Sorry. I'm glad you're staying."

I smiled a little. I could see that Peter cared about Jacob and he wasn't scared or worried to be with him, even though Julian was in the room. I tipped my head sideways and looked at Julian and he was smiling at them.

He looked down and kissed the side of my head. I turned back and sat quietly drinking my tea as Kendal and Peter talked about the last time he had driven her home and the car had broken down. The story sounded horrible and frightening, yet they were laughing about it.

Both Jacob and Julian were laughing as Kendal told how Peter had made her get out and push the car and she had fallen in a mud. As I sat and watched them, it occurred to me that they were all more than friends. They were all secure with each other, even Jacob who was clearly the submissive of the group, was secure with his place among them.

It made me think of my life with Layton. I still wasn't secure with my place, not even with him and that made me feel sad. Suddenly feeling worried about my place in this world, I lifted my hand and touched Julian's. He immediately took it in his and stroked it, tipping my face to his he looked at me as he had done throughout the car journey.

Again, I didn't know what he was looking for, but he seemed satisfied and let my face go. He sat forward and leaned his face against mine, while still stroking my hand and we sat for a while until the conversation died down.

Kendal moved towards me across the floor and held out her hand. "Will you let me see your hand, Isaac?"

Remembering my agreement to Julian, I gave her my hand and she sat and undid the bandage.

"What happened, Isaac?" I looked at Peter as he sipped his tea.

"I... I broke a glass." Julian stroked his hand over my hair, trying to soothe my journey into the room and the people that were in it.

"Are you another one that should be kept out of the kitchen?"

He was smiling and I bit my lip and looked at Julian. Julian looked at Peter.

"Actually, Isaac, is a very good cook, he made pancakes. It helps that he loves his food, unlike Jacob who would starve if someone didn't remind him to eat."

I looked at Jacob. He didn't seem worried or look starved. Kendal poked my hand and I dragged it away.

"Sorry, Isaac. I wanted to see if it was healing." I slowly gave it back to her. "I think we can just put a plaster on it now and I will take the stitches out before you go home." She smiled at me. "You look tired, honey."

"Yes. I think it is time to end this day." At Julian's words, Peter kissed Jacob and then stood.

Kendal got her bag and put a large plaster over the stitches. She kissed my hand.

"It's really nice to have you here, Isaac. I have left a sandwich in the fridge if you're hungry in the night."

I looked at her. "Thank you."

Jacob came and sat next to Julian on the floor. He leaned his head on Julian and reached out and touched the wrist of my sore hand. Kendal kissed Jacob and then Julian and there were a lot of goodbyes between everyone.

Peter crouched down to me, took my hand, and kissed my fingers gently. His closeness made my breath catch as he spoke.

"Goodnight, Isaac. It was nice to see you again."

Before I could move the feeling, he left the room with Kendal. I listened for him and could hear them talking about the car breaking down again, which now that they were away, made me smile.

"They're funny together." I looked at Jacob as he spoke and smiled at him.

Julian pulled my face round to him. "I know you are very tired; would you like to eat before heading to bed?" I shook my head.

I could barely breathe let alone eat something. Now that it was just Jacob and Julian, I felt a bit more at ease.

I felt exhausted but my mind was churning with thoughts, thoughts that only being with Layton in the basement would settle. I wanted to be in my bed, naked with him and just let him have me.

Julian spoke again. "Right then, sleeping arrangements." I saw Jacob look at Julian, pleading with his eyes and Julian looked at me. "You may sleep with Jacob in his room, but you are both forbidden to touch." He looked at Jacob who nodded.

Jacob held out his hand and after pausing for a moment I took it. Jacob was safe and now that the house was calm and less crowded, I felt comfortable to go with him.

CHAPTER THIRTEEN

Jacob took me to his bedroom which was across the hallway on the opposite side. The room was large, had a double bed and a large private bathroom. He stripped naked and I followed his lead, glad to be rid of my clothes. After using the toilet and brushing our teeth together, I followed him to bed. He spooned me and it felt good to feel his naked body against mine. He lifted his head and kissed the side of my face, and I lifted my hand and touched his.

"Are you still worried about being here?" I shook my head.

"Not so much. I miss Layton, being away from him makes me uncomfortable. Do you feel like that when you are away from Julian?" I felt him half-shrug behind me.

"Only when he's away for a long time. I like being with Peter and Kendal, and Eden when she comes by but after a while, it's like something is missing inside me. I usually take myself to the basement if I'm at Julian's. No one goes down there uninvited so I can be on my own and just think about him. If I'm here, I usually go for a walk into the woods, it helps my thoughts. He owns all the surrounding land so it's very safe."

I turned my head slightly towards him. "You go outside on your own? Don't you get worried?"

I heard his smile. "No, not really. I'm used to being on my own, I've never been much for company. Sometimes I like to think about when it was just Julian and me and I didn't have to be watched over all the time."

He said he didn't care for too many people, yet he had sat quite comfortably in the room with all of them. I loved being around people yet, I was the one struggling. Maybe it was because I had spent so much time alone these past few years that I now craved the attention from others.

"Do you like Peter?" He was stroking my body as he spoke.

"Yes. He loves me..." I could see that. "Not like Julian does, I don't think he likes other men in that way." That wasn't how I had felt. Acting surprised I turned to face Jacob.

"Really? But he was so comfortable with you…with Julian, touching and kissing?" Jacob smiled.

"Yeah, he is, I don't know why. He's not Dominant…well not like I know a dominant…" Again, that's not what I had felt. "He's controlling… in a softer kind of way, which makes it easy to be with him. Sometimes, if Julian and I have been playing and Julian gets called away while I'm healing, Peter looks after me. I prefer Peter to look after me than Kendal as she can get angry with Julian if I'm suffering, whereas Peter just gets on with things."

I thought about it for a while. Peter must be extremely comfortable with Julian and this world to accept so much. I recalled the evening with him and Kendal talking and laughing and a thought occurred to me.

"Does he love Kendal?" Jacob sort of shrugged.

"I don't know."

He didn't seem bothered, but I was intrigued and curious, probably more than I should have been. We had the same submissive minds, the same desire to please but then after that, we were very different. He seemed happy just being with Julian and nothing else really mattered to him beyond that, but I wanted to know everything, well as much as I was allowed to know.

Maybe that's why my mind hurt so much? Everything I saw or did made my mind burn with questions, I wanted to know more. As a slave, I had never questioned anything, it wasn't allowed and I had been content to let them have me and to stay in my safe submissive world. Now it didn't seem so safe anymore, nowhere seemed particularly safe, just Layton, only when I was with him. The thought reminded me that he wasn't with me, and I let out a moan on a breath.

Jacob pulled me closer to him.

"Settle now boys and sleep." Julian's voice startled me and I looked for him in the room.

He had stripped off his clothes and was only wearing his jeans as he walked towards us and bent, stroking Jacob's face and then mine. He looked at me for a long moment. "Can you settle, Isaac?"

I wasn't sure and I shrugged my shoulders. I was so tired, my body ached from loving Layton, but my mind was buzzing, the thoughts so loud in my head.

"I will stay in the room until you settle." He turned and switched off the light and I immediately went into a panic as the room was plunged into darkness.

Jacob stroked my arm and held me tightly and then Julian switched on the light in the hallway and left the door open a little which made me breathe a little easier. He disappeared into the darkness of the room, and I lay and tried to let my thoughts be about Jacob and his body, his touch on my skin.

I curled my body into my slave pose, my wrists and ankles together trying to find some comfort from it. Jacob fell asleep quickly and his breathing became shallow, his body heavy against mine. I closed my eyes and tried to find the same peace in my mind, but it wouldn't come.

For what seemed like hours, I lay listening to Jacob and then watched as Julian silently left the room. I battled the need to go with Julian or stay here with Jacob and if Jacob had stayed close to me, it would have been easier, but he moved away from me in his slumber. He took his touch away and I knew I couldn't stay here; it didn't feel safe.

I sat up and looked at the open door. I didn't want to get into trouble but just lying on the bed was making my mind hurt, too many thoughts were churning in my head. I felt alone, which on its own wasn't a new feeling. I had always been alone as a slave but now I didn't have the comfort of my room, Layton, or the basement.

I moved to the edge of the bed, slid to the floor and sat next to my boots with my knees curled into me and my arms wrapped around them, watching the open door. I didn't know where Julian had gone so I felt stuck. I touched my fingers to my boots and brought Layton's image to my mind.

My thoughts swung between staying in the room with Jacob or leaving the small comfort I found here and finding Julian. Being with him offered my mind some semblance of safety and I needed to feel it in this strange place. The need for it far outweighed the punishment I would endure for misbehaving.

I sat for ages as my mind warred over the need to be good and stay where he left me, or the safety that I wanted to feel. I stood up and looked back at Jacob sleeping on the bed. The covers lay at his waist and although his body was relaxed, I could see his muscled body defined in the light from the door. His hair was strewn across his face, but I could see the peacefulness of his features as he took each breath. He was safe and secure in his mind, in this place. I turned back towards the door and walked quietly out of the room.

I had no idea where Julian had gone. The hallway was well lit and I looked at the doors to my right and then at the doors to my left. I knew the door to the left was the sitting room where we had all sat and had our tea, it was slightly ajar so maybe he was there. I padded slowly towards the open door and looked in from the doorway. The room was dark, but I could see Julian's outlined body lying on the sofa. I couldn't see if he was awake, so I walked towards him waiting for him to speak or hold out his hand to me. He didn't move.

Layton was always awake when I needed him, and I didn't know what to do. If I woke him, would he be angry? I sat on the floor next to him and curled my legs into my body and leant my head on them.

I wondered what Layton was doing, was he missing me? Was he thinking of me? Was he feeling as lost without me as I was without him? No. This was his world, he was comfortable and secure in it way before I had come into his life. He would be sleeping with Orion or teaching him about being a slave, loving him, comforting him. It hurt to think about it. I needed him and it hurt that he wasn't with me, loving and comforting me.

My stomach growled with hunger, and I turned my head to the side on my knees and looked at Julian. I couldn't see his face in the darkness, only his outline, again I wondered whether I should wake him. If I went and got the sandwich that Kendal had left me would that be misbehaving or me being independent?

It was so confusing not being a slave. If you wanted something as a slave you begged for it and you either had to earn it or you were forbidden. It was simple. I turned and laid my head on the sofa.

I would give up the want of the sandwich for his touch, I would forget about it and lay with him. He never moved so I turned and stood and walked back into the hallway. I walked around the corner and found the kitchen where I had sat with Julian. It was in darkness but again, the light from the hallway let me see into it enough so I could see the fridge. I would get my sandwich and eat it in the hallway where it was light, then I could go back and sleep with Jacob.

Maybe that's why I couldn't settle because I was hungry? I walked into the kitchen to the left of the table and opened the large fridge. It was so big and when I opened it, it bathed the whole room in light. It was full of food of all descriptions and colours and I felt myself smile. I had never seen so much food in one place. I saw the sandwich that Kendal had left, I took it from the shelf and sat cross-legged on the floor in front of the open fridge. I liked the light and seeing all the food, it made me forget my thoughts.

I unwrapped the sandwich and took a bite while looking at the stuff on the shelves. There were foods in there that I had never heard of or seen before, things of strange colour, like a fruit or a vegetable, which I found myself touching and biting into to see what they felt and tasted like. I found orange juice in the door, and I opened it and drank from the bottle. Like a child at my first party, I wanted everything I had been forbidden.

I liked the juice and thought I had better find a mug to put it in, so I stood up and started searching the kitchen cupboards. After opening a few, I found a mug and took it back to the fridge, sitting cross-legged again. I poured some juice into the mug and finished my sandwich while I looked at the other food in the fridge.

By the time I had finished, I had a collection of food beside me that I wanted to try. Apples and cheese and a funny looking sauce dip that was green in colour, yoghurt, some green stick thing, and some jam which I opened and dipped my hand in and then sucked the sweet substance from my fingers. I couldn't remember the last time I had tasted strawberry jam. I closed my eyes and savoured the taste, god it was so nice!

I bit into the green stick which tasted disgusting after the sugary jam. I put it aside and bit into the apple instead. I drank more juice and then ate some cheese and then tried the green sauce, which was vile, so I left it. I found strawberries and I ate a few, then a few more, opened the yoghurt and started to dip the strawberries in it.

My mind was alive with excitement at so many new things and foods that I hadn't tasted in ages, some since I was a child. Boiled eggs, chicken on a bone, some cold soup thing and more strawberries, the green stick thing dipped in jam was better and then I discovered that everything dipped in jam was better from potatoes to cucumber.

I ate until I felt sick and sat leaning back on my hands waiting for the feeling to go away so I could continue my tasting, but it didn't. I looked around the kitchen and saw a bin. I dragged it across to me and sat back on the floor in front of the fridge and hung my head over it. I groaned as the feeling gripped my stomach and leant against the fridge door, needing the air to cool me down.

I wretched and leaned forward over the bin as the spasm shook my body and the food I had eaten, returned. Over and over, it left my body sometimes not giving me time to take a breath, which scared me and made me cry quietly. When my stomach seemed empty it stopped and I lay back against the fridge for a moment, the coldness of it making me shiver.

"Isaac?" I jumped at the sound of his voice and lowered my head. "I take it you have finished raiding the fridge now?"

I nodded but kept my head down. It was always best to be completely submissive when you had been caught doing something that you knew was wrong. I felt my stomach spasm again and quickly grabbed the bin and wretched into it. He moved into the kitchen, to the sink and then came and crouched beside me, waiting for the retching to stop.

I looked at him. "I'm sick."

He didn't look very happy. "I can see." He wiped my mouth and face with a cloth. "Has it passed?" I nodded and he took the bin from me. "I don't think strawberries, celery, potatoes and..." He picked up the opened jam pot and looked in it. "...and half a pot of strawberry jam go very well together."

I bit my lip. "But I wanted to try them. I was hungry and they all looked nice..." I felt my stomach spasm again. "...not finished."

He quickly gave me back the bin and I retched over it. My stomach was empty and my spit drooled from my mouth, even though my body didn't want to give up until the last drop had been expelled.

He wiped my mouth again and I looked at him panting. "I don't want to be sick anymore, I don't like it."

He smiled. "Then maybe next time you are hungry, you will eat just the sandwich and not the whole fridge. Did the little sugar rush appease your need?"

I was still leaning over the bin and I nodded, then after a moment I looked at him and shook my head.

He smiled. "No, not the sort of rush that you wanted, I'm sure. Your body knows what it wants, Isaac, your mind is just trying to salve your need. It will soon want the same thing; it just needs a little time to get there. Are you finished?" I nodded and he took the bin away again. "Right, let's get you and this mess cleaned up."

I looked at the food and the mess that surrounded me and bit my lip. "Sorry." I looked at him.

He leant and kissed the top of my head. "The consequences were yours. I'm sure next time you are hungry you will only take what you need and not what you want?" I nodded. "Why didn't you stay with Jacob?" He was clearing away the food on the floor, reattaching lids and binning half-eaten food. I picked up the lid to the jam pot and gave it to him.

"Because you left the room. Will Jacob be worried on his own?" Julian shook his head.

"No, Jacob is quite used to sleeping on his own." So was I, more than used to it but I didn't like it.

I sighed and Julian sat on the floor with me. "Jacob knows there is always someone around if he needs them. That is something you will learn, Isaac. Layton will see that you are always looked after. As a slave, you should have always had someone there when you needed them, but you didn't and bad things happened, now you worry when you are alone. The more you live in this world, the more secure and comfortable you will become, and you won't feel so vulnerable."

Jacob appeared naked in the doorway behind Julian. His body was like Julian's, muscled and beautiful and I found myself taking my fill of him.

"What's happening?" Julian smiled and turned and held out his hand which Jacob took. He was still half asleep and squinting against the light. "You were gone, Isaac, I came to find you."

"Isaac was hungry. You can go back to sleep, Jacob, I will watch over him tonight." Jacob nodded and kissed Julian before looking around at the kitchen. Still half asleep he spoke as he left.

"All the cupboards are open." Julian smiled and looked at me but didn't answer.

I pulled my knees together and wrapped my arms around them. When I was with Layton, I felt beautiful, my body felt beautiful, here with them, I felt like the odd one out.

Julian touched his hand to my face. "Mm, he is very beautiful, isn't he? I like Jacob to hang for me, sometimes for many hours when we play. It requires a great deal of strength, so he keeps very fit. You have different strengths, Isaac. You should never hide your body because it is different." He stroked his fingers over my ear through my hair and I shivered so he touched his hand to my body. "You are freezing. We need to get you out of the fridge."

He smiled at me. "Do you want to lay with me on the sofa?" I nodded.

It still felt strange to be here and being with Julian was where I felt safest. He held out his hand and I put mine in his and as he stood, he pulled me to my feet shutting, the fridge door.

There were still empty cartons on the floor, and I looked at them feeling guilty for my earlier indulgence. I looked from them to Julian. "I'm sorry. I will clear it up if you say."

He kissed my hand. "You are forgiven this time. It has been a very long day for you, and I think you have learnt your lesson. Kendal will return here in the morning; she will see to the kitchen. Let's get you cleaned up and settled. You must be very tired." I shook my head.

"I'm not." He smiled at me.

We walked through the hallway and to the door after Jacob's room which was another bedroom with a large bathroom. Julian let me brush my teeth and sat me on the floor while he wiped my body with a cloth and then dried me. We headed back to the sitting room. He stripped off his trousers and lay on the sofa. He took my hand and pulled me between his legs and wrapped his arms around me.

"There is nothing more comforting than the feel of skin against skin." I had to agree with that and turned and lay my face against his body as he stroked my hair.

I wasn't sure why I did it, but I lifted my head and kissed his body and then touched the tip of my tongue to his skin. I was glad when he pushed my head back to lie on him. "Don't play with fire and tempt me, Isaac."

His words scared me and I settled against him. I didn't want to be punished. "Settle now."

"Can we talk, I can't sleep?" He pulled a blanket from the back of the sofa, covered me, and stroked his hands over my back.

"You should have come and woken me when you were struggling."

"I did but you were asleep and didn't wake up."

"I wanted you to try and settle without me, but I think it was a little soon. I came for you as soon as I heard you were in trouble." I pushed myself into him, encouraging him to have me more and I felt him smile. "I wasn't abandoning you, just trying to let you find your way. I will always be around if you need me. Are you missing Layton?"

I nodded against him. "Can we see him in the morning?" He continued to stroke my body with his fingers.

"Well, it is morning already. Let's see how the day goes. Jacob wants to show you around his house. You are very safe here, even when you cannot see me. Layton is missing you too."

I sighed. "I don't think so. I think he's busy with Orion."

I heard him smile again. "A little jealous, are we?" I didn't answer. "I have five missed calls on my phone. So yes, he is busy, but he is thinking of you."

"Can I speak to him?"

"No. He knows you are safe with me, and you know you are safe. Speaking with him will just make it harder for you both. Try and sleep now." The fact he was thinking about me made my mind settle a little.

"I know I was sick, but can I have breakfast when I wake up?" His body flexed under me as he laughed.

"If you sleep a little." I closed my eyes.

"Is Peter coming back?"

"Sleep, Isaac."

"I don't think I can." It was the last thing I said before I slept.

Toast, bacon...or sausages. I couldn't decide as I let the aroma fill my mind, in my half-asleep half-awake state. I dragged the smell in through my nose deeply, I could almost taste it. My pillow shook under me, and I touched my hand to it to still it. It was warm and smooth, and I opened my eyes to look at it. Skin, Julian's skin. I turned my face up towards him and he was smiling at me.

"Even in sleep, Isaac, you are drawn to food. Are you feeling better?" I nodded. "You slept very peacefully." He stroked his hand across my head then pulled me up his body and kissed me. I lay my hands on his chest and looked at him.

"Would you like me to service you?" His face went serious and I looked down at my hands as my thumb stroked his chest.

I had said something wrong, but I didn't know why. Layton always liked to take his pleasure in the mornings, and I remembered that Julian did too. I looked back at him. "You don't want me to, do you? Is it because you have Jacob here?"

His face softened and he wrapped his arms around me and pulled me to his body kissing my head.

"I would like nothing more than to play with you, Isaac, and have you pleasure me. You are very beautiful, and I remember how sweet your mouth was, but you are not mine. You are not a slave, and you are not mine to play with. It doesn't mean that we will never play but you need Layton's permission." I stroked my fingers across his body and nodded.

"Okay..." I thought about it for a moment then looked at him. "You play rough... when we play, can you play nice? It scares me."

He laughed and I smiled at him starting to feel more confident with him. He held my face while he kissed my lips gently and then stroked his fingers through my hair and looked at me.

"Chaos. Do you want to go and join Kendal and Jacob for breakfast?" I nodded. I felt so hungry having lost my last meal.

"Are you coming?" Julian nodded.

"In a bit. I want to rest awhile and shower. I will join you shortly." I kissed his body before kneeling up between his legs.

"Thank you for watching me. Should I get dressed?" I preferred being naked, but I wasn't in the basement now. I wasn't sure what the rules were here. Julian put his hands behind his head and smiled.

"You are in Jacob's house. I am sure he wouldn't care whether you were dressed or not, but Kendal might be surprised to see you naked at the breakfast table. I think you should do whatever you feel like doing. Do you remember where Jacob's room is?" I nodded. "And you know where the kitchen is." I bit my lip and nodded. He smiled. "Off you go then."

I got off the sofa and walked towards the door. I stopped and turned around. "Thank you for letting me stay with you and having me." I turned and walked out the door.

In the hallway, I could hear Kendal talking to Jacob. I wasn't completely comfortable being naked here, so I went to the bedroom and pulled on my jeans from yesterday then made my way to the kitchen. I stopped outside the door and bit my lip, a little worried about just walking in. Jacob was eating at the table and Kendal had her back to us both. I wished Julian had come with me now as my confidence wavered a little. I was just about to turn and go back to him when Kendal turned and smiled at me.

"Hello, honey. Come and sit, I'll make you a nice cup of tea."

I moved slowly into the room as Jacob turned. He was only wearing a pair of boxer shorts as he got up, smiling. He kissed me before taking my hand and guided me to sit next to him. He didn't let go of my hand as we sat.

He looked at me. "Did you sleep?"

I nodded. "Yes... I'm sorry I couldn't stay with you, I tried to, but my mind was busy."

He smiled. "Busy in the kitchen eating?"

I looked down away from him and chewed my lip.

Kendal passed my tea.

"Jacob..." Kendal spoke his name in a warning. She looked at me. "Were you poorly, honey?" I nodded.

"I'm sorry I made a mess... I think I ate too much." She smiled at me.

"Yes, the kitchen certainly looked harassed this morning. I don't think it has seen so much action, ever. Did Julian look after you?"

Jacob kissed the hand he was holding, and I nodded to Kendal.

"He ate everything in the fridge!" He smiled at me. "You were sitting in the fridge eating."

I scrunched my shoulders, feeling uncomfortable.

"Jacob, stop teasing him. You're making him worried." She looked at me. "Ignore him, Isaac. He doesn't understand. I expect you're hungry now...?" I nodded and she smiled. "I'll make you something." I looked at Jacob.

"Sorry. I only meant to eat the sandwich; I didn't mean to make a mess."

He leant over and kissed me. "I don't care what you do, I like having you here. Were you that hungry?" I shook my head.

"No, not really... I think I'm struggling with all this freedom. I've never seen so much food and I wanted to taste it so I did... because I could and even when I felt sick, I didn't stop... until I was sick."

Jacob creased his face in a pained look. "I hate being sick, it's not nice, is it?"

I shook my head and half-smiled.

"Usually, I am given my food. I don't usually have a choice, but the fridge was full of choices, and I wanted them all... so I tried everything. I don't think I will do it again though."

Jacob nodded understanding a little better.

Kendal spoke without turning. "There's no worry, Isaac. No one expects you to understand the things you feel. You're still healing, still finding your way in this world. It's okay to get it wrong, that's how you learn. What matters is that someone is there to help you when you get into trouble." She turned with my breakfast plate in her hand. "There you go, poppet. Eat that up."

I smiled at the food. It was the dream I had. Toast, bacon, and sausages with a poached egg. Jacob dropped my hand and I started to eat.

"Thank you."

Kendal smiled at me as Jacob spoke. "I want to show you something today."

I looked at him as I ate and then Julian entered the kitchen, walked behind Jacob, swept his hands over his shoulders and wrapped them around him as he kissed his head.

"Good morning, Kendal. Come, boy, leave Isaac to eat. Come and shower with me so he can have a little peace while he settles." Julian reached out a hand and stroked my face. "You can stay with Kendal until we return?" I nodded.

Kendal walked around to Julian as he stood, and hugged him. "Someone didn't get a lot of sleep I hear?" She kissed him and he swept his fingers through her hair, smiling at her.

"Thank you for clearing it. It was a better night than I expected... a little busy but he settled in the end." She moved away and continued to wash the dishes.

"You want tea, J?"

Julian had moved back to Jacob. He was caressing his face with his fingers. "In a while when I return, thank you." He looked at Jacob and I could see the lust in his eyes.

I knew that look; I had seen it many times over when I was a slave. He required Jacob to service him. I wondered if Layton was getting Orion to service him this morning. As I thought about it, I spoke out loud.

"Do you think it will be long until Orion has a Keeper?"

Julian smiled. Had he heard my thoughts? He moved over to me and pulled my face up to his so I was looking at him upside down.

"No, not long. Are you worried?" I nodded a little. He stroked my face. "You are just feeling a little jealousy. I will promise to try and sort a Keeper today. I will speak to Kellen."

He kissed my mouth upside down and then released me. He took Jacob from the kitchen and I finished my food while Kendal sat at the table with me.

"Do you want anything, Isaac?" I crossed my arms over in front of me.

"I'm used to being told what to do. Now I'm asking for things I shouldn't and can't stop when I get what I want. How do you know when you can have something and when you can't? How will I know when I'm supposed to be independent and when I'm supposed to submit to their will?" I looked at the table and sighed.

Things were so much easier a slave. I looked back at Kendal who was looking at me sympathetically.

"I asked Julian if he wanted me to service him this morning." She smiled.

"Wanting to please the person you're with is a hard habit to break, isn't it?"

I nodded and held out my hand across the table. I felt alone and I didn't want to be. She must have understood because she took my hand and held it. "What did Julian say?"

"He didn't look pleased, which was confusing. He said I wasn't his to play with." Kendal nodded.

"Well you're not, you belong to Layton."

"I don't know what that means... I thought I did, when I'm with him it's easy but when he's not around, I'm not sure who I should be pleasing." Kendal nodded.

"I think it means that you don't have to please or play with anyone except him. You shouldn't offer yourself to anyone, Isaac, not without talking to Layton first anyway. Has Layton spoken to you about playing with others?" I shook my head.

"He said I was forbidden to kiss Jacob but if Julian wants me to play then I should, shouldn't I? I should do what he says while I'm here."

"Yes, you should do what Julian says. He will always keep you safe. I don't think Julian would ask you to play unless he had asked Layton first. If that's what they have agreed, then I would expect Layton to tell you that is what he wants you to do."

"What if I want to play with Julian... or Jacob?"

She turned her head to the side and looked at me a moment before answering. "Did you want to service Julian this morning? I mean play or did you just feel the need to come?"

I shrugged my shoulders. "I wanted to come I suppose, but pleasuring others makes me feel... like a have a place." She nodded.

"I understand that. It took me a long time to find my place with Julian. I wondered why he took me from slavery when he didn't want anything from me. I offered myself to him a few times before I felt comfortable. I would get upset when he turned me down. I think I was so used to people using me, I found it difficult to take emotionally from them without giving something in return." I looked at her.

It was hard to imagine Kendal as a slave she was so strong-minded, but she certainly understood.

"If I'm not here to serve anyone, then why do they want me here?" She smiled and rubbed my hand.

"Because they just like being in your company, Isaac, they just like you. Your world for a long time was just about sex and punishment and healing. Now you're learning what friendship is and I can understand that you find it confusing. Friends don't need to earn anything or pay for anything from each other. They can just be with each other in the same room because they like each other. They look after you when you are low or in trouble and they do it because they want to, not for any other reason, not because they want to play." She waited, looking at me but I didn't say anything, so she continued. "Jacob liked you before he even knew you well. Now he really likes you. He doesn't have friends that are like him, and I think he likes that you get it, understand it. Peter and I are his friends but he is still submissive to us. He is way more comfortable with you, Isaac, I can tell by the way he teases you, he would never do that with us.

"Julian saw and liked you as a slave for a long time. He makes it a rule not to get too close to slaves but the more time he spends with you, the more he sees the person you are and not just the slave. Your mind works differently to Jacob's, and I think it intrigues him to see such a curious mind on one that is also willing to submit. It is rare, Isaac, to find such a person with so many wants and needs but who can readily give them all up and submit to another. I think it is why you are finding it so hard too."

I looked down at the tea that sat cold in the cup. "I don't mean to be curious. It's just that are so many things that are different, things that I had forgotten. Things like going to the bathroom when I need to... I feel like I'm misbehaving." She smiled at me.

"Yes, that was a difficult one to learn. I wasn't a slave very long, whereas you have been for many years. This freedom Layton has given you and the things that you are learning are going to feel strange for a good while. Everybody understands, Isaac... well maybe not Jacob so much but he has always had some freedom and independence. He was a slave for such a short while... if he teases you, it's because he doesn't understand how different this is for you.

"Layton, Julian, Peter and I, all understand, and we are all here to try and help you make the transition easier. You will have to try and separate the playtimes... when you are submissive... from the times when you are allowed to be your own person. At the moment, you are slipping from one to the other and it's hurting your mind. When you and Layton play, what triggers you to submit to him?" I shrugged my shoulders.

"I haven't played properly since... since..." I bit my lip. She looked at me waiting. "I don't know. I can't remember my last few visits and the ones I do remember... I don't think I was... a good slave for them. I submitted to him because he scared me, he hurt me. Now my body is calling out to feel something more, to hurt but I'm still worried. Layton says we have to be patient, so I don't know what triggers it, I haven't got there yet."

I looked at her to see if she was surprised but she was just sitting listening and nodding. "I think Layton is right." She picked up my cup. "Would you like another tea?" I smiled at her and nodded. She got up and filled the kettle.

It didn't feel weird talking to Kendal about what Layton and I did. It felt good to share things with her.

"Do you talk to Jacob about being punished?" She turned a little to look at me.

"Jacob is very quiet and Julian is very private. I understand the need you have, Isaac, this need to feel the pain and suffer for them, but I don't like to see my friends hurt. Jacob accepts his healing and endures it to show his love for Julian. He is quite settled and doesn't feel the need to share with me. I used to care for his wounds all the time but now Julian does it, I think he prefers it that way. Only if Julian is called away do I have anything to do with it.

"Jacob prefers Peter to look after him, he's not quite as vocal as me. Sometimes their pain, their marks, and wounds make me question this world. I'll always talk to you, Isaac, if you want to share and if you don't then that's fine too." She turned back to the counter.

"Layton and I make love." She turned her head and smiled and I smiled back.

I don't know why I wanted to share that, but I did. "When I woke up, I didn't want sex for a long time, losing myself in it made me scared."

"And now?"

"Now it's... good again but I know there's more... like I know the pleasure can be sweeter. Do you and Peter play?" She turned all the way around and looked at me.

"Why do you ask that?" I looked away. She didn't want to share.

"Sorry, you don't have to answer. When you look at each other, it's like you love each other so I just wondered." She smiled at me; it replaced the shocked look she had initially turned with.

"Peter and I do love each other but no we don't play." I looked back at her.

"Don't you miss it? You used to be a slave like me?"

She looked intensely at me. "Isaac!"

I looked away again. "Sorry." I seemed to be saying sorry more times than I had ever said yes sir these days.

She turned with the tea in her hand and passed it to me across the table. She sat with hers opposite me.

She hadn't answered so I thought she wasn't going to but then she spoke. "It's different for me. I was a slave a long time ago and really, I should never have been where I was. I spent most of my days dreading my visits, the Dominants scared me, and the clients scared me. They didn't love me like I wanted them to." She shrugged a little. "So, no I don't miss it, not from them." Kendal drank her tea and I saw a little sadness in her face which made me feel bad.

"Didn't your Keeper love you?" She smiled a little and shook her head.

"No, not really. The Keepers were not very good back then, there was very little understanding of a slave's needs. The Keepers council did not exist so there were no rules or guidelines for Keepers, anyone could be a Keeper. Most of them were clients with a desire to punish and who saw it as free playtime."

"I'm sorry." She tutted and smiled at me.

"It's not your fault, honey. All these years on though, and still the system let you down, didn't it."

I didn't answer. I didn't want to think about it.

"Peter would love you if you wanted to taste it again..." She glared at me. "...Sorry."

She shook her head. "Peter and I are not together, Isaac, not like you and Layton or Julian and Jacob. We are good friends that spend time together when we get the chance."

I didn't say anymore. I was sure there was more to their relationship than that. I had spent many years silently observing people, I could see more to her and Peter even if she didn't.

"I like Peter." I wasn't sure where that had come from, so I changed the subject. "Are you staying here today?" I drank my tea as she nodded.

"Yes. Julian asked me to stay today. He's going to speak to Kellen about a Keeper for Orion. Layton is still too angry with him to be civil."

I put my cup down and frowned. "Good because I'm worried he's going to love Orion more than me."

Kendal laughed out and I just stared at her. It wasn't funny to me, it hurt. "Aw honey, why would you think that?"

I shrugged and played with my cup. "He is spending lots of time with him... probably getting Orion to service him, comforting him... getting things from him he can't get from me. I remember how good he is at making slaves."

She got up and sat next to me and wrapped her arm around me and pulled into her body.

"I don't think those things make someone love, Isaac. I think love is much deeper than that."

"It made me love him."

I heard her smile. "No, it didn't... it played a part it in, but really it isn't what brought you together, it is how you met. Layton loves you, Isaac, not because you play or service him. He makes love to you. If it was those things that made him love you, then he would keep you as a slave, keep you submissive. I bet he doesn't make love to Orion?"

I sat up and looked at her. "That's because it's against the rules, he told me."

She touched my face gently. "You worry too much. Being away from him is making your place with him vulnerable and making you feel insecure. I promise when you see him later you will forget this worry. You should tell him how you feel." I shook my head.

"I don't want to get in the way of his job, he likes the slaves, he likes helping them and he's good at it. I like helping them too when he lets me, but Julian says I shouldn't be friends with them." Kendal nodded.

"I think Julian doesn't want to see you get hurt. It's easier if slaves do not get attached to others, it makes their life easier. The same goes for you, Isaac. It's not good for you to get attached to them. I'm sure Layton knows what he's doing, he understands the slaves better than anyone. You should tell him though what your thoughts are, he would rather you tell him than worry while you are away from him." She paused for a minute and looked at me. "You are doing so well this morning, Isaac. I was surprised to see you still here this morning when I came in. You were a bit overwhelmed last night. Have you been doing your little mind warp thing?" I shook my head.

"I tried to in the car on the way here, but Julian wouldn't let me go. Layton said I shouldn't do it... only when I'm with him, he said it's not safe. I do it when I want to show my place to him, be submissive to him and sometimes, when things get overwhelming, it's easy just to… go and just submit to it. I don't feel safe to go here, too many people and a strange place. It's like being on a visit, I have to stay in the room to keep myself safe." She nodded in understanding "I tried to stay with Jacob but when Julian left the room, I didn't feel safe."

"Yes, Jacob told me you were with him when he fell asleep." I smiled.

"He had so much peace, even without Julian with him. I only sleep like that when I'm with Layton and even then, the nightmares still come... sometimes." Kendal nodded and smiled as she got up and boiled the kettle again.

"Yes, well this is Jacob's home, he has lived here a while and feels safe here. Jacob does suffer though when Julian is away for a while. Unlike you, he doesn't take his mind away he takes his whole self away. He usually disappears into the woods or his room and just becomes withdrawn."

I was just thinking it sounded like the same thing when the voice at the door made me jump.

"Good morning... well afternoon now."

I turned to see Peter standing there and then looked down to my lap then saw Kendal turn and smile under my lashes.

"Peter, what are you doing here?" He moved towards her and kissed her cheek, smiling.

"I came to keep you company." I watched from one to the other.

Peter walked around the table and sat next to me. He rubbed his hand over my head and kissed my forehead. "Morning, Isaac." I looked slowly and shyly up at him.

"Hello." He smiled at me.

"Did you sleep?"

I scrunched my shoulders. "A little."

I looked quickly at Kendal, but she was busy making more tea. I looked back at Peter. "I got into trouble with the fridge and ate everything, then I was sick." He laughed out and looked at the fridge and then back to me.

"Well, the fridge seems to have held its own, it's still there." I smiled at him.

He was funny, which was strange because Julian was so serious. I wondered how they had become such good friends.

"Where's Jacob?"

Kendal answered before me which I was glad because I would have said something completely different to what she did.

"Showering." Peter nodded.

"Is Jacob going to show you around the house?" I nodded.

"I think so... is it very big?" He smiled while shaking his head.

"No. There is just this level and a basement." I looked away when he said that. He touched my face and turned it back to him. "Nothing bad happens here, Isaac. Jacob has a gym in the basement and a computer. Maybe he would let you use it; you would like the computer. I'm sure it would keep you amused for ages; he doesn't use it much." I shrugged my shoulders and felt stupid.

"I don't know how to use it; I have never used one before. I have seen them in the shops though when I was... in the other world." He nodded.

"Of course, I could teach you. We would have to ask Layton first though. Would you like that?" I wasn't sure if I wanted it or not. How did you know if you had never tried it?

"I don't know... maybe." He ruffled my hair, just like Layton did and smiled.

"Okay well, we will ask Layton first." Kendal gave a cup to Peter and he smiled at her.

I felt awkward now sitting here with these two, so I crossed my arms over in front of me and looked at the table.

"Isaac? You okay honey?" I lifted my head and nodded at Kendal and then dropped it again. I couldn't stay here. I felt in the way, I stood up and looked at Kendal.

"I think I'll go to the sitting room..." I turned walked a step and then turned back. "Is that okay?" I looked at Kendal and she smiled and nodded.

I knew I could go but it felt wrong not to ask for permission. I turned and left the kitchen and walked into the sitting room which felt bigger now there was just me in it. I walked to the sofa, sat on the floor, curled my legs into me, and leant my head on my knees. I wished Layton was here with me; I would like it more if he were here.

BABY BOY

CHAPTER FOURTEEN

"Isaac?" I turned my head and looked at Peter. He was standing in the doorway again with his cup in his hand.

I didn't answer, I didn't know what to say to him. I was worried I would say something silly or something that would get me in trouble.

"Kendal is worried about you; she doesn't want you to be on your own. Are you worried?" I shook my head. "Are you feeling sad?"

I turned my face back and rested my chin on my knees again. Peter walked into the room and sat beside me on the floor.

"So what did the fridge taste like?"

I tried not to smile and turned my face towards him. He smiled at me and hooked his arm behind me and rubbed my neck with his fingers.

"Not sad, a little alone. It's strange really because I spent so much time alone and never thought anything of it. Now I can't seem to find any peace in it, not like I used to."

"Well, this is a strange place to you at the moment and you don't have any physical wounds anymore, so your mind is free to think of other things. Not that I know about these things." He smiled at me.

"What do you know?" I wondered how much he knew about the slaves and Keepers.

He never seemed phased by anything he saw or was asked to do. Although he said he didn't know about things, I was sure he knew more than most.

"I know that this must be extremely hard for you. I know that for the last six years you have been kept in a room that you thought of as home and now your world has become vast and full of things that are so exciting you cannot resist them or so alien to you that it scares you. It's okay if you get it wrong, hell, I get it wrong sometimes and I have lived in this world for a long time." I couldn't imagine him ever doing things wrong.

"I had a Keeper; do you know what they do?" he smiled at me.

"Yes, they look after their slaves."

"Yes, well, sometimes. Does Julian get angry with you when you get it wrong?" He shook his head and smiled.

"No. Julian rarely gets angry and if he does, he never shows it. Does anger from people scare you?" I nodded. "Why?"

"When people get angry, they get loud. They shout requests and orders, and it becomes confusing. It usually results in me being punished. Have you ever been punished...played with a slave?" He shook his head.

"No. Are you finding it hard to leave your slave life?" I nodded and looked down at my feet.

I fleetingly thought of Marcus before answering. "It was safer... easy... just to be in my room. I was treated the same every day and every day was the same." I looked from my feet to him. "There were no fridges." He laughed out.

"Yes, I can imagine a fridge full of food is quite tempting when you have never been allowed the choice before. It must have seemed like Christmas... Do slaves celebrate Christmas?" I shook my head.

"No. I couldn't even tell you what day of the week it is now, I wouldn't know what the date is. I remember Christmas from when I was little... it wasn't as nice as a fridge full of food." He turned a little towards me.

"Really? Can I ask you what you remember?"

He could ask me anything, I was so drawn to him. I found myself speaking about things that I never spoke about with anyone.

I shrugged my shoulders. "My mum screaming and the man that fucked her every night beating her. He chucked my dinner on the floor and told my mum I did it. I got sent to my bedroom and wasn't allowed out. It wasn't just Christmas, it was every day I got punished, that's why I left home when I was young... I don't think anyone even noticed." He shook his head.

"That is your memory of Christmas?" I nodded.

"That's my memory of every day. I don't want to think about it." He pulled me to him and kissed my head.

"Then let's not. Do you want to sit here with me until Julian and Jacob return?" I nodded against him. "I think you will start to enjoy it here; you just need to give it a little time to become familiar to you. Are you looking forward to Jacob showing you the house?"

I felt quite happy just sitting here with Peter. I understood why Jacob was so comfortable in his company. He was easy to be with and even though I didn't know him that well, I felt safe and secure with him.

"Maybe. Will you drive me back home later?" He rubbed my arm with his hand.

"Of course. Are you looking forward to seeing Layton?"

I nodded and felt my stomach churn just thinking about seeing him. I was just about to tell Peter about it when Jacob and Julian walked into the room. Julian immediately walked over and crouched down to me and touched my face, looking concerned.

"Were you worried?" I looked at Peter then back to Julian.

"A little but Peter was watching me." I looked at Jacob. "Are we going to look at the house now?" Jacob smiled and held out his hand. Julian stood and I looked at Peter. "Thank you for sitting with me." He smiled at me.

"Anytime, Isaac."

I took Jacob's hand and he pulled me to my feet. "Come on, I want to show you something."

I looked at Julian to see if it was okay to go and he smiled. "Jacob, remember this house is new to Isaac." He looked at me. "If you are worried, I will be here, Isaac."

I nodded and turned, leaving the room with Jacob.

He took me back past the kitchen and outside to the back. We stood on a wooden decked floor which Jacob said was the porch. He pointed to the woods, showing me the direction to Julian's house and I vaguely remembered Julian taking me out this way when he took me to the nettles. I held Jacob's hand tightly.

"I don't like it out here, can we go back inside please?" He looked at me. He was fully dressed in jeans and a shirt, he stepped towards me and wrapped his arm around my shoulders.

"Does it scare you being outside?" I nodded.

There was so much space, too much for me to be aware of everything that was going on. The woods looked frightening, dark; it wasn't a place I wanted to go. I looked up at him.

"Please take me back inside, Jacob." He kissed the side of my face.

"Of course, sorry, I didn't mean to scare you." He took my hand and turned pulling me with him and as we entered the house again. I took a deep breath, relieved to be back inside and safe.

He looked back at me. "Did you go outside much when you were a slave?" I shook my head.

"Only when being moved or going to a visit." And when Julian took me, but I didn't say that.

It was clear that beyond his world here he had very little understanding of what happened in this world. I kind of liked him more for that, he had no expectations.

"I love being outside, but I understand how it would scare you. I'm sorry." I smiled at him a little.

Jacob was a good person, and I knew his intentions were good. He had only tasted the life of a slave for a short while and had little understanding of what it was like to be cocooned in that world for many years. I was finding this hard, and it made me think about the slaves that went back to the other world. How did they manage? How did they go on to live with the vanillas, without people like Layton and Julian to help them?

We walked back through the hallway and passed the sitting room. I looked in fleetingly to see Julian and Peter sitting and talking before Jacob pulled me forward, past the door. He took me to the very end by the front door and I stopped, not willing to be taken outside again. He turned and looked at me.

"I don't want to go outside again." He smiled.

"We're not going outside. I thought I would start at the beginning." He waited, looking at me. I nodded and tried to smile.

He was trying so hard to make me feel welcome and I could tell he was containing his excitement at having me here. I was completely overwhelmed by everything I was seeing and feeling. The freedom Jacob had and felt here was so new to me. I felt so unsure and a little lost and felt the need to scamper back to the sitting room to sit with Julian and let him have me. I took a few deep breaths and tried to settle my heart that was hammering in my chest.

This was my new life and I had to try and move forward. I couldn't hide with Julian or Layton forever as much as I liked that thought. Jacob was still standing watching me and he rubbed his thumb over my hand that he held. He was giving me time to decide what I wanted to do even though I knew he wanted me to stay with him. I nodded again to him.

"Okay. I'm going to try and stay with you." He smiled and leant in and kissed me.

"If you want to stop or go back to Julian just say. If you want to know anything, just ask." I nodded at him.

He turned and faced the first door. "This is the basement door; it takes you downstairs to a huge place. It is mainly full of gym equipment but there is a computer down there and a small sofa and sitting room." He put his hand to the door, and I squeezed his hand and he looked at me.

"I'm not sure if I'm ready to go down there." He dropped his hand from the door.

"Okay, then we won't go. Is it because it's the basement?" I shrugged my shoulders.

I wasn't even sure of the reason why myself; I wasn't stupid enough to think that everyone had a dungeon in their basement…but then this was Julian's domain.

He continued. "The basement at Julian's house is where Julian and I play. It is where he punishes me, but it is also where he loves me. It doesn't hold bad memories for me, it's where I feel the most at ease and safe. Kind of like the basement where you stay with Layton I suppose?" I nodded in agreement.

Yes, that was where I felt safest and most at ease. Even though I had been punished and played with there, it held no bad memories. Other basements though did not fill me with such good thoughts. Other people's basements were where I slaved and where I went to fulfil their needs and take their punishments and was rarely loved while I did so.

I wanted to explain to Jacob. "Most of my visits took place in the basements of people's houses, locked away where no one could hear you cry out in pain. The actual place doesn't scare me but where it takes my thoughts and my mind, that scares me. I'm not sure of those thoughts anymore, not sure whether I want them or not anymore. I'm not ready to face them yet." He nodded.

"I understand. Apart from that time Kellen took me, my time in basements has always been safe. My play and punishment have always been given in love of me and what I am to Julian. Maybe when you are more settled with your place, it won't hold such bad thoughts?"

He meant when I played again with Layton. Even the thought of that made me feel a little uneasy. The image of Devon came to mind as it always did when I thought about taking any punishment or pain.

"Maybe." He kissed my hand.

"Come on, I still have something for you." He walked down the hallway and explained each door.

The spare room where Julian had taken me in the night, which he said, had been newly built recently. He opened the door fleetingly and we peered in, there was a double bed and a small amount of furniture which I hadn't taken note of before. He said it was where Kendal or Peter stayed sometimes. As we headed back towards the sitting room, we reached another door to our right. "This room is for you."

He opened it and stepped inside but I didn't move, he turned and looked at me. "I asked Julian if you could have your own room so you could stay here."

I looked at him not understanding. I didn't want to stay here. I wanted to stay in the basement with Layton. Had Layton agreed to this? Is this what he wanted? Did he want me to be away from him permanently and stay with Jacob?

"I don't want to stay here." I shook my head at him and stepped backwards, pulling my hand from his.

I turned and looked at the hallway, there was nowhere safe here, nowhere I could go. I felt the panic take my air and all my thoughts and I leant against the wall until the floor felt like it was falling away, so I slowly slid down the wall to the floor.

I needed Layton to have me. I could feel my mind drifting and though I knew I shouldn't go; I couldn't stop it. I breathed quickly and looked at Jacob who was staring at me confused.

I shook my head at him and whispered my words. "I can't stay... I can't stay."

From far away I heard Jacob call for Julian and then watched as he knelt on the floor with me. I put my hand out and I didn't know if I was wanting him to stay or if I wanted him to go. A hand pulled my face round and I looked into Julian's eyes. Somewhere in my head, I felt the smallest amount of safety just looking at him and gave up the fight to stay awake. I felt his fingers sweep my face.

"Can you come back?" His words were distant, foggy in my head.

I let my head fall into him with the last of my sane thoughts. I found my peace as I felt him easily scoop me up from the floor.

I could hear the chatter and noise surrounding us, but it didn't matter in this place. It wasn't anywhere I could ever explain but it was safe and warm and although I never saw it, there was a door somewhere that I could open and leave when I felt ready to. I didn't want to leave, I wanted to stay here until Layton came back. If he never came for me, then I wanted to just stay here on my own and never come out again. I didn't like the world very much; it didn't feel safe to be in it.

I could feel the fingers stroking my hair and the blanket that was wrapped around me as I shivered. I knew it was sign that I was heading back to the harsh reality of the world. I didn't want to go, I wanted to stay until I knew he was there, but my safe space seemed to be getting smaller and smaller, pushing me out.

I moaned as I was propelled quickly back into the place I didn't want to be. I pushed myself into the warm body that held me, trying to stay away from it but it was too late. I lay on Julian. Years of using all my senses to understand my surroundings had heightened all of them and I knew it was him because I recognised his scent.

I gripped his shirt in my fingers hating this return journey, especially as I knew Layton was not here, I felt vulnerable. He kissed my forehead and continued to stroke my hair with his fingers.

"Isaac?" I didn't answer I didn't want to be back. "You can just stay here until you are ready to talk. Would you like tea?" I nodded against him.

I looked around the room as much as I could without moving. We were in the sitting room on the sofa, and we seemed to be alone, for which I was glad. I didn't want to feel like I was being watched, it made me feel like I had to try to be good and I really wasn't feeling good at all.

I wondered what Julian was thinking about my mind trip. Was he angry with me for going? I felt so sad inside, so lost. I felt like I had been ripped away from a life I was just getting used to. One moment Layton and I had been naked in bed and I had felt so happy and secure, and now I had been passed to strangers with not a clue what I was supposed to be doing.

This wasn't home and he wasn't Layton and it all felt so wrong. I felt a tear run down my face; I couldn't live in this world. Layton wanted me to, but I wasn't good at it, I was only ever good at one thing and that was slaving for others. It was the place I felt safe, and I never got into trouble and as much as I didn't want to go back to it, I had to accept that there was no other place for me.

I didn't seem to fit anywhere else, no matter how much I tried to be the independent adult. I felt another tear follow the last and I moved my hand to sweep their tracks from my face.

Julian took my wrist and looked at the wetness on my fingers before tipping my face up to his. "Talk to me, Isaac." I shook my head and pulled away from his hand, laying my head back on him.

He let me be for a while and just stroked my face. Kendal brought in the tea and set it on the side then crouched down to look at me. I didn't look at her or speak and after a while, she stroked my arm before getting up and leaving the room again. I sat up and looked around the room before looking back at Julian.

"Where's Jacob?" Julian smiled.

"He is with Peter and Kendal. He is a little worried that he upset you." Julian wrapped the blanket around my other shoulder and I laid back on him.

"I'm sorry. I didn't mean to upset him or cause trouble. Maybe you should take me back because I think I need to go back. I tried to stay but I can't. I'm not good at living in this world so I think I should go back. I know Layton wants me to live here but I can't, I tried it and I can't do it anymore. It hurts and it makes trouble for everyone. I don't want to keep saying sorry, I don't want to be a trouble anymore, I don't want it to hurt anymore." Julian stroked his hand over my hair.

"Help me understand, Isaac. Do you want to go back to Layton?" I nodded. "Because it hurts being here at Jacob's house?" I shook my head.

"No not just here, here in this world. I can't do it. I think I need to be on the other side of the doors at Layton's house, where it's safe and I don't have to think and constantly feel bad for not doing things right. It's what I know. I know I'm good at it and even though I don't want to do it all again because I'm so tired, I think I should go back. There is no place for me here, I don't fit."

He kissed me before pushing me to sit up and looked at me. "Let's drink our tea while we talk." I sort of nodded, being led by him and he handed me the cup.

I held it in both hands and loved the warm feel of it on my fingers. I sipped it and looked at him while he tasted his, then he put his cup down and looked at me. "Do you think that Layton wants you to stay here?"

I nodded. "Jacob said that I was to have a room here so I could stay. I didn't mean to make him upset but it's too hard to be here. It's too hard to live in this world constantly thinking and making decisions that are usually wrong. Do I want to eat? Or wear clothes that I don't find comfortable? Stay here or sleep with Jacob or stay in my own room? I wouldn't know when to come out, or even know if I was allowed..."

Julian held up his hand and I stopped talking and looked down into my tea. He pulled my face back to look at him. "I love that you are sharing with me, but your mind is working too quickly for me to keep up. Jacob didn't mean that you were to stay here forever. Your worry has created its own story." He let go of my face and gestured that I should drink my tea, so I did while he continued. "Layton loves you and he wouldn't want you to stay here forever and I'm not sure I cope with your chaos permanently.

"You are very new to Jacob, who has met very few people he can relate to, submissive people like himself. He really wants to be friends and he wants you to come here and be comfortable and feel secure. He wanted to let you have your own room, so you had somewhere to go when things got too much. He finds it difficult too sometimes, to live in this world but he has places to go that make him feel safe when he feels unsure. He was just trying to make a safe place for you here, but he's overwhelmed you. He would like it if you stayed here, he said he wants you to be here where it's safe when Layton can't be with you. I think he likes you a lot." Julian smiled at me and touched my face fleetingly with his fingers before picking up his tea and drinking it.

"Now I feel bad... again. I don't want to keep getting it wrong, it hurts people."

Julian smiled and put his cup down. "You have not hurt him. I have tried very hard to explain to Jacob what your life has been like when you were a slave. He doesn't understand that it felt safe and secure to you and that this all feels wrong. He says things to you that make sense to him, but you find hard to understand. Neither of you is wrong, you just need to find an understanding of each other. Someone is always here, Isaac, if things don't make sense. It doesn't mean you don't fit or do not have a place here.

"I know being a slave seems easier, being a slave for others is so uncomplicated. It is made that way for the slaves so all they need to do is think about pleasing others. All their days are mapped out for them, so they have no worries, no thoughts to get in the way of their desires because we want them to stay and sate those desires.

"Living in any world is complicated, being given choices is something that you will learn to deal with, like the fridge incident. Next time you are hungry and go to the fridge, I am sure you will only eat what you need instead of taking everything you want?" Maybe.

I remembered how good that jam had tasted and… and this was exactly my point, I couldn't trust myself, how could anyone else?

"But what if I can't make the decision? What if I do want to eat everything? Not just want, what if I do it? What if I eat all the jam? Sometimes it's just too hard and then I get into trouble." Julian smiled.

"It really doesn't matter, Isaac. It only matters that you are safe, beyond that, everything else is always fixable. You know if you went back to being a slave, you wouldn't be able to have jam, or tea, or even see Layton. I'm not sure that would make him very happy either."

I looked down at my tea. "I know... I don't want to go, I just know I was good at it, I never got into trouble, well rarely and I always knew what I was doing." I looked back at him. "Do you like me being here causing you chaos?" He laughed and touched his hand to my arm and rubbed it.

"I love you being here. When you leave later the place will seem very quiet. Will you come back again?" I thought about it. It hadn't been that bad, had it? If Layton had to go away again, I would rather be here with Julian and Jacob than anywhere else, especially with Peter being here too.

"Maybe. Will you always be here? Will Jacob and Peter?"

"I will always try to be here when you come and visit, Isaac. If I cannot, then I will make sure Peter is here, okay? I think you like Peter, don't you?" I nodded. "Now. What else did you say was bothering you?" I looked away. "Oh yes, clothes, clothes that don't feel comfortable?" I looked at my jeans and then at him.

"I do like them... just not all the time. I know I can't be naked here." He smiled at me.

"You can be naked here if you want, no one will care, Isaac. Would you prefer to wear linens around the house instead of jeans?" I nodded. They were slave trousers, but they were comfortable and looser than jeans.

"Can I? I know they are slave trousers, but I'm used to them."

"Of course. They are more comfortable for the house than jeans. Jacob always wears them or boxer shorts when he doesn't want to wear clothes. I will get you some for next time. Would you like to see Jacob now? Maybe help choose the colour of your room?" I laid back on Julian and he wrapped his arms around me and kissed me. "I promise you will find your place in this world, Isaac." I lay there for a while taking comfort from Julian's touch.

"Can you stay with me? I don't think I want to be away from you again." He kissed me.

"Of course. I should have understood that you still need to feel the security of a Dominant close by, then maybe we could have stopped your little mind trip. Shall we go and see Peter and Jacob then?" I nodded against him.

He moved me from him. I stood and waited while he stood and stretched before taking my hand.

"Was I gone long?" He smiled.

"A while."

"Sorry." He turned to me and tipped my face to look at him.

"Isaac. These things that you do are not your fault. You do not have to say sorry to me or Jacob or any of us." Well, that was good.

"That's good because I'm getting fed up with saying it. I never had to say sorry this much as a slave." I smiled at him which he seemed to like because he kissed my lips.

"That's because you were too well behaved, you're going to be missed. I love the way you just come right out and say things. Come on."

We walked back into the kitchen. Everyone was sitting at the table and it made me uncomfortable so I looked down. Jacob stood, walked over to me, and hugged me.

"Are you back now?" I nodded and he kissed the side of my face. I wanted badly to say sorry again, but I held it inside me.

"Isaac, thought that when you said it was going to be his room, that he was not going back. He thought it meant he was going to stay here permanently."

Jacob looked at me. "You can if you want..." He looked at Julian. "Can't he?"

Julian smiled at him and caressed his face. "No, he can't."

Peter and Kendal laughed a little and Jacob looked a little put out. It felt good to hear Julian say that, but I felt bad for Jacob.

I looked up at him. "But I will come back and stay... sometimes." Jacob smiled.

Julian spoke to Peter and Kendal. "I am going to spend the rest of the day with the boys. It's what I should have done in the beginning. I will talk to Kellen tomorrow. Today I am going to enjoy the company of these two."

Jacob seemed over the moon to have Julian spend the rest of the day with us and I was pleased too. Things seemed so much easier when he was around. Kendal stood and kissed Julian on the cheek.

"I think that's an excellent idea, J. It means... I am free to go shopping." Peter groaned as Kendal got her stuff together.

Julian looked at Peter. "You don't need to hang around. If you have stuff you want to do, I can drive Isaac home later." Peter shook his head and looked at me as I waited for his reply.

"I promised Isaac I would take him back, besides if you lot are going to paint, I want in... unless you want me to go and find my own fun? You do know though that would mean me shopping with Kendal?"

Julian smiled and looked at me. I liked having Peter around, he was relaxed and funny and I didn't feel like I needed to make conversation with him.

"Are we painting?" I looked from Julian to Peter.

I had never even touched a paintbrush let alone painted anything. Jacob stood behind me and wrapped his arms around me.

I turned my face toward him. "Have you painted before?" He shook his head.

Julian turned and looked at me. "You don't need to worry. This is going to be fun... Peter and Jacob assure me."

Peter and Kendal laughed as Kendal put on her coat.

"Try not to make too much mess boys. I will be back in a while and I will make some supper." She kissed me. "Try and relax, Isaac, and enjoy all the attention and boy time."

I nodded to her not feeling at all relaxed about it but wanting to please her. Peter saw her out and when he returned, he walked straight to me and took my hand, smiling at me.

"I am under strict instructions to stay with you at all times." He caught me off guard and I forced a smile to him. He squeezed my hand and looked at Julian. "What are we painting then?"

Julian was smiling at him. "Isaac's room. We need to get changed and Isaac needs to choose a colour for his room." He looked at me. "Jacob has chosen a few colours that he thought you might like and if you cannot decide then we will help you."

I nodded at him, feeling completely overwhelmed. I gripped Peter's hand tightly, glad now that Kendal had given him his instructions to stay with me.

"I can't change, I don't have any clothes here?" I looked at Peter. "Shall I just stay in my jeans?" Peter shrugged.

"Don't worry, neither do I." Both Peter and I looked at Julian.

He shook his head, smiling. "Come on, let's see what we have."

We were in the bedroom, what would be my bedroom. We were all in linens. Peter and Julian were wearing black ones and Jacob and I were wearing white ones. Mine was tied around the waist with an old tie, as they were Jacob's and far too big for me. The room was empty of everything, there wasn't even a bed or carpet on the floor, which kept bothering me while I was supposed to be thinking about paint.

They were all waiting for me to choose a colour from the five paints lined up in front of me. There was white, grey, blue, and a bright red which reminded me of blood, so I stayed away from it. The other colour was light brown which I didn't like. I looked at the three of them watching me and then back at the paint.

Peter came and stood with me and held my hand. I shook my head and looked at him.

"I can't decide." I hung my head. This was never going to be a good idea leaving it to me. "I don't know what colour. I'm sor..." I looked at Julian.

Julian stepped towards me and smiled. "It doesn't matter, Isaac. We can paint with all the colours." I shook my head.

"I don't want blood on the walls or that dirty one." I pointed to the brown looking one.

Peter laughed and kissed me. "No, you're right it's horrid. Jacob, did you pick that one?"

Jacob smiled at Peter. He picked up one of the brushes that were laid out on the floor. "Can we paint with the others then?"

I looked back at the paint. I couldn't remember what colour the walls had been in my room when I had been a slave. It seemed really important now and I wished I had taken more notice. The quiet room where Orion had stayed had been white. Layton had said it was to settle his mind and right now, I needed something to settle mine. I looked at Peter.

"Just this one." Peter smiled.

"Excellent, Isaac. White, it is then." I looked at Julian.

"Do you think that's okay?" Julian smiled at me.

"I think it's a really good decision. Well done." I smiled at him.

Peter dropped my hand, opened the tin of paint, and poured it into four small pails. He handed me a brush and one of the pails. I stood waiting while he gave one to Julian and Jacob. I watched as Julian took Jacob over to one of the walls and started to show him how to paint.

Jacob was watching Julian and I could see the love he had for him as he listened to him, hardly paying any attention to what Julian was showing him. I wanted to show Layton my room, I wanted to show him that I was painting, I wanted to show him that I loved him.

I could feel that feeling inside me like something was missing. I looked down at my brush and the pail of paint.

"Isaac?" I looked up to Julian who was watching me. "Do you want me to help you?" I shook my head.

Peter walked up behind me and ran his hand over my back, I turned and looked at him. "Do you just put it on the walls?" Peter smiled at me.

306

"Something like that. Put it on any way you like, Isaac, it's all going to be the same colour so it doesn't matter. Come on, you can help me with this wall." He gestured to the wall on our left, I turned and walked over to it. I dipped my brush in the paint and slopped it on the wall.

I looked at Peter to see if it was right. He smiled and did the same with his then I watched as he stroked the brush over the paint spreading it out across the wall and I did the same. We painted for ages and I loved it, it was messy and wet and after a while, I was covered in it. My whole hand and brush were completely white. I dropped the brush on the floor and did handprints on the wall. It felt so good and was so exciting I dipped my other hand in the paint and did both hands.

"Jacob look!" I looked across to Jacob to show him.

Julian turned and laughed at me. "Isaac, you are meant to be painting the walls with the brush, not your hands." I smiled at him a little unsure and he smiled back.

I turned back to my paint and picked up my brush and started to paint over my handprints. I got tired after a while and sat on the floor and painted a little but mainly just watched Peter.

"Have you painted before?" He looked down at me.

"Yes, lots of times, mainly Julian's house." I looked at my feet and then back to Peter.

"Do you like feet?" Peter laughed.

"What a strange question. I suppose I do. Do you like feet?" I smiled and touched the brush to my toes, coating them in the paint.

"I never really thought about it until I met Marcus. He was a client when I was at Kellen's house, and he has a foot fetish. He loves my feet. He likes to do different things to them, punish them and then look after them." I covered my whole foot in white paint and then held it up for Peter to see. "I think he would like this." Peter smiled.

"Did it hurt having your feet punished?" I shrugged my shoulders.

"A little but he always looked after me. He loves me and now we are friends. He wants me to stay with him when he next visits but I'm not sure."

Peter was on a ladder now, finishing the ceiling with a roller. He stopped and looked down at me.

"Are you worried about it?"

I turned and put my foot on the wall, making a footprint.

"I worry that he won't like me if I can't go."

Julian spoke from across the room. "Layton has told me about Marcus. He said he is a good person, Isaac. If he is your friend then he will not worry that you can't go, he will understand." I nodded to Julian.

"I think he's nice, but I don't think Layton likes him." I was painting my foot again. Peter was back to painting the ceiling.

Jacob came and sat with me and started to paint my other foot.

Julian started to paint again but spoke as he worked. "Layton is jealous, Isaac, he feels the same as you do about him being with Orion. He does like him; he is just worried that you will like Marcus more than him." I looked at Julian.

"I could never do that! Marcus kept me sane, but Layton saves me from myself. He makes my mind quiet so I can breathe."

Peter stopped painting and looked at me. "That is a very beautiful thing to say, Isaac."

I looked up at him and smiled. "I couldn't breathe when I was away from him, it hurt every day." I looked at Jacob who was still painting my feet. I knew he understood. He looked up at me and smiled.

I whispered to him. "Watch this." I looked at my feet and shouted to Peter. "Peter! Quickly look."

Peter immediately jumped from the ladder, came over, crouched down and looked at me. I put both feet on his body and pushed him over. Jacob and Julian laughed, and I smiled at him as I looked at the two footprints on his chest.

"Isaac!" For a moment, I worried that he was angry, but he smiled at me, and I let my smile return. "You're mischievous! I had managed to stay clean." He stood up and picked up his roller and flicked it at me, but Jacob got in the way and took the brunt of the flying paint which made me laugh. His face, hair and body were covered in white dots of paint.

He looked at Julian. "Peter put paint in my hair!"

Julian laughed and shook his head. "It was meant for Isaac."

Peter was climbing back up the ladder. I wiped the paint dots on Jacob's face, smearing them in small white lines. Enjoying the pattern they made, I continued down his body.

"You're a mess, Isaac." I smiled at Jacob and kissed him.

I remembered then that Layton had forbidden me and I looked at Julian. He was looking at me and I looked down to my lap.

"I wasn't playing." I looked at him fleetingly and looked down again.

"Yes, but it's forbidden." I nodded.

"Okay... can I paint him then?" Julian smiled and Peter laughed.

"Yes... he never said anything about that I suppose. Although we are all meant to be painting the walls, not each other." Jacob looked at Julian.

"Painting each other is more exciting than painting walls. Isaac is nearly all painted anyway."

Everyone looked at me which made me uncomfortable and when no one spoke I smiled at them all.

"It's more fun than painting walls." Both Peter and Julian laughed and went back to painting.

Having not been forbidden I picked up my brush and proceeded to paint Jacob.

BABY BOY

CHAPTER FIFTEEN

Peter and Julian finished painting the rest of the room while Jacob and I took turns painting each other. It felt like a sort of group playtime, without any pain or actually touching each other, it was sensual and relaxing. Jacob was sexy and hot. I loved tracing his body with the brush. He was sitting cross-legged and I was laying with my body across his lap, my head on his leg as he swept the brush across my back.

I wrapped my wet painted arms around him, feeling extremely submissive and content. It had been fun playing with paint and my mind felt quite peaceful laying here with him. I closed my eyes and let my body relax in the feel of the brush against my skin.

"Are you sleeping, Isaac?" I shook my head, but I was tired and could easily sleep here with him.

I was just about to fall asleep when I heard Kendal. "Boys! Look at the mess!"

I lifted my face from Jacob and peered around him to see her standing in the doorway. She stood looking at Jacob and me with her mouth open. I smiled at her. "Isaac, is that you under that paint?" I nodded.

Peter and Julian were clearing away the brushes and paint and Julian spoke to her. "Yes, they have had... fun I think."

Kendal scowled at him. "Yes, I can see that." She looked at Peter. "Why do you have footprints on you?"

Peter laughed. "Isaac stood on me." He looked at me and smiled before looking back to Kendal. "Do you like the room? Isaac chose the colour." Kendal looked around the room and smiled at me.

"I love it, Isaac. White is simple and soothing." I laid back against Jacob and he wrapped his arms around me. "Are you tired, honey?" I nodded. Julian wiped his hands on a cloth.

"Yes, it has been a very long day. I think it's time to get cleaned up and have something to eat before we take Isaac back." I looked at Julian excitedly.

"Is it time to go home?" He smiled and nodded.

"It will be by the time we get cleaned up and have something to eat. Come on boys, let's get you two into the shower." Julian held out his hand and I took it. He pulled me up and then Jacob.

Peter walked over and took my hand.

"Come on, I'll help clean you up." He walked me through to the bathroom and Julian and Jacob followed.

Kendal shouted after us. "I'll start supper and get towels and robes for you all."

As soon as I walked into the bathroom, I was hit with memory after memory, like electric shocks in my head. I remembered Rourke and the things he had made me do here.

I stopped walking and squeezed Peter's hand. He turned and looked at me. "Isaac?"

I looked at him trying to keep the memories from consuming my mind, trying to stop the panic.

"I don't like it here."

Julian was immediately at my side. He touched my face to look at him. "Do you remember?" I nodded. "They are slave memories, Isaac." I shook my head.

I hadn't been with a client, I had been with my Keeper, and I had needed to feel safe and loved but he had continued my misery and I wasn't ready. He shouldn't have made me feel those things, he should have made me feel safe.

"I wasn't a slave, I was Isaac. I was with my Keeper, and he made me feel bad things here. I don't want to remember them, I don't want to be here."

I stepped back as if the action would take the bad feelings and memories away, it didn't. Peter had stepped back with me. He hadn't let go of my hand, which I still gripped tightly in mine. I knew if the touch was broken, I would go and I was trying not to, I was trying very hard to stay with them.

Julian nodded in understanding and looked at Peter. "Can you take him to the big bathroom?"

Peter smiled at me. "Of course."

Julian took my face and made me look at him again. "If Peter takes you away from here, can you stay with him?" I looked at Peter and nodded slowly.

He was safe, I had only known him a short while, but I felt secure with him. Julian nodded to Peter and he scooped me up in his arms. "Try and keep him with you." Peter nodded.

"Put your arms in, Isaac, otherwise we will get paint everywhere." I curled myself into his body and wrapped one of my arms around his neck, pushing my face into his shoulder.

314

I felt him move and I closed my eyes waiting to be away from that place. As he walked, I took the opportunity to inhale deeply through my nose and take in his smell for the first time. He was hot and sweaty, and his scent was strong, but I liked it, it reminded me of playing, surrounded by warm and sticky male bodies.

"Right, Isaac, let's get you cleaned up, that paint must be making your skin feel tight."

His voice made me jump but then I breathed him in again, the voice and the scent of him filled my senses, creating a blanket of comfort. I could feel we were still moving so I didn't answer or open my eyes.

"Did you like painting?" I nodded against him as Jacob's image came to mind and I forced myself to answer.

"I liked painting Jacob." I felt him laugh under me.

I felt so tired I could easily let sleep take me here with him.

"Right, here we are."

I opened my eyes, and we were in the large shower room that Julian had taken me to the previous night. He let my feet drop to the floor and when I didn't release my hands, he pulled them from him gently. "I'm not leaving, I just need to turn the shower on."

I nodded and let him go. I turned to look in the big mirror and stood to look at myself. I was completely white, from face to feet, my blue eyes looked large and bright, and my hair looked off white against the painted skin. The shower came on and I breathed in and pushed the linens from my body, stepping out of them, staring again at my reflection.

The trousers had left their outline on my legs and body. My skin didn't look so white against the white paint. Peter had stripped off his linens and he joined me in front of the mirror, wrapping his arm around me. His skin was dark brown and looked almost black against my painted skin. I was so drawn to looking at it, finding the difference so vast yet beautiful.

Seeing him naked for the first time took my breath for a moment, his cock was flaccid but hung heavily down his inner thigh. I had to stop my eyes from lingering and drawing his attention. The attention I wasn't completely sure I wanted even if the thoughts were bouncing around in my mind.

The images in my head made me smile and he spoke to my reflection. "Feeling better?" I nodded back to him. "Come on, this is going to take a while."

He pulled me from the mirror and under the spray and I turned to him. "Can you wash my hair?"

He smiled and nodded, looking slightly confused by the request. "Yes, of course, sit down."

I dropped to the floor and sat just out of the shower spray. He unhooked the showerhead and then sat with his legs around me. He rubbed his hands over my body, washing as much of the paint off that he could, then he turned me around to face him, got a cloth and some lotion, and started to gently rub my face to remove the rest of the paint.

"We will get the paint off first then we will soap you down properly, okay?"

I nodded and sat watching him as he concentrated at getting the paint off. I loved his concentration as he dabbed and patted at my face and mouth, his deep brown eyes were sunk deep behind his brows, casting a shadow and making them look like black pools. He had a beautiful full mouth and his top lip had deep v in the centre. His arms were thick muscle, and his chest was like a solid platform, sweeping into the six-pack ladder down to his cock. His thighs and calves were thickset like his arms, and I could feel their strength as they surrounded me.

My mouth did that thing again, where it sounded the words before I had time to think. "I like you."

He smiled looking at me quickly before looking back to my ear where he was cleaning. "Good, because I like you too, very much, Isaac. I think you are fun to be around, it's been a long time since I've enjoyed an afternoon of painting. Considering the things you have seen and done, you are quite grounded…with a little crazy curiosity. Do you remember much from before you were a slave? Did you go to school in the other world?"

He rinsed the cloth under the water before going back to cleaning.

"I remember some things, mostly things I missed like food and tea…and clothes, although they are not as comfortable as I remember. I went to school when I was little but when I got older I didn't go much. As long as I stayed out of the way of people, no one seemed to notice or cared what I did. I don't want that bathroom in my room."

I knew I would never use it on my own and didn't want to have to go in there again. If I was going to be made to stay in my room, I didn't want the bathroom, not that one.

Peter smiled as he wiped the cloth around my face and in the creases of my nose.

"Do you want to share the memory of what happened there?"

I shrugged my shoulders, unsure if talking about it would help it leave my thoughts or send me off on a mind trip for safety. I didn't know how much Peter knew about my time here, I didn't want to spoil our liking of each other.

I looked at him. "It's not very nice."

He stopped cleaning and wiped the cloth across my lips. I looked down to my lap.

"Well, I kind of gathered that from the swooning you were doing. Is it hurting your thoughts? Did Rourke punish you there?" I nodded.

"He hurt my thoughts. He made me do something that made me feel upset to put me in my place and I wasn't ready. I don't want to tell you." He swept his hand over the side of my face.

"That's okay you don't have to. Can you look at me?" I lifted my face and looked at him. "Memories are painful sometimes; they can make you think about things that you didn't like and want to forget. Does Layton know what happened?" I nodded.

"I had forgotten, well I wasn't thinking about it and then it made me remember. I don't want to remember that every time I go to the bathroom." He was washing my neck and arms now, he bent my arm and scrubbed at my elbow to remove the paint.

"No, of course and I'm sure Julian will do something about it. I'll tell him, okay?" I nodded. "Give me your hand, let me get the paint out of your fingernails." I held out my hand and he kissed my fingers before scrubbing them with a small brush.

I think it's because he was naked and so very close, that my mouth kept drooling over him and saying things before I realised I probably shouldn't say them.

"Do you like men?" Peter smiled as I held my breath a moment to see if I was going to get in trouble for asking such a question.

"Yes, but not in the same way you do. I like to love women."

I watched him for a while and everything he did, from the way he held my hand to the gentle rub of his fingers across mine, told me otherwise. He was carefully cleaning the paint off my bad hand, and I had to question his answer, or it would plague my mind because it didn't fit.

"But you kiss Jacob and me and hold my hand and touch me, like now, like you feel something else, like love." He never looked at me as he cleaned the other arm and hand, but he smiled.

"Because I do love Jacob and I love you and I want to help look out for you. I know how important touch is to Jacob and you for comfort and security, but I don't see your bodies in the same way that you see each other. I like my playtimes to be with ladies."

He looked at me then and smiled. He seemed very sure.

"I have had some visits with lady clients. They punish harder than men clients, but their bodies are so soft I didn't like fucking them if they requested it. I don't think I pleased them very much because they never really asked for me back." He was scrubbing my feet and I leaned back on my hands.

"I like them because their bodies are soft. Surely it would make sense if you prefer men that you would only have male clients?" I shrugged my shoulders.

"I went where I was told to go, to whoever wanted me. I think maybe whoever pays the most money. Do you still have my biscuit?" He laughed and nodded.

"Yes, safe and sound. Julian gave it to me to look after. Are you hungry?" I nodded.

"I'm tired too but I still want you to have me and wash my hair, please?" He looked at me questioningly.

"Have you?" I smiled at him.

"Yes, have me. Layton does it usually. He washes my hair and loves me, and I don't have to think about anything." He smiled at me.

"Is this one of those mind trip things?" I shook my head.

"No, I don't think so, I like it. It makes my thoughts quiet." He was smiling, shaking his head and I smiled with him. "It's like having tea I think, it's soothing." He looked at me.

"Ahh, okay. Do your thoughts always hurt you?" I shook my head while he washed the last of the paint from my foot.

"No, not when I was a slave. Now I feel like I have a lot to think about and this world makes my head hurt. It's confusing and when there are lots of people or there's lots going on I can't make my thoughts stop, like the memories. Sometimes it all comes out of my mouth at once. Julian calls it chaos."

He smiled, reached out and touched my face and stroked his thumb across my cheek.

"Yes, I can hear that. Come on then turn around... let me have you." I smiled at him and turned around, putting my back to him.

I moved back between his legs until I could feel his thighs touching my legs and leant against his firm body. He wrapped his arms around me and kissed my neck. "You are very easy to love, Isaac. I can see why it would be easy for people to take advantage of you."

He wet my hair with the shower and then rubbed the shampoo slowly into my hair and as he rubbed his fingers through my hair, I relaxed on him. It wasn't the same as when Layton did it, but it was nice to just lie here with him and I was sure he could learn. "Tell me when you have had enough." I would never have enough of this attention, I could sit here for hours and let him have me like this.

I debated not telling him but then thought about it. If I wanted him to learn I would have to share some of my knowledge. "Layton does it until I shiver... but I always try not to shiver because I never want it to stop." I cocked my head a little to look at him and saw him smile which made my stomach roll.

After that, he seemed to get it. He washed my hair and body with little or no interaction from me either vocally or physically. He moved me as he wanted and needed, keeping me close, keeping his touch firm and caressing. He kissed and touched me like he was exploring me, in a way that made me feel weak and breathless and so subservient to him, that all he had to do was say the words and I was his. He never asked for anything in return so I let him have me until I couldn't hide in it anymore and shivered.

"Isaac, does that mean you are cold?" I shook my head, not wanting him to stop, not wanting to leave my new friend who seemed to love me, even though he liked ladies.

I shivered again as the air made my wet body involuntary react. "Isaac?"

I sighed heavily and turned my head into him and opened my eyes sulkily.

"Can you have me again, when I come here?" He held my face to him and stroked his fingers over my cheek.

"I would love to have you again, Isaac." He didn't seem in any hurry to move and just looked at me while he stroked his hand over my head. "You are giving me crazy thoughts." I smiled at him, feeling sure we were in the same place.

"Like the ladies do?" He smiled at me shaking his head which confused me, then without actually answering he pushed me forward to sit.

He stood and hooked the shower back on the wall and washed himself clean of paint while I watched him. He looked down at me and held out his hand and I took it so he could pull me up. He took me under the spray and warmed my body under the water before turning it off and wrapping me in a large towel. I stood holding it while he quickly dried my hair and then dried himself.

He stood and looked at me and pushed my hair back across my head with his hand. "Do you brush it?" I shook my head.

"No just do this." I took my hand from the towel and ruffled my hair. He smiled and leant in and kissed the tip of my nose.

"I shall remember for next time. You look handsome." I scowled at him and he smiled. "Not handsome?"

"I want to look beautiful." He hugged me.

"That's what I meant. Come on, put the robe on and we can have supper."

I wasn't sure I was ready to move on from our sharing, I still felt we were in the middle of something that we hadn't quite finished. I wasn't quite sure what it was though so when he helped me with the robe and then put his on, I just stayed silent. He held out his hand and I took it. We left the bathroom and headed to the kitchen.

Kendal was there on her own. Peter sat and pulled me to sit next to him.

"Julian not here yet?"

Kendal shook her head, smiling. "No, I think he is having trouble getting paint out of Jacob's hair." Peter smiled back and looked at me.

"Oops." I smiled back at him.

Kendal checked my hand and replaced the plaster, and then made us tea and hot rolls with soup and as we started eating, Julian and Jacob joined us. The room became noisy with the conversation that I couldn't keep up with, so I stayed quiet and ate my soup listening to them. Peter and Julian were telling Kendal how Jacob and I had spent more time painting each other than the walls and Jacob spoke now and again adding his side of the story. I watched him as he listened to them talking. He was like me, happy to sit and listen most of the time, only speaking when he wanted to share his feelings about something.

They spoke about my room and the bathroom, but I stayed silent, still not feeling all that comfortable about speaking to the whole room. Julian touched his hand to the side of my face, and I looked at him.

"Would you like carpet in your room, Isaac?" I shook my head.

"Wood floor... and no bathroom… thank you." Julian smiled.

"You need a bathroom; I will sort it out. Jacob says you need a new one to make new memories. Does that sound okay?"

I liked new memories, I liked the ones that Layton and I made, and I liked my new memories of Peter. I nodded and smiled as I looked at Peter.

"Can I have a bed?" Peter smiled and Julian laughed which made me look at him.

"Of course, you can have a bed. Next time you come we will have it all ready for you."

"Can Layton come next time so I can show him?" Julian nodded.

"I think that would be a good idea. Are you ready to go home?" I nodded and smiled.

My heart jumped at the thought of being with Layton again.

"Come on then, let's get you dressed." I looked at Peter and put my hand in his and waited for him to take me. Julian laughed. "Have I been replaced?"

Peter smiled at me and then Julian. "Yes. I think he likes the undivided attention."

Julian nodded and ruffled my hair. I looked down away from Julian in case he was annoyed.

"It's okay, I know it's hard to share when you are used to having one on one attention." He looked at Peter. "Are you okay with it? He is very... demanding."

I turned to look at Peter as he looked at me and tried to look sorry for being demanding. He smiled and kissed my forehead.

"Yes, it's fine. I'm sure he just needs the security." Julian laughed a little.

"Apparently not, Layton says he is always this busy." Peter looked at me again and smiled.

"Really Isaac? Are you always this entertaining?"

I shrugged and looked down. I didn't mean to be. I liked to be with people, especially people I liked a lot.

He touched my face and lifted it back to look at him. "It's okay, I like having you." I half-smiled. "Come on, let's get you dressed then. I'm sure you would prefer Layton's company to mine." I smiled at him; he already understood some things. He stood and took me with him to Jacob's room.

I was dressed back in my jeans and t-shirt and sitting cross-legged on the bed holding my boots while Peter was dressing. He had given me the socks and boots and asked me to put them on while he used the bathroom. I didn't want to wear my socks and although I knew the boots would pain me without them, I stuffed them in my jeans pocket to hide them.

I kissed my boots and put them on my feet. The blisters from before were healing and even though my feet were still red in places, they didn't hurt which I found disappointing. I wanted to feel the burn and sting of it again.

I pulled at my laces so they were tight, hoping it might create a feeling that would stop the niggle and was just tying them when Peter sat on the bed and stopped my hands. He looked at me and held out his hand.

"Socks?" I sighed and dropped my head. I didn't know how he knew. "Come on, Isaac, where are they? I saw you put the boots on, there were no socks on your feet."

I pulled them from my pocket and looked at him to see what he would say. He took them from my hand and put them on the bed, then he started to loosen the laces on my boots.

"Are you trying to punish yourself?" I shrugged my shoulders. "Why do you do that? Do you think Layton would like it?"

I shook my head as he pulled each boot off. He held my feet and rubbed his thumb over the red marks. "You still have blisters from the last time, surely they are still hurting you?"

I shook my head. "Not enough, I needed to feel it more. I need to see if feeling it makes me think of Devon and... the thought of it makes me horny."

Peter put on my socks and smiled at me. He put one boot on and started to do up the laces.

"When you have your room here, you will be able to sort your own needs out." I didn't understand.

"What, punish myself?" He smiled at me and shook his head.

"No. I mean you can come, pleasure yourself, masturbate, so it doesn't niggle at you all day."

"I don't think I'm allowed to pleasure myself. I belong to Layton and I have to be ready when he wants me but I will ask him." Peter nodded.

"I see. When you were a slave, what did you do when you were not allowed to come or play?" I looked at my boots.

"I misbehaved so I got punished harder until it hurt and then I didn't think about it."

"And is that what you're trying to do now?" I shrugged and looked at him.

"I don't know. I just know I needed it to stop the feeling inside of me." He smiled at me and held my face while he kissed my cheek.

"I have a lot to learn, Isaac. It's a difficult time for you. Julian has said that you are not ready to play properly yet?"

I didn't answer as I wasn't sure about that. The things I was feeling inside me were confusing me. "I don't know how to help you, but I do know that if you were mine, I wouldn't want you to come back to me with new blisters on your feet. Next time you come to stay here; I will talk to Layton about how to help you through these difficult times."

"I don't understand the things that I feel inside. Layton says that needing something and wanting it are different. I don't know what I want and what I need, they seem to be all mixed up with worrying about it all. He says I'm not ready but there are times when I think I am, and it burns inside me." He looked at me concerned.

"Is it burning inside you now, the need for it?" I shrugged and then nodded.

He reached out and caught my hand and pulled me to him. He turned and sat me between his legs and wrapped his arms around me, leaning his chin on my shoulder and kissing my neck. "I can't make it go away but I can have you, so you don't have to think about it for a while?"

I wrapped my arms around his and leaned into him nodding. Like waiting with your Keeper.

He stroked my arms with his fingers and rubbed my neck and whispered in my ear that I was beautiful and kissed me. The feeling he created in me was how I imagined a Keeper should make their slave feel and I closed my eyes and started to drift into sleep as my thoughts got quieter until the door opened and I heard Julian speak.

"Ready?"

Peter looked at me. "Are you ready to go home?"

I opened my eyes and looked at him sleepily, nodding "Thank you... for having me."

He kissed me and slowly moved me forward and stood up. He watched me for a moment before smiling and holding out his hand to take mine. Without thought, I pushed my hand into his large palm, and he wrapped his fingers around my hand tightly.

Jacob stayed with Kendal while Julian and Peter took me home. Peter drove and I curled up on the back seat with Julian. I was so tired but the closer we got to home the more excited I got and asked a few times how long until we were home. He gave me my jacket back that he had taken from me in the car yesterday, but I didn't like wearing it and I just lay my head on it. When I felt the car slow, I sat up and looked at Julian and he smiled at me.

"Yes, we're home, Isaac." The car stopped and Peter came and opened the door. Julian got out first and I followed eagerly.

Peter handed me the bag with my biscuit in and kissed my head. "I'll see you soon, Isaac."

I was so focused on being here I took Julian's hand in a hurry to get home. We walked a few steps towards the door and then I felt the feeling, the feeling that something was missing, which was strange as I was looking at the door that would take me to Layton. I stopped, which made Julian stop and turn and look at me. It took me a moment to realise what didn't feel right. I turned and looked at Peter who was leaning on the car watching us.

I looked at Julian. "I need to tell Peter something." Julian nodded and let go of my hand and I turned and walked to Peter and pushed my hand into his.

He smiled and held it as I stood there for a moment trying to work out what it was I wanted.

He brought my hand to his lips and kissed my fingers that were wrapped around his. "You're home, Isaac. Layton is waiting for you."

"Yes, I know but I don't want to leave you and I don't know what to do about it." Peter hugged me; he kissed the top of my head.

"Well, you certainly know how to make someone feel good." He held my face and looked at me. "I am not going far; I'm going to be at Jacob's and I'm going to help finish your room. I will speak to Layton and try and see you in a few days if he says that's okay."

Not feeling completely happy with the situation I nodded slowly.

"Will you make a new bathroom?" he smiled.

"I will."

I stood thinking about it for a moment. I had to go. I needed Layton. I looked up at him.

"Bye... thank you for my biscuit."

I got up on my toes as far as I could and kissed him full on the lips so I would remember him before turning and heading back to Julian. He was standing watching and he held out his hand, I walked towards him and took it. We walked to the door that I knew would take us straight into the basement and I turned and looked at Peter just before we went through it. As soon as we were inside, I took a deep breath. I was home.

CHAPTER SIXTEEN

The bottom door was locked but Julian unlocked it and stepped through, and I followed. As soon as he pulled the door shut, I dropped his hand and walked into the basement, searching for him. My heart was beating so fast inside my chest as I quickly swept my eyes around the large space, looking over at the sofa and the cage, I headed towards them. He wasn't there and I turned to Julian, already feeling the upset building inside me. I was just about to say something when I heard my name.

"Baby Boy." I turned quickly and there he was standing in the doorway to the bedroom.

I stumbled quickly to him, fell on my knees at his feet and wrapped my arms around his legs. Strangely, the upset feeling didn't leave, and I tried to muffle a sob of relief, which failed, as my heart hammered in my chest, deafening me. He ran his fingers through my hair, and I closed my eyes and held him tighter, completely unable to form any words.

I heard Julian speak but I didn't let go. "I'll ring you later, he's very tired." I heard the door open. I didn't want him to think I wasn't thankful even if I was glad to be back here. I whispered my words.

"Bye, Julian."

I heard him smile as he spoke. "Goodbye, Isaac."

The door closed. I didn't move. I breathed deeply filling my senses with him and he continued to play his fingers through my hair. I revelled in his touch. No one felt like he did.

He swept his fingers down my face and lifted it to him. I looked straight at him, taking my fill of his face as my eyes filled with tears. No one looked at me like he did.

"Fuck, Baby Boy, I missed you." He dropped to one knee, the other bent beside me, breaking my hold on him and took my mouth with his.

He held my head roughly at first while he ploughed his tongue into my mouth and I let him have me, opening my mouth to him so he could have whatever he wanted. When he slowed his tongue invasion of my mouth and his hold loosened to a gentle caress of my face, I clung to his arms and let my tongue touch his, joining him in the exploration of tasting and feeling each other again.

He pulled away and looked at me and then kissed me again quickly, wiping the tear that pooled on my cheek. "So, so beautiful, Baby Boy."

I reached my hand up and tentatively touched my fingertips to his face, tracing all his facial features, reading him with my touch, and then swept them slowly across his bottom lip. He took my hand and kissed my fingers gently. "Did you miss me?" I nodded at him.

"I couldn't breathe." He smiled at me and swept his hand over my face and leant down and kissed me again.

"Did you have a good time?" He was rubbing his thumb over and over my ear and I shook my head. He laughed silently as I smiled a little and nodded. He swept his hands down my arms and then lifted the one that I held the bag in. "What's this?"

I smiled at him and sat back on my feet and opened the bag. I pulled out the biscuit. "It's the biggest biscuit ever!" He laughed and nodded.

"Do you want to get naked and share it with me?" I nodded excitedly.

I loved it when he knew what I needed, what I wanted. I dropped it back in the bag and he stood up, pulling me with him. He scooped me up in his arms and I wrapped mine around his neck and kissed him. He turned off the basement lights and walked into the bedroom shutting the door.

We both undressed and he made tea and we sat on the bed with me between his legs, his arms wrapped around me. The tray of tea and the bag with the biscuit sat between my legs and I took the biscuit out and broke some off and gave it to him. I dipped my biscuit in my tea and put it in my mouth and turned to look at him smiling, feeling so relieved and happy to be back with him.

He smiled, half laughing, and I tipped my head into him feeling completely content. There was nothing that compared to this feeling, being here with him, feeling his body next to mine, surrounded by him and feeling free to be me, not having to worry about right or wrongs. I turned sideways on so I could look at him and we just sat and enjoyed each other being together again.

He shared his tea with me when mine became undrinkable with bits of biscuit and I sat drinking while he smothered me with his touch and his love. He took the cup from me when it was empty. We sat looking at each other for ages, touching and stroking each other's bodies, taking our fill of each other. He turned off the main light, leaving the lamp on beside us and I leant my head against him and kissed his body. He lay back against the pillows, taking me with him and wrapping his arms around my body and his legs around mine.

"Only you make me feel like this." I pushed myself up on his body to see him. "Just you, just Layton, no one else... ever." He pulled me to his body again and kissed my forehead.

"Yes, Baby Boy, I feel the same, just you, it's always been just you." I closed my eyes and just felt his fingers stroking over my body.

"I love you... does it count?" He laughed and squeezed me.

"I love you too and yes this time it means everything to me."

He pulled me up his body and turned us on our sides, so we were looking at each other. He kissed me and stroked his fingers over my face before scooping his arm under my head and pulling me to his chest. I wrapped my arm over him and closed my eyes again.

"I need to sleep now." He kissed my head.

"Off you go, Baby Boy, I have you." Sleep had never taken me so quickly.

Morning, or whatever time it was, was like waking up in luxury. A warm body under me and a warm arm wrapped around me with gentle fingers stroking me. All made even more perfect because they were Layton's. I didn't open my eyes but just lay there listening to him while he was on the phone, although he was doing more listening than talking. He would just say the odd thing before listening again.

I hoped there wasn't a problem upstairs and he had to leave again. I gripped him tightly, not wanting him to go anywhere and he moved his hand to my head and played with my hair. I kept my eyes closed, not wanting anything to change the peace I felt as I listened to him.

"Really?" It didn't seem urgent, he still felt relaxed under me. "Well, that would be good, yes. Just get him to ring me... No, we've not spoken yet..." Layton laughed. "No, I have no idea what you did but he was exhausted... I will call you later when I have heard it from Isaac."

I pushed myself up and looked at him worriedly. He smiled at me and touched my face as I squinted at him through sleepy eyes. "No, our day has just begun. I'm sure I will be given the full story... Isaac's way... Okay, thank you again for watching him, it really was a great help."

He closed the call and chucked the phone on the bedside unit and wrapped both arms around me as he rolled me onto my back so he was on top. I laughed and looked at him.

"Who was that?" He kissed me.

"That...was Julian." I felt uncomfortable.

"Oh... did he tell you I caused trouble?" Layton smiled at me, stroking his fingers over my forehead and playing with my fringe hair. He didn't seem too worried.

"No. He rang to check on you, make sure you were well, that you weren't too traumatised from your stay with him." He planted small tender kisses around my face and neck as I spoke.

"I did trip when I was there but only because I thought I wasn't coming back." He stopped kissing me and looked at me.

"Why would you think that?"

I pulled my arm from under him and stroked his face with my fingers.

"Because Jacob gave me a room and I thought you wanted me to stay there forever. I thought I had to stay there, in Jacob's house, in my room." He frowned at me.

"I never said that I wouldn't see you today. You know I would tell..." I put my hand over his mouth to stop his words. He kissed my palm and I slowly moved it from his mouth. "Sorry, Baby Boy. I know you have trust issues." I shook my head.

"Your face was doing that fist thing. I know that you do what you say, I know that, but people change the rules all the time and it gets confusing. I always trust what you say, I always trust you but when I'm not with you it gets lost in my head." He smiled at me.

"Julian said you were a little overwhelmed. I should imagine your mind was working overtime just trying to keep you there. Who watched over you while you found your peace?"

I lifted my head and kissed him now his face was back to normal and he smiled at me.

"Julian watched me. I wanted to stay there until you came but my mind wouldn't let me." He nodded.

"Well, I think you knew you were safe, Baby Boy. You were so worried that the slightest thing had you hiding but I think you knew you didn't have to stay there. Tell me about this room." I smiled at him.

"I painted it! And I painted Jacob, that was fun, more fun than painting walls... I kissed Jacob... I know you forbade it, but I wasn't playing, we didn't play." I looked at him to see his reaction, but he was just watching me, so I continued. "Julian said no too but he let me paint him. I did handprints on the wall and footprints on Peter. Peter brought me the biscuit on the way there when I got upset in the car. Julian said I couldn't have hot chocolate because I would have erotic thoughts... can we have hot chocolate?"

He laughed silently and kissed the side of my face. "Definitely, I will make some later. What else happened?"

"I need to go to the toilet. Can you stay there? Can we stay naked in bed for two days?" Layton laughed.

"Two days? That's a long time, Baby Boy." He moved off me so I could go. I sat up and looked at him.

"I know but I want to make love to you, and I want you to make love to me and I want to tell you about someone... Peter. He likes ladies, he likes to make love to them because they are soft, but he still says he loves me." I got off the bed and looked at him. "Don't move, I want to come back."

He was laying on his side with his head leaning on his hand, looking extremely sexy. It made me not want to go to the bathroom at all, it made me want to just go back and touch him. I thought about it, stepping back to him but he spoke as if he knew.

"You may go to the bathroom; I'm not going anywhere... well I'm going to make tea but I will be back here waiting for you."

I walked off to the bathroom. "Okay."

When I returned, he was laying as he had been, but he had a cup in his hand. I got on the bed and he pushed himself to sit up, looking at me and smiling.

"What?"

"I was just thinking how well you are doing and looking forward to spending two days naked with you on our bed." I smiled at him.

"Really? Can we? You don't have to go upstairs?" He shook his head and handed me my tea.

"No. Orion is learning his slave poses with Leon and Julian is going to see Kellen about a Keeper for him today. Hopefully, he will know someone free at the moment and allow me to have him." I was kneeling next to him, touching my body to him while we both drank our tea.

"Kellen will help, I'm sure. He looks bad on the outside but he's good on the inside. He just wants people to see the bad things."

He reached out and held my face and I looked from my tea to him.

"How can you see any good in him after the things that happened, that he allowed to happen in his house, to you?" I shrugged and moved closer to him leaning against him.

"I know there is something good inside him, I feel it. I think he's lost or maybe he just likes being the bad person." Layton smiled and moved so I could snuggle closer.

He drank the last of his tea and put it on the side and then played with my hair. "So, what trouble did you get into?"

I sighed and looked at him, I didn't want to tell him. I tried to ignore the question and I looked at my tea and drank the last bit, taking longer than I needed to.

"Isaac?" I gave him my cup and laid down with him, putting my back to him.

I pulled his hand round my body and held it tight. I didn't want him to know that I had caused chaos in Jacob's kitchen when I had been trying to be independent. He didn't say anything, and I moved his hand to the side of my face and held it there.

"So, what do you think about this room then, that Jacob has given you?"

"It worries me. I liked painting it but when I went to the bathroom, I remembered bad things, things about Rourke." I turned my face a little to look at him. "Do you remember them?" He frowned a little at me.

"The things he made you do when he was trying to get you to be a slave again?" I nodded and turned away again. I held his hand against my face wrapping my fingers through his. "Yes, I remember. Did Jacob's home make you remember the time that you spent there?" I shook my head.

"No, not really. The room looked different, felt different but the bathroom looked the same and I couldn't move the memory from my head. The same when Jacob took me outside, I didn't like it because of the nettles. I don't know how to stop the thoughts and make them not hurt." He rubbed his thumb over my cheek as I held his hand.

"So, what did you do then?"

"I asked Jacob to take me inside so I could forget, and Peter took me away from the bathroom. I didn't tell him though what happened there, I didn't want him to know the things that Rourke made me do."

Layton kissed my head and put his mouth to my ear. "Well, Baby Boy, I think you did amazingly. You didn't hide from them, you asked to be taken away from them. So, you did stop the bad thoughts. You cannot stop memories, remember? You can make new ones, so you don't have to think about the bad ones. It's okay that you didn't share with Peter too. You don't have to tell people everything, it's up to you what you want people to know about you. Did Peter ask you to tell him?" I shook my head.

"No. He asked me if I wanted to share, and I said I didn't, and he didn't mind that I didn't share." I paused before speaking again feeling very unsure of my thoughts. "I like Peter. He said I'm very easy to love." I looked up at Layton.

"I can tell you can't I, that I like him? Does that make you jealous? Julian said you liked Marcus, but you were feeling jealous. When I think of you with Orion, I felt jealous. Did he service you? I asked Julian if he wanted me to service him in the morning, but he wanted Jacob to do it. I saw him looking at Jacob with need in his eyes when he took him from the kitchen. When Julian took Jacob… Peter watched me." Layton was smiling at me.

"Take a breath, baby, I can't keep up with the questions." I turned to put my back to him again.

"Sorry. My head is full." He bent and kissed my head while I played with his fingers.

"I know. You spent an entire day and night away from here and I know how hard that must have felt. That it filled your head with thoughts and feelings that made you worry. I will listen and try to answer all of them, okay?" I nodded and he pulled my face back to look at me upside down.

"Being away from you, from each other is new and yes I feel jealous when you share things with other men, but I know you love me and you know I love you, yes?" I nodded my head as much as I could with his hold.

He kissed my forehead and I turned then to face him, keeping my body as close as I could to his. I looked at him and touched my fingers to his face gently. I needed to clarify these feelings because the word love just didn't seem to cover what I felt when I was with him.

"It's different with you, it's more than the word. It's something inside me that feels different when I am with you, feels complete. I don't know how to explain air but that's what you are when I'm with you. Even when you don't let me breathe it, I can still feel it inside me. I let people have me when you're not around because my thoughts won't stop but they don't have me as you have me. You don't need to be jealous because they never have my air, only you do that." Maybe Peter too, well he certainly took my breath away sometimes. He was looking very serious at me.

"Baby Boy, that's a very beautiful way of explaining what you feel." He sighed and stroked the side of my face. "Orion did service me this morning." He paused looking at me. "Servicing your Dominant is good training and shows your place." Yes, I remembered. "Making Orion submit to me, to my will, is part of my job. It has always been part of the work that I do here with the slaves. They must all learn to earn my respect and my love and understand they work for me.

"Do you understand that, Isaac, from when you were a slave?" I nodded and stuck out my bottom lip to show my dislike of sharing. He continued. "Because of this world that we live in, because of the job I do, my life here can never be just yours, Baby Boy, but... it is only you that has my air." He was watching me. "I like the slaves, Isaac, being with them fulfils a need in me. When I play or I am serviced by Orion or any of the slaves it is like having... Oatmeal biscuit." He was smiling at me, and I looked at him and frowned.

"They are really nice...?" This wasn't making me feel better at all. He smiled as he nodded.

"Yes, they are, and they give me a sweet fix when I need it, but I'm always thinking about and wanting... hot chocolate more. Hot chocolate is sexy and erotic and fills my mind with things I never thought possible." I looked at him and smiled.

"Am I hot chocolate?" He smiled back.

"Yes, you most definitely are, always. It doesn't matter how many times I have an oatmeal biscuit, there is always room for hot chocolate, I will always want you." He looked at me for ages. "I never want you to feel jealous, Baby Boy." I leant forward and kissed his mouth as seductively as I knew how.

"Do you want hot chocolate now?" He laughed quietly.

"Mm, very much. I know you must be aching to come. I know you asked Julian this morning because you needed your pleasure sated, but I want to keep you wanting a little longer. We are going to play a little later when your mind is settled again with me."

I stuck out my bottom lip at having my pleasure forbidden. He leant forward and caught it between his teeth, pulled it from mine, sucking at it before letting it go. The action made me moan and push my cock into him.

He smiled. "Yes, I know it's burning you, later I promise." He kissed my nose and swept his hand across my hair. "So, Peter...you like him a lot?" I nodded.

"Yes, he doesn't know how to have me but I'm teaching him. I don't have to share him with Jacob... I mean he likes Jacob too, but Julian has Jacob. It got confusing being with Julian when Jacob was around, though he didn't seem to mind when Julian had me. I just like being with him.

"Julian said I can just come and find him if I need him. Jacob wanted me to sleep with him and Julian said I could. I wanted to, but when Julian left, I couldn't stay there. Jacob fell asleep and my mind was busy, so I went to find him." Layton smiled at me. "Shall I take a breath so you can keep up?" He laughed and nodded.

"Yes, that would be good." I took a deep breath and looked at him. "Who did you go to find? Julian or Peter?"

I shook my head a little. "No, Peter didn't stay at Jacob's then, he took Kendal home but they both came back the next day. Jacob's house is very busy." Layton nodded and smiled as he continued to play with my hair.

"It sounds it. Were you worried?" I shrugged a little.

"Sometimes. Do you think I will have to stay in my room? Julian said Jacob gave it to me, so I have somewhere to go when things get too much. I'm not sure how having a room works. My last room was my home, and it was safe to be there on my own, but I was never to leave it unless I was collected. Which was fine because I never wanted to leave but I'm not sure I want to stay in that room on my own. Should I just go in there and stay there? Can you come and see my room? The rules aren't clear."

"I would love to come and see your room. I don't think this room is like your old room. I don't think you have to live in it, it is somewhere in Jacob's house that you can put your stuff and your clothes and go there when you don't want to be with anyone else." I couldn't imagine wanting to be on my own ever, not there.

"I don't have any stuff. Just me and my clothes and my boots. What else do people have?" Layton laughed.

"Lots of things that they don't really need. Can you tell me more about Peter?" I shrugged.

"Not really, I haven't finished getting to know him yet. You should get to know people who are going to have you. Are you jealous?" Layton smiled and shook his head.

"No. I want to know more about the man that is learning to have my Baby Boy. Do you trust him?"

I nodded. "Yes."

"Mm, well he bought you a cookie so you would say that. Does he let you do anything you want?"

I shook my head but answered differently to explain. "Yes, although he wouldn't let me wear my boots without socks. He said if I was his he wouldn't want me to come back with blisters on my feet. He wants to teach me to use the computer, he's going to ask you if I can? He wants to come and see you because he said he doesn't know what to do when I want to be punished. He said I could pleasure myself in my room." I looked at Layton and smiled. "Can I?" Layton looked serious again.

"No to both." I sighed.

"I told him that." Layton's face softened. "I know the rules." He looked at me confused.

"Do you? What are the rules?"

"I have to ask permission to come so that I am always ready when you want me." He pulled me into his body and hugged me.

"You amaze me, Isaac. There will have to be some compromise I can see. I like that rule though. As for Peter, we need to wait and see if he calls. You may have decided he will have you, but he needs to decide what's right for him." He smiled at me again and kissed me before stroking my hair again with his fingers. "What trouble did you get into then?"

I looked at him. The rule about only telling people what you wanted them to know didn't apply to him, I knew. I bit the inside of my lip.

"Shall I make more tea?" He smiled and shook his head.

"Why can't you tell me?"

"I can, I don't want you to know."

"Why?"

"Because it was a stupid thing to do and even while I was doing it, I knew I shouldn't have, but I couldn't stop myself." He was still smiling at me.

"Doing what?"

"Do I have to tell you?" He nodded.

"Yes. Or I can ring Julian and ask him to tell me."

I half kicked my leg against the bed in frustration. He moved his legs over mine and continued to look at me.

I sighed. "When I left Jacob sleeping and got up to look for Julian, I got hungry and went to eat the sandwich that Kendal had left for me in the fridge." I paused. "I found it and ate it... along with everything else that was in the fridge." He laughed at me. "I was really sick."

I looked at him hurt but he just raised his eyebrows at me. "You ate everything?"

I shrugged. "Well, I tried everything a little. I threw up in the bin and made a mess in the kitchen. Julian came and got me and cleaned me up. Everything looked so nice... I just wanted it." He smiled at me softly.

"It's not stupid, Isaac. It has been a while since you have had so much choice and I understand that you are trying to appease your body while it asks for many different things. Even with independence comes consequences from the things we do. You left the world six years ago and had everything taken from you so you could concentrate on being the best slave that you could be, having those things back is going to feel overwhelming and confusing for a while.

"I love you, Isaac, nothing you do is stupid, and I missed you more than I thought possible. I missed your talking and the way you look at me when you're unsure. The way you look at me when you are sure. I just missed everything about you." He kissed my lips gently and I stroked my hand over his face and then through his hair.

"Is Orion still angry? Is he healing now?" I watched his lips as he spoke.

"Yes, he's healing. He has good moments and bad ones and he's beginning to understand what is expected of him. This is a very difficult time for him, he swings from being upset to angry to very submissive. He only ever gets attention when he is submissive, so he learns to earn the things he wants. He will get there soon." He tipped my face, so my eyes looked at his. "Marcus called for you while you were away." I looked at him excitedly.

"Is he back?" Layton shook his head.

"No, not yet. He said he would be back in a week or so. Are you excited to see him?" I nodded and he smiled.

"Yes, but I'm still not sure about going away with him."

"Well, there is no need to worry about it yet. You can decide when he gets here." I pushed my face to his chest and held him tightly and he held my face to him and kissed my head.

"Are you pleased with me? I stayed with Julian. He said I could come back if I needed to when I was struggling but I knew you wouldn't like it, so I tried so hard and stayed there even though I wanted to come back... from the moment I left." He wrapped his arms around me and held me to him.

"I am so pleased, Baby Boy, I wasn't sure you were going to last the night. You are doing so well. You have managed to share with me without tripping and took yourself to the bathroom. You have trusted people and made new friends." I pushed my face up to look at him and smiled.

"I'm good, aren't I? I've been good?" He smiled at me

"Yes, very good. What is it that you are trying to earn?"

"I want to play, I'm not scared anymore, I want it." He moved a little and looked at me.

"Not scared at all?" I shook my head.

"No, I want it." He smiled.

"Mm, you do have it bad, don't you? It's not safe to play when you have no fear, Baby Boy. It's also no fun. Your need for it is driving your mind, making you forget your limits, it's a dangerous time." I pushed away from him and turned my back to him.

"I hate you." He stroked his hand over my back.

"That's okay, Baby Boy, I still love you. I understand your frustration, your need for it is starting to affect your thoughts. It's an addiction and you will say whatever you feel you need to, to get your fix." He pulled at my arm and I pulled away from his hold. "You need to find a balance in the things that you feel, Isaac. You need to keep the fear of it and mix it with the need you feel for it, instead of jumping from one to the other." I didn't move and he leant and kissed the back of my neck making me shiver. "I'm going to make something to eat for us. Would you like to help?" I didn't answer. "It will help take your mind off it." I turned and looked at him.

"I can't find the balance. Being with you makes me want it. You said if it scared me, I wasn't ready. Now you say because I have no fear we still can't play. You know my limits; I trust you, so why can't we play? I don't understand what you want." He reached out his hand and touched my face and I moved it from him.

"When I play, I take my lead from you. Yes, I do know you, but pain limits change all the time. Your mind is still healing, your emotions and feelings are running confused inside you. You should always have the fear of punishment, Isaac, it's what makes it safe, it gives you your limits. At this moment, you just want to feel the pain because you think it will make this feeling you have go away.

"When your need for it doesn't leave you, you will ask for more and more punishment, trying to sate the feelings inside you. It will end up as just pain and that will put you right back to not wanting it again. Being punished should fill you with a little fear, a little excitement, and thoughts of pleasure. I need to see those things in you when we play so I can watch over you and sate your need safely without causing you any damage. I know it's burning inside you; it has been a long time since you played and you have not been allowed to come today, which is adding to your discomfort. We will play a little later, when your mind is in a better place. You are still reeling from your day of independence and that is definitely not where you should be when we play."

I turned more towards him, having a little hope now.

"I know where my mind should be when we play, I do. I can go there whenever you ask... I can go there now and stay there 'till you say I'm ready..." He shook his head.

"I don't want you to take yourself, Baby Boy, I want to take you there. There is no fun in going there on your own, remember? Doughnuts without sugar?" He smiled at me.

I didn't like it, but he was right there was no fun or pleasure in going there on my own. I rolled over onto the bed and hid my face in the cover. I felt him run his fingers down my back and it made me quiver. I turned my face towards him, laying it on the bed.

"I don't hate you." He smiled and leant forward on his knees and kissed the side of my face.

"I know."

"If I behave can we play? Can I taste it a little?"

"Maybe. Do you want to help make dinner?" I nodded still with my head on the bed.

He held out his hand and I took it in mine. I pushed myself up on my other hand and moved towards him. I needed my place with him to be safe, I needed it confirmed. He opened his legs and I sat in between them and curled up into him. He wrapped his arms around me and stroked his fingers through my hair, giving me exactly what I needed.

He kissed my head. "I have you, Baby Boy." I sighed heavily.

"Will cooking dinner make it go away? I don't like feeling it asking all the time." He tipped my face up to him.

"It will stop you from thinking about it, it won't make it go away... seeing as you have been so good staying with Julian, I will let you choose pudding." I smiled at him. "I see you've had your bandage removed?" He held my hand with the large plaster covering the stitches.

"Kendal did it, she said it's better." Layton put it to his mouth and kissed it.

"I'm hungry." He laughed.

"I knew you would be, come on let's go." He moved me from him, got up and then pulled me from the bed and we headed to the kitchen.

My helping with dinner consisted of me sitting cross-legged on the kitchen floor while he cooked. I felt settled again, enjoying being back with him, enjoying watching him, chatting endlessly, letting my thoughts spill from my mouth and not worrying whether I was saying the right or wrong thing.

Layton decided as I was so settled, that we should eat where I sat and joined me sitting on the floor. We ate steamed fish and vegetables from lap trays and then ice cream and fruit, which wasn't my first choice. Layton said that custard and ice cream didn't go together which I disagreed then relented when he said he wouldn't have any. We spent the rest of the day naked on the bed. He told me about some of his Keepers and about his time spent with Orion. I told him about some of the old Keepers that I had had when I left here.

He was massaging my shoulders as I sat cross-legged between his legs.

"Tell me what you miss about being a slave, Baby Boy." I tipped my head back to him so I could half look at him.

"The peace in my mind mainly. I understand why the slaves are kept submissive. I miss quiet, lazy healing days with my Keeper, where I would lay on my bed and be comforted. When the pain was just receding and simmering inside me, but I would still want the attention. Doing things like this, like we're doing. Where my Keeper would be working the ache from my body from hanging or holding poses. My favourite day was number three, day three of healing. I would still be able to feel my wounds, but it wouldn't hurt my thoughts. My mind and body would still feel full from playing and I would be fussed over, touched and comforted and get lots of praise." He kissed my head.

"What would happen on day four?" I screwed my face up.

"The feel of it would start to fade, the marks and welts would be disappearing, and I would already be able to feel the new feeling growing inside me, the start of wanting it again. The worst part of it was, I knew I would have to endure it growing for a good few days before I was allowed to go for viewing again. Actually, today feels like day four... only now I don't know when my torture will end."

I looked at him again and sighed which made him smile. He pulled me back to him and swept both his hands down my stomach and between my thighs and parted them. My cock twitched and I pushed my legs wider feeding the feeling. "Are you teasing?"

"I'm testing something." He moved his feet onto my knees either side, pushing them to the bed, stretching them open wider. My muscles ached with the pull, and I closed my eyes and let a small moan escape my open mouth. I felt my cock grow hard and I opened my eyes and looked at it.

"You don't need to test it, see, my cock knows who its master is, it knows when you want it."

He pushed his feet down harder on my knees pushing them to the bed, making me wince a little, making my cock throb. He pulled my hair making me look at him.

"You are a sneaky little fuck, Baby Boy, trying to make me play."

He dropped his feet to the bed releasing my knees and kissed me. He carried on, looking at me for a moment while I tried to hold onto the ache he had caused in my hips. I could feel the rush of blood around my body, my mouth opened slightly, breathing quickly.

I relaxed my head into the hold of his hand and looked back at him. "I've seen what I wanted." He leant forward and kissed my open mouth. "It's time to shower, come on."

Completely ignoring my asking cock, he pushed me forward and slid from the bed, turning and holding out his hand. I paused for a moment, feeling annoyed that yet again my needs were being ignored, before doing as he requested and sitting up and taking his hand.

We brushed our teeth and I was cleansed and washed. I was sitting on the shower floor between his legs as he finished rinsing my hair. It was my favourite time with him, when he took me away from the harshness of this place and my world became just him and his touch.

He turned off the shower and pulled my face up to look at him.

"I want you to stay in this place, Isaac." Well, that wasn't going to be hard to do, it was my favourite place. "I want you to stay quiet and if I request you to speak you will call me Sir. Do you understand?"

My heart skipped a beat and I went to answer but he put his finger across my lips. I nodded slowly… my breathing quickened.

It was playtime.

CHAPTER SEVENTEEN

"I want you to stay in this place until you hear the name that only I call you. Until then, you are not free to ask for anything, you are just mine to do with as I please. Your body is mine, your mind is mine, and your orgasms are mine. This is going to be a tough journey, Isaac. Not all your needs will be met, and you will recall things from your slave days that you had forgotten and may not wish to remember but if you feel it, then that's because I want you to feel it. You can show me all your feelings and emotions, Isaac, but the only one that will get you anything is complete submission. Do you understand?"

I nodded. He stroked his hand around my face. "I know you're happy to be here in this space when you are free, this is just going to be a little taster so I can see where your mind is when things are taken out of your control."

He pushed my head forward and moved away but I didn't move even though I still wanted his touch. He returned and knelt behind me and started to towel my hair. "I'm just going to make it a little easier, give you a little more time to give yourself to me." He kissed the back of my neck. "Just let me have you, Isaac."

I closed my eyes and relaxed, letting my hands lay loose against the tiled floor. He dried my hair and my body and dried each leg and foot and I let my body relax so he could have it. He put down my foot and watched me for a moment before speaking. "Are you safe, Isaac?"

I nodded slowly to him. My need for him to have me was so strong it was hard to have a coherent thought, even to answer his question.

"Good boy." He stood up and dried himself as I still lay naked on the shower floor. "Take yourself on your hands and knees to the bed and take pose for checking."

It had been ages since I had been asked to do it and a small moment of doubt flickered through my mind before I pushed it away and moved, crawling on my hands and knees to the bed. I spread my knees and feet and bent over the bed, laying my head on its side and placing my hands out either side of me. It was the slave pose for having your hole and cock checked; something that happened every day when you were a slave. I stayed there for ages before he joined me in the bedroom, wearing his black linen trousers and carrying a black box.

My heart skipped a beat as he walked around and placed it on the bed. I must have flinched or shown some movement.

"Yes, you know what this is don't you."

I didn't answer as I was not permitted or expected to. I curled my fingers into the bed covers, feeling slightly anxious and a little curious. He opened the box then, left it, and walked around behind me and touched my arse. He swept his hand over my back and then down to my hole and rubbed his finger over it.

"Such a beautiful hole you have, Isaac, it's always eager to be filled." I felt his finger push against it and just as it opened, he took his finger away.

He returned his finger and pushed it against my hole teasing it, just as it opened for him again, he removed it. I pushed my arse back, wanting it and got my backside spanked five or six times. I was shocked at first but then realised my error in asking for something.

I was to be submissive at all times and lay here and let him play with me, let him have whatever he wanted. I dug my fingers into the bed cover in frustration as he left me for a while, never speaking or touching me while he sorted through the black box. I wished I hadn't moved now, but I had been so eager to feel him inside me, I wanted to feel the pleasure I knew having my hole filled would give me.

He was sorting through ropes, finding the lengths he wanted and retying the others neatly. I could just see him above me, not clearly unless I turned my head and I wasn't going to do that, I wanted him to return to me and give me some attention, so I stayed still and waited. He leant over and patted my face roughly with his fingers.

"Lesson learnt, Isaac?" I nodded against the bed. "Each time you move or ask, you will receive nothing, each time you misbehave, the length of time you are ignored will get longer. You want sugar, don't you?" I nodded.

Yes, I desperately wanted sugar, it was no fun being here waiting... well it was a little exciting... but nothing like the feelings that flooded me when he was touching me, adoring me, having me.

"If you want sugar it has to be earned so let's start right back at the beginning and see what you remember." He walked around the bed again, this time carrying some rope and knelt on the floor behind me. "Come back on to the floor on your knees and fold your arms behind you."

I did as he asked and slipped back from the bed on to my knees and placed my arms folded across each other behind my back. He ran his hand up between my shoulder blades and into my hair, pushing my head forward to my chest then swept them back over each shoulder, following the arms down where they met each other. He started to bind my wrists in rope one at a time and then each wrist to each arm, touching my fingers regularly, asking me to move them now and again to test the tightness of the rope on my circulation.

The rope was then wound around from wrist to elbow keeping them solidly bound to each other. He rubbed his hands up to my shoulders which were pulled back tightly.

"That should appease you a little." He pulled me back against him and stroked his hands down my body.

My balance was completely taken from me and if he let me fall I couldn't save myself. After tensing up for a moment I relaxed in his arms and the restrictions of the binds. "Mm, that's right, now you're remembering what it's like to be bound aren't you."

I felt slightly out of it, and he kissed me and stroked my face.

"I have you, Isaac. Are you safe?" I didn't answer and he pulled my face to look at him. "Come back a little, Isaac, I need you to stay with me and answer me."

I dragged my mind so his image became clearer in my head and nodded to him and he swept his thumb over my lips. "Speak your answer."

I whispered my answer. "Yes, Sir."

"Good boy." He bent and kissed my mouth, teasing it open with his tongue and then tasting me.

I let him have it, holding my mouth open for him until he pulled away and looked at me. I could see the desire in his eyes, and it matched my feelings, the difference was, I was forbidden to do anything about mine, it was all in his control. He pushed me up onto my knees and back over the bed, then left me again to get something else from the box. Crawling onto the bed in front of me, he sat with his knees either side of my head.

"Lift your face to me." I lifted it as much as I could with my arms bound behind me and he put a metal ring in my mouth. "Open it wide." I stretched my mouth open as much as I could and the large ring sat behind my teeth, stretching and holding my mouth open to him, the ringed hole for his cock when he wanted me to have it.

He buckled it behind my head tightly and then looked at me again. "You are being very good, Isaac." He pulled his linens down over his cock which was protruding, already hard, towards me. "Look what bound hot chocolate does for me."

He stroked his hand over his long shaft, teasing it forward in front of my face and I wanted to taste it. It was so close to my mouth, and I pushed my feet into the floor pushing myself forward towards it, forgetting the rules in my need of it.

He pulled his linens over his cock and slid from the bed, and I moaned in my gag, looking at him. I was ignored and I moaned again as my need pulsed around my body. I pushed my feet into the floor again in frustration hoping to draw him back or get his attention. He ignored me and took the box from the bed and put it on the floor and sat with his back to me. I kicked my foot into the floor over and over, I didn't want to be ignored, I wanted him to have me.

He never turned when he spoke. "It's easy to forget isn't it when the need for it burns inside you. You are mine, Isaac, you will have what I want you to have when I want you to have it, not what you want. This is to remind you of what submission is. It's not just words and it's not submitting to me as you do out of play. This is much deeper than that and I want you to remember what it's like when you have all your control taken away."

I moaned to him as my blood raced around my body, feeding my cock, making it hard and I pulled at my binds, which made them hurt, which made me moan again. My spit drooled from my mouth, and I lay my head back to the bed and closed my eyes.

If I wanted him to come back, I had to stop fighting and find my peace, get my mind back to where it could serve him. I knew where my mind should be, I used to find it easy to give up and just let them have me but at the moment, it was full of only my need, my worry about not having the control to save myself. I had forgotten.

I had forgotten how hard it was to serve someone and forgotten how to give up my wants and not ask. Millions of thoughts were slipping in and out of my mind. Be independent, be submissive, don't take your own mind, let me have you, take what you want, you're forbidden. It was so confusing. I lay quiet and still trying to take my mind back to where it was safe. I felt the bed dip and I opened my eyes.

"I said it would be difficult, Isaac. I have just spent many weeks trying to teach you independence, now I ask for you to leave all those thoughts behind and completely submit to my will." He stroked his hand over my face and wiped the drool from my chin. "Are you safe?" I thought about it for a moment while looking at him.

This used to be so easy, I used to be able to give myself without thought for my own pleasure or need. Even though I was struggling with my thoughts now though, I knew I was safe with him. I nodded.

"Good boy, I have you. Relax in your binds, Isaac, let the rope hold you." He sat and stroked my body with his fingers, and I could feel my thoughts settling with his touch. He pulled my face to look at him. "That's it. Are you going to behave?" I nodded at him.

He got off the bed and fetched more rope and disappeared behind me. He bent my leg, so my calf laid against my thigh and held it there while he ran a finger over my hole, teasing me over and over with the sweet touch but I didn't move.

"Good boy!" While I wallowed in my praise, he bound my ankle to my thigh and did the same on the other side, making me totally immobile on the bed.

Once finished he traced his fingers over my legs up to the soles of my feet so gently, hardly touching, that it tickled, and I moved them, squirming under his touch. He took his hand away until I stilled my feet, then he returned to them and continued to gently tickle them.

I kept them as still as possible, pushing my face into the bed covers and moaning as I held them, quivering from his touch. He laughed a little then knelt on the bed and turned me over, so I lay on my back on my folded arms, my legs spread wide. He stroked my belly and swept his hand over my semi-hard cock, which immediately came to attention and filled with my blood.

"Beautiful, a beautiful hard cock for me, Isaac." I watched as he leant down between my legs, licked at my cock head and I moaned in my gag. "Remember your orgasm is mine so you do not come until I request it." He played with my cock in his hand, then licked the precome from it with his beaded tongue, rubbing it over the sensitive part at the base of the head.

I wanted to come, I was already ready, and I knew if I breathed into it and fed it, I would come. I whimpered to him and shook my head. "Do not come. I always come first unless I say otherwise, then I will decide if you may come, do you understand?" I nodded at him. "Speak so I know it's very clear."

"...Ess... Cir." He smiled at my effort to form the word around my gag.

"Push your spit out, Isaac, I don't want you to drown." I pushed my tongue forward over and over and then turned my face and pushed it out of the side of my mouth.

He leaned over and wiped the spit as it trickled out and wiped all around my face. He moved off the bed and took off his linens before returning, crawling up the bed, then lifted his leg over my body so his knees were on either side of my head, sitting a little on my chest with his cock reaching out towards my face.

He reached down and took hold of my hair in his hand and pulled my face up to his cock and pushed it in my mouth through the gag. I slid my tongue over his shaft as it pushed to the back of my throat, and he slowly began fucking my mouth. He had all the control, how deep he went, how quick or slow I could have it. I couldn't even wrap my lips around him.

"Look at me, Isaac, while I fuck your throat." I looked at him while he thrust inside my mouth, choking me.

All I could do was slide my tongue over him and I revelled in giving him that pleasure. I looked at him as I slid my tongue over and over his pulsing cock. He let go of my hair and my head dropped back to the bed. "Fuck, Isaac, I need to go deeper."

He moved off me and stepped to the floor, leant over the bed, and dragged my body to the edge so my head hung over the side. He rubbed his cock in his hand and tapped it against my chin. I was now upside down and all I could see were his balls swinging with his movements, balls I would have loved to suck into my mouth.

"Mm, this is much better. Now I can fuck you right into your throat." My heart skipped in my chest as he swept his fingers over my throat to my chin.

I could hear his smile in his voice when he spoke. "Was that a little fear I saw there, Isaac?" He put the head of his cock in my mouth. "I can cut your air supply off like this and pleasure myself while you suffocate."

He reached between my legs and touched my cock, keeping it pulsing and needy with his touch and his words. He thrust in my mouth and held his cock there until I wriggled for air. "I may forget to let you breathe in my excitement."

I moaned around him as my body fought for oxygen. He was Layton and I felt secure in the knowledge he wouldn't harm me, but he was scaring me a little, causing my mind to panic. He withdrew his cock, and I took my air quickly. He pushed it back in and held my face in his both his hands.

"I could make this head of yours sleep and while you lay in your darkness, I could just have what I want." I tried to move my head and he held it tightly. "I'm not finished, Isaac."

My body convulsed as it tried to rid the obstruction from its throat so it could have its air again. I couldn't breathe and he was controlling it and that was frightening. What if he did get lost in his pleasure and forgot me? What if his pleasure was so sweet, he didn't care about my air? I wiggled my feet in their binds as my body convulsed again. He withdrew completely and lifted my head.

I looked at him, tears streaming from my eyes, running sideways into my ears, my spit drooling across my nose from my gaping mouth. He crouched down and kissed my wet slobbery face. "You're okay. If you want to come today, Isaac, then you have to work hard to please me. You must let me have you. Now stay still while I fuck your face."

Fear and excitement. I wanted to come, so I wanted to please him but having your air taken was scary. He smiled then stood and held his hand over my throat as he put his cock in my mouth again. "That's it, good boy, just let me have it."

He moaned his pleasure as he started to thrust rhythmically inside me, making wet squelching noises as my salvia lubricated his path. I held myself as still as possible for him, relaxing my throat, trying to ignore the reflex to gag, until I couldn't stop the retching.

He pushed his cock in, moaning, enjoying the spasm of my throat on his cock, closing his thighs to hold my head still to him. I wriggled my body under him, fighting for my air and I felt his hands touch my squirming body. "That's it, suffer for my pleasure, Isaac."

I needed air and I pulled at my binds and tried to get away from him, gurgling around his cock for mercy. He held my face tightly and watched as my body was racked with fear, fighting for its life. He withdrew and I gasped over and over, crying and moaning my upset.

"Okay. You can have a little sugar for being so good." He pushed my legs apart in their binds and their stretch made me moan out. He took my cock in his mouth and started to suck it, sweeping his mouth over it.

With the ache in my hips and the feel of his mouth on me, it wasn't long until I was quivering on the edge. I let the pleasure pulse through me and I tensed my body as the orgasm asked, moaning and pushing towards it, I wanted it so badly. He left me and stood watching me as I fought against it, and I lifted my head and moaned to him, asking. My body was aching from its binds and the orgasm it had tasted but been forbidden. The pain and the pleasure were working together inside me, to make me want it all.

He smiled at me and swept his hand over my face. "This is what I want to see, Isaac. You lying there for me, looking at me with your need begging me to ease it, showing me I can have anything, even your air so that I will let you have your pleasure. It shows me you know your place when we play."

He swept his hand around my face again before sliding his cock through the ring at my mouth and fucking my throat again. Around the squelching noises in my throat, I begged for my air again until my body did it's best to remove the obstruction, retching and heaving sticky bile and saliva from my stomach. It ran out of my mouth into my nose and eyes as my body used all its power to dislodge him.

When he took his cock from me, I gasped noisily and shook my head, trying to free the sticky fluids from my mouth and face. He pulled my head up to watch me struggle and then as I silently cried my upset, he wiped his hand around my face, clearing my nose and eyes of the foamy liquid.

"Good boy, I'm always going to keep you safe but it's still going to hurt for a while." He bent and kissed the side of my face and then took the gag from my mouth.

I opened and closed my mouth to release the ache from my jaw and swallowed the pooled saliva. He pushed his balls to my face. "Suck my balls while I decide whether you may come or not."

I opened my mouth and lifted my head and sucked at his warm smooth balls. I swept my tongue over them and took them into my mouth and listened to him moan. He leant forward placing his hands on my body and swore under his breath as he gently thrust his cock over my chin.

I pulled at them with my mouth and then sucked them again. I wanted to do a good job, I wanted him to let me come. "Fuck, Isaac, I do love your mouth. I could come over you right now just feeling your mouth on me."

He pulled himself free and knelt on the bed around me and grabbed my body and dragged it back onto the bed so my head wasn't hanging over the side. He sat back, pulling his arse open and sat back on my face.

"Lick my hole, show me how much you love it." I touched my tongue to it, and he sat harder on me, moaning.

I licked at him over and over, pushing my tongue into him and he moved up and down, fucking himself on my tongue, moaning with need. "Harder, Isaac."

He pushed his arse over my face, smothering me with his need to feel it. I couldn't move so I sucked at his hole and then licked it again, spurred on by his moans of pleasure. He took himself away again and knelt beside me, looking down at me. My cock was pulsing hard between my bound legs, and he touched it fleetingly, making me quiver with need. It made him smile. "You want it bad, don't you?"

I nodded at him. It was taking all my will not to beg for it. He touched my cock again and watched me try and take the orgasm that was simmering through me. "You're not to take it, Isaac, not before I have had my pleasure and fun with you."

I looked at him, hurt, and he smiled as he touched my cock again. I breathed quickly, trying to push the feeling away and he watched, enjoying the control he had over me. He took me to the edge of pleasure until it was painful to forbid it and then would take his hand from me and watch the pleasure and pain of it on my face.

My moans went from needy cries to angry groans as I was forbidden the prize that I so wanted, my release. As I writhed on the bed, he pleasured his cock until it dripped with juices which he made me lick from him. He turned me on my side, and I groaned as my body hurt from its binds. He held me there while he played with my hole, he lubricated it with gel and played his finger in and out of it.

My legs twitched with the need to open them and when I did, he took his finger from me. "If you want to feel your hole filled you need to hold yourself still on the bed."

I closed my knees together again and waited. He gave me back his finger and fucked me with it again and I moaned with pleasure as I struggled to keep my knees together so I could have it. When I felt the orgasm ask, I opened my legs and thrust my cock forward and my pleasure was removed. I closed my legs and he made me wait, wait until I was laying quiet and still on the bed again.

I was waiting again now but he didn't return his finger. He moved from the bed and I lay still, waiting. I couldn't see what he was doing, and I knew I was forbidden to move, so I lay and waited. In front of me on the bed was dropped a bamboo cane, a crop, and a leather flogger. I lay looking at them, breathing hard knowing he was watching me. I could feel his eyes on me. He lay down next to me, spooning my body, stroking his fingers over my bound hands and arms down my back and over my arse.

"No reaction? No reaction to the things that could take your pleasure and make you writhe in pain if I wanted them to?" My heart skipped in my chest. "That's better but not enough to keep you safe. Your need for them is overriding your fear. You have forgotten their touch, forgotten the feel of them, you only remember the pleasure they gave you because you don't want to remember the pain."

He swept his hands over my body, over my chest and my now painful shoulders. "I know these are paining you, Isaac." He kissed my shoulder. "You are making it fuel your cock, turning it into your pleasure." He touched his hand to my cock, and I opened my knees. I heard him smile and he let it go. "The need to come is burning you and blinding you. If I let you come now you will still only remember the pleasure these binds gave you. I want you to find pleasure in them, I want you to find your pleasure in the pain I give you, but I want you to earn it.

"You will wear the binds until I can see the pain of them is starting to override your pleasure of them until I can see you remember why you should fear them." He touched my face and turned it to him. "Do you understand?" I looked back at him.

He was my world. I couldn't move, I could only breathe when he allowed it, have pleasure when he allowed it. I didn't really understand what he was saying, asking of me but he could have anything he wanted. My pleasure was in his control, and I wanted him to pleasure me, I wanted to come for him.

I nodded slowly to him and he smiled. "Yes, you would do anything for me at this moment, wouldn't you?" He stroked my face. "It's good, Isaac, it's a good place to be, I know. Your lack of fear is making it feel so safe, your need to have your release is making you extremely submissive. I will keep you safe while you remember, while I play. When I can see what I want, you can have your release...if you still have the energy to take it." He turned my face back to the bed and slid his hands over my arse. "Now I want to have my pleasure."

He rubbed his fingers over my hole, rubbing some more lube over it and then over his cock. He pulled my legs tight into my body, making me moan out on a breath.

"Shh, now, Isaac. Just let me have you, you look so fucking hot bound and at my mercy. I just want to take you." He moved his body closer to mine and I could feel his cock at my hole.

He put his hand over my mouth and pushed his cock inside me, stifling the cry that left me as my hole was stretched quickly. "Behave for me now, boy." He wrapped his arm around my legs, pulling them tighter to my body and started to thrust in and out of me.

He still had his hand over my mouth, and he pushed my head into the bed as his pleasure took his mind. I moaned into his hand with each thrust as it pained and pleasured me. The force of his hold had me completely immobile to his thrusts.

I was not Baby Boy now, I doubted in his mind if I was even Isaac right now. I was a body with a hole for him to take pleasure in and he did so without thought. I gave up the fight for my orgasm and relaxed my body, letting him have it. If I behaved and let him have me, then maybe he would let me have some pleasure. He must have felt my body relax for he kissed my back and praised me.

"Good boy, Isaac... you are such a beautiful fuck." He took his hand from my mouth. "Thank me, Isaac... thank me for filling your tight little pig hole," I spoke with each thrust of him.

"Thank you… Sir... for filling... my tight…pig hole." I moaned to him. I wanted to touch my cock and pleasure myself.

"That's it, moan for me, it's so fucking hot when I can hear you moaning for it and know you can't do anything about it." He thrust hard inside me, and it made me open my mouth and cry out as he pushed deep inside me. "Fuck, Isaac."

He withdrew quickly and pushed me over onto my front, he parted my knees and pulled my arse apart and watched as he pushed his cock into my hole. "Fucking beautiful."

He pulled it out again, making me screw my face up. It was one of the most intense feelings of fucking, being entered and being left. I heard him smile, enjoying his play and he did it again, pushed his cock head in and then withdrew it, moaning with his own need.

"I just need to come, Isaac... are you going to behave?" He thrust inside me, making me stutter my answer.

"Yes...Yes, Sir." Behave.

It meant to lie still and relaxed and open your hole so they could fuck you hard. He pushed my knees out wide with his knees and leant over my back with his hands on either side of me, pumping his cock into me while I lay completely helpless, mouth open, moaning in the pleasure and pain of it. He was lost in his play and even though it was uncomfortable and hurt a little, it filled me with gratification that it was my body he was lost in.

It made my cock pulse, along with having my hole fucked. There was nothing like this feeling of being used and helpless, it made me burn inside with need, the need to be treated bad and be punished but loved at the same time. He kissed the back of my neck in praise of my submitting body.

"Good little fuck boy." He pushed himself upon his knees and dragged my arse back to keep me with him then held my feet making them pull against the rope on my legs. "Ah, fuck..."

He pushed deep inside me making my body jolt and spasm with need and he emptied his life into me, crying out over and over. His body dropped forward over me as he lay sated for a moment before slapping my arse hard with his hand and withdrawing from me.

He turned me over roughly, looked at my cock, semi-hard dripping with precome. I was breathing hard, and I looked at him, begging, I wanted to have my release for being good. He reached over and picked up the cane and showed it to me. The thought of it made my blood race around my body and my cock throbbed to him. He smiled and shook his head.

"Please, Sir...please may I come?" His smile disappeared from his face, and he threw the cane on the bed.

"You were told not to ask for anything. Do you think that misbehaving will get you punished?"

I thrust into the feel of my cock. I wanted anything right now. Either would give me the release that I sort, I knew.

He shook his head. "You cannot tease me with your need, Isaac. Mine has already been sated. When you show me the truth of what you are feeling, then I will release you from everything that is hurting you. Now for misbehaving, you will be ignored. I'm going to shower; you are safe on the bed as long as you don't struggle."

He moved off the bed and then turned and leant over me and looked at me. He pushed down on one of my shoulders, making me moan and he looked at my cock as it asked for more.

"I understand why you hide from it, Isaac. I would never let it hurt your mind, but you have to feel it just a little so you can have limits. Limits keep you safe." He watched me for a moment. "Are you safe?"

Yes, I felt completely safe. I was here with him but angry at being forbidden my release and that made me shake my head.

He smiled. "I saw you work that answer out so I can see that is not true. Don't forget I know you better than anyone else, I can read your thoughts. I will only be gone a few minutes and then we will sit together. I will leave you on your stomach, the ache will burn you soon enough."

He pulled me onto my front and I lay my face on the bed and watched him leave the room. Still, my body ached for its release.

When he returned, he checked my circulation on my hands and loosened some ropes. It allowed my hands to breathe a little, but it did not release my arms from their pulled back position. He was back wearing his linens again and he was sitting on the bed, watching me. I was begging to be touched. I had been good for him, I had let him have my body so he could take his pleasure and in return, I had been left and ignored. It was getting harder to find the pleasure in my binds, but when he was near me like now, I still burned to be touched by him. I still felt my orgasm asking. I looked at him, showing him, and he stroked his hand over my face.

"Your mind is so strong, Isaac. I know you are suffering but that's not what you are showing me. You are trying to control me even though you are bound and immobile. You are submitting your body to me but not your mind and that is not acceptable when we play. It does not earn you your pleasure or anything else you want." His phone started to ring and he sighed. "If you were engaging me, you would have my undivided attention but..." I looked at him as he collected his phone and looked at the caller.

"Oh, this will be interesting." He smiled at me before answering it.

"Layton." He was watching me. "Hello, Peter... Yes, I have been hearing all about it from Isaac and think that's a good idea. I have been giving it a great deal of thought also... if you're free, now would be a really good time to come over, assuming that living in this world and being friends with Julian means that you're not easily shocked?"

He laughed into the phone. "No, you are quite safe, I promise. You want to know more about Isaac, and I have an opportunity for you to see and learn first-hand. We're just tasting a few things again and he's misbehaving, which is making it challenging and interesting for both of us... if you are interested in learning of course?" He stroked his fingers over my forehead.

"Excellent. Do you have any linens?... If you could please, anything more will worry his mind... Yes, just come to the main entrance and Leon will bring you down... I look forward to seeing you." He closed the phone and looked at me and smiled. "Well, this is exciting and unexpected. We are about to find out, Isaac, if your choice of a Keeper is a good one."

Peter was coming? No, no I wasn't ready. I moaned out to him, shaking my head. He put his phone away and sat beside me.

"You don't get to choose and if you were behaving and submitting to me as you should, then you wouldn't care because only my wants would be important. If you want Peter to have you then I want to see if he is prepared for what that involves. It's not all warm cosy showers and pillow talks."

Even though I wasn't allowed to talk right now, it was really important to me that he didn't forget those things. I whispered my words between the aches in my body he was making me suffer. "I like…those things."

He smiled down at me. "I know you do and you would have Peter believe that's all you want…and need. I know that you've already had thoughts of him fucking you, holding you down making you take his beautiful black cock in your hole. I bet you've already seen yourself sitting at his feet, felt it inside, this special place you want with your Keeper. That only works if he wants it too and it wouldn't be fair to either of you if I let you start a journey together that isn't open and honest from the beginning."

I hated him for being in my head… and for the pain that was starting to seep into my mind.

"So, while you're relearning and tasting your submissive place with me, where you're very safe, I think it's a perfect time to bring Peter in. Peter needs to taste it too; he needs to see you. He needs to see that even though you need and want it, you hate it, that it hurts not just physically but mentally. That sometimes you struggle with your place. Hopefully, he'll hang around long enough to see that in your place you also find serenity, peace and security. That it gives you a purpose and fulfils your desires to serve and you get to earn the prize of sweet pleasure and pain induced orgasm…and how much you love that."

He reached out and stroked his fingers through my hair and I closed my eyes to intensify the touch. I wanted one of those orgasms.

"I like…them too." My words were whispered and slightly panting in my mind fog that was starting.

"Yes, I know but they have to be earned remember? Doughnuts with sugar? Look at me." I opened my eyes and looked at him. "No one is going to play with you, no one except me is going to touch you. I have invited Peter to come and watch but your pain and your pleasure will be what I decide, they belong to me. Do you understand?" I nodded slowly.

"Speak your answer, Isaac. It's important that you understand that today you are just serving me so you're going to be very safe."

"Yes, Sir… just you." He smiled at me.

"Good boy. Now we are going to move out into the basement to make room for our guest, but first…you spoke twice without permission…" Before my mind could form a thought of what that meant, I got two hard slaps across my arse making me tense and moan. "That should help your journey a little," I growled my annoyance at him, and his raised brows made me look away and puff my anger into the bed covers.

My binds were starting to niggle and become painful, and I was desperately trying to keep it from overwhelming my mind. I screwed my face up, trying to push it from my mind and he stroked his fingers over my ruffled brow.

"Let it in, Isaac. Let me look after it and you." I moaned and moved my face from his fingers. "Okay, let's get you moved before you really hate me."

I hated him now. He was bringing Peter here and I wasn't ready. I wasn't sure Peter was ready for what he was about to witness. I wasn't even sure if I was ready for what Layton wanted from me.

This wasn't fair…on either of us, I had just found him and not even had the chance to tell him things. I hoped he didn't scare him away because I would be angry…I hoped I didn't scare him away…I needed him.

I was dragged across the bed and pulled onto my knees and then manhandled over his shoulder. I got my arse slapped a few times as he turned and headed towards the door.

This was either going to end with me gaining a new Keeper or losing a friend, either way it was now out of my control. We walked through the door into the basement…

To be continued….

AFTERWORD

Many thanks for reading my books. I hope the characters are drawing you in and you grow to love them like I do.

If you would like to leave me a comment or feedback or just drop me a line saying hi, then please head over to my website or catch me on Facebook where I usually hang out.

BOOKS IN THIS SERIES

ISAAC – The Isaac Series Book 1

LAYTON – The Isaac Series book 2

SLAVE – The Isaac Series Book 3

BABY BOY – The Isaac Series Book 4

PETER – The Isaac Series Book 5

JUST BREATHE – The Isaac Series Book 6

OTHER BOOKS FROM THIS AUTHOR

JULIAN – A stand-alone book (these characters return in The Isaac Series)

SECRETS AND PROMISES – This book features characters from The Isaac Series

ABOUT THE AUTHOR

Taylor J Gray is a self-published author of Dark erotic and taboo stories. She was born in the suburbs of London and although she's moved about a bit she hasn't moved far from where she started. Taylor is married and lives with her partner, two dogs, and two cats. Her husband is very supportive of her work. She has worked in various roles and one of her favourite jobs was being a cinema manager but, even in school, where she used to write for her friends, her passion has always been writing stories and poems.

She has always loved the worlds of fantasy and fairy tale and reading and watching stories that don't quite fit into the normal. She's always wanted to write a romantic love story with a twist of something a little bit spicey hot and ended up with her first story Julian. Her interest and role in the BDSM community and the deep and trusting relationships they share led her to write stronger and more powerful stories about their desires and needs and her second story Isaac was born. She loved him so much she made a series! She still considers what she writes as a love story.

She is an ardent supporter of gay rights and the LGBTQ community and totally believes in love is love.

"The human mind and body is such a beautiful thing."

BABY BOY

Printed in Great Britain
by Amazon